Ben Pastor, born in Italy, moving to Texas. She lived for thirty years in the United States, working as a university professor in Illinois, Ohio and Vermont, and presently spends part of the year in her native country. *Tin Sky* is the fourth in the Martin Bora series and follows on from the success of *Lumen*, *Liar Moon* and *A Dark Song of Blood*, also published by Bitter Lemon Press. Ben Pastor is the author of other novels including the highly acclaimed *The Water Thief* and *The Fire Waker*, and is considered one of the most talented writers in the field of historical fiction. In 2008 she won the prestigious Premio Zaragoza for best historical fiction.

TIN SKY

Ben Pastor

BITTER LEMON PRESS
LONDON

BITTER LEMON PRESS

First published in the United Kingdom in 2015 by
Bitter Lemon Press, 47 Wilmington Square, London WC1X 2ET

www.bitterlemonpress.com

This edition published in agreement with
Piergiorgio Nicolazzini Literary Agency (PNLA)

A CIP record for this book is available from the British Library
ISBN 978–1–908524–51-5
eBook ISBN 978–1–908524–52-2

Typeset by Tetragon, London
Printed and bound by CPI Group (UK) Ltd, Croydon, CR0 4YY

*To Isaak Babel
and his silence*

MAIN CHARACTERS

von Bentivegni, Eccard, Colonel, chief of *Abwehr* central office
Bernoulli, Kaspar, Judge, German Army War Crimes Bureau
Bora, Martin-Heinz, Major, German Army
Kostya, POW and Bora's Ukrainian orderly
Lattmann, Bruno, *Abwehr* officer
Malinovskaya, Larisa Vasilievna, Russian soprano
von Manstein, Erich, Field Marshal, Commander, Army Group Don
Mantau, Odilo, Gestapo Captain
Mayr, Hans, Colonel, German Sanitary Corps
Nagel, Master Sergeant, German Army
Nitichenko, Victor Panteleievich, Orthodox priest
Platonov, Gleb, Soviet Lieutenant General and POW
von Salomon, Benno, Lieutenant Colonel, 161st Infantry Division (ID)
Scherer, Jochen, Panzer Corps officer
Selina Nikolayevna; Avrora Glebovna, Platonov's wife and daughter
Stark, Alfred Lothar, District Commissioner for Occupied Territories
Tarasov, Taras Lukjanovitch, retired accountant
Tibyetsky, Ghenrikh "Khan", Russian Tank Corps commander
Weller, Arnim Anton, non-com, Sanitary Corps

The unpredictable wins, the obvious loses.

SUN TZU

Prologue

He had to listen. He had to go out and listen.

From Merefa to the river, as the bird flies, it was less than twenty-five kilometres. By the country lanes (there was hardly anything else but those around) and if you wanted to avoid villages and towns, the distance meant a zigzag now at right angles, now curvy and oblique, around ditches and ravines scarring the earth, eastwards and south. Birds filled the ravines; forgotten and devastated farms at the bottom let birds nest in their ruins, inside their charred ceiling beams. You heard the birdsong come as if from below the earth, as if birds of the afterworld were singing sweetly, or mermaids were calling with treacherous insistence. Then you reached the edge, and down the grassy or chalky slope five or fifty metres below you stood or lay the carcass of a hut with bent poles and rotten straw and broken windows, full of birds that went on singing despite your presence. Russian birds, Ukrainian birds would have had to give up singing long ago had they fallen silent every time an army had rumbled or stolen through in the past two, ten, hundred or hundreds of years. And the same applied to the wind, and the gurgle and chuckle of water in the river as it bent in and out, looping the bank.

Martin Bora stared at the map, elbows on it, chin resting on his hands. That he had to go out and *listen*, and not only for

11

military reasons, was all he was actually capable (or willing) to think of for the moment. The itinerary to a place – not a town or a collective farm or isolated house but a solitary place – stared back at him as a thin broken line on the off-white network of numbered squares. Here Merefa, a small town now a suburb of Kharkov, with its shrine to the Virgin of Oseryan at the end of a westbound lane; there the Donets they called "northern" in these parts, fringed with woods wherever war hadn't razed them to the ground, still swollen with the receding spring flood that here and there had made lakes and bogs of the low-lying fields. In between, the zigzag of dusty paths, landmines, booby traps, the less than occasional sharpshooter: the hair-raising unwritten geography he had to add in pencil when he knew enough about it, for himself and others. But also a singular peace of mind across those kilometres, with death that sounded like a skylark or a rustle in the bushes, pure and unalloyed as he was pure and unalloyed these days, after Stalingrad had tempered him, freed him of all dross. Or so he thought; so he hoped.

It was warm already. The sky resembled the pale tin ceiling of an old building; occasional rainless clouds across it mimicked the pattern on the tin sheet. Below it, the living moved, and the dead lay still. The dead found in the small woods called Krasny Yar numbered five by now. Peasants, Russians; Bora knew little more about the story. He thought of them because his eyes met the name *Krasny Yar* on the map, written in Cyrillic and printed over in Latin letters. He was going nowhere near there, but not for the reasons the Ukrainian priest bellowed about; there was no more a devil in the woods than there was real hope of winning this war, even though as a Catholic and a German officer Bora believed both in the devil and in the final victory.

He stood to gather his gear in the one-floored schoolhouse he shared with his Ukrainian orderly and a sentry. It was the right place to spend part of his days: modest and unmarked, in case Russian planes made it past the German-held Rogany airfield to strafe or bomb recognizable structures. More often than not, he'd go alone. No escort, not even a driver. He sedately collected field glasses, compass, map case, pencils; and then camera, rifle, ammunition, anything else he'd take along for the trip.

Seeing the wedding band on his left hand surprised him for a fraction of a second. He'd started wearing it on the ring finger of that hand, contrary to German usage, because army vehicles and equipment often broke down in the Russian front's dust or mud or snow, and he had to reach into tight greasy spaces to fix things. It was his resilient tie to life, that single gold band, being the link to Benedikta and all she meant to him. That she was angry at him for volunteering to go back to Russia after nearly dying there did not change matters between them. Her lovemaking before his departure proved that anger *was* love.

It was part of the reason why he had to go out and listen.

Wedding band and identification disc had to routinely be left behind. Bora removed them, entrusted them to the small safety of his trunk. He'd leave the large map here as well, and although he'd circled in red the wooded lot where dead peasants kept turning up, he wouldn't even drive by there. No, no. There was no time to look into such things. Come June – July at the latest, if the date were, unwisely, further postponed – everything on this map and all its adjoining charts (Poltava, Kramatorskaya, Belgorod and on to Kursk) would be up for grabs again, and likely to be churned into extinction.

Well, at least he wasn't killed en route to the river. Snipers, partisans, a way of life (or death) for the lone German out in the Russian open, were only slightly less of a problem than they had been in Ukraine. In the partly wooded area south of Bespalovka, where his regiment-in-the-making had its camp, Bora left the army car and continued on horseback. From there on, no wheeled or tracked vehicle could venture safely. Ditches, bogs, canals, wet turf replaced solid ground. Russia made mounted troops useful again, precious again, and those who hadn't accepted the conversion of their glorious First Division to the Panzer Corps, like Bora, after biding their time and bleeding themselves white in infantry units, saw their chance again. And so the old class of young decorated officers, the von Boeselagers, Douglas von Boras, Salm-Hordtmars and Sayn-Wittgensteins, all related one way or another, had high-quality regiments designed for them. Armed reconnaissance, guerrilla warfare and invaluable support on vehicle-unfriendly terrain meant danger, excitement, absolute love for tradition – and the possibility of going out and *listening*.

Soon enough Bora was riding into a thicket of coppice – mostly birch, and willows further on, which peasants used for building and basket-weaving. Even the larger trees were new growth, planted long after the October Revolution. The trail was narrow, two feet across at most, less here and there where branches hung draped in fresh leaves. Boots, cavalry saddle, the horse's flanks all became moist in the process; although it hadn't rained, there was humidity in the air so close to the river. Even if he didn't go out of his way to think, because *feeling* was much more useful at certain stages of reconnaissance, it came to Bora's mind as he proceeded that it was in a shady area like this, circumscribed, that a few kilometres north of here those Russians had been mysteriously killed, culprit unknown. His orderly whispered of death by staves, blades, of eyes put out: killing such as peasant warfare had known five hundred years ago and more, and which conflict in today's Russia was seeing once again.

He rode on, alert but somehow unmindful of himself, wondering if here, too, there were corpses lying about. But after the Germans' Second Coming to Kharkov, as he called it, it would be surprising if there weren't. In March they'd fought tooth and nail over every square inch of territory, and if now the Donets could serve as a frontier between the opposing armies, it was only after they'd paid for each square foot of land with soldiers' and hostages' and prisoners' blood.

Where the birches gave way to willows, sky and water became visible beyond the tender green. Totila's hoofs began to sink a little, but he was a patient, sure-footed animal and he kept going. Only the occasional sucking sound was produced as the horse's shod hoofs pressed into or lifted out of the soft earth.

Bora noiselessly parted the supple branches the minimum that was needed to advance. Eager to listen, he'd let the bird-song go through him for the last several minutes, thin sounds and chirping, warbling phrases that pierced him from side to side like sweet arrows. Soon the lap and purl of shallow water eddying and circling would be heard, where willows too thinned out and twiggy brushes, canes and reeds took their place. Bora dismounted and walked through the wet grass towards the riverbank. Stepping carefully (as if a landmine wouldn't blow him to shreds the moment he touched it or tripped the wire), his eye fell on the delicate halves of a bluish eggshell at his feet. On one of the branches overhead, the young bird must have hatched recently: there were fragile smears of pale moisture still visible inside.

Bora avoided crushing the shells under his boots. His Russian orderly came to mind, who'd started keeping hens for eggs. *When I'm not around,* Bora thought, *he lets them scratch about by the row of graves by our outpost. Calls them droplets of his blood and his consolation on earth, because he's a peasant at heart. Poor Kostya. Drafted when the war first began (if I think how I was playing the young embassy officer in Moscow as late as May two years ago, when my bags were already packed in East Prussia to attack the Soviet Union!), he hasn't had time to fire a shot in anger. His entire regiment surrendered to the first German officer it met. He has a young wife in Kiev he worries about, is meek and good-hearted. Compared to him, I am a black soul.*

There was no clearing by the bank; leaves reached the water's edge and tall canes bent this way and that to form a chain of broken canopies. Insects sparkled in the air like handfuls of gold dust over the slow current. Bora crouched where he could; he leant forward, dipped his fingers in the river and listened.

It was a spot, unmarked on maps, nameless as far as he knew, like so many spots he'd stood on at the risk of dying, made precious by that possibility. Less than a square metre on the left bank of a river that flowed into the Don, capricious and meandering, getting lost, flooding. From the Don they'd all retreated as they'd retreated from Stalingrad. And across this lazy current sat the Russians. It was just a matter of listening. Inner quiet, slowing of the heart. The horse loosely tied and waiting in the back. Bora could feel every muscle tense or relax in the crouch, lungs taking in the marshy air less and less frequently. Closing his eyes, the small, nearly inaudible sounds around him became distinct – water streaming or making a whirlpool, birds singing far and near, tremulous leaves picking up the barest breath of wind, the horse's lips ripping a green shoot from the ground. From the other bank, birds calling, men elsewhere or silent, engines absent or turned off, villages, farms, towns, army camps, homesteads empty or mortally quiet.

Already in Stalingrad, towards the end, when all of them had grown close to madness one way or another, long pauses of stillness had become necessary to him. Bora grazed the water with his fingertips, listening. Each pore, each cell was a hearing organ, strained and yet giving itself up to whispers and silence alike. His entire life was present to him in these moments (boyhood bike rides, the sun on a doorway, holding hands with a girl, the Volga at Stalingrad, Dikta's throat when he kissed her, a lizard, his stepfather in Leipzig, things not yet happened but just as present; anxiety come to a point too high to be felt, and turned to lack of sensation, a sublime void). Mosquitoes swarmed on his bare arms, flies bit, toads leapt in the mud. The sun rolled like a huge cart of fire across a tin ceiling, a tin sky.

Bora opened his eyes. He estimated the width of the river at this point, its depth, the invisible but existent ford. Calmly he stood up, untied his horse, regained the saddle and paced into the water across the Donets, towards enemy lines.

1

*The determination of the value of an object must be based
not on its price, but rather on the utility it can bring.*

ST PETERSBURG PARADOX

3 May 1943. Early afternoon, near Bespalovka.

I write this diary entry after a fruitful and lively session with my
regimental staff in the making. They didn't like me going off on
my own, but I know what I'm doing.

Regarding my little foray, you'd think the Soviets would man
the bank where there are shallows. We've been sitting for a couple
of months staring at each other along this river. But it's true that
you can't guard every blade of grass, stack of rocks and river bend.
On the map, the woods on the Russian bank (flatter than ours,
with bogs and false rivers where we have low cliffs) appear criss-
crossed by a number of paths, actually overgrown now. Part of the
tree cover has been blasted during the last battle (or the previous
one; it's been two years that we've been going back and forth), and
during mud season the shell holes have become pools. Elsewhere
it has dried up, but water keeps seeping through even at a good
distance from the river's edge. No tank, ours or theirs, is safely
coming or going across for another month at least – that's for sure.

There's a minuscule island in the middle of the ford, all trees
and canes. Once I crossed over to it I had to dismount and wade
to the opposite bank, stepping around carefully. The Russians
are close by, and no mistake. Recently smoked papirosyi butts,
the occasional tin can: not scouts, that much I know. We don't

leave evidence. On a hunch, even though everything was still (even the birds, which should have put me on the alert), I kept advancing, because across the woods, on the edge far from the bank, there used to be a village we razed the first time around. However little shelter the ruins may afford, I told myself, there's a cemetery with a good fence around it, and if it's regular troops manning the area, they have no doubt set up there. In fact, there they were. No dogs, which was lucky for me. Dogs would have smelt the stranger from a distance. A platoon busily working, without a sentry to keep an eye on the environs. What I saw and photographed was worth the trip, anyway, especially the 76 mm anti-aircraft or anti-tank gun.

Returning, I don't know what came into my head. In the woods facing the islet where I'd left Totila, there was an old woman gathering sticks, and instead of stealing past her, I stopped to give her a hand. Half-blind, she didn't realize I was a German: only a soldier. She called me "little soldier", even though I was twice her size and could have picked her up with one hand. She spoke Russian, so I assume she's one of those moved in by the central government after the Ukrainians were starved off years ago. A witch from the old march tales, she seemed: in rags, bent over. That's how they made up stories like Baba Yaga and her flying mortar, I thought. Next, she'll show me her house on chicken legs, which you're supposed to address so it'll let you in. In fact, she only asked me if I were "one of the boys at the graveyard", by which she meant the platoon I'd spied on. I boldly said that I was. She then grabbed a stick and tried to thrash me with it, the fool, cursing me out for digging in her yard "to bury all those metal pots". Pots? Landmines, of course. It means they're not planning to move soon, at any rate: otherwise they'd be clearing the terrain, not mining it. Do they expect our tanks to cross over the shallows before then? It seems the Soviets have been mining every inch of cultivated and fallow land in this section for weeks; the few peasants still around are in revolt. As – by her own admission – the old woman and the others keep gardening among the "pots", it's safe to suppose they're anti-tank mines, or else they'd have been blown to smithereens. She was still ranting when I left.

Little does she know. Far from being her "little soldier", in a month I've been able to do most of the planning for the regiment, to be called Cavalry Regiment Gothland, bearing as its insignia the leaping horseman of my 1st Division (not the horse's head like Regiments Middle and South), plus the clover leaf of its parent unit, the 161st ID. Out of the 27 officers slated to fill the commanding positions, I have thus far managed to pull together 18, from the many places where they ended up after our 1st Cavalry Division was disbanded late in '41. Except for one, so far all readily expressed the willingness to come. The senior non-coms (Regimental Sergeant Major Nagel foremost among them; I'm ready to insist with Gen. von Groddeck – and even Field Marshal von Manstein – that his presence is imperative) are in the works. As for the troopers, I trust my officers will do a good job of recruiting. It's inevitable that a number of locals will be necessary, both as scouts and interpreters; four of us officers speak Russian, although I'm the only one technically qualified as an interpreter. I pointed out to Lt. Colonel von Salomon that it is preferable to have ethnic Germans. If we fight under our byname for Ukraine, "Land of the Goths", it is only right. The problem is, a good number of Russia's Germans have been transferred to the Warthegau. Others have fought for the Soviets and were made prisoners: these I don't trust and I'd rather do without. Cossacks are much prized, but I don't particularly care for their methods. I am and remain a German cavalryman: swashbuckling, sabre-rattling and hard drinking aren't what I'm looking for. Am I being difficult, at this stage of the war? Well, I may be difficult, but it is my regiment, and within reason it is at my discretion (and good judgement) that it must come into being.

Driving from the Bespalovka camp back to Merefa, Bora changed his mind about Krasny Yar, and decided to take a detour there. He travelled along a dirt lane, straight and white like a parting in the hair, between fields of new grass where larks sang and quails called out with their three notes, clear like water drops. Were it not for the skeletons of Soviet trucks and the cannibalized remains of other vehicles by the roadway, it would have seemed a peaceful landscape. Silos and low roofs, long metal sheds, stables and tractor shelters pointed to the presence of collective farms, mostly abandoned during the fighting at winter's end. Only stray dogs lived there now, which German soldiers, depending on their mood, shot dead or took along as mascots. Occasionally, farm boys stared from behind the fences. Krasny Yar lay beyond, an unidentified spot on the horizon no road sign pointed to. Bora had driven past it when going elsewhere, without stopping.

When he arrived, the impression of dislike he'd had driving through earlier was confirmed. The destitute hamlet and the wooded patch where corpses had been turning up bore the same name, yet the place wasn't beautiful – *krasny* – at all, and neither was it enough of a ravine to call it a *yar*. A piece of sloping ground at most, at the end of a dirt road passable only as far as a fork that diverged widely. On the left, the trail died amid the handful of crumbling huts. On the right hand, what trace there was had ceased to exist, ploughed by tanks that had left behind track marks as deep as graves. The edge of the woods bristled a couple of hundred metres beyond, where the earth rose into a weary swell and then sank.

Bora's rugged personnel carrier could negotiate the tracts of even space remaining across the fields, but seeing German soldiers in the village, he stopped at the fork, and after surveying the edge of the wood through his field glasses, he left the vehicle and walked towards them. Infantrymen, which put him at ease. Here was where one could just as likely find men of the 161st ID or SS belonging to *Das Reich*, whose area of control extended behind the infantry sector and west to the city of Kharkov.

The infantrymen saluted. Two had taken off their summer tunics and were drinking from their canteens. Another was putting away a folding shovel. The non-com among them came closer. "Going into the Yar, Herr Major? Flies'll eat you alive," he commented drily. "We just buried another."

Bora rolled down his shirtsleeves, buttoning the cuffs to reduce the surface available to insects. "Who was it this time?"

"An old Russki peasant as far as we can tell, Herr Major. The head was missing – badly chopped off, too."

The patrol belonged to the 241st Reconnaissance Company of the 161st ID, newly strung out from north to south on a strip of land that ran with a slight elevation from north-west to south-east. The non-com showed Bora the fresh burial, and related the rumours about the "weird deaths" that circulated among the troops. "Comrades from other patrols report stuff disappearing around here. Shirts, socks, cans of boot grease, all in full daylight. And inside the Yar you orient yourself by dead reckoning, because compasses malfunction. The Russkis claim the place is haunted. Not that I believe any of this nonsense, Herr Major, 'cause the Russkis will try to spook us if they can't do anything else. Fact is, the Russkis don't like it at Krasny Yar either."

"Tell me more about the man you buried."

"Peasant clothes, barefooted, with the long hanging-out shirt they wear out here, hands tied behind his back with an old piece of wire, half rusted through. We could have left him where he was, but my sister's a nun; I thought we ought to bury him even if he's a Red." The non-com gladly accepted a cigarette (Bora did not smoke these days, but carried a pack to offer occasionally). "In the rotten farms around here there's just old folks and kids, Herr Major. The farm boys come begging, but the old cross themselves if you mention Krasny Yar. Some of us end up doing it on purpose, to see them react – it's pretty funny. In the woods, nothing worth reporting other than the dead man. Coming back we saw one of the farm boys had followed us, and fired into the air to make him stay away. That scared him off, which is better than ending up dead, too. Seems the Russkis have been telling stories about this place for years. They go a long way to avoid it and have done so forever; the old folks say it was already this way when they were children."

Bora glanced back at the line of trees. "I'm going in. Keep an eye on my vehicle, will you?"

"Yessir. We won't be on our way for another hour and a half."

"Good." Bora checked his watch. "It's 16.00 hours now; I'll be back before 17.00."

The non-com squashed the cigarette butt against the breech of his rifle. "By the way, sir, after the burial the priest trekked in there."

"Which priest?"

"The batty one: the Russian."

"Father Victor?"

"The one from Losukovka."

"Victor Nitichenko, that's him." Bora turned, heading for the Yar.

The small woods rose up suddenly out of the grassy expanse. Here there were none, and there they were, trees that grew thick at once, disorderly as they'd surfaced from among the stumps of the old ones, cut years before. Bora had thus far kept away on purpose, pushing this place and the events that had occurred here to the edge of his mind, because he had other things to worry about. But Krasny Yar and the Krasny Yar dead did not quite go away; their presence remained perceptible.

"Keep straight ahead," the non-com had indicated, even if "straight" in the woods does not mean much. In a few minutes, however, following what seemed to be a trail left by small animals – or by elves, if the woods had been enchanted – Bora realized that in fact he could almost walk in an unswerving line. Out east, as in the days of the German tribesmen and Romans battling at Teutoburg, forests were measured in hours, or days. Walking directly (not while reconnoitring, when the going was much slower), this was at most a couple of hours' worth of woodland, yet within its boundaries had thus far died five – no, *six* people.

Bora knew that some of the murders dated to the last occupation of the area by German troops. It had been local *krest'yane* – farmers who hadn't been killed, deported, or who hadn't fled in two years of war – who reported the disappearance of this or that relative, a fact in itself that made it unlikely the missing had joined the partisans. In every case the woods, or the fields immediately around them, were the last places where the victims had been seen; and Krasny Yar was where their bodies were found by searchers.

It was true what he'd been told: the magnetic needle trembled and gyrated. Eventually Bora put the compass away. According to the non-com, the mutilated corpse was discovered about a kilometre into the wood from where he'd entered ("always leave the patch of firs to your right. The spot's on the rise with the lightning-blasted tree, near the hollow"). It must be close to a kilometre now. The firs were there, dark green. No rise, no tree and no hollow yet in sight. Fallen branches snapped under his boots; a tangle of creepers which had grown rank since the snow melt shot up through the first cleft in the ice. Wet spots, spongy and treacherous, were betrayed by the capricious mosses around them. Bora bypassed them to regain the elfish trail. Common birds called from distant trees. The soldiers before him had advanced in a broken line; Bora's expert eye read small signs in the bruised greenery showing how they had fanned out.

After a short time, in the thicket to his right, he spotted something moving, progressing against the dark of the ragged firs. Or not progressing, exactly: something that swayed, stealthily passing from one point to another. The Losukovka priest, he told himself, the one from Our Lady of the Resurrection of the Dead, Nitichenko. He'd come to pay his respects to Bora at his arrival in Merefa, because he now lived with his mother by the pilgrimage church in nearby Oseryanka.

Russian priests were specialists at recognizing the authority of the moment; and besides, it had been the German Army that had allowed him to reopen his Ukrainian rite church, and to say mass. "Poor among the poor, called to serve at a great distance from my parish church, in Ostroh and Staraya Kerkove, Krasnaya Polyana and Sloboda Solokov…" For no specific reason, Bora did not care for him. It was not surprising that he moved so cautiously. It was the clergy's way in this country. *It is the attitude so many of us have in life,* Bora thought. *But not mine.* He didn't want to give the priest the satisfaction of thinking he could spy unseen, but didn't feel like calling his name out loud either. He kept an eye on the black shadow in the trees while he continued steadily to the slope where he'd just noticed the blasted tree. Split and torn through, it leant over one of those hollows found in wooded areas not far from rivers (the Udy bordered Krasny Yar to the north-west): a pit like the hole that leads to hell, a magic kingdom, or a treasure cave. *Thinking in mythical terms comes easy in a place like this.*

The rise sat in a blade of afternoon sun that cut through the foliage at a slant. Flies reeled in the light undisturbed; great clusters of them buzzed above the blood-soaked ground. Bora climbed the rise and slackened his pace. He chased the insects before reaching the edge of the hollow, but the flies hovered around him. In the snarl of grass and creepers, he noticed a coarse wooden button on the ground, which he picked up and pocketed. There were traces all around like those made by boars when they root for food, digging with their tusks in the dead leaves. They most likely pointed to a struggle at the time of the murder; or else they'd been left by the soldiers as they recovered the body or uselessly searched for the missing head. Where they'd hauled it out of the woods – an uncommon mercy there and then – the forest floor was equally discomposed.

The idea that a severed head lay somewhere near was strangely disquieting for one who'd driven fear into corners unreachable by reason. Not that Bora thought he ought to be afraid. It was a near-superstitious disgust for the blind eye, the dead jaw, the symbolic meaning of a bloody skull separated from the torso. *In Khartoum, my great-grandfather's head was exposed by the Mahdi's followers for days. It was Great-grandmother Georgina who travelled there alone ten years later to demand the skull, still on display in the residence of Abd Allah. She took it along in her little Victorian trunk, under the admiring escort of the Mahdi's successor, who – seeing his offer of a jewel refused – asked her to marry him, and was turned down.*

The odour of blood was imperceptible in the open, although there must have been plenty of it spilt. In the springtime grass, flies formed hairy knots, sucked what they still could from the soaked earth; dispersed by a sweep of Bora's arm, they landed on him, but preferred the dead man's blood. The non-com spoke of the Yar as being shunned, but Bora could have said that no place was off limits, much less safe from war in Ukraine; it would be worse in a few weeks, as it had been a few weeks earlier. The cycle of war around Kharkov had the inexorable nature of a pendulum. "The other bodies, who found those? Do we know?" he'd enquired.

The non-com had shrugged, puffing on his cigarette. "They say the priest found one. The others, sir, I wouldn't know."

I'll have to send out Kostya to ask around. At a prudent distance from him, the shadow to Bora's right hesitated, hanging like a black tatter forgotten on the washing line.

"Victor Panteleievich!" Bora called finally. "Father Victor, come out."

Nitichenko heard him, but did not react. Perhaps he was annoyed at having been discovered; perhaps he was afraid. Bora resorted to the usual gesture adopted when the locals did not listen to him, which was to unlatch his pistol holster. It was a calm movement, little more than a transfer of the right hand towards the left hip, but it usually had the desired result. The priest picked his steps through the trees, emerging into the open at the edge of the hollow. He saluted with exaggerated humility, looking up and sideways as cats do when they study a rival before deciding whether to attack or turn tail.

Without staring directly at his feet, Bora noticed the priest had no shoes on. The first and last time they had met, Father Victor had been wearing calf-high boots that creaked at every step, most likely worn for the occasion. Perhaps he usually went barefoot; or else there were other reasons why he chose not to wear footwear that might give him away in this wood.

"*Povazhany* Major," he said in a contrite tone, "I came to say a prayer for this poor Christian's soul."

"We don't even know that he was a poor Christian," Bora replied. "He could be a committed atheist, or a political commissar." In Russian the word "Christian" merely referred to a peasant, but Bora was irritated by the priest's attitude.

"Whoever he was, *povazhany* Major, he was dreadfully punished for his sins."

"Oh yes? How do we even know that? That he was a sinner, I mean."

"We're all sinners before God."

"That's true. So he wasn't one of your parishioners?"

Father Victor, wearing his long hair tied in a ruffled ponytail in the old manner, answered that he hadn't seen the corpse close up and didn't believe so; even if – he abjectly added – the number of those who came to hear mass even from far away had grown after the Germans' return.

"Who told you there had been another murder in the woods?"

"I dreamt it at night, esteemed Major, as clear as a picture, just as I dreamt the other one; and that's why I came here with the permission of your men" (those of the 241st Company were not at all Bora's men) "as I did a year ago for that poor daughter of God with a cut throat."

"And who was she?"

"A half-wit girl from the Kusnetzov farm, south of Schubino."

Bora checked the time on his watch. "And the other bodies? In Merefa I heard of search parties organized to seek those missing from nearby farms, and how they were all found here one way or another."

The priest moodily raked the hair back over his ears, looking elsewhere. "This has been going on a long time – a long time. We don't know how many died in all. Women, children... Those killed since the war started, I can show you where they were found. Even if in my dreams I've seen them moved, dragged elsewhere from where they died."

"Moved by *whom*?"

"The dreams didn't say, *povazhany* Major. But it is an unclean spirit that dwells in this wood, and has for a whole generation. Maybe more than a generation."

Sure, sure, we need to hear this nonsense too. Bora latched his pistol holster. "I want to take some photos. Show me where the other corpses were found, before it gets dark."

Other times – ever since coming to Russia – he'd had to deal with superstitious priests, more gullible than the oldest among their followers. They filled people's heads with tales and lies, they populated nature with angelic and diabolical forces worse than in the days of the tsars. They were myopic, bigoted and dangerous. On one occasion he'd reached the point – he who was otherwise so measured – of slapping a deacon for denouncing as a partisan dispatcher a poor farm girl who'd refused herself to him.

TUESDAY 4 MAY, MEREFA

The following day, Bora had once more relegated Krasny Yar to the back of his mind. He had chores to do in Merefa and Kharkov. First, however, came a meeting with the 161st Division chief of operations, Lieutenant Colonel Benno von Salomon, who acted as liaison between the division and Bora's cavalry regiment-in-progress. Von Salomon travelled often nowadays, and this morning he was in Merefa after conferring with District Commissioner Stark, whose office was just out of town.

Von Salomon, with his long bloodhound face and the slow, precise lawyer's speech he carried over from civilian life, failed only on principle to formally grant Bora's request, promising all the same that he'd get German "or at the most, ethnic German" troopers within a reasonable time. They briefly discussed how to procure cold bloods – mounts used to harsh climates – and whether some of Bora's former colleagues might be interested in returning from the Panzer Corps to the cavalry. "Not that I expect it," Bora admitted, "but personally, if I had to choose between a desk job in the armoured troops and front-line duty in a saddle, I'd have no doubts."

"It doesn't mean their commanders will release them."

"They will as soon as they see the Field Marshal's signature, Herr Oberstleutnant."

More numbers followed, estimates, the minutiae of an organizational plan. Von Salomon read Bora's typewritten notes with his face low, underscoring every line in pencil as if to impress words and ciphers in his memory. "Good," he said at last, smoothing the pages on the teacher's desk, all that Bora had to offer as a drawing table. "I'm glad *you*, at least, are keeping your lucidity. It's not universal, you know. We all cope with the size and scope of what's around us as best we can."

"Yes, sir."

There's always a moment when the narrow door of formality between colleagues opens a crack more to reveal a space where a few liberties – if not exactly familiarity – are allowed. Von Salomon had already created this space by remarking on Bora's lucidity. Later, putting away his pencil in a monogrammed leather case, he added in a low voice, "Just think, it was reported to me that a certain colonel in an artillery regiment demands that all his officers be born under the zodiacal sign Leo. 'The sign of conquerors,' he says. And a dear friend, whom I do not identify by name out of respect, has been collecting hair clippings from his fallen soldiers in an album, arranged by colour. I'm afraid he has filled more than one volume by now." The leather case found the breast pocket, slipped inside it. "You're aware that in the first winter on this front... well, in that first winter all sorts of things happened. Before Moscow we built a fence with the bodies of Russians run over by tanks: they and their long coats had turned flat and stiff like cardboard cut-outs. We used them as road signs, too. So you will appreciate it if these days I tell you how it reassures me to deal with a young man who has kept his right mind."

"I am grateful to the colonel."

Von Salomon had already remarked upon Bora's impeccability in a complimentary way at their first meeting, an unusual show of approval for a higher officer. "Impeccable" meaning in fact "unlikely to sin", it was about as far as any of them felt (or were) at this time of their warring lives. But Bora was not deluded; von Salomon referred to appearance and comportment. He did make a point of keeping up the appearance of a German officer, if nothing else. The stiff upper lip ("Stoicism", Dikta called it, in her less spiteful moments) was a family trait. He'd thought a little less of the lieutenant colonel after the compliment. Not because he didn't appreciate it, but because he was sure he did not deserve it.

"In your own way, Major, those of you who kept their lucidity are impregnable fortresses."

Ein feste Burg... It was Luther's hymn about God as inviolable citadel. As a Lutheran, von Salomon was surely not ignorant of Bora's descent from the reformer's wife, even though he might not know that the landed Boras from Bora (or Borna) itself had remained Catholic with the stubbornness of Saxons who do not give in to anyone, not even other Saxons. Whatever the case, it was excessive praise, and Bora said so.

The lieutenant colonel shook his balding head. "No, no, allow me. I speak from experience; I met my demons in the winter of '41. If you haven't been told – and I'd rather you heard it directly from me – I was repatriated in the winter of '41 after a serious nervous breakdown. They sent me first to Bad Pyrmont, then to Sommerfeld, closer to home. It was just exhaustion, not insanity. As you can see, I have recovered perfectly."

Bora nodded. Bad Pyrmont, at the border with Switzerland, was merely a spa, the same one where his stepfather had gone to brood over Nina's first refusal to marry him in 1912. But at Sommerfeld the army had built nothing less than a sanatorium for the mentally unstable.

It was an unsolicited apology on the part of his superior in rank. Any comment would be superfluous. Yes, Bora had overheard how von Salomon had not come unscathed through the Russian experience, so he was careful (he would be, in any case: military sobriety required it) to keep the mildly expectant attitude of the younger officer. That the man had been repatriated for health reasons as early as the winter of 1941 did not change matters, even though increasingly erratic behaviour, coupled with the tendency to weep over setbacks, was wholly unacceptable in a lieutenant colonel, such as von Salomon had been since 1941. He'd served valorously enough to be decorated once back at the front, but promotion to full colonel still eluded him.

With the coming of spring, he seemed to be flagging again a little. Bora thought of a colleague's worried comment a few days earlier, when he had travelled to Generaloberst Kempf's Poltava HQ to get official support for the organization of his unit. "But then," his colleague told him over a mug of beer, "it could be worse. We've got folks here who are superstitious about walking on the shady side of the street, or leaving their quarters with the left foot. Did I tell you about the captain at Zaporozhye who collects live flies in a glass jar, just to see them cannibalize one another and eventually die? That's sick, isn't it?"

However von Salomon took Bora's discreet silence about health matters, he seemed anxious to change the subject. "How's the update coming along?" he asked.

He meant the painstaking work of gathering details about Soviet guerrilla methods in handbook form: the distilled essence of interrogation, wire-tapping of all kinds and on-sight observation, Bora and his colleagues' ongoing project ever since 1941.

"Satisfactorily so far, Herr Oberstleutnant. It'll soon be ready for use as a third edition of the *Partisan Warfare Handbook*, or as an addendum to what we have already. It's a stand-alone text. Naturally, we're adding items every week." Bora said it to convince himself, trying not to think of the difficulties he was encountering as an interrogator.

"Good, good." Von Salomon stood to place the typewritten sheets about the cavalry unit – meant for Generalleutnant von Groddeck – inside an already overstuffed briefcase. The meeting might have ended here, except he'd apparently heard about the deaths at Krasny Yar, and was "rather intrigued".

"Are you familiar with the place, Major?"

Krasny Yar, again. Bora said he wasn't, not really. "I only went there for the first time yesterday, Herr Oberstleutnant."

"Will you tell me about it?"

Bora bit his tongue. Those Krasny Yar corpses kept coming up, adding trouble to trouble, surfacing in conversation in the same way they surfaced in the woods. Managing the unexpected is always difficult, even in peacetime; when abnormality reigns, the unexpected is intolerable, mostly because you don't recognize it at first. You simply stagger when yet another weight is added. Lucidity, on the other hand, was something he took pride in. What else was there, when one had gone beyond courage and beyond fear? Both words were meaningless now, as if his mind (or soul) had developed calluses and no blow would register upon it until it bled.

He told the colonel what he knew, sketchily because he had errands to run and wanted to make it to the district commissioner's office before a queue grew in front of his office. "None of the victims died from gunfire, so possibly the killer doesn't want to be heard, or perhaps he has no firearms. The dead were mostly women or the elderly, which might make one suspect the attacker may not be in his physical prime; but then, as I understand, mostly women and older people went into the Yar. Our soldiers in the area were never harassed: for the reasons above, or because the killer feared we would then mount a full-scale operation. That's all the solid data, Herr Oberstleutnant. The rest is peasant gabble."

Thankfully, von Salomon had lost interest midway through the exposition. When they parted ways in downtown Merefa, each bound to his next task, the colonel insisted on seeing Bora to his vehicle. Walking between two buildings, he pushed his younger colleague aside with a sudden, barely controlled shove, so that Bora would be the one to step into the shade. It could have been a coincidence, and Bora was careful not to show he'd noticed. As he started the engine, however, he saw the colonel in the rear-view mirror still rigidly keeping to the sunlit centre of the lane, forcing a courier's motorcycle to swerve around him and skirt the wall.

Only three kilometres lay between what Bora called his Merefa outpost (the small schoolhouse on the road to Alexandrovka, with a sombre row of graves outside its courtyard) and the office of Gebietskommissar Alfred Lothar Stark. Despite this, he had time during the brief stretch to face two stocky Russian fighter planes heading for him, hedge-hopping back from who knows where – without ammunition, otherwise they wouldn't have spared the solitary army car. They swept over him so low that he slammed on his brakes and nearly went off the road. He'd just accelerated again when they veered ahead of him, cutting across his path this time. Bora was able to decipher the white letters – *Gitlerji* – painted on one of the fighters. Whatever curse they were addressing Hitler with in Cyrillic, they attracted the attention of the German pilots stationed at Rogany, who appeared from nowhere, skimming the roofs with machine guns blazing. And even if they barely missed Bora, they scored a direct hit on a picket fence, pulverizing it along with the ridge pole of the *izba* beyond, only to vanish behind the rooftops after their fleeing enemies, towards Oseryanka.

When Bora reached his destination, an ominous plume of black smoke to the west marked the place where one of the Russian fighters had most likely met its end. The sky was otherwise free of noise and of the peculiar happy blue of the season. As a pilot's brother, on principle Bora did not wish evil to flyers in general. All he could do was hope that there was another reason for the black cloud out there.

The building that served as Stark's brand-new headquarters had in the old days been the residence of a German manufacturer, such as one found in and around Kharkov before the Revolution. Whether descendants of Moravians settled here long ago or technologically advanced newcomers, Germans had frequented the region for years. The brick construction, gabled and tall, with the date 1895 inscribed on a limestone scroll under the peak of the roof, could have stood anywhere on German soil. Although the long-disused factory behind it had perished during the fighting, the house was still referred to as the *Kombinat*. A branch of the Kharkov railroad led directly to the factory and the residence from the old-fashioned little architectural jewel still called – the war notwithstanding – New Bavaria Station. The *Kombinat*'s façade bore signs of the house's old elegance, including stained glass in the bullseye windows by the door, miraculously intact. And this even though (Bora knew; he'd gone in a couple of times before) the interior had been partitioned into cubicles years ago to host *Rabfak* worker–students of the Kharkov Technical Institute for Engineers, and later the aeroplane factory employees. Only the ground floor maintained some of the old glory, and the district commissioner's office was just inside the main entrance, to the right.

Bora was in luck. No queue: only Russian prisoners on their knees, waxing the floor. In the small parlour to the left, a brown-jacketed assistant enquired as to his business; he then leapt from behind his desk, stepped across the corridor and opened Stark's double door just enough to put his head through. Whatever he was told, the assistant simply slid both wooden leaves wide open and went back to his desk.

"Major Bora," Stark called, seeing him on the threshold. "Come in, come in. What have you got for me today?"

Bora walked in. The panelled, well-lit room was overly spacious, but then space was needed for the amount of paperwork that started and ended here; in just a few weeks, the Gebietskommissar (Geko, as he was nicknamed) had set up an efficient system of managing people and resources in the area that the army countenanced mostly because it hampered the Security Service's overbearing. Whatever Stark's office had been earlier – most likely a parlour – it had some pretence of elegance: a high ceiling, coffered, a chandelier shaped like a transverse metal bar, on which etched opaline glass bulbs the size of melons lined up; glass cabinets; a spotless, carpetless oak floor. Stark himself, in his gold-brown SA blouse, radiated both optimism and a busy man's problem-solving attitude. Asking Bora what he might have for him only revealed his trust that officers would spontaneously turn in captured goods or civilians for labour. They'd met a week earlier on account of the mounts Bora still needed to bring his unit to full strength, Stark displaying an impressive knowledge of the horseflesh yet available in the Kharkov Oblast.

Bora said, "I actually have a couple of questions for you, District Commissioner."

Stark gestured for him to sit down while he continued to converse with someone on the telephone. "Not the insecticide again, Colonel… I've got your requests here. I read them; I understand. But we're strapped for it; we need it for other hospitals. Believe me, if I could, I would. I shipped it all out last week. Well, bricks we *do* have; I got a load straight from Nova Vodolaga. If it's bricks you want, and nothing else, I can favour you." Covering the mouthpiece, Stark looked over. He saw that Bora remained standing, and took it to mean he was in haste. "Yes, Major?" he enquired.

"I need five women —" Bora began to say.

"*Five* women?" Stark lowered the receiver, smiling in a friendly way. "That's the cavalry for you. You need *five* women?"

"— to do the wash ing and cleaning for us, Herr Gebietskommissar."

Stark grunted a "Yes, goodbye" into the mouthpiece, and returned the receiver to its cradle. Looking over the top of his glasses, he leafed through the typewritten sheets in a neat folder of his. "Well, if that's all you horse boys need them for, Major, I've got five babushkas your grandma's age."

"They'll do."

"Have them picked up tomorrow morning sevenish at the Merefa station, and then stop by to sign the paperwork. What's the other question?"

"Well, it *was* insecticide until I heard you a moment ago. I did try to remedy things on my own, but – I brought along a list the medical corps gave me. I think it's a crescendo, in terms of efficacy. Pyrethrum, for example. I don't know where to find it, even though I have access to three out of the four other components – coal oil, ether and turpentine. Naphthalene I think I could scrounge from maintenance if they have some to spare."

"Pyrethrum? We've got none."

"Potassium arsenite was my next bet. Other ingredients: ten parts of milk is fine, but where do I find molasses?" (Stark shook his head.) "So, I'm down to sulphur dioxide, even though without pressurized bottles we'd have to burn it on a gas cooker for – what, seven hours or so? With wooden huts and straw roofs, it's not a great idea. For best results, hospitals recommend hydrocyanic acid, better if Zyklon B, poured on floors and sealed off. But the ventilation time —"

"*Please!*" Stark raised his hands in an alarmed gesture. "Leave the hydrocyanic acid alone; don't even think of it! You'd kill yourselves *and* your mounts. I'll see if I can get you bottled sulphur dioxide. You'll have to ration it like water in the desert, though. For a closed room, 100 grams per square metre will do, in about five hours."

"When may I send for it?"

"I said I'll see if I can get it. Send someone on Friday if I don't call you back." The phone rang again as Bora left, and Stark picked up the receiver while shaking his head. "*Zyklon B*," he muttered. "What are they thinking?"

Bora thanked him and left. As golden pheasants went, District Commissioner Stark was better than most. Physically, he'd have resembled a sturdy pheasant even without the administrator's telltale brown-yellow blouse. The fact that his office had just been set up here within the bounds of militarily administered Ukraine represented an escalation in the infighting among the Party, the SS and Rosenberg's Ministry for Eastern Occupied Territories. The Army steered clear of the tiff, but Bora's "new father-in-law", as he called his wife's stepfather, was too close to the Party's inner circle for him not to have heard about it.

By all accounts, considering that it was his charge to extract all that was possible from this region, Geko Stark did it with some basic humanity. Perhaps his early days as a newspaperman had a role in that. He'd given up a rich post as a Gauleiter to serve here, and now operated from Merefa like a tranquil spider in its web, keeping in touch with his assistants on the road. Stark's strong voice (the voice of an industrialist, more or less his own grandfather's voice at the publishing house, clear and distinct) reached Bora in the corridor, where he had stopped to read communiqués on a bulletin board. The Russian prisoners waxing the floor drew back on their knees, making room for him, without raising their heads. Yes, Stark was organizing things. Soon everyone would have to come knocking here to get what was needed. If Generaloberst Kempf resented having such gross civilian interference in his sector, he kept it to himself, or had other things to worry about. Leaving the *Kombinat*,

Bora overheard Stark bellow, "And where am I to find *those*?" over the phone, whatever *those* were.

Eventually all of Ukraine (Gothland, now that Himmler had renamed it) would be under civil administration. If there was time. To Bora it made little difference whether he had to go to Army supply or to a former SA in order to get what he needed. But for SA Oberführer Magunia of the Kiev General District, not to mention Ministerial Director for Ukraine, Erich Koch – who by squeezing blood out of turnips had exasperated the sleepy locals into armed resistance – finding oneself next door to a spurious Area District under the cool-headed, effective Alfred Lothar Stark might be a nuisance. Magunia had taken his vengeance by granting him no more than a skeleton crew, so that the Commissar had to do most of the work himself out of the busy little office at Merefa. Whatever insecticide *he* used, there were no flies in his office, but the moment Bora stepped out, they were a nuisance again. On the other hand, there was no running water anywhere; jerrycans had to be hauled for the most basic needs. Toilet bowls – when available – reeked; sinks reeked. Latrines reeked of carbolic acid over the stench of human waste. Bora chased the flies from his path. The five babushkas he'd send for in the morning would have to do the troopers' washing on the bank of the closest river, like in the beginning of the world.

With just enough gasoline in his tank to make it to Kharkov and back, Bora started out for the third meeting of the day, and it was barely 9.30 a.m. His additional task at the moment, as if bringing his unit up to full size were not enough, was what he'd been painstakingly trained for: interrogating Russian prisoners, mostly high-ranking officers and the occasional party bureaucrat. For him, ever since the start of the campaign, interrogating those political commissars who hadn't been executed on the spot had gone hand in hand with reconnaissance duty and the frequent, bloody skirmishes with the enemy. They'd given him headaches, those ideologically obdurate young men whom he often only got to see after they'd already been beaten or tortured. In some cases he succeeded in extracting something out of them; in most cases, he failed and could do nothing as they were dragged out to the gallows or the firing squad. As of this spring, he had been faring better with disheartened Ukrainian partisans, and best of all with privates and a few grudging non-coms. Officers were a mixed bag: some committed suicide (but not as often as commissars did), and others could be talked into saying what they knew, which was sometimes – not always – of real use.

With colonels, and more recently a handful of generals, each represented a case in its own right. Bora had a good record with them. Among them, however, General-Lieutenant Gleb Platonov was a thorn in his side. Old fox that he was, he hadn't answered a single question put to him by Army interrogators since his capture in mid-April aboard a plane that had got lost in the fog and crash-landed on this side of the Donets. Surviving his badly injured pilot, he'd managed to burn the papers he had with him before the Germans reached the accident site. Identification had only been possible through photographs until a couple of his unranked Russian prisoners, who had nothing to gain from keeping mum, confirmed who he was.

Bora, to whom the prisoner had been sent as a last resort due to his extensive interrogation experience, bristled with irritation even as he drove to South Kharkov. For over ten days Platonov (referred to as Number Five) had sat in front of him with his mouth shut, blinking every now and again, impervious to all arguments. Bora kept the pressure on, but knowing the man's past – how, tried and jailed during Stalin's purges, he'd only been fished out when war made it necessary – his hopes of breaking him were dim. Platonov used the poor health of his three years in Siberia to his advantage; more than once he'd passed out (or pretended to), forcing Bora to call for medical help and the expected shot of caffeine or whatever else eventually brought him to. The medic from a nearby hospital who periodically checked Bora after his bout with typhoid pneumonia said he couldn't be sure the prisoner suffered from any real pathology. A student drafted before finishing his degree in medicine, Weller had flown out of Stalingrad with the last wounded before the trap closed; now he compensated for the limitations of his non-commissioned rank with thoroughness tinged by melancholy. In his words, "Whatever the prisoner's state, surgeon's orders are that his health be closely guarded, Herr Major." As if Bora didn't know.

The Germans had given Platonov decent quarters in the Velikaya Osnova district at the southern edge of Kharkov, where the Lopany River bent like an elbow and the beleaguered railroad tracks on the opposite side formed a comparable, lesser angle. The area was like an island: the river and the tracks coming down from the South Station nearly touched the river north of the district, and tracks and river crossed below it. The building adapted as a special detention centre stood on Mykolaivska Street, less than a kilometre from the war-damaged hospital on Saikivska. The hospital had once stood in a garden setting, but was sparsely manned these days and being hastily repaired by the Germans. Bora and many others referred to it merely as 169, the number that marked it on army maps, as army units changed and street names alternatively transcribed into German from Russian or Ukrainian only created confusion.

Grabbing his folded tunic from the front seat and stepping inside, Bora asked, for the sake of asking, "Has Number Five said anything?" When the expected negative reply came, he showed none of the crankiness he felt. "There, Mina." He patted the watchdog, a large Belgian shepherd the men here had adopted and aptly renamed after defusing the Soviet anti-tank charges she carried strapped on to her body. "There, girl, let me through. Is she pregnant, or are you making her fat?"

"We're making her fat, Herr Major. She eats anything. You ought to see her catch flies."

Platonov's secure quarters were on the third floor. Bora climbed the stairs, telling himself the obvious: sometimes captured enemies give you a hard time, sometimes they collaborate at once; most of them have to be worked on. But, damn it, Lieutenant General Platonov had withstood Stalin's methods. Bora wasn't in a hurry but would be soon, since Platonov stood to know about the latest STAVKA plans, the line-up of Soviet forces in the Kursk salient, and – most importantly – details about the reserves massed at the back of them.

At the first landing, he stopped to remove his pistol belt in anticipation of wearing the tunic over his summer army shirt for the sake of protocol. As if it were worth it. Platonov strongly disliked him, and if in his arrogance (his rank and connected importance allowed him) he addressed his jailers as "brown vermin" and "fascist garbage", to Bora he said nothing at all, not even "good day". The same routine repeated itself day after day: he stood, Platonov sat, and told him nothing. Ten minutes or an hour made no difference to his silence; and neither did an entire night of patient reasoning on Bora's part.

But then… At the start of the second week of detention, Bora discovered through informants that Platonov's wife and daughter, reportedly victims of Stalin's Purge, lived in Poltava, some 150 kilometres south-west of Kharkov. Far away, but by Russian standards practically next door. Through all kinds of bureaucratic snags and difficulties he'd arranged for the women to be picked up and brought to Kharkov as soon as possible. It was a matter of days now. This morning, Bora planned to show the prisoner a photograph he'd ordered to be taken of his two relatives: indoors, without recognizable landmarks or objects other than this month's calendar on the wall. *See, we have your women*, it meant. *Unlike Stalin, who told you they were dead, we haven't even arrested them. Yet.* It could be done in a friendly or in a threatening way, without in the least contravening protocol; such an exchange of precious goods might be irresistible for a man who hadn't seen his family in six years.

Third landing. Flies circled in the narrow corridor leading to the rooms adapted as cells, all empty at the moment except the general's. Above, on the fourth floor, there was only one more room set up, where Bora occasionally spent the night when interrogations dragged late into the dark hours. Regardless of the stifling heat, Bora now put on and buttoned his tunic, buckling his pistol belt over it. When he slipped the photo of the prisoner's women inside his left breast pocket, his fingertips touched the button he'd picked up in the woods.

No, he didn't look forward to facing Platonov's bad-humoured leanness again. Dark and tall once, he'd grown stooped and grey by the time of his rehabilitation, but in the way rock only grows harder. You'd never believe he had nightmares and the guards sometimes heard him cry out at night.

Entering the room, furnished with every comfort that could not be used for committing suicide, Bora surprised himself by thinking of Krasny Yar. Touching the button had sufficed to take him back there. How was it possible that a bushy piece of land with a handful of murdered Russians in it kept bobbing up to the surface when millions had died thus far? It annoyed him. *The Russkis will try to spook us if they can't do anything else,* the non-com had said. Well, maybe.

Platonov, seated in a green velvet armchair, would not even raise his eyes towards him. For a change, Bora didn't open his mouth either. He took the prisoner's indifference in his stride, and walked around the small table to face Platonov as he sat with his eyes doggedly turned to the floor. Having been briefly in enemy hands himself a year and a half earlier, he fully understood the refusal to give information. He'd done the same; the Russians had broken his left arm for it. But then he'd managed to escape. Despite the velvet seat and lace doily on the table, Platonov would no more be given the chance of fleeing now than he'd been given by Stalin back then. As a rule, Bora normally remained standing, but this time he reached for a stool and seated himself across from the prisoner.

Platonov looked up. Bora met his glance, as one would acknowledge a fellow passenger on a train. For close to twenty minutes they sat facing each other, Bora steadily keeping his eyes on Platonov while he stared past him at the opposite wall. Neither man moved, shifted his weight on the seat or even caused its wooden frame to creak. There was a solitary fly in the cell, and Bora could hear it land and take off from various objects.

To the prisoner, it was perhaps one more form of nerve-wracking challenge to resist; to Bora it amounted to an exercise of mental discipline, devoid of emotion. And although no one could know what Platonov was thinking, Bora let a myriad other sensations, all unrelated to the place and moment, go through him without thinking about them, in the same way a breeze on a water's surface doesn't affect it enough to make it ripple. Platonov's seamed face, marked by pain and overbearing, might equally indicate a similar ability to abstract himself, or else the stolid, spiteful intention to withhold communication now and forever.

Finally Bora rose to his feet. Tight-lipped, he unbuttoned his breast pocket, took out the photograph and laid it on the table, face down. By the time he curtly rapped on the door to be let out, the prisoner had made no attempt to turn the print around or even reach for it; he might have lowered his glance to it, but Bora didn't stick around to see whether this was the case.

Letting things settle in Platonov's mind was all Bora could do for now. He started back for Merefa, and at the Udy River crossing he began to think some luck was already coming his way. A makeshift filling station had been improvised by army engineers in a clearing by the road, too good an opportunity to pass by. The officer in charge was unsympathetic at first; lorries and half-tracks took precedence. In the end he agreed to give him half a tank, but remarked, "You know, you cavalrymen ought to travel on fodder. Where's your horse, Major?"

Gasoline being at a premium, it was best not to argue. Bora replied with the truth: that time was too tight this morning for a ride. He'd driven uneventfully as far as the Kremesnaya turn-off when a motorcycle courier overtook him in a storm of fine dust, signalling for him to slow down, much as a traffic policeman gives directions to an unruly driver.

The army vehicle came head to head with the still-running motorcycle, and stopped. "Major Bora?" the courier enquired, raising the goggles on his forehead.

"Yes. What is it?"

"I was told at the Mykolaivska Street detention centre I'd find you along this road, Major." The courier took a folded sheet out of his pouch. "There's a high-priority communication awaiting you at Borovoye."

"Borovoye?" Bora scanned the message, which bore the name of an *Abwehr* colleague usually stationed at Smijeff, on the Donets.

The courier turned the motorcycle around, in the direction of Kharkov. "You could go back five kilometres and take the first dirt road to the right, but I don't recommend it: they're still clearing it of mines. You might as well keep on to Merefa at this point."

"Thank you; I know the road from there."

What his foul-mouthed colleague Bruno Lattmann might be doing at Borovoye, in the middle of nowhere, was not indicated on the sheet. The place was at least thirty kilometres from here, which in Ukraine meant anywhere between one and two hours' travel. There was nothing at Borovoye as far as he knew. His first thought was that the courier would bring news of Platonov: that he was ready to talk – or that he'd smashed his head against the wall. Now, Bora didn't know what to think.

The dirt trails were a nightmare of ruts and crumbling shoulders once away from the minimally maintained roads. On both sides, fallow fields, burned farms, flocks of peasant women around the occasional water troughs and long stretches of absolute, undulating solitude went by.

Son of a Deutsche Welle radio executive, Lattmann was a close friend. When they'd last met ten days earlier, the conversation had ended on a personal note, not unusually for them. "Can you confirm she's still living there?" Bora had asked.

"Yes. I thought you'd have gone to see her already."

"I haven't."

"What are you waiting for? For the front to turn again?"

"It was a long relationship, Bruno. I'm in two minds about it."

"Well, this is probably the last chance you have. A year ago things were different, but now... If it matters to you, you'd better make time to see her."

Recalling the conversation, Bora sped as much as the road allowed. Yes, he'd have to go and see Larisa. He promised himself he'd do it. At Stalingrad, towards the end, he'd told himself, full of regret, *I'll die without seeing her again.* Now he resisted again. *If there's time, I'll go.*

Not that Lattmann would be sending couriers or urgent messages about private matters. When Bora reached Borovoye, just before noon, he found a small radio shack newly set up there, and his *Abwehr* colleague pacing back and forth in front of it.

The first words Lattmann said were, "Fucking hell, Bora, I've been chasing you all morning!"

"I've been busy all morning."

"Drop *everything.* We've got a top-ranking Russian commander who waded over this morning from across the Donets. News came in via radio, coded and in Morse. Seems he contacted us beforehand on our radio frequency to keep us from shooting at him. Says he's defecting."

"Really." After Platonov, Bora wasn't looking for another disappointment. "Are we sure?"

Lattmann took him by the arm and led him out of the shack, away from the radio man. "Listen to this. He asks specifically for the head of our Office of Foreign Intelligence III."

"Specifically?"

"By name. And rank. It's possible he might know about Colonel Bentivegni, you'll say. Well, he also speaks serviceable German, and seems to know lots about us."

Us meant Counterintelligence to those in it. German-speaking Russian officers were not infrequent; the generation before Bora's had learnt Russian while training secretly in the Soviet Union during the Weimar days, and vice versa. Bora remained cautious.

"Does he. Hm. And who does he say he is?"

"*He* says he's Tibyetsky."

Bora felt a nervous sting down to his fingertips, like an electric shock. "The 'Tibetan'? The one they call Khan?"

"Right."

"Jesus Christ. Jesus Christ, we had him facing us in Stalingrad. He's into *all* of STAVKA's planning. Can it be...? It'd be the lucky break of the year!"

Lattmann grinned. "You're the interrogator; you be the judge. He came rumbling up in a brand-new model of tank the Panzer Corps will drool over. Big stuff. Scherer, whom you know, was called in for armoured support in case it were a trick, and cordoned off the place."

Other than Konev and Rokossovsky, Khan was the prize catch of a lifetime, never mind the year. To hell with Platonov and his convenient swoons. Bora could hardly contain himself. Tibyetsky was as elusive as his assumed name. (Like other old revolutionaries, he had two or three aliases.) Bora had studied him as far back as Cavalry School and the War Academy, and what Khan had later achieved at Stalingrad, at Smolensk, was legendary. Hero of the Soviet Union, awarded the Red and Gold Stars, and God knows what other medals... All hope of taking him prisoner had been out of the question. How likely was it that he should defect – and now? *If I think how he thundered over the loudspeakers while we were spitting blood in Stalingrad so we'd surrender, if I think he bowled us over just four months ago...*

"Bruno, when can I see him?"

Without being asked, Lattmann placed a jerrycan of gasoline in the back of Bora's vehicle. He habitually chewed his nails, and his fingertips always gave the impression of having been nibbled by fish.

"Go at once. Scherer is anxious for you to get there. The Russian is still inside his tank and won't get down until we assure him an official contact will be made with Bentivegni in Berlin-Zossen. So I checked with our Kiev people. Given the mess on the Tunisian front, Colonel Bentivegni is reported 'somewhere' in Southern Italy conferring with commanders there, more's the shame. By the way, it was coincidence that Scherer and his unit were in transit to the 11th Panzer Division's new deployment area; imagine how desperate they are to get their hands on the tank. I needn't tell you that the *Abwehr* must have the defector first before RSHA gets hold of him; the Central Security Office would transfer him then, and we wouldn't get another chance." Given that when alone with Bora Lattmann usually spoke of the RSHA as "Kaltenbrunner's thugs", it was a sign of his haste that he'd simply called SS-Gestapo intelligence by its acronym.

Bora flew over every rut and pothole along the next twenty-odd kilometres; any forgotten landmine in the criss-cross of dishevelled lanes zigzagging between Borovoye and the river could have blown him sky-high.

2

The immediate area along the Donets, south of the ford Bora himself had used the day before, was cordoned off by troops, a sign of the importance and secrecy of the event. All around stood heavily armed soldiers and artillery from the 161st, in case it were a ruse, and, further back, armoured vehicles and three tank busters from the 11th Panzer at the ready. The place where the Russian tank had stopped was on the nearside of a slight incline fifty or so metres from the river bank, undetectable from enemy lines. On its oversized turret the commander's cupola was open, and a man in a leather jacket and visored cap stood leaning, with his arms crossed over its rim. Distant grass fires to the east, invisible from here, caused infinitesimal flecks of grey ash to rain slowly over the scene, resembling bits of foil.

Without drawing close, Bora took a long look through his field glasses. Photos of Brigadier General Tibyetsky existed, none taken close-up since the start of the war, but he had seen several from the late '30s. His heartbeat accelerated; Bora could feel it in his throat. Between January and June 1941 until a week before the invasion, as assistant to the military attaché in Moscow, he'd gathered all available information about the Red Army's higher ranks, including the tank corps general most likely to give Germany a run for its money once hostilities began. It made Bora's head spin to think of him less than fifty metres away now, on this side of the Donets. As mysterious as his nickname, earned after his revolutionary activity in the steppes of Central Asia, he went by Tibyetsky but that, too, was an assumed battle name, like "Stalin" or "Molotov". Bora also knew him as Petrov and Dobronin, and there might be other aliases. If this defection was a trick, it was a luscious one, a trap he longed to jump into headlong.

The Russian had meanwhile taken his own field glasses in hand, and was surveying the array of troops facing him. Eventually, he turned to the shaded spot where Bora's vehicle was parked, and there was an exchange of stares through their respective lenses. Cinders slowly swirled in the air between them. The mound of steel and the man on top of it stood motionless behind that lingering, erratic reel of minute specks.

"It's about time you got here, Scotsman."

Caught up in his observation, Bora was startled by the voice nearby. A flushed and smiling Scherer stood by him. As a former cavalryman and colleague from the heady days of the invasion, like others at that time he'd referred to Bora as *Der Schotte*, because of his mother's lineage. "He won't deal with any of us, Scotsman," he said, out of breath. "Look at that turret, will you?" He pointed to the T-34. "What a *beast*. The tank alone is worth instant leave to Germany. If he's rigged it with explosives, I'm ready to defuse it with my teeth. I'm having an orgasm over that tank."

"Well, I'm having an orgasm over *him*." Bora put away the field glasses, dry-mouthed with anticipation. "If he isn't Ghenrikh Tibyetsky, I'm not standing here with you. Has he said anything?" It was the same question he'd asked about Platonov; but who cared about Platonov now?

"Other than what I told Lattmann? No. Won't let us get any closer, and threatens to blow his head off with his sidearm if we try. When we mentioned there'd be somebody from Counterintelligence coming, he answered to not try and deceive him as he's informed about the officers working for Colonel von Bentivegni in this sector."

"*Really.* He may be bluffing."

"Whatever. See if you can get him to climb down."

Bora took a deep breath. Unhurriedly he walked through the soldiers' cordon, coming within five metres of the Russian tank and maybe a foot from the mouth of its formidable 85mm cannon. "Komandir Tibyetsky" – he addressed him in Russian – "welcome. You asked to speak to an IC officer?"

Khan let the field glasses dangle from the strap around his neck. He replied to the salute curtly. "I asked to speak to Bentivegni. Colonel Eccard von Bentivegni has to come here for me."

"Yes, of course." It was a challenge not showing how ready they all were to accommodate him. Bora counted to ten before adding, "It can be arranged. I'll need a few days."

"A few days? No." Irritably Khan turned away. "No."

"May I ask why?"

A fleeting pause followed, less than a drawing of breath. "My comrades' bodies are inside this tank, and in this weather 'a few days' is not acceptable."

Khan's crewmen were *dead?* It could be true. Where Bora was standing, a burst of machine-gun fire from the gunner's hatch would literally cut him in half. Somewhere, the instant of absolute panic turned into a kind of nervous bliss. The lazily raining ash flakes, so fragile they dissolved as they touched men and things, were at odds with the thrill of the moment. "Well, Commander, we haven't fired upon your vehicle. How can it be that they died?"

"I shot them. You don't suppose I could cross over with their approval."

No; and if this was truly a defection, not with the approval of Soviet units on the other bank, either. In any case, whatever his plan, however Khan had managed to slip away, his exploit could result in a cannonade from across the Donets at any time. Bora wished his heart rate would stabilize. They were much too close to the river here. The idea of losing the prize before having a chance to speak with him was intolerable. "Three days is the best I can do, sir." Highly strung as he was, he tried to make light of things. "I'm not God."

Khan still looked away from him. Clearly he, too, didn't want to give others the satisfaction of reading his thoughts. He must suspect the German officer was striving not to betray his enthusiasm, and in turn kept silent about the reason (which must be a colossal one) that brought him here. An innovative T-34 was in itself a passport of immense value; the fact that a commander in his position had eliminated his crewmen to come across indicated a superior motive that might well require Colonel Bentivegni to fly to Rogany, or to the closest landing patch.

Bora waited for an answer, heart in mouth. The mighty armoured box, a monument to its own firepower, faced him with its tons of steel. The T-34 as Bora knew it (*tridsatchetverka*, the "Little 34") came to less than half the weight of a German Tiger, but agility, plate and cannon made it a frightful enemy. A few steps behind him, Scherer bragged to someone about the heavily armoured cupola ("That thing is *huge* – I bet it can hold three men by itself!"). Yes, and more: beyond plate, firepower, brute size, this was the shape of things to come. Tibyetsky stared down at him with a frown, alone on his perch. But suddenly to Bora the crest of the rise behind the tank, shielding it from a river that coincided with the front, was the threshold of a doomsday vanguard. From here to the Don, to the Volga, to Siberia, behind the general, he could imagine millions of Russians lined up in multiple depths beyond it. A storm of ashes from infinite fires whirled over them. The idea of an apocalyptic herd of such mastodons surging over the top of the rise staggered him. Taking Khan away from the firing line was an absolute priority.

"Commander Tibyetsky, sir, may we have proof that your crewmen are inactive?"

"I said they're *dead*."

"May we have proof of it?"

Khan twisted his mouth in contempt. "No." And then, impatiently, "What difference does it make? I could blast you like skittles by myself, if I chose to, tank busters and all. Are you Major Martin-Heinz von Bora?"

He pronounced it *Geinz*, not Heinz, but it was impossible not to blink in the face of recognition. "I'm Bora."

"May I have proof of it?"

Bullseye. Bora knew when he was bested. "Commander, you have my word that I will expedite the connection with the office you seek."

"I demand to speak to Bentivegni myself."

"By all means. But it can't be done from inside your vehicle."

Khan took a last domineering look around, at the armed men and beyond them. From his vantage point he must have been able to see a long way, into the rolling fields and wilderness stretching between here and Kharkov. Grasping the rim of the cupola, he straddled it with his powerful, booted right leg. "Three days: I can see you're not God."

Bora breathlessly made a mental list of steps to take and levels of clearance to obtain. Within the next half-hour, Tibyetsky climbed down from the T-34, turned in his pistol to him, grip first (Bora checked the magazine and gave it back in the same way), and allowed German soldiers to climb in. He supervised them as they extracted one by one the corpses of his four crewmen, all shot at close range, presumably by the bullets missing from his Tokarev.

Ashes were no longer filling the air. The scent and aftertaste of burning stubble hovered above him as Bora made his plans. Immediate communication with *Abwehr* in Zossen, some 1,200 kilometres away, could only be established by short-wave radio. Bora was familiar with a powerful TFA station set up by the 161st not far away, in the Beriozovy Yar woods north of Losukovka. Soon he was ready to accompany the general there, while Scherer, who had driven the T-34 under tree cover, would follow with his men and armoured vehicles.

The radio shack was a two-room makeshift cabin along the dirt road that parted the woods like a scar, running along the bottom of a shallow ravine that ran from south-east to north-west. A blindfolded, disgruntled Khan dismounted from Bora's vehicle and reached the place on foot, escorted by the major. Behind them, in the Russian tank, Scherer crushed everything in his path.

Bora's destination for army-related intelligence was Field Marshal Manstein's headquarters at Zaporozhye, and as far as his *Abwehr* headquarters counterparts; normally he'd send coded messages through the usual channels, a relay system based on the network of intelligence listening and transmitting posts in the occupied East, first among them the *Abwehr Nebenstelle*, the branch office in Kiev.

This time he contacted the headquarters in Zossen directly, only to receive confirmation that Colonel Bentivegni was unavailable. When Bora reported it Khan grumbled about the delay, but he had little choice.

"It's a matter of waiting until they physically track him down, Commander Tibyetsky, then they'll call back with a secure date for the colonel coming here to meet you."

"Yes? It had better be within the three days you said, Major."

Generals are the same worldwide, Bora thought, having one at home. After sending a message to Manstein's office in Zaporozhye, there were more delays waiting for a reply from that end, too. Bora sat with Tibyetsky in the dirt-floored room that served as quarters for the communication crew. At one point the Russian asked for bottled water, which the Germans didn't have. Bora offered his canteen, but – whether he feared being poisoned or drugged, or else didn't like the offer – Khan demanded that the major himself bring him a sealed drink from inside the tank, along with other amenities of his, including cigars.

Bora left him under armed guard and complied. In the cramped belly of the T-34, momentarily vacated by an enthusiastic Scherer, he was less affected by the dead crewmen's blood than by the stacked shells and ammunition boxes. What struck him most, however, were the fresh American-made provisions Russian tankers enjoyed. A memory of Stalingrad's misery, especially on the German side, pierced him: as if canned goods, calorie-packed D rations and powdered milk were telling him, even more directly than the massive hull they were in, that Germany couldn't win this war. He scrupulously gathered what the general asked for, recommending his tank corps colleague set the rest aside, away from the soldiers' understandable greed.

Soon Khan was sipping a Fanta-type fruit drink from the bottle, one such as Germany had started producing after Coca-Cola had become an enemy brand and was no longer on sale. "Where am I to wait for Bentivegni's arrival?" he asked.

"In a safe location, Commander Tibyetsky."

"My tank?"

"Likewise. And if you have no objections, your crew will be interred today in the closest civilian burial ground."

"I have no objections. They had a clean death: they were lucky."

Bora tended to agree, apart from the minor detail of friendly fire. "As matters stand, and with all respect, regarding your journey to the safe location I'm sure you'll understand we have to take precautions, including a change of clothing. During some stretches we may have to resort to a blindfold. In all cases I'll be at your side, regrettably with a loaded gun."

"A *loaded gun*. Indeed! So why did you let me keep my own sidearm, Major?"

Bora stayed on this side of a smile. "I wouldn't advise you to try to use it."

"Oh, what the hell," Khan said out of the blue, casually and in passable German. He gave Bora his pistol and sat back. "Let's wait until we hear from your superiors before we decide how to travel."

The Tokarev gun, safety catch engaged, slipped into Bora's briefcase. His watch read 2.15 p.m. Any time now the radio reply from Bentivegni's office would arrive. The man draining the bottle in front of him, strawberry blond, stocky, was more the Russian general type than Platonov, and yet they said he wasn't even Russian by birth. In his fifties, Tibyetsky looked the picture of health, without a wrinkle on his face, radiating a sort of glow. His top-quality boots, fine leather jacket over a well-sewn tunic shirt and breeches reinforced at the knee spoke of good discipline and self-care.

Bora was glad he had kept up his own warring looks, despite the season and the fortunes of war, because it wouldn't do to look less than spruce before a Frunze Academy graduate (and instructor) such as this. Picking up the empty bottle and tossing it into the wastebasket, he said, "I've admired you ever since Cavalry School. Your exploits in Finland, and then in Mongolia against Sternberg's 'Wild Division'… Your victory against Baron Sternberg's Whites at Urga in '21 was exemplary, although your comrades didn't make the best use of it. Shchetinkin stole your thunder by executing him, I think."

With a freckled forefinger, Khan dabbed the corners of his mouth. He watched Bora for nearly a minute before observing in an amused voice, "You won't soft-soap me into talking, you know."

The words stung. Bora had some difficulty concealing his annoyance. "Flattering a general-rank officer from any army would never cross my mind, Commander. I was making conversation. In my youthful regard for your military skills, silly as I was, I even came up with a little theory about your beginnings, which isn't worth reporting here."

"My *beginnings*? I doubt it."

"Well, you must understand that my stepfather and other members of the family fought against the Revolution in the Russian civil war: for us at home it was a frequent matter of discussion."

"I want one of my cigars," was all Khan said.

Bora had them ready in the briefcase; he took one out and

lit it for the general. They were Soyuzie brand, individually wrapped inside a daintily carved wooden box.

Behind the pungent smoke, Khan rounded his lips around the cigar, half-closing his eyes. Unreadable as he was, the squint might either mean he silently had agreed to listen to what Bora had to say, or else that he felt no interest in the argument. Bora would have to take his own counsel regarding the conversation. *What is he here for,* he kept wondering, *what is he, other than a tank commander? Why is he letting us know he's acquainted with our names and tasks? It's not an intelligence officer's way of acting, but then again... I hope they do locate Colonel Bentivegni and let him know he's here.*

"So, Major, how did you learn about me?"

"Other than studying your tactics? I watched all the 8 mm reels about you: speeches at the Frunze Academy, tank manoeuvres, your testimonial at Lenin's funeral —"

"You didn't watch *all* my reels."

"Well, I watched all that I could find."

Khan seemed tickled. "Young officers: how similar the world over you are. Luckily youth makes you as dumb as you are ambitious: you'd be dangerous otherwise."

If he weren't who he is, I'd never let myself be talked down to this way. Bora checked his watch to avoid betraying his irritation. By the way Khan smiled, however, it was possible that he had read Bora's thoughts.

At 2.35 p.m., confirmation of Manstein's keen interest in the T-34 arrived from his chief of staff at Zaporozhye. Zossen's *Abwehr* reply followed right after. Bora left the room for the time needed to hear and decode the messages, and was soon able to announce Bentivegni's readiness to meet personally with General Tibyetsky on Friday 7 May at the latest. Thankfully Khan seemed inclined to accept the time frame. In reality, to his surprise, Bora had also been tersely directed not to make use of a blindfold or other restrictive devices. Silently he started jotting down notes to himself, but glanced up when the Russian, mouthing his cigar, said, "Weren't there instructions for you as well, Major Bora?"

Bora would not answer. Khan smiled, stretching his booted legs. Without his cap, the reddish stubble on his meaty head glittered with beads of perspiration; the wooden building was very warm. "I rather thought so," he commented when the blindfold did not make its reappearance.

There was much yet to do, and not much time to do it. Calls were placed to half a dozen command posts and offices across the Kharkov region before Bora was actually ready to go. Outside the cabin, meanwhile, Scherer had used branches and netting to disguise the T-34's type and marking in preparation for transporting it. He was now dying to start out.

"It's twelve kilometres from here to the Smijeff–Gottwald rail station," Bora walked out to tell him. "Driving this thing across country it'll take you, what – half an hour or so? Once there, you're to load the tank onto the Kharkov-bound freight train and travel with it to the Kharkov–Lasevo station."

"Isn't that in the Tractor Factory district?"

"Precisely."

"I thought it'd been razed in the fighting!"

"Not quite." Bora handed him a scribbled notebook page. "Get the T-34 inside Building G for the time being. Here are more precise directions. I'll meet you there as soon as possible, to ensure all is well."

"Anything else?"

"Yes. I'll need a non-commissioned officer's Tank Corps suit, boots and a head cover that'll fit Tibyetsky. An identification tag and a credible *Soldbuch* too, better one without a photograph. Can you help? I'll have enough trouble as it is motoring with him from here to where I'm going."

Soon Scherer came up with the items, minus the footwear. "If he takes off his jacket, he can wear blouse and trousers over what he's got now. Sorry about the boots; I can't help you there."

"I'm thankful for what there is, Jochen." Bora draped the reed-green canvas clothing over his arm. "I'll return the tag and *Soldbuch* when we meet at the Tractor Works. And don't let the tank out of your sight: the Field Marshal wants to take a look at it himself."

Scherer smiled under the black skull-badged cap. "They'd have to kill me first, Scotsman."

Rumbling and screeching over a bed of flattened shrubs and small trees, the T-34 headed out of the Beriozovy woods, towards the clearing where the 11th Division tank busters waited in order to accompany it.

Another hour went by. Feeling under pressure to maintain the appearance of absolute control, Bora straddled the cabin's doorstep. As for Khan, he unhurriedly let the cigar go out in his mouth as if this weren't a pivotal moment in his life and he hadn't fired four shots into his crewmen's heads.

At last a requisitioned City Soviet president's car, a sturdy pre-war GAZ-61 sent up from Smijeff under the escort of armoured cars, came bumping along the ruts of the forest road. It was only at that point that Bora handed the Panzer uniform to the Russian. "If you don't mind, sir."

Khan took a contemptuous look at the clothes. Showing no sign of accepting Bora's invitation to wear them, he uncrossed his legs without haste. "Lighter, please," he said. "I want to finish my smoke before we head out."A moment later, however, he changed his mind about the cigar, dropped it to the dirt floor and squashed it under the sole of his boot. Before handing over the leather jacket he conceitedly took out of its breast pocket a photo of himself emerging from the tank's cupola with a chestful of decorations, and began to change.

From the Donets, the quickest way to Kharkov was by the highway that ran through Schubino and Bestyudovka. Bora instructed the GAZ-61 army driver and the escort cars to take that route by themselves, while he'd transport the general in his vehicle up the dirt lanes that linked hamlets and farmsteads in long direct stretches. Keeping to the ravine road through the woods until he came to the Udy River and Papskaya Ternovka, he planned to continue north-west of Ternovoye, cross the rails north of Bestyudovka, then skirt the woods again. Straddling the sectors of the 161st and 39th Infantry Divisions, by long detours and winging it, he might avoid SD- and SS-controlled checkpoints. If all went well, he'd reach the Kharkov suburbs at Babai, and along unmarked paths his destination in Velikaya Osnova.

From *Abwehr* sources, Bora had a good idea of where Security Service units operated between the Donets and Kharkov. Partisan warfare was heaviest south of here, where the 15th ID had been bled white by guerrilla attacks, so the SS paid keen attention in that area. Still, entering the heavily manned city with a Soviet general in a Panzer outfit – and not losing him to the SS – would be the trickiest part of the journey.

Bora considered how he'd come to depend on the adjective *sonder* attached to his orders on this front: "special, particular", paradoxically the same prefix that typified the most brutally aggressive SS mobile units. But *sonder* meant you usually got through, or could negotiate your way across sectors; as an interrogator, he needed that flexibility. Yet he never forgot that in old German *sonder* could also mean "lacking, without".

Minutes later, oddly credible in his new outfit, Tibyetsky watched as his handsome jacket was folded into a knapsack and the photograph slipped into Bora's map case. He asked for a fresh cigar. Bora handed him the box, but the Russian only took one. "You must have gasoline to burn if you send three vehicles off on a ruse."

Bora checked the time: 4.20 p.m. By this time, Scherer and his staff must have reached the railroad station and would have perhaps already loaded the tank on to the waiting train. "For some things, Commander Tibyetsky, gasoline is worth burning."

*

During the first few kilometres, Khan gave Bora the silent treatment. At one point he spoke to himself, opening with a sneer the army document supplied to him. "Let's see who I am supposed to be. A forty-year-old. How flattering. A carpenter by trade, perhaps with a large family to keep on a sergeant major's pay."

Whether or not he meant to modify the impression he'd given of refusing all conversation, it was only while they were skirting the hamlet of Ternovoye, past broken-down fences where vetch and creepers reached to a man's height, that he addressed Bora, who was of course dying to be spoken to. "What were you saying earlier, Major? Not about my *beginnings*, as you called them: about your relatives' table-talk interest in the October Revolution."

Bora glanced over. "It was a little more than table talk, Commander. We were directly involved on both sides of the family."

"So you said."

"My stepfather and a few older cousins went straight from the trenches of the Great War to the Russian border... Take an acquired great-uncle of mine – that is, my maternal great-aunt's brother-in-law: he went missing in 1919."

"Thousands did."

"Well, we lost Uncle Terry, as we called him at home. Great-aunt Albertina Anna was married to Jan Terborch, a German of Dutch descent; in 1918 his younger brother, lately of the Saxon Horse Guard, enrolled in the Brandenstein Brigade against the Bolsheviks. It was in Finland that we lost him, after his 'flying detachment' of mounted youngsters led the attack against the town of Lahti, cutting the connection between the Red Guard units in the east and west of the region. He's got a gravestone – technically a cenotaph, since there's nothing of him there – in Enschede. I wrote a school paper about him."

"I see." Khan flicked ash from his cigar on to the car floor. "I see," he repeated. In fact, he seemed wholly removed from the words he was hearing. Under the lids, his grey-blue eyes had the lazy mobility of a cat's eyes. What thoughts might revolve in a high-ranking defector's mind at a time like this – what hopes or fears, and how irrelevant a younger man's point of view on anything might be to him – Bora could only guess.

"Do you play chess, Major?"

"Do I? Only passably. I'm too impulsive at times."

"I see."

Another long silence followed; Bora had to bite his tongue to avoid breaking it. The combination of tension regarding his precious passenger, burning curiosity and this odd sitting side by side with the man who helped obliterate the Sixth Army in Stalingrad troubled him. He revealed none of it, and under the circumstances, claiming impulsiveness was at best improbable. Khan kept an indolent, attentive eye on him. The cigar had burnt down to a stub, which he carelessly put out on the metal of the car door and then replaced between his lips.

Bora paid attention to the road. It was unsafe to try to cut across the clear stretches of level flat land that temptingly ran on either side. What with minefields and the presence of unexpected ditches and invisible bogs, prudence called for keeping to the zigzag of dusty lanes, straight or crooked *dorozhki* of beaten earth and gravel. Through the side openings of the vehicle birds' voices flowed in occasionally, as did the scent of wild grasses that grew stronger in the afternoon, strongest at sunset. Poplars, nameless shrubs shone like silver along brooks and canals.

One, two, three army checkpoints came up, at bridges and crossroads. In each case Bora promptly stopped the vehicle a few metres back and turned off the engine. The military police let him pass every time, without paying much attention to the Panzer non-com in the passenger's seat. Then it was fields and ravines again, demolished farmhouses, rank grass and flowers going by, concealing or half-concealing the thickly manned expanse on this side of the Donets.

Khan looked outside. At last he spoke, the cigar butt lodged in the corner of his mouth. "So. What marks did you get on the paper concerning your relative?"

Bora was grateful to be addressed again. "Top marks, Commander. Mostly because I engaged in a sort of *samokritika*, by self-critically mentioning my hunch that Uncle Terry hadn't fallen after all; far from it: that he'd gone on to a glorious military career in the Soviet Union."

"Intriguing. Give me a fresh cigar."

Bora did, holding out the lighter to his passenger. "*Such are the vagaries of fate*, I commented, listing the arguments in favour of my thesis. You'll appreciate it took some gumption for an officer cadet to make such an assertion in Cavalry School."

Khan took a puff. "You may have a cigar, too."

Not to mention his weeks in a Prague hospital battling pneumonia, Bora had quit smoking in June 1941, clearing his nostrils and lungs for heightened perception during reconnaissance duty. A cigar was the last thing he needed, but he deftly took out a second Soyuzie and lit it.

They smoked from the upcoming crossroads to the other side of the tracks north of Bestyudovka without a word, facing away from each other, sending an acrid cloud up to the canvas top of the car and out of the side openings.

"May I ask you a question, Commander Tibyetsky?"

"Only if it doesn't relate to my present task."

"It doesn't. During the civil war, would you have defeated Ungern had his troops not mutinied on the way to Tibet?"

"Absolutely. He was finished."

Silence again. Near Babai, less than ten kilometres from the Kharkov city limits, Khan seemed to lose a shade of his coolness for the first time. Had he betrayed himself? No. Bora simply *felt* it, and couldn't have said why. The sensation was gone as soon as it came, and what in the Russian had actually occasioned it?

By the time they reached the city gates, Khan was again a paragon of composure, on the side of a traveller's boredom.

Eyes closed, he kept his arms loosely folded on his hefty chest.

"Did any of yours go crazy last winter?" The question came wholly unexpectedly. Pointless to wonder whether Khan had enough information about Bora to know he'd been at Stalingrad; besides, Stalingrad was on Bora's mind but not necessarily his passenger's. Bora's delay in answering could in itself be a reply. Khan bit his cigar, without opening his eyes. "Some of ours did. Not to speak of civilians. If you don't have a strong ideology, you go mad."

"Well, I think you can go mad regardless of ideology."

It ended there. They were now in the industrial periphery of the city, where unkempt open spaces alternated with built-up manufacturing areas; sluices and service roads ran side by side along torn fences, blind walls. Ruined smokestacks, like towers beheaded, formed pyramids of reddish bricks. The secondary lanes Bora was following, muddy with broken pipes, wormed through piles of rubble.

Looking out for the first time in several minutes, Khan remarked, "Not exactly the high road to town."

Silently Bora considered his options. The most hazardous part of the trip lay just ahead, in the last two kilometres leading to the Velikaya Osnova district. Overhead the day, perfectly clear until now, was beginning to turn. A ridge of clouds to the west would soon swallow the setting sun, and there might be rain coming. Bora took it as an omen. "From here on, for credibility, the lower in rank ought to drive," he said, braking and then stopping for the time needed to switch places with Tibyetsky. "I'll give you directions."

No sooner had the station and its many tracks leading to the Donbas become visible ahead, with the south-eastern brick factories, than another checkpoint barred the way, and it was manned by the SS. "Whatever the level of your spoken German, put this under your tongue," Bora told Khan on the spur of the moment, handing over the first thing he found in his pocket, the button recovered from Krasny Yar. The Russian, however, was ahead of him. He'd already placed the unlit stub of his cigar between his upper molars and right cheek, inventing an abscess that might justify any imperfect speech.

"Documents please, Herr Major." The SS men leant over to look inside the vehicle.

Bora carried several typewritten passes allowing him to move around alone or with a driver at any hour of day and night. He presented his paperwork, and the examination was soon followed by "Fine, thank you, Herr Major."

When Khan's turn came, however, the SS scrutinized the Panzer Corps *Soldbuch* a long time, flipping the pages back and forth. They said nothing; only kept reading a few steps away from the vehicle. Motionless in the passenger's seat, Bora looked at them. They were young, untried, replacement fellows whose training surely amounted to a handful of weeks. He ostentatiously pulled back his left cuff to check his wristwatch, because doing it in a furtive manner would give his anxiety away. "Is there something wrong with my driver?" He judged his irritation just right. "You can keep him here if you want to; I haven't got time to sit here all day."

The SS promptly gave the papers back, and made room for the vehicle to pass.

Once in Velikaya Osnova, the officers traded places again. A tickled Khan spat the cigar stub out and a wad of saliva after it. "You wouldn't have really left me behind back there."

Bora calmly looked over. "What do *you* think?"

"That it takes one to know one who's ready to shoot his way out of a tight spot."

They met no more delays, nor did they converse, until they reached the detention centre. Bora drove through the car entrance into the inner courtyard, away from the street, parked and came to open the general's door. Khan put one leg out to dismount, the same leisurely movement he'd made to emerge from the tank's cupola. He remained seated a moment more, looking up at the German. "What marks did you earn for the paper on my early career?"

"Top marks, same as for Uncle Terry's."

"Ah. Good student." Exiting the vehicle, Khan adjusted the canvas blouse on his hips. "And probably a good chess player. We'll have to talk about it some time. Even if I can't imagine when."

On the third floor, the rooms set up for special prisoners were lined in a row from one end of the corridor to the other. Platonov occupied the room farthest from the landing, but even so, the cries from his nightmares would be all too audible from the same level. Bora directly led the way up one more floor, to the single room set up for the interrogator.

Every level of the structure had been inhabited by visiting German businessmen and engineers in the late 1930s. Naturally, every suite was thoroughly bugged; then, as now, the windows were high and had solid, artistic grilles across them. In this room, modern wallpaper in a zigzag pattern resembled stylized factory roofs, smokestacks trailing vapour. During the battles for Kharkov, the fine furnishings had disappeared: the *Abwehr* had had to hunt all over for decent beds and a bare minimum of comfort.

Khan looked inside before stepping in. "I've seen better."

It would not have done to reply that he'd have much preferred for a defector to be flown out of the Rogany airfield directly to Berlin, and it was unnecessary for Bora to remind Tibyetsky that he was merely honouring his demands to wait in the area for Bentivegni's arrival. "Your things will be brought up next, so you can change. The photo of yourself and the cigars, too. May I provide anything else, Commander?"

Khan sat on the bed to test the mattress. "Yes, my provisions. No need to prepare my meals, Major. As you saw, I brought along enough sealed food for two weeks. I'll touch nothing else. In the morning, a single chocolate ration is all I require."

"Understood. I must, however, insist on a routine medical check before I leave."

"What? Don't make me laugh. Do you really think I plan to commit suicide after going through all this effort?"

"I must insist. If you prefer, I'll remain present in the room."

"That's ridiculous. Send the damned quack in, and make it snappy."

Weller happened to already be in the building, checking General Platonov's blood pressure. He followed Bora upstairs, promptly carried out the check-up, found nothing out of the ordinary with (or on) Khan, and left.

Bora's watch read 6.13 p.m. Time to meet Scherer at the Tractor Factory. Before leaving the detention centre, he enquired about Number Five with a variation on the usual question. "Has he asked for me?"

"No, Herr Major."

"Anything else to remark?"

"Only that he hasn't called us names, Herr Major."

It was just like the bastard, Bora thought, to react to the first news about his family in years by simply not insulting his jailers. He stopped to scratch Mina's fat back on his way out of the building. Dusk was closing in fast, even though the clouds hadn't yet risen to fill the sky. He took Moskalivka Street to Rybna, crossed the bridge over the Kharkov River and headed down the long Old Moscow Highway/Staro–Moskovskaya road to the Tractor Factory district. Soon he was driving alone on the wide boulevards leading out of the city. Side streets petered out, the steam factory and the Russian army cemetery went by, and still Bora followed the German signs in Gothic script that read *Nach Ch.T.S.*

The *Kharkov Traktorenwerk Siedlung*, a small industrial city at the edge of the city, had suffered much in the repeated battles for Kharkov. In the near dark, Scherer was waiting off Narodna Street, in front of Building G. Bora gave him back the Tank Corps suit and the rest.

"Did you have problems getting here, Jochen?"

"None, other than it was a bear loading the tank on to the damn train."

"The convoy?"

"It's parked around the corner. Was already here when we arrived. Not very happy; Russki fighters strafed them around Bestyudovka. No casualties, but a round barely missed the car. If you want the GAZ-61 back in Smijeff tomorrow, my men and I will go along part of the way, to rejoin our unit. Make sure you take along the trunk with the Russian's foodstuff; he's got all kinds of goodies in it. So what's the Field Marshal going to do, send for the T-34 or have it disassembled here to study it?"

"He's flying in himself in the morning, so they might work on it in Kharkov. Or in Zaporozhye."

Scherer took a wistful look at the menacing, dark bulk filling up the hangar behind him. "It'll take more than what we presently have to confront this model if they plan to use it in large numbers. It's so new, the paint on it is still fresh. I wonder how many of them they've got in the hamper."

"However many they have, we'll make good use of this one. Start the tank up and follow my vehicle down Ivan Frank Street. There's a better place to keep it for the night."

After leaving the T-34 safely awaiting Manstein's visit in an underground shelter on Louis Pasteur (Lui Pastera) Street, Bora decided on a hunch not to take a shortcut to Merefa through the southern districts, in case Platonov changed his mind and wanted to see him tonight. Less than two hours had gone by, but the guards at the detention centre reported that Number Five had insistently been asking for the interrogator during the past fifty minutes. Anxious as he himself was, Bora decided to let the old man dangle a little longer, and climbed to Tibyetsky's room instead. There, he found Khan fast asleep, so he had the guard place the trunk by his bed, and walked away without waking him up.

Gleb Platonov looked like death. Grey-faced, haggard, he sat with the photograph of his relatives face down on the table. "Where was this taken?"

Other than his name and identification number, it was the only sentence Bora had ever heard him speak. "I'm not required to say," he answered dryly.

"Who had it taken?"

"Not required to say that, either."

"It shows this month's date. Has to be your doing; German doing."

"Does it?"

"I demand to know —"

"I'm not accepting demands, General."

"I ask to know —"

Bora moved his head from side to side, an indifferent sign of refusal. Platonov must be in a state of absolute turmoil at this time. Whatever Stalin's reason for making him believe his women were dead, right now he had no way of knowing whether they were imprisoned (they weren't); he couldn't even be sure they were in German hands, since the calendar in the snapshot was Russian – Bora had made a point of it. For all Platonov knew – and this must be the cruellest doubt in his mind – they could have been executed in the days since the photo was taken. Keeping the image face down was meant to lessen the unavoidable pain of enquiring about them. Bora turned it face up. There was a kind of ache for him as well in seeing them: the women were beautiful, and affected him in his own way. Platonov's love for them was legendary; he'd reportedly tried to kill himself in prison when told of their deaths. It stood to reason that if his women were now brought forward, they were alive, and in German hands. Clear-minded logic suggested it. But Platonov might be other than clear-minded this evening. After his release, he'd fought for nearly two years in the name of a system that had stripped him of all ties and shreds of hope, forging him at last into a war machine out of his utter, infinite lack of expectation. But now… Bora felt a stable lack of pity, which didn't mean he ignored the man's feelings. To him, it was a matter of getting what he wanted, taking care not to show that he had no intention of harming the women; if on one pan of the scales lay Platonov's anguish for them, the other was weighed down by his stoicism in Stalin's jail, when he thought he had nothing more to lose.

Platonov could not bring himself to say out loud that he'd believed his family lost until today. Under his breath, he mouthed, "I thought – it's the first time in six years I've seen an image of them."

"I can have them safely escorted here to meet you." Bora's only sign of familiarity (intentional, as everything was in his behaviour with prisoners) was that he stood there with his hands in the pockets of his breeches. His fingertips met the button from Krasny Yar, and for a second the dead in the woods, the cut throat, the severed head were with him in the room.

"Swear to me it's true, Major." When Bora said and did nothing, the prisoner's voice turned grave and low, like a repressed sob. "What do you want in exchange?"

"My needs haven't changed." From the briefcase at his feet, Bora took out a questionnaire he'd typed in Russian, a number of sheets held together by a paper clip, which he laid on the table. Platonov ran his eyes over the first page, and pushed it back in disgust.

"Bring my family to me."

Bora firmly replaced the questionnaire under Platonov's eyes. They stared at each other across the narrow space separating them. After confronting Khan's physical exuberance in the afternoon, this was the cut-out, the abused leftover of a man; a few hours and a single photograph had crushed what remained of one who'd withstood torture. Bora had to think of his Stalingrad days to summon bitterness and avoid all empathy.

"No. I don't want to wait until morning. I've waited long enough."

It was the first and only suggestion that the women were due there the following day. Platonov was visibly shaken. He might have suspected until now it was a trick, so Bora took advantage of the moment. "I can tell you they spent four years in hard labour south-west of here, at the Kremenchuk power station. We freed them in '41. They're quite well, as you can see from the photo. I understand your wife lost three toes of her right foot during her sentence, but given the circumstances it could have gone much worse. Your daughter Avrora Glebovna is reported to be in good health as well." Bora did not look away even after Platonov began to tremble. "As long as they're under my tutelage, General, I vouch for their safety. However, should I lose that oversight, believe me, anything can happen. I have a wife; I speak as a husband to a husband. The moment the ladies enter this building I'll personally and on my honour answer for them. But I'm not inclined to endure further delays: I want guarantees, too."

It was strange, but it had happened other times with prisoners about to give in: that their protest suddenly became hollow, spoken in a dull tone that belied the forcefulness of the objections put forward.

"*Guarantees*? I am a Soviet lieutenant general."

"And I'm a German interrogator. Soviet authorities didn't even let you know your relatives survived your disgrace: we bring them to you."

"It could be a ruse."

"No, no. It's a barter, General Platonov. And when bartering, IOUs don't work."

Platonov clutched the armrests of his green velvet seat to keep from trembling. His lower jaw hung half-open like a very old man's; a frightful weariness seemed to have overtaken him, making him come unglued. He gave the impression that he would start losing his limbs piecemeal at any time, like a broken puppet.

The one thing that could be used against him Bora was using

now. He heard himself say, "Here we go, General", and, as if from a distance, he could almost see himself neatly squaring the pages on the table, evaluating the effect of the handsome charm that had so often got him through in his young life.

As if looks spoke the truth. As if Stalingrad, leaving him sane, hadn't carved out of him most of the civility he'd previously been one and the same with! *This is the devil's work*, he was thinking, dismally. *I've gone from the role of a naive Adam in Eden to playing the serpent. And yet the serpent too has his reasons.* Whatever Stalin's plan had been in making Platonov believe his women had been killed, it must be intolerable to start hoping again at this point, and at the hands of the enemy. Everything in the prisoner's desperate posture begged for mercy; Bora had to be careful not to show a particle of the sorrow that tried to cut a rift into his firm resolve.

"Let me go once more through what we have been through for the past several days. You have been working closely with Colonel General Konev. We know you met with Marshals Zhukov and Vasilevsky in April, and we rather think you were to help organize the front around Voronezh. I understand your reticence to speak, and more so to elaborate on details, whether or not they can be termed military secrets. So I prepared this questionnaire, which itemizes possible changes brought by your High Command to the composition of tank destroyer, armoured and rifle divisions. We wish for you to mark off the option closest to the truth. And we wish to know what the role of the general officers listed at the bottom of the questionnaire is expected to be in any upcoming operation."

I, we. Bora's careful dosage of the personal pronoun drew an imaginary line between what the German Army wanted and what he, Bora, was willing to do to meet him halfway. "From the moment Selina Nikolayevna and Avrora Glebovna were brought to my attention," he continued, "I have strong-armed others" (he didn't say, but Platonov understood he meant more politically inclined colleagues, or the SS) "in order to keep them under Army care. Since we speak of guarantees, let me repeat: I cannot guarantee their permanence in Army-controlled territory, under Army custody, as time progresses, whether or not you collaborate. But if you collaborate *now*, I promise you the ladies will be in this building by mid-morning tomorrow, and I'll do everything in my power to secure their future comfort. It's true, I did argue with colleagues over them. I stuck my neck out, as they say, and all for nothing until now."

Platonov lowered his eyes to the sheet in front of him. He'd regained his frowning hardness through God knows what effort, but he looked so careworn and pale that Bora felt he ought to say something to be on the safe side. "Kindly do not fall ill on me, sir. I won't accept it. Think of the matter this way: if you hadn't succeeded in destroying the papers you carried when we captured you, we'd have the information already."

"Has someone new arrived this afternoon?" Taking time was an old technique: Platonov must be running out of ideas if he resorted to it. He tried to change the subject. "I heard steps. Who else is here?"

Bora took out a pencil. "I'm sure you'd like to know, General." He laid it on the table. "We'll promptly and thoroughly check anything you mark off, so please do not offend us by jotting down the first thing that comes into your head."

"I need to think."

"No. You need to give me what I want. Tomorrow I'll give you what *you* want."

"And if I don't?"

"If you don't, my part of the bargain is off, and I certainly will not risk another disagreement with my colleagues on account of your relatives. I am not walking out until you start writing. I *could* stay in this room all night if I have to; I'm used to losing sleep. But I won't. One hour is the time I will give myself to call about your family coming. I won't offer twice. It's now ten minutes to eight."

Most of the options on Platonov's sheet were numbered. All the prisoner had to do was to circle the right number. With all the appearance of calm, Bora sat in front of him, right elbow on the table, resting his chin on the knuckles of the same hand. Oddly, compassion had dwindled to nothing inside him. Faster and faster, impatience rose and strained in its place.

"You've seen enough of me by now, Major, to perceive that I cannot —"

"It's seven minutes to eight."

"And using this – this method…"

Bora thought of the hours he'd spent cajoling him, reasoning with him, trying to convince him, and now that he was so near to breaking Platonov his irritation bordered on physical pain. Platonov sweated, and stared at him.

"I cannot, Major."

"Six minutes to eight."

A cornered animal can grow stiff or collapse, bite or crawl. Desperate cleverness can be resorted to and bring success, or utter failure. Platonov's eyes seemed to burrow into his interrogator, sounding him for heartlessness or hesitation. "But maybe I could – I could give you —"

"What? You could give me *what?*"

"I could give you" – Platonov's face was a skull covered with sad flesh – "something else."

It was empty blather; Bora had heard corralled prisoners drivel on before. The attempt to divert his attention infuriated him. *You will give me what I want,* he was about to shout, but then he held back. A drowning man will promise anything to be saved, to be thrown a rope; and there are moments when *anything* may be even more than what you were looking for. "Define *something else.*"

"How much does a German major earn?"

Bora didn't think he'd heard right. A senseless urge, like a blackout of reason, brought him to within an inch of taking out his pistol and shooting the old man in the face, seated where he was. Only the pinprick of a thought – that Platonov might be counting on such a drastic way out – stayed his hand the time needed to regain control. *I kept it together when all was lost,* he forced himself to think. *I kept it together when all was lost. I can keep it together now.*

"General," he spelt out, "it is now five minutes to eight. Fifty-five minutes and ninety-seven questions to go."

By the time Bora walked out, half of the sheets had been marked. Platonov was visibly too agitated to continue, incoherent, gasping for air, so the medic had to be summoned again. The melancholy Weller faithfully arrived, and the prisoner was reportedly tranquil and resting shortly after 9 p.m. when Bora made his call to request that Platonov's family be sent to Kharkov. In the morning he expected to get the rest of the information out of him, before personally going to pick up the women at the Osnova train station.

He was psychologically tired. All this trouble for information that Khan Tibyetsky might soon be voluntarily and tenfold supplying the *Abwehr* with. But every prisoner must be squeezed for what he knows, and the more you learn, the more you can cross-reference details.

It was pitch dark when Bora reached Merefa. At this hour every night, fever returned like a reliable friend. It didn't bother him much, even if in the height of summer he might end up suffering with the heat more. He took it in his stride, because they told him it would last a few more weeks, or months. There were far worse things.

Still, he was on edge. The events of the day weighed giddily on him. What he'd finally extracted from Platonov paved the way for more results; the simultaneous arrival of a ranking defector exceeded all hope... Bora worried for the sake of worrying. As if when things coincidentally went the way they should a void of tension appeared, which had to be filled.

Worry filled the gap, because there was always something to be anxious about.

He didn't expect to hear from the sentry that Nitichenko, the Russian priest, was waiting for him outside the schoolyard, by the row of graves. "That creep," he grumbled. "At this hour? What for?"

The sentry didn't know. Bora walked into the triangle of faint light from the open door, where a picket fence beyond the graves emerged like a monstrous set of fangs from the earth.

"Victor Panteleievich, what are you doing here?"

"*Povazhany* Major, *bratyetz* – little brother, our Lord sends me to you."

"No less." Bora breathed in the cool air of night. Two years in Russia had accustomed him to these familiar modes of address, and he no longer wondered why old women called him *daddy* or *grandfather* or a priest *little brother*. "I don't believe I'm worthy."

"You make use of irony, *bratyetz*, but we are all under the Almighty's eye and fist."

"Yes, some more than others. What can I do for you?"

"You must set fire to the Krasny Yar woods."

These Russian baboons. Irritably Bora half-smiled in the dark. "If the Almighty wanted to see all the places razed by fire where people are killed, Victor Panteleievich —"

"Only those where the devil's work is done." Left hand spread on his chest, right hand raised, in the slice of eerie kerosene light Nitichenko resembled Rasputin the Mad Monk more than a minister of the Ukrainian Autocephalous Orthodox Church. "From the ruins of war-ravaged villages the *domovyki* have been chased into the wild."

The devil's work. Hadn't he thought of his interrogator's role in the same terms? Bora inhaled the night air as if its coolness could bring his fever down. "The *domovyki*? If that's so," he said, "it doesn't seem to me a good idea to try to chase those house spirits from the woods too. Besides, wouldn't they have departed as soon as communism came?"

"This may be true, brother in Christ. And Krasny Yar has been cursed ever since."

"Well, Krasny Yar isn't under my jurisdiction, Victor Pante-leievich. And if your blessings didn't get results, what do you expect fire will do? I'd rather not have the spirits getting it into their heads to come and room with you, or with me."

"You continue to make use of sarcasm, Major. It is a foolish thing."

Bora gestured for the sentry to remove the priest. "Not nearly as much as believing in goblins. Go home, now, and be thankful that I'm in a good mood."

Inside, Kostya had laid out some dinner, canned food Bora had no desire to open or eat. The mail had come, some of it hand-delivered by colleagues, slips typed or handwritten, often devoid of envelopes. There were no letters from home, but a note bearing Stark's signature informed him that a sealed envelope lay waiting for him at the Ministerial Director's office in Kiev.

Instantly Bora's hopes were up: SS Standartenführer Schal-lenberg, Dikta's mother's new partner, had recently travelled to Kiev, so the privileged, unopened envelope might come from her. Or maybe not. He was prudent: he'd learnt to take small bites out of hope, and forbade himself to think beyond what the note said. He'd know soon, at any rate, as Geko Stark had promised to forward the mail promptly.

Seated on his camp bed, Bora read the rest of the mail: mes-sages of soldiers who asked to serve under him, who petitioned to be chosen for the new regiment. Many were those who'd been with him at Stalingrad, or those he'd gathered along the way escaping the mortal trap, dragging them through the Russian winter to salvation – if returning to the German lines was such.

It troubled him that they considered him a talisman, one of those fortunate commanders under whom the enemy doesn't kill you. The duties of his new unit not only implied danger, they were danger itself, daily, different from that of a siege only because you can move while they shoot at you. And yet they called him *Unser Martin* among themselves, familiarly, "our Martin", claiming the proximity of trust. They sought recommendations from their present commander, chaplain, army surgeon: and the majority of them had never even mounted a horse. To how many of them could he say yes, granted that regulations allowed for their transfer?

Every day, whatever Bora did, Stalingrad was there, like a droning refrain. At night, he removed Stalingrad. He did not allow anguish to cross the space, at times physically reduced, around himself. Sleep came heavy, brutal, like a seal that made his mind impermeable to memory. At times it occurred to him that criminals lead similar lives, wilfully depriving themselves of entire portions of their experience, a self-mutilation necessary to keep going. He had no indulgence towards himself, not ever. *I know myself and treat myself accordingly*, he reasoned. *I know who I am, the choices I made.* And he never went further in that scrutiny. He hadn't gone to confession in nearly two years. He mechanically attended field Mass whenever possible, but in Russia even praying had become mechanical, a question of formulae. In Stalingrad he had not prayed, not even when the situation was that of one who has already begun sinking into the abyss. Perhaps because he feared that the Christian's last powerful hope, that God will listen, would be disappointed. Perhaps because God had nothing to do with Stalingrad.

His lucidity, the lucidity von Salomon envied in him, was polished like a mirror (or a sheet of ice); Bora did not allow the smallest speck of dust to rest on it. It was an extreme process of scouring that removed with acid all blemishes and flaws.

3

Past midnight. Bora was still unable to sleep. Platonov's demented offer to buy him off – with what? What could he consider as even remotely attractive to a creed-bound German officer? – still agitated him. *Has he misconstrued my leniency so far? Have I somehow given the impression I'd be open to personal gain? I don't see how. He spoke of a major's pay, so it's money he had in mind, or other valuables. He doesn't seem the kind of officer who'd try bribery. Or did he already try that card during the Purge and get massacred for it? The only concession I made, against my better judgement, was that his wife will be informed she is to meet him. My plan was to have the women collected and put on a train without explanations (we owe them none), but this is a small compromise. Tomorrow, before they arrive, I'll make him keep the rest of his bargain. How do I feel? Three-quarters done; to think the Kiev Branch had given up on Platonov. But partial victory tastes bitter after his offer to buy me off.*

Fever contributed to his restlessness. In a twilight state, images overlapped before him in a confused reel: Platonov stealthily offering a handful of gold, the sealed envelope from home containing money instead of a letter, even Colonel von Salomon telling him he'd have to pay in marks for his unit's mounts. Bora sat up in his cot to drink quinine in half a glass of stale water from his canteen. He'd better put Platonov out of his mind if he wanted to remain level-headed with him in the morning.

He stood to empty his pockets. Out came keys, cigarette lighter, a few coins. Last of all, the button from Krasny Yar. Hand-carved from hardwood, it was the sort of large fastener on a Russian peasant's coat. Did the latest victim lose it during the struggle that ended in his brutal beheading? Had he not used the butt of his cigar Khan could have stuck it in his mouth to conceal his accent before the SS, but knowing it came from a corpse would be irrelevant to someone who had shot his men point blank without batting an eyelid.

From his trunk, Bora took the cloth-bound, sturdy diary that had survived Stalingrad, and opened it to a fresh page. This diary and the letters to his family were the only things saved from the disaster; whatever few other Russian items he still had dated from before the siege, as he'd left them in this same trunk in Kiev and recovered them since. He sat down at the teacher's desk, uncapped his gold-tipped fountain pen – Dikta's gift – and began writing.

The defector is Hendrick Terborch. No doubt about it, and notwithstanding his many aliases, even though I was five when I last saw him. Obviously, I don't think for a moment that he absconded here because I serve in this area. He did so *in spite* of it, possibly because he was assigned along the Donets with his armoured brigade. It goes without saying that I know more about him than I let out, including the role he played early in the great officers' purge five years ago. Rumours are that he turned in a few colleagues. After all, he came through that ordeal unscathed while throngs of others were lucky (such would be his term) if they received a bullet in the nape of the neck without having to undergo torture.

Thus, officer corps being what they are, it is little surprise that all those involved knew one another, including Number Five-Platonov and Terborch-Khan Tibyetsky. As a matter of fact, Khan was working for him when Platonov was arrested at Stalin's orders, and from what I gather he did nothing to succour his commander, although it must be admitted that not many ran the risk during those days, because it meant signing their own death sentence. Whether or not Khan went as far as supporting the imputations or merely sat by, watching Platonov go down at the trial, can only be conjectured.

In any case, it is prudent to keep them apart and unaware that they share the same building. The risk is that Platonov might be blinded by pride and clam up again. As for Khan Tibyetsky, I'll be glad when they take him off my hands; security-wise we aren't nearly as well organized in Kharkov as we ought to be.

Questions: what made a Hero of the Soviet Union change his mind about Russia, given that back in '19 he burnt all his bridges behind him? Did he have enough? Has he seen the error of his ways, as they say? What does he want from us? What else has he to offer other than the tank model Scherer drools over? It'd have been awkward and possibly unadvisable, but why didn't he pick up on the line I tossed him, mentioning my relative? He can't have thought me so dense that I wouldn't have recognized him, having also admitted to studying his daring feats. I, on the other hand, couldn't very well openly admit that this apple falls closer to the tree than is comfortable for either of us, as officers and members of our class and family. Clearly he sees no advantage in revealing himself to his sister-in-law's grand-nephew, a young major who can in no way be of use to him.

Tomorrow I'll stop by to see how he is faring, as soon as I give a last push to Platonov. Should the old crank play games again, I'll have to threaten his women's well-being, and I'm perfectly able to make it sound credible.

These Russians are exasperating. Tonight, far from going away as he was told, that dingbat priest gave me an earful about the dead in Krasny Yar for another half-hour. It's an odd thing, though. The place apparently does have a dark connotation. Only because they're desperate for food and fuel do the locals venture into it, seldom alone: those who were killed had risked it because they had no one to accompany them for whatever reason. If I'm to believe Father Victor, of the 6 adult victims recovered (there were others, children, who except for one never were found), two were bludgeoned to death and had their eyes put out (older men), while three women (ranging more or less from 18–35) suffered multiple stab wounds. All were identified as living in an area that goes from Ternovoye to Selionovka, including the farms known as Kusnetzov and Kalekina. The last victim, whose head is missing, remains unknown; according to the 241st Company he was in his 60s at least. In every case particular ferocity seems to have been exerted. A maniac, one would think, or a totally clumsy blunderer. What is the rhyme or reason to such crimes? How are they linked? The priest doesn't know whether anything was stolen, but given the times, it's unlikely the victims carried valuables. That's why I think of a maniac, or a desperate fugitive, like the Rex Nemorensis we read about in Roman mythology: a condemned criminal let loose in the woods until another felon is sent to try and take his place.

When I first heard about the matter last month, I enquired at the 161st HQ whether a search could be organized to stop rumours (and killings) once and for all. The reply wasn't encouraging: I was told to ignore what happens to civilians, and Russians to boot. Additional reasons: Krasny Yar isn't strategically relevant (true, but what's strategically relevant when our biggest headaches at the moment are partisan bands, for whom two rocks and a log are shelter enough?) The woods are partly mined – by us or by the Reds, I don't have that detail, and don't really have a clear idea of the contours of the risk zone. The non-com I met there would have told me if there was danger. Seems we haven't yet decided whether we'll clear them or finish mining them in weeks to come. Most importantly, no German soldier has been harmed in or around Krasny Yar.

Should the official disinterest surprise me? When we first arrived at Merefa, I reported to the German War Crimes Bureau that we'd discovered the bodies of executed German soldiers in this schoolyard, along with the corpses of many civilians. The 161st Division judge promised to "send someone", which in time I have learnt to suspect is another way to say that nothing will happen. In nearly four years of war we've all grown overwhelmed with the sheer amount of violations from all quarters. Back in Poland and even at the start of the Russian campaign we had a system going: reports regularly flowed from the field through divisional command, and we even had "flying judges", unattached to specific units, sent directly from Germany to investigate. I haven't given up on the "Merefa Schoolyard" case, as I call it, all the more since there are two or three other important pieces of news I hope to report if the right counterpart comes about. Krasny Yar isn't one of them exactly, but if a judge arrives and looks half-interested, I'll add it to the list. Lt. Colonel von Salomon tells me I'm "too picky", a strange choice of words under the circumstances, because I think myself thorough but not fastidious. 20 German soldiers and at least twice as many Russian nationals fatten the earth where Kostya's hens scratch for grubs: it isn't picky to urge for a fair enquiry.

Enough. I've got a busy day tomorrow. If I belonged to my older relatives' generation (and had a bed at my disposal), I could say *And now to bed*, as Victorian diarists used to do. But a camp bed is what I have, too uncomfortable to honour with a diary line.

WEDNESDAY 5 MAY

Something nagged at him the moment Bora opened his eyes, a kernel of foreboding that something negative lay just around the corner. Not waiting *for him* directly – it would be useful if warnings came that way; his destiny would be manageable then – but in relation to him, involving him somehow. He lay staring at the ceiling trying to tell himself it wasn't so, that anxiety trailed behind other, less admissible feelings. Towards dawn he'd dreamt of his wife. Dikta slowly, lovingly taking his clothes off, in a room whose ceiling was so low over them it nearly touched the bedposts. They'd never lain in such a room, but she'd more than once undressed him – though always in great haste. As a rule, Bora made himself not think of her, because it was difficult enough as it was. Being away, not lying with her, having to make do. *Making do* implied a few unalterable rules: cold showers, long hours, staying well away from Russian girls. Dreams he tried not to have, or to forget immediately. Starting the day with Dikta on his mind, aching for her, was absolutely no good. He'd rather worry.

Kostya, who'd already left for the Komarevka station in a two-horse droshky, set aside a pail of icy well water ready for him every morning. In his shorts, Bora stepped barefoot into the cold shade outside the school building, and emptied the pail over his head and shoulders. *Nitichenko is starting to spook me, damn him. I'll kick him from here to Losukovka if he shows up again.* He shaved, dressed, drank a tin of coffee and headed out of Merefa towards Kharkov with a painful sense of tightness at the pit of his stomach, his typical mode of transferring stress to the body, where he could clench his jaw and bear it.

7 a.m. At this time, Kostya would be picking up the babushkas who'd do the regiment's wash. The day promised sunshine, despite a few flesh-coloured clouds from the endless east (it was Russia, Russia and then again Russia, all the way to the Pacific Ocean). Bora mentally reviewed what he'd tell Platonov in case he balked at completing the questionnaire – *I swear I'll threaten to kill his women if he crosses me* – but in fact was still thinking of Dikta. In the dream (or else in his elaboration of it), she knelt on the bed wearing a satin garter belt and nothing else. Rose-pink satin, the colour of clouds and all the slippery or lacy things she wore under her clothes, meant to exalt rather than cover, like sea froth between Venus' thighs. The last thing, the last thing he should be thinking of.

Meanwhile, he'd reached the *Kombinat*. In the grassy patch in front of Stark's office, Russian prisoners were hauling water from a trough. They froze when the German vehicle came to a screeching halt nearby. Without a word Bora jumped off, grabbed the bucket from one of them, set it on the trough's edge and dunked his own head into it. Coincidentally, District

Commissioner Stark was stepping out of the door for a smoke, and remained there, open-mouthed, with the cigarette in his hand. He was still staring when Bora restarted the engine and sped away.

Nothing's about to happen. He kept drumming the thought into his mind while he crossed the temporary bridge over the Udy. *There's nothing unusual, nothing's about to happen.* Nothing unusual at the checkpoints, at the corner of Novomirskaya, past the railroad tracks, entering the Velikaya Osnova district. Yet the moment he turned into Mykolaivska, Bora *knew* things were wrong, despite the usual appearance of the street.

As soon as he set foot inside the special detention centre, he heard Mina's furious barking at the foot of the stairs. "We just phoned the hospital, Herr Major," the guard on the ground floor informed him. "Number Five really took ill this time. Will you go and see him at once?"

Bora didn't need to be told; he was already climbing the steps two at a time. With a first-aid kit over his shoulder, Weller overtook him at an even faster pace, grabbing the handrail to speed himself up. "Surgeon's coming," he shouted, and ran ahead.

Platonov's door was wide open. The general lay on top of his bedcover, fully dressed, grey in the face, eyes closed. The sergeant heading the centre and two guards stood by while the medic felt for vital signs and started preparing an injection at once. "Usually this brings him around," he said, barely turning his face towards Bora. "This time, I'm not sure. It's his heart, I think."

"The men thought he was sleeping," the sergeant volunteered, "but he wouldn't move when they shook him."

After giving the shot, Weller renewed his checking and tapping: quick, neutral motions that might equally suggest hope or impending failure.

Bora was trying not to let his anger get the better of him. Finding anything that resembled a responsibility for what had happened seemed the only way to cope with his disappointment. "What did he have to eat?" he pressed the guards.

"Nothing, Herr Major. We were about to bring him his breakfast."

"Did he take any medication? Weller, did you give him any?"

The medic shook his head without looking. "The *Oberstarzt* specifically forbade that he be handed any medicine to take on his own."

"Sergeant, how did he seem last night?"

"Other than that he hardly touched his dinner, Herr Major, he slept through until midnight. At 02.00 hours we checked on him and he was pacing back and forth, talking to himself. At four he lay down again and had nightmares, because we heard him cry out in his sleep like he always did. An hour ago he started groaning, but that was no news either. Then he went quiet, and we only realized we ought to send for help when he wouldn't wake up."

Weller, who'd been crouching by the bed, stood up when he heard the heavy steps of the army surgeon from Hospital 169 clattering up the stairs. He walked in, nodded to Bora, sent out the guards and launched into some expert, thorough ausculta-tion and work of his own. Another injection, more searching for life signs, and, finally, a pause.

"He's gone."

Fuck, Bora thought, without reacting openly. Before he could think of what to say, the surgeon – a weary-looking man who seemed in need of medical attention as much as any patient of his – confirmed, "Myocardial infarction."

"Are we sure?"

The surgeon's eyes, bleary and yellow with jaundice, blinked twice. His pallor – like von Salomon's obsessions, like the stubbed, blackened thumbnail on Weller's hand as he put away the useless medications – was a sign of the times. Details stood before him so starkly as to become symbols. Bora waited for an answer with heart in mouth. *We are all bruised, inside and out. Those of us who didn't die, that is; who didn't lose fingers and toes to frost, who weren't blinded or maimed. War marks us all, sooner or later. Other than by fever, I wonder how I am marked.*

"There was hardly anything that could have been done, Major. A quick but natural process."

The disappointment was nearly too much to take. Bora suppressed the thought that Platonov's wife and daughter were arriving by train within the hour.

"He's the first prisoner I've ever lost."

That was not strictly true. It did not take into account the prisoners executed after Bora had failed to make them talk, or those who had told what they knew, but had been taken away just the same and shot against his will. He was reacting badly not only because of what else he could have learnt from Platonov with the lure of his womenfolk; it also seemed to him that the old man had purposely, perversely succeeded in silencing himself forever before his last surrender.

"Yes?" The surgeon sounded unmoved by Bora's statement. "Well, Major, he was a sickly man. I saw him when they first brought him in, and whatever happened to him in years past has undermined his health. He bore signs of repeated forms of stress and abuse."

"I want a post-mortem."

Before them, Platonov seemed unnaturally long and narrow on the bed, as if death had stretched him out at both ends. Sourness, and the contempt with which he must have spat out his last breath, remained stamped on his face. The surgeon stared at Bora. "I don't think we need to look for blame. This was bound to happen whether you, I or the medic were here or not; probably even if the prisoner hadn't been kept under pressure lately."

"I want a post-mortem, Herr Oberstarzt."

Bora's resentment failed to get a response. The surgeon dropped his shoulders: he'd obviously long ago learnt not to fight useless battles. "As you wish. But it will confirm what I'm telling you."

"*Please.*"

"Very well. I've got my hands full now, so I'll run an autopsy first thing in the morning. Is that soon enough for you?"

"Thank you."

"All right, then. Weller, come along: there's nothing else we can do here. I'll send an ambulance for the body."

On the fourth floor, flies circled the landing. Bora reached it, carrying in his briefcase Platonov's few personal items, including his women's photo and the blank sheet and pencil he'd issued him in case the prisoner decided to add information, which had been left untouched on the table. Thorough as he was, Bora saw partial failure rather than partial success, and knew himself well enough to anticipate how he'd dwell on this failure from now on. *I should have stayed in the room. I should have kept pushing him. I shouldn't have given him a chance to escape by death.* In the corridor, all was quiet. Bora hesitated at the top of the stairs before entering Tibyetsky's room. The handful of nights he'd spent there, waiting for Platonov to talk, seemed such a waste of precious time now. He felt no sorrow whatever for the old man: only anger at knowing he'd have to deal with his wife and daughter in fifty minutes' time.

According to the guards Khan was up and about, so Bora, who had the key to the room, knocked briefly as a formality and stepped in.

A transient, artificial ceiling of cigar smoke ebbed away upon his entrance, dissolving in a pungent wave.

"Komandir Tibyetsky."

Flemish merchants, well-fed city dwellers portrayed by Dutch painters in their comfortable interiors: Hendrick Terborch surfaced through Khan Tibyetsky as he sat bootless, sipping soda from an inexplicably ornate tall goblet, rimmed in gold. Army Supply had found it somewhere, that remnant of pre-revolutionary splendour, and had set it aside with the rest of the mismatched furnishings for the special detention centre.

Bora had never used it. It was the sort of goblet you could find in Renaissance Bruges, or in Amsterdam.

"Major Bora."

This was a separate world from downstairs; other rules applied. Remote as their relationship might be, the two men faced each other in the unspoken awareness of a common past – theirs were the well-to-do North European cities, the solidity of aristocracy and landed gentry, a cultivated breed of men and women accustomed to seeing what they shared across and despite national borders. All Khan was doing amounted to a dipping of lips in the sweet drink, seated on the bed with a partly unwrapped chocolate ration by his side, and the photograph showing him in all his glory on the bedside table. Bora on the other hand, pale after Platonov's death, had to seal off his turmoil in order to concentrate solely on the minor task of paying a visit to his prize guest.

"So," Khan added, "we do meet again, and so soon."

Bora closed the door. *He doesn't remember me, cannot remotely recognize a child one-sixth my present age in me. Yet he knows who I am, hangs from that tendril of family history, and doesn't give it away any more than I do. He wouldn't ask; I wouldn't volunteer. I wouldn't ask, either. We are as much or as little related as any two human beings on the face of the earth.* "I stopped by to see if you have all you need."

"All but a good rest. The man below was crying out half the night."

"We had nothing to do with it."

That wasn't precisely true, and a hasty justification was the last message Bora wished to convey. But the words escaped him: he was for a fraction of a second merely a young man in front of an older, more experienced one.

Khan smiled without removing his lips from the goblet's rim. "Someone without enough ideology to keep him sane?"

Any reply could be misinterpreted, so Bora avoided giving one. A few minutes and he'd have to get going to reach the train station, meet Platonov's women. He glanced at the open trunk against the wall, whose rich lend-lease contents he'd checked the night before to make sure cans and boxes were sealed and harmless.

"An American candy bar, Major?"

"No, thank you."

"Do sit down."

It was Terborch inviting him, as if this were his parlour and Bora a visitor. Or else it was the brigade commander speaking. Bora sat down automatically on the stool facing the bed.

Khan studied him. "Good breeding, army breeding: you did at once what you were told." Idly turning the goblet in his hand, so that the drink swirled a little, he was in turn unreadable and serene. He nodded towards his black-and-white likeness as a much-decorated commander. "Believe me, Major Bora, I am conscious of my preciousness. I *made* myself precious and my own best game piece. Young officers like yourself ought to learn this kind of chess-playing."

Bora looked away, for fear of appearing grieved or intrigued or impatient or anything else. The morning's events had made him numb; Khan's confidence had cowed him somehow. *His grave,* he thought, *his empty grave has fresh flowers every day, brought by his ancient sweetheart, my great-aunt's age. My stepfather refused to read my research about him: he rejects the very thought of betrayal. Does a man whose grave was wept over decades ago still belong to the order of nature? Can he die? Or did he die long ago?*

"Tell me, Major: did you just lose the man downstairs?"

Lying would be useless: Khan understood German and there'd been considerable confusion below a few minutes earlier.

"Yes."

"Uh-uh. You'll lose this war, too. For all practical purposes, it's lost already."

"*That* I doubt. You would not be coming over to us if it were."

The goblet, with a yellow-orange residue at the bottom, came to rest on the photograph, in the middle of a bedside table that, miraculously, matched the bed. Khan sat back on the mattress with his shoulders to the wall, stretching his stockinged calves. He finished unwrapping the candy bar – a 600-calorie cocoa and oats ration – and munched on it. "Or because it *is* lost, and when the aftermath is over, the move will once more be worth it."

They were still conversing in Russian; there was just enough distance between mind and spoken language to allow for some unguarded sincerity. Whatever crossed Bora's mind, whether it was mere impulse or the need to be spiteful, he said, "The *man below* was Gleb Gavrilovich Platonov." And because he tended toward punctiliousness, he removed the goblet from the photograph.

"Imagine that." The amiable Flemish burgher sank back into Khan Tibyetsky until there was nothing left of him. Out of focus behind him, the wallpaper pattern of smokestacks and jagged roofs turned into a garble of geometric thunderbolts. His meaty head seemed to radiate pale lightning. "*The vagaries of fate*: isn't that how you put it, in the paper about your relative?" He was smiling widely, which Bora found outrageous, yet fitting for the man (commander; hero; defector). "You look annoyed, Major."

"And you look pleased."

"We are a fatalistic race."

"My research actually suggests you're not Russian-born."

Khan shook his head from side to side, like a teacher commiserating his pupil. "But that was a schoolboy's homework, Major, by your own admission. You are standing: what, leaving already? A question before you go. How is my tank, my iron horse?"

"Safe. In a safe place."

"As it should be. You know those ashes falling like snow by the Donets yesterday? I set fodder and stubble on fire to cover my trail. You'll agree it doesn't get any more Russian than that."

"Echoes of 1812."

"Moscow on fire before Napoleon? Of course, today is 5 May. It would come to mind on the anniversary of the Great Man's death. No, I was thinking of the witch Baba Yaga flying in her iron mortar, and erasing her traces by sweeping behind. Baba Yaga, that's me. It doesn't get any more Russian than that."

Like a chess piece, the goblet went back where Khan had originally rested it. There would be no acknowledgement: there was no real reason for Bora to stop by other than routine, and perhaps the need to buffer his distress at losing Platonov, now that Khan was so much more important than the Platonovs of the world.

"I have to go, Komandir Tibyetsky."

Khan grinned openly. "But that's not my real name." And he kept Bora in suspense until he added, returning the spite used to inform him of Platonov's death, "My real name is Dobronin."

Mina was still fidgety when Bora left, running up and down the stairs with the hackles stiff on her back. She smelt death, agitation. *I'm like her right now,* he thought, *and have to regain my self-possession between here and the train station.* As late as the point at which he started the engine, Bora considered sending someone else, to avoid facing mother and daughter with the news. But it wouldn't do. He'd go, look them in the eye, and express his regrets. A strange word, regret: he didn't at all regret extracting information through emotional blackmail, but he'd present his regrets formally. *I've done worse things than telling wives their men are dead: I killed their men. What of it? They killed us by the tens of thousands, and their war against us is as filthy as ours, often filthier.* All things considered (it was a short drive to New Bavaria station), he quickly consoled himself by thinking that at least Selina Nikolayevna would understand as soon as she saw his expression. She was a general's wife after all. She'd utter something like, "Has anything bad happened to Gleb Gavrilovich?" And he'd only have to nod his head.

But if nothing had been spared the Platonov women, nothing would be spared him either. The train was late, which gave him more time to ruminate. In a day of perfect sunshine, on the platform a strong tepid breeze from the western gullies brought the green scent of trees, and pollen like ripples of gold dust. Bora stood still, busy resisting the need to pace back and forth and chasing the cowardly, small temptation to think of Dikta as he'd dreamt her, a powerful antidote to any other kind of tension. When the locomotive pulled in, delivering materiel, cattle and whatever else the quartermaster's office or Geko Stark had still managed to sweep up in Ukraine, Bora had nearly given in to the temptation, but rapidly collected himself.

As soon as the women stepped down in their flower-print cotton dresses, such controlled hope and happiness glowed from them that he again regretted having come in person. They were even more handsome than the snapshot had promised. The girl, especially: tall, ash-blonde. At seventeen or eighteen, Dikta must have been like this. At forty, Dikta would resemble the mother. Like a Renaissance triptych – *The Ages of Woman*, or other allegory – two portraits missing the middle one, which was Dikta as she appeared now. Bora's unprepared heart sank. *I won't tell her two Russian women look like her past and her future; she'd resent it. But if in years to come she'll seem like Selina Nikolayevna does now, only more elegant, more accomplished, mine, I will be blessed.*

The Platonov women had seen him. Even in German hands, under German escort, expectation made them both smile, a resiliency that was both shy and irrepressible. Bora walked toward them, deceived by that strength.

When he did give the news – quickly and in plain words, a crude merciful brevity mitigated by the concern in his voice – he wasn't ready for the scream Selina let out, as if years of suffering and separation, terror and the titbit of hope he, Bora himself, had offered her only to take it back, were the last blow she could take. She screamed like a madwoman and fell down before he could catch her. As she crumpled, the wind on the platform lifted the light cotton dress above her knees: in a wave of cloth the whiteness of her thighs flashed bare before him. Avrora, who'd remained standing, petrified, pushed Bora back when he leant over to adjust the clothes on her mother's limbs; and as she knelt, for a moment the wind also took her skirts, so that he was angry at himself, mortified for staring before turning away (smooth, no stockings, a glimpse at the clean shapeliness the modesty of Russian women jealously kept from sight – *They're good girls,* the rare, better-minded commanders reminded their soldiers, *show them respect*).

If this ever happens to my mother... Bora thought, feeling revolted at the idea. *How did she react when they gave me up at Stalingrad, presumed dead? I don't want to know; I want to believe her Victorian upbringing supported her even then, will support her regardless if Peter or I should fall.* He raised his hand to keep away a rifle-toting soldier who came to see what the commotion was. *"From now on, you boys have no mother, no wife, no sweetheart. A man can't keep steady if he minds his women."* *It's the sole advice the general gave us when we left for war.* Why didn't Bora think of how Dikta might have taken the bad news last December? After all, Selina Nikolayevna was Platonov's wife, not his mother.

It seemed an endless scene, but moments actually went by before Selina came to and broke into convulsive weeping even as Bora helped her to her feet. Only then did the girl allow herself to shed tears. Bora addressed her because the mother seemed incapable of coherence. "We did not manhandle your father," he said awkwardly, as if a German officer had to justify himself to a civilian, and a Russian at that. "His heart gave way because of previous hardship."

The original plan had of course been to take them to the special detention centre, and then to temporarily house them at Merefa. Now, once out of the station, Bora accompanied the weeping women to his vehicle, telling himself *they see nothing, notice nothing, grief does that, numbs you to your surroundings... Or else they'll remember forever this station, this breeze, and the man who gave them the bad news.* He said, "Avrora Glebovna, Selina Nikolayevna, I have arranged for you to stay at Father Victor Nitichenko's house in Merefa until you can go back. It's not far. We'll return the general's body to you as soon as possible," he added, forgetting he'd asked for an autopsy and the corpse would be in no condition to be shown.

During the ride – thirty kilometres seemed very long under the circumstances – the women didn't speak a word. Other than the greeting when they first met Bora, before learning of Platonov's death, they'd only replied to what he told them afterwards with anguished nods. In the passenger's seat, where a few hours earlier Khan Tibyetsky had been a cumbersome presence, Selina Nikolayevna still cried to herself, silently. Her daughter sat in the back; she had a tight-lipped, sorrowful, proud expression: Dikta's face when Bora had last seen her in Prague, and told her he'd volunteer again for the Russian front. Avrora Glebovna stood in for Dikta a precious instant: their eyes met in the mirror, and he looked away with a singular stab of the heart. *She's gone even beyond hate. She's so young, but suffering has replaced time in the process of making her age inside. Why does Dikta at times look like this, stare at me or away from me like this? We love each other but remain two single people. There's nothing I can tell this girl to explain, comfort, justify. There's nothing I can tell Dikta to make myself truly understood by her.*

Had Platonov been a good father to her? Fathers have odd ways of showing their devotion, not always through kindness.

Bora avoided the rear-view mirror. Once in a while, he stole a glance at Selina's hands, narrow, long-fingered: despite the years of hard labour they were fine, delicate hands. The type of hands that can be unsuspectingly strong, this he knew from Dikta: fingers and wrists capable of governing a spirited horse, of deeply stroking a man's back while making love to him… The rear-view mirror was not safe, and neither were Selina Nikolayevna's hands, resting slackly in her lap. He looked forward to reaching Merefa and leaving both women there. *When the time comes I'll have Kostya pick them up and bring them to Hospital 169, and then to the train station. I don't want to see them again. It's not my job, and I don't like my role with them.*

At the Lednoye checkpoint, manned by SS, he showed the women's identification papers as workers, without giving details. He left the vehicle to explain briefly that he was taking them along as domestic labour, and even though the SS observed nothing openly, a look at the two beautiful passengers made them think otherwise. They were smiling when Bora drove off.

"Why did you tell them you're taking us to your command, and not to the priest's house?"

The question caught Bora off guard, as he didn't know Avrora Glebovna understood German; and besides, it was impossible she'd heard him from inside the vehicle. Through the rear-view mirror, she met his gaze long enough to add, "Mother was deaf for a time, after the accident. I learnt to lip-read with her. She has forgotten how, but I still can."

"I'm taking you to the priest's house."

"That's not what you said."

Bora tilted the rear-view mirror so as not to see her eyes. To Selina Nikolayevna at his side, who stared at him questioningly, he repeated, "I'm taking you to the priest's house, be sure."

There were moments – this was one – when serving in the *Abwehr* seemed to him light years away from his nature and his education. Driving close-mouthed toward Komarevka and its brick and tile works, he considered his stepfather's reservations about his choice of counterintelligence. *Ever since we were boys, he hammered into us the importance of frankness. To him, it all amounts to spying, and anything to do with the term "spy" falls under the same rubric in his mind as conspiracy, treason and assassination. It galls him to think that a stepson of his was trained to manipulate documents and people. To him, honour means facing the enemy on the battlefield; even politics is taboo for a real soldier in his view. When I first advanced the hypothesis that Uncle Terry might have met his end quite differently from the blaze of anti-revolutionary glory we assumed had devoured him, he was incensed. The possibility that a relative of ours had crossed over – no matter how many times removed he was (and acquired by marriage besides) – sounded like anathema. He wouldn't read my papers; he wouldn't discuss it. To this day, it's a subject he won't let me broach. Great-aunt Albertina Anna says she has forgotten the whole thing, all the more since her husband (Terry's own brother) has been dead fifteen years.*

We're like this in our family. Comportment has to match essence, or at least dress it up to the extent that good behaviour is all you see. But what about me? Lying, misrepresenting my and others' intentions, forging communications, using my knack for languages to express anything but the truth – I've done all of that along with going into the field as any other first-line officer, one season of war after the next.

As God willed, they reached the house of Nitichenko's mother. In front of the little single-floored building, a whitewashed *shatka* with blue shutters and a pitched straw roof, sheets hung out to dry flapped hard in the breeze. The priest wasn't in but the ancient woman was, a servile little person who'd lived under the tsars until middle age. She bowed in front of Bora and went as far as addressing him as *barin*, Master, and *Your High Nobility*. On the other hand, the only words the Platonov women said were *yes* and *no*, listlessly. Even Avrora had tumbled back into silence. They'd only taken along a small canvas bag between them for the trip, and walked the few windy steps between the vehicle and the priest's door holding their skirts close to their bodies. Selina limped slightly, but did not lean on her daughter's arm.

From now on, theoretically it ought to be all downhill for the day. Bora drove the short distance to the *Kombinat*, where he was to sign the receipt for the babushkas supplied by District Commissioner Stark. A queue of military men and civilians blocked the entrance to the building, and he only cut his waiting time by pulling rank. Inside, stacks of medical supplies marked with their Kharkov hospital destinations cluttered the hallway. Disinfectants, remedies against pinworms and lice, rolls of flypaper. Geko Stark sat at his desk, going over a document. He noticed Bora through the double doors, but didn't invite him to enter immediately. "Just a moment, Major," he said, and went on reading, spectacles across his forehead.

The few minutes' delay, spent staring at the chandelier's etched-glass bulbs, actually gave Bora a chance to double-check his composure.

"Sorry to have kept you waiting," Stark was soon telling him. "Please come in." And then, as if mistaking the reason for the officer's presence here, he added half-seriously, "If you lack running water where you are, Major, I can't help you much."

Bora had already said, "What do you mean?" before recalling that Stark had seen him dunk his head in the pail earlier that morning. It seemed like another world, another life since then. He surprised himself by thinking that even the erotic dream about his wife belonged to *that* world, not this one. For an impractical second Bora longed to be away from here, from his duty, from the war: to be in any world but this. At Stalingrad he'd nearly succeeded in escaping reality by imagining other things and other places; he'd kept sane by believing himself elsewhere, while countless others lost their reason and lives around him. He finally acknowledged the commissioner's comment. "It's just that I get a fever occasionally, and need to cool off."

"Interesting method. The letter Standartenführer Schallenberg left for you hasn't yet arrived from Kiev, so you must be here for the babushkas. Do they satisfy?"

"I haven't seen them yet. I sent my orderly."

"They're supposed to be a hardy lot. Sign here, and in case they don't pan out, let me know and I'll get you five more."

Bora read and signed a paper similar to those that certified receipt of animals or materiel.

"Please sign this copy as well. A fever, you said? You do look under the weather." Stark's observation called for excuses Bora would rather not make, but once again chance gave him a reprieve. The telephone rang, and the district commissioner ("Yes. Good. Only if you confirm. Yes. Good.") was tensely paying attention to the call for a moment. Headquarters communication, Bora knew, had a way of sucking one's attention in. The interval, at any rate, allowed him to appear and sound indifferent a moment later when he said, "Thank you for the concern, Herr Gebietskommissar. I'm quite well."

Stark looked at him as though his mind were still on the phone call. But he must have been thinking of something else entirely, because he said, "Wait," and stood up. He removed the belt and pistol holster all ranks habitually wore, and slipped it into a right-hand drawer. "Are you in a hurry to leave? If you aren't, there's something I'd like your opinion about."

It was hardly appropriate to say he needed to stop by Hospital 169 to make sure Platonov's body had been moved there and to ask for it to be left in presentable shape for the family. Bora was non-committal; still, he didn't actually say no.

"It'll only take a minute, Major. Follow me outside."

Behind the main house, a vast gravelled area separated the living quarters from the old factory. Ravaged by war, its walls had been picked clean of rubble and stood orderly and clean, the carcass of an unknown sea mammal. Other service buildings, however, storerooms and garages, were still in use. Russian forced labourers hauled sacks and bags down from army trucks; at the officers' coming they stood at attention where they were and bowed their heads. "Keep going," Stark barked at them in Russian. "No one told you to stop." To Bora, "I'd like to think we're here to civilize this crowd, but it's more like herding cattle, believe me. The goad and the stick are all they ever understand; I know from my old managerial days at Derutra. This way, please." He led Bora to a brick building that must once have housed tractors. "The first time we met I think you understood I know horses. I'm aware you're looking to supply your regiment with worthwhile mounts, and wish you the best at this point. But if there's one thing I can't abide, it's to see the right horse go to the wrong rider."

"The *wrong* rider? I beg your pardon!"

"No, no," Stark hastened to add. "Sorry, I didn't mean you or yours. Why, Major, I followed your exploits as a horseman before the war. As a former newspaperman and sports enthusiast, I was disappointed that you gave up on the Olympics on account of volunteering for Spain, although as a German patriot I approved."

"Some things are more important than others, District Commissioner."

"Aren't they, though? Take a look inside."

Bora knew there was something exceptional in the building even before registering the soft stamping sound on the dirt floor. In a makeshift stall built against the long side of the large empty room stood a narrow-bodied, high-shouldered horse, chestnut in colour, with slender, strong legs and small hoofs, a concentrated image of lightness, power and speed.

"A *Karabakh?*"

"A Karabakh entire, Major, fresh from the farm. Caucasian, Armenian, Tajiki in equal measure, not for the faint-hearted. A beauty meant for a Marshal of the Soviet Union: they don't come finer than this. Four years old, name's Turian-Chai, beautifully broken and ready to go. What do you think?"

Bora took a knowledgeable look at the horse's small, sculptured head, tranquil and intelligent. "I heard the purebreds nearly went extinct some forty years ago, but he's larger than the mixed race from the Don. He's spectacular: croup and legs of a runner."

"Right you are: at the old Volkovoy farm near Taranovka they timed him at one kilometre per minute. I'd bet money he's one of Alyetmez's descendants, of the Tsar's stud farm. Three of our general-rank officers have got pre-emption rights on him."

"I can see why." Bora wouldn't step over the threshold. He didn't want to come close enough to appreciate the stallion fully and be tempted to long for it. The horse had noticed him, though, and widened its nostrils, sniffing calmly.

Stark straddled the entrance with a horse-lover's grin on his face. He had pink, compact, smooth skin; it made Bora think of the marzipan cakes they made in Lubeck. "In full daylight he shines like spun gold," he bragged. "I rather think SS-Brigadeführer Reger-Saint Pierre will claim him, but there's always a chance he won't. The other two don't know a gelding from a mare."

"It might not make a difference to *him*." Bora nodded half-heartedly toward the horse.

"Does to me. I feel strongly about it. So strongly that if the Brigadeführer turns him down, if the other two aren't up to it (they aren't) and I can't find a worthy rider, I'd sooner make stew out of him. Don't look at me that way; I've done it once before with a Turcoman colt." Stark spoke looking at the horse and not at Bora, as though Bora were no more than an accessory to his plans. "So, Major. Are you interested? Yes or no?"

Bora, who even in Stalingrad would have starved to death before feeding on horseflesh, had to keep his exhilaration in check. "Day or night, let me know immediately if he becomes available, Herr Gebietskommissar."

"Please understand I'm not doing you a favour; it's the horse I'm doing a favour to. If Reger-Saint Pierre says no, I've already made up my mind that it's you or the cooking pot. Enough said." Without waiting for Bora to walk back with him, Stark waved curtly and hastened toward the *Kombinat*. "Kindly be on your way; I've got a string of people waiting to talk to me before I can get a bite to eat."

Driving north to Kharkov and Hospital 169, Bora tried desperately to hide his feelings to make room for reflection. Out of sight went – or were supposed to go – dejection and residual anger at losing Platonov and a certain embarrassed shame at the way Selina Nikolayevna had tearfully watched him drive away from the priest's doorstep. Given its remoteness, even the possibility of salvaging a fine horse from the butcher made him anxious rather than full of hope, and had to be dismissed. He needed all the clarity he could summon in preparation for reporting the Soviet general's death to the Kiev Branch Office that evening.

Some time in the past couple of hours, his wristwatch had stopped. Bora had forgotten to wind it the night before, and now he didn't know what time it was exactly, save that it must be well past 11.30 a.m., if not close to noon. The hands on the face read 10.06, the time he'd left the station with the Platonov women. He had eaten nothing in twenty-four hours, but didn't have the ghost of an appetite. Worse, the tightness in his stomach wouldn't let up. Waiting for a freight train to grind slowly along the tracks from the Donbas, a constant headache, annoyed him more than usual. *Why am I rushing? The old bastard is dead. I'm in a hurry for the sake of being in a hurry only because it gives me the illusion of achievement.*

A gale still carried shreds of harmless clouds across the sunny sky; but it was dying out closer to the ground, and it was warm. Once past the tracks, Bora found the boulevard leading to Kvitki Park and the Lopany Bridge blocked by a slow-moving convoy of army trucks, under the escort of armoured cars and anti-aircraft guns mounted on Opel three-tonners. He impatiently decided to go around the obstacle by taking the north–south route two streets down. It meant he would cross Mykolaivska near the special detention centre: not the place he'd like to see at the moment. But he preferred moving to lagging behind, so he cut across the district he'd come to know well, marked by mounds of rubble cleared from the pavement, some of it already overgrown, other fresh heaps replacing the houses that had once existed there.

It was a regular grid of streets. Up came Svitlanivska, Olexandrivska. He'd begun to cross Mykolaivska, ready to go one more block to see if he'd overtaken the convoy. Catching a glimpse of military police vehicles across the pavement, right in front of the detention centre, somehow chilled him to the bone. The scene in itself was neutral, but normally the vehicles were not in sight; a *Feldgendarmerie* officer standing near a staff car belonged there even less. Bora's mind stopped racing for a numb second; a swallow darting between buildings caught his attention and he was lost after its agile sweep for that moment, as if any object, any occupation were preferable to what he might discover next.

The military police officer (a mature captain, rather agitated) told him, "It happened just after 09.00 hours, but I'd barely arrived here myself. We didn't know where to reach you, Major – the men did their best."

Bora had a commanding officer's antipathy for the expression "one's best", but he couldn't find the will to voice a critique, or anything else. Followed by the captain, he rushed inside.

Shots had been fired in the building; Bora smelt gunpowder before seeing the evidence. Behind a closed door, Mina barked ferociously: she had obviously been locked up to keep her from being felled or running away. The sergeant in charge stood at the foot of the stairs, whiter in the face than the wall behind him. "It was a raid, Herr Major, a regular raid. Headhunters, outranking us. They blocked both ends of the street. We thought they were after hidden Jews or locals, but instead they burst in. They fired into the lock when we wouldn't turn in the key without signed orders just because they were asking for it. They broke his door down and forced him out, kicking and throwing punches —"

Headhunters were SS police. Bora heard himself shouting, as if someone else in his place were furious, as if he didn't know in any case that the SS had authorization to proceed. "Without signed orders? Do you mean they barged in without accountability to anyone? Who led them? What unit did they belong to?"

"They wore *Adolf Hitler* cuffs, under an Untersturmführer. There was a staff car waiting below, which they pushed him into at gunpoint, and then they were gone."

Leibstandarte Adolf Hitler, the 1st SS Panzer Division. Trying to find out more and collect himself at the same time was a challenge. "*Where to*, Sergeant? Out of town, into town? Did you follow them?"

The military police captain intervened. "They'd have had to shoot their way through the road blocks, Major. One of the men just told me he raced to the attic, and from there he saw the car take a left on Beleshivska. That's all."

An exasperated Bora ran up to the fourth floor, where Khan's door had been smashed by rifle butts and the room showed evidence of a struggle. He was reasonably controlled when he came back down moments later. "Sergeant, what did the licence plate read? SS, *Wehrmacht?*"

"It was an Opel Kadett with a civilian plate, Herr Major."

An Opel Kadett with a civilian plate. Bora already had an idea. He ordered the captain not to leave the premises until his return, and sped in the direction the car had reportedly taken. From Beleshivska Street one could, in theory, reach every location in downtown Kharkov, but once across the tracks he continued down Osnovinska, and travelled northwards the length of Seminary Boulevard to the great prison at the crossroads. He made no attempt to seek access there, and instead parked in the narrow side street by the boundary wall. On foot, he rounded the corner so that he could take a look at the vehicles parked along the sidewalk by the entrance of what had been the dreaded Soviet jail. Bora knew his *Amt VI-Ausland* Security Service Foreign Intelligence counterpart in Kharkov by sight, and had made it his business to know his licence plate as well. If his Opel was there, it more than suggested that he'd led the raid.

The Opel sat parked across the street. Striving to keep calm, Bora walked past it. It was useless touching the hood to check for residual warmth from the motor; the day was sunny, and enough time had passed since Tibyetsky had been taken. Given the time of day, however…

On the same side of the street and down a bit from the prison, on Kubitsky Alley, there was a small eatery where surviving cooks and waiters from the Krasnaya and Moskva hotels now served German officers. It had been a restaurant connected to the nearby central rail station. Spartan, best known for its use as a temporary army morgue after the first battle for Kharkov: its pea-green walls and linoleum floor hadn't changed since. Bora went straight there, looked into the anteroom, and when a faded waitress approached to show him to a seat, he strode past her to reach a table where a young man in civilian clothes sat eating half a roast chicken.

The man (more or less Bora's age, very fair, with the sloping forehead of a badger) raised his eyes and continued to slice the meat on his plate. Bora did not salute, did not take a seat; he stood there less than five seconds before saying, "He defected to us; he is under Army guardianship." His voice did not rise above conversation level; nothing in his appearance betrayed the rage he felt.

The plain-clothes Gestapo officer finished chewing the morsel he had in his mouth. His hands, delicate and fastidiously manicured, had buffed fingernails. When the serrated knife he held went through the chicken breast, clear juice oozed from the tender meat. "He was under *Abwehr* guardianship, Major. We heard out Brigadier General Tibyetsky and are fully aware of his requests. But he can just as well wait for your Zossen superior while in our care."

"It's unheard of. I demand to see him."

"No. He's not yours."

"He's not *yours*."

"Cool your heels. You're not the only interrogator on the face of Russia, you know."

Those sitting at the other tables were connected with the prison one way or another; at the opposite end of the room, three *Leibstandarte* tank corps officers sipped beer and kept an eye in their direction. Bora only glanced at them. "Tibyetsky won't eat or drink anything but his own provisions."

"Then he'll starve. We're not in the habit of treating

Bolsheviks like nursery brats. Take your huff now and get out, Major Bora."

"It doesn't end here."

"It *does.*"

In his mind's eye, a well-placed kick overturned the table and sent chicken and plate flying. Outwardly, Bora turned on his heel without apparent haste and left.

Letting things settle, however, was the last thing he intended to do. He reached his vehicle and hightailed across town to the old Tschuguyev road, and, with just enough gasoline to get there, on to the Tractor Factory district and Jochen Scherer. After refuelling he headed south, mostly cutting across the open fields and at risk of driving over a mine, to Borovoye, where Lattmann walked with him to a safe distance from the radio shack to hear the news, and poured out a flood of obscenities as commentary.

"How the fuck did they find out we had Tibyetsky? All communication was encrypted!"

"They must have tapped our lines, know our new codes. Are we certain about our personnel?

"I vouch for mine here, Martin, and that's all."

"What about Kiev?"

Lattmann rolled his eyes."I think the Kiev Branch is safe. Besides, you said you'd sought Zossen directly."

"Right, and yesterday morning I was alone in the room when I did. Could it be someone in Zossen?"

"Not in Bentivegni's own office, I don't believe. But if we're tapped, we're tapped everywhere. Hell, this is fucking serious."

"It was a ten-minute blitz, carried out as one does against hostile forces. They broke in as soon as I left for the rail station, so they might possibly have timed my departure. They couldn't have known I'd stop by the district commissioner's office on my way back; but even if I hadn't, what with the train's delay, what with having to take care of the general's women instead of driving them directly to the detention centre, I wouldn't have returned to town in time. Not even if I drove straight to the station and back."

"Well, if Khan refuses to negotiate with them —"

"The *Leibstandarte* tank men will be disappointed if they want to learn from him where we took the T-34: I never told him. But it depends on what he wants out of his defection, Bruno. Through *Amt VI*, the Reich Security Central Office may be able to offer it, or pretend they do. At the restaurant, that damned Odilo Mantau looked like the cat that ate the canary. Khan's open show of familiarity with our nomenclature is odd; I don't know if it's arrogance or foolhardiness. If he's an *Abwehr* operative or has otherwise been working for us, he probably came over because his cover was about to blow, but to me he wouldn't say a thing: he was keeping everything for Colonel Bentivegni. If I'm correct, he's ours by rights, and this morning's raid is a direct attack against counterintelligence on Kaltenbrunner's part."

They were standing in a green patch of low grass, where Lattmann paced back and forth with his arms folded. "Oh, shit, oh, shit," he hissed under his breath, red to the roots of his wiry crew cut, and began to chew on his nails. "Our asses are on the line. We saw how they brought down General Oster last month."

"Not to speak of Old White Head."

A mention of Admiral Canaris, exonerated in the spring from *Abwehr* direction, was sure to incense Lattmann even more. Never mind that to the eyes of younger officers the commanders were not without fault. "It's starting to smell like a goddamned purge. What do *you* think?"

Bora looked away from his friend's nail-chewing. He shook his head, which of course didn't mean he had discounted that possibility. "They expect me to try to directly contact Bentivegni's office or even III C, where Breuer is our liaison to RSHA, but I'll bypass them. I'll avoid Kiev as well. I'm off to Rogany, to see if the pilots there will let me use Luftwaffe short-wave equipment.

Some at II JG 3 are my brother Peter's old colleagues; I trust they will."

"The Central Security Office will track an incoming message to Bentivegni even if you call from an airfield!"

"But I won't." Bora reached for Lattmann's left wrist and tilted it to read the time on his watch. Restarting and winding his own, he said, "I'll get in touch with our people in Rome and let them scout out the colonel for me. It's imperative for him or for another III C top rank to fly in as quickly as possible. On my way here I stopped by the Tractor Factory to warn Scherer in person, before someone got the idea of snatching the T-34 from under our noses. He and I handled the tank's transfer directly, so they couldn't possibly track us, and in fact the SS Tank Corps policemen never showed up on Lui Pastera Street. Besides, Field Marshal Manstein was better than his word: the T-34 had already boarded the train for Zaporozhye at dawn. Yes, at this hour Scherer and his men will be gone as well. Say, who have we got in Rome now?"

Lattmann gave respite to his battered fingertips and cracked his knuckles instead. "Until the end of the year it ought to be Ralph, Ralph Uckermann: you know him, he's married to an Italian girl. He's still recovering from his Stalingrad wounds, but he's back on active duty. You watch, Martin, the Security Central Office will either close us down or take us over; I don't know what's worse."

"*I* know what's worse." Bora started walking towards his vehicle. "You never saw me just now, Bruno. Don't even tell Bentivegni if he asks."

Evening came before the day's chores were done. Bora reached Hospital 169 with a throbbing headache, the sign of a rising fever. Dr Mayr, the army surgeon, was in the operating room, and there was a long wait before they could talk. Bora spent an interminable hour and a half by the clock on the ward wall, walking up and down past a number of closed doors. Without as much as removing his bloody gloves, the *Oberstarzt* heard his request and indifferently agreed to leave Platonov's body in presentable shape, but otherwise acted ill-disposed towards the visitor, dismissing him with a "Yes, yes, goodnight."

An entire wing of the hospital building, in imminent danger of collapse, was boarded off with nailed planks. The wards Bora walked past on his way out housed those maimed by mines and grenades, or severely injured while hunting (or being hunted by) partisan bands. *They're tearing us apart piece by piece,* he gloomily told himself. *When it's over, Russian soil will be fertilized by shreds of dismembered German flesh. We killed millions, they killed millions. All of us manure for the fields out there.*

In the vestibule, something stopped him cold. As if thoughts could materialize, his impression was that someone, disembodied from the knees up, was emerging at an angle from the earth, someone who halted when he did, stood still even as he did. It took him a few seconds to recognize the image of his own tall, spur-clad riding boots reflected in a broken mirror leaning tilted against the wall on the floor by the doorway.

It was unadvisable returning alone to Merefa in the dark; Bora did not bother to leave the hospital garden where he'd parked. He had a handful of hard tack in his vehicle: he chewed on it, drank from his canteen and fell asleep in the front seat.

4

Thursday 6 May, Merefa. Written at the outpost, 7.38 a.m.

Washed and shaved at Hospital 169 this morning, and sucked on the bottom of my fuel tank in order to arrive here. Kostya is off with the specific duty of getting me a 25-litre can of gasoline, even if he has to steal it. A review of more potential officers for the regiment begins at 8 a.m. sharp. The same was supposed to happen for non-coms this afternoon, but I have to pick up Colonel Bentivegni at Rogany at 4 p.m. (see below), so their interviews will be postponed. The non-coms are particularly important. I do hope I can get Nagel back, because I can trust him with the choice of filling the positions at those levels: one less thing to worry about. After Stalingrad he was promoted to Regimental Sergeant Major. I recommended him for a decoration as well, and will see that he gets it if he hasn't already. My life will be easier if I have him, but it may be early June before he arrives.

I'm still reeling from yesterday's events. By the time I fell asleep behind the wheel, Kiev learnt of Platonov's death (they were understandably put out); Colonel Bentivegni was informed of Tibyetsky's unconscionable kidnapping (I can't use another word) and anticipated his arrival in 24 hours' time; for what it's worth, I delivered Khan's provisions to SS Hauptsturmführer Mantau, about whom I know more than he imagines. We all spy on one another, and after the so-called "Ten Points" we had to agree on a year ago with Amt IV, the Central Security Office has leeway to interfere with our activities in the occupied territories. Mantau belongs to Amt IV E5, so I can only make a fuss about the mode of Khan's removal. As it was (and still is) my strong suspicion that they might try to shut down our special detention centre, I drove back there after connecting with Bentivegni, to make sure I'd left nothing behind for Odilo Mantau to rummage through, just in case.

What a difference a day makes! Yesterday at this time the old man was still alive, and Khan/Uncle Terry was sipping orange drink from a gold-rimmed goblet that now lies in pieces on the floor. I stepped on glass shards when I first went into his room after the raid. Later, when I returned in the afternoon to retrieve his empty trunk and vainglorious photograph (it reads *Narodnaya Slava* – National Glory, no less! – in pencil behind it), I thoroughly searched the premises, as if there were clues for me to follow. What was I looking for?

It is checkmate, nothing less. No use recriminating about Headquarters' insistence that Khan be kept in Kharkov, after I all but begged them to let me fly him out of Rogany or Krestovoy. He'd have been safe at our interrogation camp near Frankfurt, or at Colonel Gehlen's Foreign Army East HQ in East Prussia. I daresay Khan would have been safer even in Merefa. Now, as the chess expert he claims to be, he will be tempted to play the Central Security Office against us, selling himself to the highest bidder. Over there, they'll do anything to learn about our network as much as they will to hear about STAVKA's plans.

As for the Kiev Branch Office, they'll start working at once on what we got out of Platonov (Lattmann will hand-deliver the packet to ensure there are no more interferences). It must be said they were against the use of the general's family to convince him to talk; I insisted it would be the only method, and still believe this. Did shock (hope, surprise) contribute to his death? Mayr said no, but he wasn't in the room while I grilled the old man. Am I sorry he died? Only because I didn't obtain all I wanted. I'd have shot him without regret at least three times during his detention, because of his arrogant attitude and (especially) for trying to buy me off.

The more I think about it, the more his attempted bribery puzzles me. I wish I'd asked him what he meant, but I didn't want to appear interested. If it wasn't mere braggadocio or a bluff, did the "something else" Platonov spoke of have any role in his Purge trial? Some of the top ranks were accused of profiteering, in addition to the usual charges of diversionism and espionage. And now, even the one man who might possibly know something about it is out of my reach. Not that Khan Tibyetsky would necessarily be inclined to tell, but he did seem – what's the word? – glad, or even relieved, that his old colleague had died. Of course, if Uncle Terry sat as a witness against him during the Purge, after Platonov was rehabilitated their relations might have been strained, to say the least.

It exasperates me that I lost two prize catches in one week; not good at all for my fine performance as an interrogator thus far. But if in the first case I might have been too heavy-handed, in the second there was nothing I could have done to keep it from happening.

Khan–Terry is an acquired and remote member of our enlarged family; still, he's a Soviet star of the highest magnitude. My connection with him was the very reason I was chosen to carry out research about him in Moscow: the *Abwehr* saw it as a plus. I wonder how it might be seen by the Central Security Office if it comes out. Oh well. Will he keep his word, and speak to no one but our own Colonel Bentivegni? Or will he be enticed into sharing the wealth of his knowledge anyway? Rightly employed, a defector's information will benefit our military aims, no matter where it is deposited.

All the same, the raid marks a serious escalation in the infighting between intelligence services. We've lost much ground since our 1936 protocol with RSHA on mutual responsibilities and areas of competence. What does it mean for us who work in the field? As Grandfather Wilhelm Heinrich was reported to have quoted African wisdom (after his stint in the German Cameroon), "Where two elephants engage in combat, the grass below is thoroughly mashed."

Oh, and a shock to start the day. The grumpy *Oberstarzt* saw me in the hospital vestibule early this morning and told me – implying that it was my fault or by my order – that his young medic is being transferred without notice. No such thing, I told him just as curtly. "What do you expect me to do? Sudden reassignment is routine." Still, I wonder. They were so put out at our Kiev office, Weller *could* be a victim of Platonov's passing. Dr Mayr waved in disgust and grumbled something about the general's post-mortem and calling me about the results before nightfall.

At 7.50 a.m. Kostya was back with the fuel. Judging by the state of his boots and white canvas trousers, he'd stepped through a sluice or wetland to get it, and Bora had a hunch where he'd gone pilfering (the army-run sheds and deposit by the river).

"Kostya," he said, "where are the babushkas? I want to have a word with them before they start work."

The young man clapped his hands, as if he'd just remembered something he ought to have said before. "They weren't on the train, *povazhany* Major. The conductor told me they were made to get off at Pokatilovka."

"A station earlier? Why? By whom?"

"I took the liberty of asking. The guards on the train said they were needed elsewhere, that's all. I went to Pokatilovka, and they weren't there either."

"And I signed them out!"

Bora immediately called the district commissioner's office. Stark wasn't in yet, but his assistant assured him they knew nothing of it. "That's highly irregular. I am not at liberty to look in the commissioner's desk, but we'll see what we can do, Major."

Until 1 p.m., Bora interviewed ten promising officers, a couple of whom he knew well and was glad to meet again. It started thundering around noon; the light coming through the windows dimmed more and more, and eventually the weather took a turn for the worse. By the time the officers left, it smelt like rain. Hoping it would not start pouring in earnest, with all that it meant to dirt roads and parking spaces everywhere, Bora walked to the doorstep to look at the sky. A radiant azure overarched the horizon of the Donets. Towards it, sweeping from the Poltava region, a storm front drew an immense fan of dusty grey, the colour of ostrich feathers: strong, high altitude winds must be driving it eastwards. Westwards, all was ink-black and gravid with lightning. It must be pouring in Kiev, where Bentivegni was expected to make a stop before flying to Kharkov. At the edge of the schoolyard, Kostya, in off-white canvas fatigues that looked phosphorescent in the muted light, gathered the hens. He pointed out the storm clouds to Bora and wagged his head to mean there was trouble ahead.

Ordinarily, it would take between an hour and an hour and half to travel to the airfield. Bora decided to leave no later than 2 p.m., to be on the safe side. When Stark's assistant called back to suggest an appointment first thing in the morning, so that the matter of the vanishing babushkas could be discussed, he took his time. Bentivegni would have many questions for him regarding Khan Tibyetsky, and possibly Platonov as well. "I won't be able to confirm until this evening," he said. "What time does your office open?"

"The district commissioner will be out of town later in the day, so he plans to be at his desk as early as 07.00 hours."

"If you don't hear from me, it means I'll not be able to make it, and we'll have to reschedule."

Heavy rain had started to fall in the meantime. Coin-sized drops punched the dirt heaped on the graves, made a drumming sound on the canvas top of Bora's vehicle; Kostya's pail let out a clacking noise as water gathered at its bottom. The ostrich-coloured clouds had folded across the sky, in a green scent of wet leaves and grass. Bora did some mental reckoning, having flown (in good weather) the route Bentivegni was to follow: leaving Berlin at 6 a.m., after a flight of two-and-a-half hours he would reach Warsaw at 8.30 a.m.; averaging a twenty-minute layover for refuelling, and considering the three-and-a-half hours of the next leg, he'd be in Kiev at about 12.20 p.m., or 1.20 p.m. local time. Half an hour of layover and two more hours in the air meant he would be landing at Kharkov–Rogany just before 4 p.m. In good weather.

But the conditions were going from bad to worse. At 1.45 p.m., Bora telephoned the airfield's Luftwaffe personnel for last-minute information about the weather in Kiev. They told him rain was reported, but knew of no particular difficulties to flights in and out of the city. He left for Rogany shortly thereafter, unaware that Bentivegni had already been delayed by adverse conditions in Warsaw, and was running nearly two hours late; as a matter of fact, he hadn't yet been able to board the Kiev-bound plane.

Despite the many spots where muddy streams had spread gravel and dirt across the road, Bora reached the vicinity of the airfield well in advance of the scheduled landing. Through the windshield, the stormy sky was dramatic, a study in contrast worthy of a grand painting. *It might be worth taking the time,* he thought. At reduced speed, he approached a dirt lane to the left and turned on to it. On his map, he'd pencil-marked (so that it could be erased) a wooded area near Podvorki, cleft by a picturesque gully known as Drobytsky Yar. Before the war, there had been a therapeutic colony in the vicinity, but it was all deserted now, trees and fleeing birds under a spectacular play of rain clouds. Bora allowed himself the small detour, putting the camera he had carried along since the Polish campaign to good use.

At Rogany, German fighters were grounded by bad weather. Four p.m. came and went, and then another hour, and another. Bora was worried. At the control tower they had no details on Bentivegni's flight, and were inclined to think it had not left Kiev. This was only confirmed after 6 p.m., when Bora was told that worsening meteorological conditions in central Ukraine had forced the pilot to cancel the flight altogether. With more than five hundred kilometres separating Kiev from Kharkov, any attempt to travel by land – unadvisable at night, on unsafe, poor roads – would not deliver the colonel to his destination before the morning. Bora had to wait another half-hour to learn that, weather permitting, Bentivegni would be departing Kiev at 7.45 a.m. the following day, and would land at around 9.45 a.m. not at Rogany but at the Aerodrome, Kharkov's landing field by the horse track, on the highway to Belgorod. "Do you know where that is, Major?"

"I know where that is, thank you."

He left the airfield in the pelting rain. An entire afternoon of work had been wasted, but there was no arguing with thunderstorms. Every hour Khan Tibyetsky passed in RSHA custody increased the possibility that he would strike a deal with them, even though – considering how temperamental he was – a refusal to meet his demands regarding food and other comforts might make him ill-disposed toward his new hosts.

Past the old Soviet Army burial ground, Kharkov's darkened, war-torn city streets eventually clustered around Bora's vehicle. Curfew had depopulated them. Less than ten years earlier, the NKVD purge had decimated the undesirable – from intellectuals to beggars – in a city swollen with peasants escaping the great famine. Grass, dirt and manure had become food for thousands in those days. Orphans had roamed, and bands of famished dogs had reverted to a feral state throughout the once-prosperous region. *And then we came*, Bora thought. *It's partly our fault that they turned on us. We could have played Ukrainian nationalism to our advantage; some of us were successfully working to that end when political orders to the contrary broke the eggs in our basket.* He found that he resented SS interference even more than the fact of it per se. Past the Donbas Station Bridge, he travelled the last kilometre in the curdling, wet dusk, rounding the corner to Hospital 169 using the map he had memorized.

"I tried to reach you to say the post-mortem has been completed," Dr Mayr told him, "but didn't find you. Do you have a Russian answering your telephone?"

"My *Hiwi* orderly. Why?"

114

"Russians should not be allowed to do such things as answering our telephones."

"Don't house servants answer telephones, Herr Oberstarzt? A phone is the only luxury I have there. Besides, Kostya is a Volga German." Kostya was in fact a full-blooded Ukrainian. Bora, raised in a class-bound family where no one showed disrespect to, or used the familiar form of address with subordinates, never ceased to wonder at how humanity stops at certain boundaries, even among those supposed to look beyond differences. But maybe the surgeon was only making a point, or using him as a sounding board. "I'd be grateful for the results."

"Well, Major, the findings are wholly consistent with my initial diagnosis: the man died of a myocardial infarction. I detected extensive scarring in the myocardium, and a ventricular aneurysm that only hadn't ruptured because it was lined with scar tissue. There is evidence of prior inflammatory processes; in my estimation he had suffered an acute cardiac episode at least once before. As for anything else, and keeping in mind I'm no medical examiner, there were no wounds, no internal trauma, no traces of poison in the system, and the stomach was empty."

The autopsy was a formality, Bora knew. Still, he couldn't tell if he was relieved or not by what he heard. "Very well. Thank you."

"If the family would care to view the body, I suggest they do it as soon as it's feasible. I haven't got first-class facilities here, let alone refrigeration."

The light was dim in the corridor where they stood. Behind a closed door, planks were being sawn to repair something or other, and the freshly cleaned wards gave out an acute odour of disinfectant. Bora breathed it in. *The bottled sulphur dioxide; I nearly forgot. Tomorrow is Friday; it ought to be picked up at Stark's office.* "I'll see that they are accompanied to the hospital," he answered. He didn't want to sound overly disposed to escort the Platonov women himself, although he had that in mind.

"When? I'm a responsible man, Major, but I need a night's rest like everyone else."

They stared at each other with intense dislike, the weary-faced physician and the straight-shouldered, frowning, *impeccable* officer. Bora felt a need to be aggressive, although the man in front of him was hardly the appropriate target. He pulled back his left cuff to read the time to conceal his belligerence and create a small break in the tension. *Does he think I'm less under stress than he is, less tired than he is? It doesn't show on me as it does on him, that's all.*

"They'll be here in an hour, Herr Oberstarzt." Bora was on the point of adding *Is that soon enough for you?* as the surgeon had done with him after Platonov's death, but he bit his tongue for the sake of civility.

"You know," Mayr charged, "you should have opposed San-itätsoberfeldwebel Weller's transfer. He deserves better, and has already seen his share of human suffering in this war."

Ah, here we are. Kostya had nothing to do with any of this. Bora felt his resentment peak. "Well, Herr Oberstarzt, haven't we all." He saluted and smartly turned on his heel, knowing how headquarters etiquette galled the less martial officers. "If he's lucky, he's been repatriated."

Outside, it was raining less. Where paving stones had been removed to build barricades in the last battle, the garden floor had become a giant puddle. Taking the car keys out of his pocket, Bora's fingers grazed the wooden button from Krasny Yar, and in his mind's eye the thick undergrowth rose up to hem him in, with its secrets and dismembered bodies. It troubled him considerably, the power of suggestion that little hand-carved disk had. *It's what, contact magic? Why do I even keep carrying it around? That spooky Nitichenko: when I get back I'm tossing the damn button inside my trunk. No, I have Dikta's letters there. I don't want it anywhere around her letters.*

Suddenly, it started coming down in sheets again. Once in Merefa, the track became impassable after he left the main road to reach the few homes towards Oseryanka, where the priest's mother lived. An army patrol redirected him, and even escorted him for a brief stretch that was like a torrent bed.

Wicker fences, woven horizontally like baskets, with jars and broken cups capping their stubby posts, appeared in front of the screened headlights when he turned into the grassy lane leading to the house. Platonov's daughter must have been standing at the window and seen the military vehicle braking in the mud. She came to open the door, and stepped back so that Bora could stand on the threshold and make himself heard in the rush of falling water. A candle was all that mitigated darkness in the room, enough for them to see each other. She said, in a hard voice, "Mother has fallen asleep for the first time since we left Poltava. She would want to come and will be angry that I didn't wake her, but it's better if I do this in her place. Unless there's an order that we both be there."

"There isn't."

Bora couldn't bear to look at her, but not – as she might think – because he felt shame, much less guilt, but because it was like standing before his wife: in the twilight the resemblance was uncanny, confusing, physically painful to him.

"Let's go, then." Wearing the same cotton dress she'd arrived in, Avrora Glebovna had nothing to protect herself from the rain. Cans and pails left outside to gather rainwater had prevented Bora from parking close to the house, and she'd get soaked even in the brief distance between the door and the vehicle. Giving him no time to think of a solution, she squelched bare-legged, in open shoes and light clothes, towards the car. Bora made her sit in the back, because he didn't want to have her next to him with the flimsy fabric clinging to her body.

During the trip, he told her the minimum necessary: her father had died of natural causes; he would be buried in his uniform, with full military honours; she and her mother would be escorted back to Poltava on Sunday at the latest. The girl's silence forced him to assume she was listening. Midway through, unexpectedly, she said, "It doesn't look like it now, but Selina Nikolayevna is worth more than the job you Germans have her doing. She has an engineering degree from the Technical

Institute of Engineering in Moscow; she used to earn 600 roubles a month. Why don't you put her to better use?"

Thank God her voice was nothing like Dikta's. Yet. It was slightly unripe, and Dikta spoke more from her throat, a voice irresistible to him. "We'll see." Bora gave a concise, almost brusque answer. "What about yourself?"

"I'm ignorant. I know nothing, and can keep on shovelling cow dung, Major."

Of course; how could he ask? She must have been made to leave school at eleven or twelve. No, surely *before* twelve, which was the age limit beyond which the children of the accused could be shot. The temptation to find *her* an occupation in Kharkov was so strong and ignoble to his own eyes that Bora blushed in the dark as he decided against it.

In the hospital's dimly lit corridor, Dr Mayr began by darting him a reproachful look, no doubt to reprehend him for the girl's wretched, sodden looks. He accompanied her inside the room where Platonov lay, with a shake of the head to Bora so that he wouldn't follow. They walked out less than five minutes later. If Avrora Glebovna was weeping, it did not show on her rain-wet face. Her eyes were narrow under the blonde brows, Dikta's angry look. Bora felt unspeakably unhappy.

"I'll give her something dry to wear," Mayr said meaningfully, "and she can also take my trench coat for tonight. Just send it back when the young lady has no more use for it."

Avrora Glebovna sat in complete silence during the return trip, wrapped in the hospital gown and waterproof cloth. At one point, Bora cut short what he thought to be a checkpoint patrolman's insistent look at his passenger ("Mind your duty, Private"), and pushed aside the probing torchlight. For the rest of the drive, he could have broken the silence, but chose not to. *I already told her mother I regret Platonov's death, which isn't even true. I don't want to sound like I'm interested.*

In front of the priest's house she left the trench coat in the back seat. A stumbling dash through the mud took her to the doorstep, and moments later – Bora was trying to leave the yard in reverse gear, laboriously – the old Nitichenko woman slogged out with the hospital gown in her arms. "Here you go, *barin*," she said obsequiously as she gave it back, but Bora didn't like the suggestive echo at all, like a wink accompanying the words. *Old hag, let me catch you doing something amiss and I'll teach you to wink.*

As he drove to Merefa, Bora resented the surgeon claiming a higher exposure to suffering. Yes, maybe in volunteering for Spain he had left nothing of himself behind, except his impatience to confront himself with life. In Poland, in the assignments between then and the invasion of Russia, there had been a young wife and some worries, some misgivings. Whenever he might leave Ukraine, however the upcoming battle turned out, grief – personal and impersonal – made up most of the baggage he didn't have the luxury of letting go of. Forgetting had always come hard to him. For some time now, the past had taken a quality of adherence; it *stuck* to him. Bora could remember moments and places with such intensity that changing parts of the past seemed possible. The rational awareness that it would not be – that things could not be – undone, renewed his grief and regret with the pain of a fresh wound. What could Mayr understand? Keeping Stalingrad out of his thoughts was a necessity: a magic circle had to be drawn within which he could be safe.

It was all the more remarkable that his men and superiors did not notice. The fact that his composure did not falter partly accounted for their lack of perception; the rest was due to self-absorption on their part, or obtuse or uninterested callousness in the ranks.

At the schoolhouse, Kostya – God knows how – had managed to prepare a good warm meal of barley and meat, for which Bora was very grateful. "Have some too," he said, "and bring a tin to the sentry." He ate sitting at the teacher's desk, while the young Russian stood in the other room feeding quietly, like a mouse.

Merefa outpost, 10.05 p.m.

Kostya at times reminds me of the Good Soldier Schwejk. He's by no means stupid, and always full of good intentions. But he does certain odd things! Today before the storm he walked all around the building saying, "May luck stick to you, may bad luck fall off you," a blessing of sorts as far as I can tell. The first thing I had to do with him was get him out of the habit of blaspheming the Mother of God, something Reds his age do without even thinking, while their fathers added political vim to it during the Revolution. I told him I'd kill him if I heard him one more time, and I meant it. Now when he answers me, he adds an S to his "yes" or "no", (*da-s* and *nyet-s*) in the old-fashioned way, the S standing for *sudar*, sir. The other day he showed up with a pocketful of Makhorka, the rough local tobacco, and told me I should chew on it to chase the fever. How does he know I'm running a fever? He's seen the quinine, codeine, bromide and other Russian booty concoctions they gave me at the hospital in Prague, most of which I meant to bestow on the army surgeon today, and forgot.

Simple soul that he is, Kostya cut out and carries around a photograph of the Soviet movie star and songstress Lyubov Orlova, a pleasant blonde with a penchant for pantaloons and cigarettes: vices, he admits, he'd never allow his wife to cultivate. If he only knew what pleasure it is to pull Dikta's riding breeches down: so fitted at the waist, her underthings come down too. In his artlessness he calls his wife "sweet", and I'm sure she is, the dear girl. Dikta on the other hand is anything but sweet. She's smart, inside and out, strong-willed, passionate, impatient. I'm all those things too, or so she says.

Poor Kostya, he's given plenty to this war: he's a prisoner; his two brothers serve in the Tank Corps, his sister is a pilot; his father, a common Krasnoarmeyets of the 29th Infantry Division, died at Stalingrad (I should think so: we bombarded them with all we had). Kostya was a plumber's apprentice when he was drafted, and his dream is to have his own shop one day. I told him that if he manages to install me a shower in this building I'll write to Stalin personally to recommend him. In all seriousness, he replied that he doesn't think Stalin will listen to a German officer's recommendation, and that in fact it might even be counterproductive. I was joking, but if he does make it possible for me to wash in the sink or take a shower, I may really be tempted to wire Iosif Vissarionovitch the line you read on the walls of public buildings everywhere: *Spasibo, tovarishch Stalin.* Thanks, Comrade Stalin.

Now for the serious things. To my great delight, my old friends Hara Bauml and Alfred von Lippe, who were in Stalingrad with the 24th Armoured Division, are asking to join Regiment Gothland. Quite a shock: Bauml is unrecognizable. Lippe tells me Bauml's brother Paul was severely wounded during the house-to-house fighting at the beginning of January, when none of us expected to come out of the city alive. He was left behind to die with hundreds of others who could not be transported, packed in their own filth on the floor of a basement once used as a hospital ward. Bauml can't speak of it to this day; it was Lippe who told me.

Regarding the regiment, their immediate concern is whether we can trust the locals who are to fill scout and interpreter positions. They all claim to be anti-Bolsheviks, and if one listened to them, one wouldn't understand how the Revolution ever succeeded. I told my two colleagues that experience as an interrogator thankfully helps during interviews. I am familiar enough with Russian mimicry and body language to know when they're telling me an untruth. Some I already turned down when I asked whether they recognized the (invented) names of pro-German leaders in Ukraine, and they answered yes. Even though it might be they lied because they're anxious to join us, I wouldn't bet my life – much less my men's lives – on it.

Rain came and went the following morning; it was unseasonably warm and still stormy down Kiev's way. Bora hadn't confirmed his appointment with Geko Stark; even so, there was the bottled sulphur dioxide to collect, and he might drop by the district office at seven, in case the commissioner was free to see him. The Kharkov Aerodrome, closer than Rogany, could easily be reached from there.

He arrived at the *Kombinat* a few minutes early. The lights were on inside but the doors remained locked, so he sat in his vehicle rereading his last revision of the *Partisan Warfare Handbook*. Engrossed in the subject, he paid no attention to the staff car pulling in alongside him. The last thing he expected was the slam of the sturdy-framed Opel door on the driver's side, an impact that jarred the light personnel carrier. The car, civilian suit and the greatly altered face looking in belonged to Odilo Mantau, who was shouting brokenly, "So you've *done* it, eh? It didn't *end there*, eh? Your Russki underling told me I'd find you here!" and other such nonsense.

Bora found that he couldn't leave the vehicle, because Mantau leant on the car door with all his weight as he kept vomiting insults. "Are you out of your mind?" he shouted back, extricating himself from behind the wheel to exit from the passenger's side.

"You and your cohorts, I'll have your heads for not letting us keep him!"

Angry as he himself was becoming, Bora tried to decipher Mantau's rant in order to piece together the message. *Not letting us keep him* was the phrase that stood out of the jumble enough for him to grasp it had something to do with Khan Tibyetsky; his next thought was that Bentivegni had ordered, unbeknownst to him, a retaliatory raid to get the defector back into *Abwehr* custody. The barely formed theory collapsed under Mantau's next charge, sputtered at him face-to-face. "We could have all been poisoned, do you realize? Every man jack of us! Good thing the candy bars were left untouched —"

Bora was one to keep his distance. An energetic shove on his part sent Mantau reeling back a full step. "Are you telling me Tibyetsky was poisoned?"

"He was *killed*, damn you!"

They came close to blows in the following frantic moments, during which Mantau accused the *Abwehr* of murdering its own defector. "The Russian workers are those you called for and then diverted to us two days ago. I threw Stark out of bed at six this morning to have a confirmation; it's no point in your denying it!"

The struggle to make sense of the disconnected pieces started again. Bora groped for an intelligible explanation. "The Russian workers? The old women? I called the *Gebietskommissar* to complain about their diversion elsewhere!"

"Sure you did. You called the day *after* they'd already been sent to us!"

Commissioner Stark, attracted out of his office by the commotion, divided the two of them, now on the verge of a boxing match.

"Gentlemen, gentlemen! Transgressing this way – it's unheard of!" ("I'll kill him!" Mantau foamed at the mouth. "If I don't kill you first," was Bora's reply.) "Major Bora, Hauptsturmführer Mantau, you are forgetting yourselves." He held them both by the arm and apart from each other, like fractious schoolboys. "We are looking into the matter now," he said, seeking to pacify them. "You both applied for Russian labour at the same time. But, gentlemen, there's much confusion behind the lines these days. Our uniformed train personnel cannot be held responsible if someone gets passengers off one station early."

Bora felt as though he was waking from one nightmare into another, where Colonel Bentivegni was about to arrive. "Someone, Herr Gebietskommissar? It must have been someone with the authority to appropriate native workers and redirect them to a different destination!"

"Well, we don't know who that person might be, do we? I'm sure the Hauptsturmführer here can search the list of local officials working for us in the rail service."

Both officers were suddenly quiet. Mantau took out a handkerchief and wiped his face and neck. Bora desperately worked out priorities in his mind, and although Khan's apparent poisoning loomed largest, the need to secure further information came first. "However they're involved, we could begin by asking the women in question," he said.

Mantau's face fell. "I ordered for the lot of them to be strung up."

"*What?* That's knee-jerk for you. What a brilliant idea! And when is the execution —"

It was Mantau's turn to look confused. He glanced at his watch and his voice trailed low. "About now."

"Jesus Christ, call immediately: stop the hanging, or we may never know!"

Without stopping to argue, Odilo Mantau ran indoors. Stark took advantage of the pause to ask Bora, under his breath, "What's got into you, Major? Don't you know who he is?"

"I know exactly who he is."

"Please keep me out of your conflict, whatever it's about. If you horse fellows have to be so troublesome, you won't get much space to manoeuvre out here. Trust me, some of us had the same gall back in '34, and had to be taught a lesson."

Being compared to an SA irritated him. Bora straightened his uniform. "I'm not a *horse fellow*, District Commissioner."

"Worse: you're a Canaris horse fellow. Will you please keep your mouth shut while you're being helped?"

Bora walked to the *Kombinat*. His watch read barely 7.15 a.m.; Bentivegni would not board his plane for another half hour. But there was no practical way of informing him in time; it all had to wait until he could give the bad news in person. Thoughts of Khan's vitality, of his death long before (or long after) it actually happened, of all that had become forever lost with him, crowded Bora's mind in the short stretch to Stark's office. Mantau was just getting off the phone, and what residual hostility he still had in his system went into the hateful look he gave his Army colleague.

Bora ignored it. "For God's sake, Hauptsturmführer, tell me what happened."

"It's too late for two of the Russian whores. I'm sparing the other three until I can milk them for all they know, but don't expect me to take down the bodies: they'll hang there until they rot."

Were he not pressed for time, anger at the stupidity of this response would have led Bora to reopen the argument. "That'll do wonders for our public image. Christ, will you at least let me know *how* Tibyetsky died?"

"As if you didn't. He was poisoned."

"How's that possible? What did he eat?"

"It was as you said – he refused our food."

"So how did the poison get into him, and how could *you all* have been poisoned?"

"I told you we don't mollycoddle those in our custody, Bora. My colleagues and I ate the rest of the provisions in his trunk. Yes, we had a small party: why not? You don't get American provisions every day. When evening came and Tibyetsky still refused to touch any food, I decided he could have his American-made chocolate rations. Those, we heard, are vile-tasting, and we didn't care to try them." Grudgingly Mantau fell silent when the commissioner, without entering, sternly put his head into the room and gestured for him to lower his voice, pulling the folding door closed to ensure their privacy. Then he took up the story again. "I took them to his cell myself last night."

"How many?"

"I don't know how many; all there were. What difference does it make? He demanded to see Bentivegni, demanded to see you. When his demands went nowhere, he threw a tantrum. He warned me he'd only eat a single ration in the morning, and for the rest of the time he'd go on a hunger strike. Why all these questions, Bora? It's clear how it happened! All there was in his stomach was chocolate and oat flour, with enough poison to kill him. They don't know yet what kind; they think it was an alkaloid, highly concentrated. Shortly after 05.00 hours this morning my men woke me up to report that the prisoner was thrashing about and asking for help. When I walked in, he was convulsing. He was fine when he awoke at 05.00, and half an hour later he was dead."

Bora spoke through gritted teeth. "But why do you think he was killed? It sounds as if he committed suicide."

"Asking for help? No."

"Christ! Didn't you have capable medical personnel on hand to intervene right away?"

"No, they're short-handed at the first-aid station; their personnel go back overnight. It took them less than a quarter of an hour to arrive, but the prisoner was gone within minutes."

A small poster on the commissioner's desk, advertising a Ukrainian folk dance on Sunday, struck Bora as something from another world. He stared at it, as did Mantau, wondering who had time for such things. "What are the alternatives? Either Khan carried poison with him in his food supply, in case he felt compelled to do away with himself, or the poison entered the rations *after* he came under your watch."

"There's a third alternative. You poisoned the rations before bringing them over."

"You have to decide whether it was us or the Russian cleaning women, Hauptsturmführer."

"It could have been arranged by you through them. It will come out, so you might as well own up to it."

Keeping his own anger in check took more effort than Bora was willing to employ. "Seen from the outside, the same charge could be levelled at its sender. It is our command that was deprived of Commander Tibyetsky's person." ("Fuck you and your command," Mantau interrupted.) "All told, who had access to him while in your custody?"

"Other than Medical Corps personnel to ensure he had nothing to harm himself with, only my picked men and myself. *And* the Russian whore I hanged, who cleaned up his cell last night."

"Hm. Who's in charge of your Medical Corps unit?"

"The SS surgeon at the first-aid station on Sumskaya. Why? Who's in charge of yours?"

"Colonel Hans Mayr, the Army surgeon at Hospital 169. And you can vouch for all your subordinates with clearance —"

"Of course, the same as you can vouch for yours. I'll find out somehow that you planned all this, so don't you dare come anywhere near the prison."

7.25 a.m. There would be time, if he moved with haste, to at least try and view Khan's body. But Mantau was still on his high horse, so Bora tried a different tactic. "We could negotiate."

"There's nothing to negotiate."

"But there is. Would you or your *Leibstandarte* colleagues be interested in knowing where we took the T-34?"

It was the one detail, orally communicated, that could not have been tapped. Mantau's blond snout scented the possibility of capitulation on Bora's part. "Where?"

"Allow me to view the body, and I will tell."

"I don't trust you."

Bora held his breath. Much as he dreaded having to welcome Bentivegni with a disastrous piece of news, adrenaline kept him functioning well for now. However, as soon as he had a moment to himself again, he'd come crashing down. "We stored the tank on Lui Pastera Street in the Tractor Factory district. Where's the body?"

Mantau's lips jutted out in a strange grimace, as if he were about to whistle or blow up a balloon. "At the Sumskaya first-aid station, near the former university hospital."

Sumskaya, less than a kilometre from the Aerodrome. Finally a glimmer in the dark. "Will they let me in?" Bora asked.

"They'll let you in."

It was like floating on a piece of timber after a shipwreck, but was all that could be done at the moment. Bentivegni would have to take it from here on. Bora and Mantau left the commissioner's office one after the other without speaking a single word, but Stark wouldn't let them get away with it. His gold-yellow, dapper bulk stopped them in the hallway.

"Shake hands, both of you. You're not leaving here until you shake hands."

They reluctantly obeyed. Mantau left the *Kombinat* first; Bora was about to do the same when the commissioner held him back. "By the way, Major, SS Brigadeführer Reger-Saint Pierre decided to accept the stallion: a week from now my fine Karabakh will be on his way to Mirgorod. Sorry about that." He slipped his freckled hand into his tunic pocket. "This ought to console you, though. From your quasi-father-in-law Standartenführer Schallenberg, untouched by censorship."

The envelope was slightly larger than letter size, powder blue, and the handwriting on it was Dikta's.

"You're blushing," Stark grinned. "I imagined it wouldn't actually *be* from Schallenberg."

Bora thanked him, and jealously put the envelope away. "I would appreciate it, Herr Gebietskommissar, if you didn't mention this morning's episode."

"I didn't reach my position by mentioning things, Major. Take along the bottled sulphur dioxide or send for it soon; it won't last if you leave it here."

"I'll take it now."

The Kharkov University hospital belonged to the outer rim of the spectacular concrete semicircle that war had not succeeded in dismantling altogether: the gigantic Derzhprom complex of office buildings on the square that had been renamed Platz der Wehrmacht as late as 1941, but which since the tank battle in March had been dedicated to the *Leibstandarte* division. They said that escaped animals from the zoo were the only ones to live in the abandoned citadel of battered cement; someone supposedly had taken photos of chimpanzees crouching on windowsills. Across from the hospital, on Sumskaya Street, was the SS-run first-aid station. Bora arrived there shortly after 8 a.m., and encountered no difficulties getting in. He should have become suspicious at that point, but there was a chance that Mantau had phoned ahead to lift the ban on his presence.

In reality, Khan Tibyetsky's body was nowhere in the building, or so the SS surgeon told him. "Are you sure it wasn't the ex-Red Army hospital two blocks from here?"

In mid-March, the *Leibstandarte* had torched the Red Army hospital with hundreds of wounded in it, on Mantau's orders. Bora's self-restraint came in handy. "I doubt it."

"Then maybe it's the *Wehrmacht* hospital in District Six."

The SS meant Hospital 169. Possible. Bora couldn't very well search the premises, and regardless of their attitude, the medical staff here did seem uninformed about a body laced with poison. He asked the surgeon for permission to telephone the other facility, and when he spoke to someone there, he received another denial. "Shortly after 05.30 hours, you say? This morning? Not here."

Bora was seething, but he'd also lied to Mantau, after all – or at least given him only half the truth. The tank had been gone from Lui Pastera since dawn on Wednesday. Once in Field Marshal Manstein's hands in Zaporozhye, Tibyetsky's new tank model was off limits to anyone but the Field Marshal's closest collaborators.

Despite the war damage, there were several medical facilities in Kharkov, and no practical way of knowing if Khan's body had been brought to any of them. Bora could not afford a wild goose chase at this point. Deep down, he hoped against hope that the RSHA had been lying all the time. Tibyetsky could still be alive and in their hands, possibly out of the Kharkov Oblast or Ukraine altogether. *Bentivegni will have to get a view of the corpse before we accept the story as true. Hanging Russians is cheap, and there's no guarantee Mantau told it as it was.*

Before leaving the SS first-aid station Bora checked the fuel gauge, an automatic reflex on this straitened front. The Aerodrome, on the highway that led north to Belgorod and Moscow, sat in an area where – aside from the pre-revolutionary horse track – a large cemetery, barracks, gardens and a massive tile factory in various states of disrepair formed the north-eastern suburbs of the city. Bora had driven that way other times, especially during his first stint in Kharkov. Larisa lived not far away, in Pomorki, and more than once he'd sat in his vehicle looking at her house from a distance, without ever walking up to her door.

An easterly breeze pushed the oppressive clouds ahead of itself, undoing their thick vapours. At this time, Colonel Bentivegni would be midway through his flight from Kiev, which meant at least an hour's wait by the runway. Outside the entrance to the landing field, Bora was tempted to make time for himself and read Dikta's letter, but he had an almost superstitious reserve about reading her words in his present state of anxiety. He fingered and hefted the envelope without unsealing it, grateful to her mother's high-ranking lover for eluding censorship. Dikta was often intimate in her expressions, always suggestive; thinking of army employees poring through words meant for him before he did had made him shy and resentful over the last three years. Its size and weight suggested there was a card inside, or a photograph. Bora kissed the envelope and put it away. *Tonight,* he told himself. *However it goes with Bentivegni, tonight I'll find a quiet moment to read it. Postponing pleasure, they say, sees you through otherwise dismal days.*

So he decided to pass time by driving north, past the Aerodrome's entrance, beyond the old brick stables and the thinning-out buildings. Up there, a west–east *balka* formed a swell beyond which the road parted the Shevchenko industrial area on one side and on the other the beginning of the vast woods of the Biological Institute, a park that had become wilderness. Already the horizon was immense; sluices and wet spots overflowed across the rolling fields. On both sides of the road, steam rose from the sodden grassland and from the ditches that ran to the Kharkov River. Above the Pyatikhatky forest, south of Lisne, hovered a grandiose scene of rain coming down in sheets and gaps opening and closing in the storm clouds. Bora drove a short way up the Belgorodskye highway, and then to a clearing off the road on the right. There, he stopped to take some photos from behind the wheel, because he'd have sunk to his ankles in the mud outside.

At 10.15 a.m. the aeroplane touched down. It was a rickety-looking pre-war Ju-52 that even at its top speed of 260 kilometres per hour could not have done much against headwinds. No wonder Bentivegni had had to wait out the storm in Kiev.

Bora greeted the colonel on the much-mended runway. He saw no point in delaying the inevitable unpleasantness, so he simply gave Mantau's version of the facts, which was all they had at this time.

Although they'd often communicated since Bentivegni had taken over Section III in September '39, it was the first time they had met in person. With the face of a bulldog under the new "standard cap" many wore these days – even outside of the mountain troops – the middle-aged, sunburned Bentivegni, in his mixed summer and winter uniform, instantly managed to layer an image of control over his total astonishment. He had shaved recently and as best he could, judging by the nicks on his chin.

"It's extremely serious news," he said in a clipped voice. Only his stiff-necked stance suggested how hard the blow must have hit him. No other form of disappointment transpired. Bora was left to wonder whether Khan had been an *Abwehr* operative or not, and if he had, for how long. What both of them were thinking (that it was unexpected but conceivable that it could have happened, and now that it had, what next?) did not surface at all.

"Herr Oberst, I assume all responsibility for what happened."

"None of this is your responsibility, Major." Bentivegni had a small knapsack with him, which he now calmly let down from his shoulders and brought to rest on the ground – a sign they would speak here, away from all ears. "What happens from now on will be. Give me details."

Bora did. Bentivegni listened while fixing his gaze beyond his interlocutor, an *Abwehr* habit which allowed the listener to appear marginally interested while (Bora knew) nothing actually escaped their peripheral vision. At the end of the report, his comment was, "We must first confirm the truth of Captain Mantau's statement. He'll try to keep it from you, but I expect you to reconstruct exactly what happened. Not the charge I'm sure you expected or were hoping for, but the organization of your regiment gives you the perfect cover to stay in this area. Assuming there *is* a death and they have nothing to do with it, the Central Security Office as a whole will take the blow as we do, although Amt IV Gruppenführer Müller will be very cross. I predict Odilo Mantau won't have an easy time of it. As for us, we knew as far back as 1939 that it's the Gestapo's job to keep an eye on the army in the field. It's our task to work around it. Unless there's a lead to follow through Mantau, act as if we have dropped the Tibyetsky matter, Major. If Gebietskommissar Stark enquires about this morning's spat, say the disagreement between you and the captain was exclusively about the Russian workers. It was very improvident of Mantau to let out that Tibyetsky had been killed, and at the district commissioner's office to boot. Either he's lost his cool – we know his history – or he meant to make a scene for reasons of his own." A sunbeam out of the clouds suddenly spread a lake of bright light around the men, dazzling them. "It'd have been preferable if there had been no argument, but on the other hand, lack of response on your part would have been read as a possible sign of involvement on our side. I assume *you* did it on purpose."

"Not really, Herr Oberst."

"Hm. Start looking into things, and locate the corpse. Over at the jail they'll be busy about now doing some quick damage control, so that news of Tibyetsky's death doesn't leak out. You say you don't believe the Russian workers were involved, but we don't know for sure. In any case, little harm done: executions of civilians need no justification. As for the Soviets, they never will acknowledge their champion even crossed over."

It was typical counterespionage pragmatism. Out of Bentivegni would come neither appreciation for Bora's care in safely removing the defector and tank from the Donets, nor an acknowledgement that Khan might have had a better chance at Gehlen's FHO camp or in Berlin.

For half a minute, maybe, the officers stood face to face in the windswept space without speaking. Pools of sunlight opened and closed on the runway. Far off, fighter planes from the home squadron, inside the hangars for maintenance, revved their engines, making the sound of giant hornets. *Looking into things* meant the risk of a collision course with the *Leibstandarte* and the RSHA. Bora listened to the angry sound from the hangars. What was it von Salomon had said about the captain in Zaporozhye who crowded flies in a jar until they fed on one another?

Under the cloth visor of the "standard cap", Bentivegni's big-boned face had a disillusioned serenity about it. "Close down the special detention centre, Major, before someone else does it for us. And send the men back to divisional headquarters for reassignment. Lost for lost, after they commandeered Khan Tibyetsky from us... You wouldn't have taken any drastic *steps* of your own accord, would you?"

The suspicion was as offensive as when Mantau had first thrown it at him a few hours earlier. Bora did not blink an eye.

"Naturally no, Herr Oberst."

"Not because he was your relative, you understand. I had to ask." It was a natural segue for Bentivegni to say, "As things are, it was expedient that you insisted on pushing Platonov off the edge. None of us at Headquarters expected to get a single word out of him."

"I didn't actually get a single word out of him," Bora admitted, "but he did fill out a good portion of the questionnaire."

"Did his women come?"

"They came."

"Unless there's something that can be got out of them – I leave it to your judgement, including the methods you might use – send them back quickly."

"Yes, sir. Selina Platonova supposedly has a degree in electrical engineering. I'm having it checked out."

Bentivegni nudged the knapsack at his feet with the side of his boot, just short of a moderate kick. "These Soviet women! They're either engineers or physicians, or else they drive tractors. If it turns out she possesses useful knowledge, we'll see that she's employed where we need her skills. There's also a daughter, isn't there? Fine: both of them will be detained from now on. We can't have them go out and tell the world their relative died in our hands. *Yes*, Major Bora. Well, you should have thought about it. Once they had been informed, their personal freedom was forfeited."

In his anxiety to bring Platonov to collaborate, Bora had disregarded this possibility. Without showing it, he now felt sick. "It might be equally practical to send them to the Fatherland as labourers, Herr Oberst."

"I'm surprised at your insistence. They'll be detained." Unhurriedly, Bentivegni's glance migrated to the camera hanging from Bora's neck. "I see you are still taking photographs," he observed.

"Yes, sir." Bora was hoping for a comment of some kind, but none was forthcoming.

"Tell the pilot to refuel quickly, Major. I leave within the hour."

The rest of the day brought no improvement. It had all fallen into Bora's hands after Bentivegni left the scene without saying what steps he would take in Zossen, if any, giving him carte blanche here. It came down to a slight stress on words: "*Solve the problem*, Major, and *tidy up* afterwards." Whatever Mantau's prohibition, Bora did drive from the Aerodrome to west Kharkov, by the RSHA prison on Seminary Boulevard. From the corner of the church across the street, he saw the bodies of the two babushkas, hanging from the wrought-iron balcony of an old house nearby. They resembled bundles of rags from where he stood. How many times had he seen improvised gallows set up, ever since Poland? Hanging was commonplace; all units resorted to it. The merciful officers limited executions to what was necessary – because, more often than not, the Soviets didn't take prisoners either. The two women, conscripted to empty slop buckets and clean floors, had gone by a tug of the rope beyond fear, mercy, anger, ideology. Beyond innocence and guilt. Envying them sounded excessive, but Bora suspected there were worse fates than hanging oblivious from iron bars.

He returned to Merefa at sundown after disbanding the crew of the special detention centre (they took Mina along) and returning the keys to divisional command – minus a set he kept for himself for future reference. The sentry and a frightened Kostya told him that panzer officers from *Leibstandarte Adolf Hitler* had stopped by and asked for the *povazhany Major*. Bora, who always took along maps, documents and other papers he wanted to keep private, grew steadily angrier and also very worried. They hadn't gone as far as opening his trunk, but before leaving they'd used Kostya's hens for target practice. There was chicken blood all over the school yard; Kostya was fighting back tears over his dead pets.

They could make his life very hard from now on; Bentivegni and District Commissioner Stark were both right in that. A measure of protection came from what Bora knew or could find out about his adversaries, or from selective collaboration. He meant to keep as a last resort the old boys' network of commanders who were his stepfather's friends, from Generals Bock and Kesselring to Field Marshal Manstein.

9.32 p.m., Merefa.

Unpleasant day. The choice of a moderate adjective helps. Rereading my Russian entries, I see how on many occasions I merely wrote the letter A (for anguish) on certain days. There's a point when remarking on things would be too much, and remaining silent far too little. How does this day fare, in the continuum from excellent to dismal? Unpleasant is a polite word my parents use at home for anything ranging from a flowerbed ruined by heavy rain to the Great War. And so, yes, it was an unpleasant day.

Gobbled some aspirin to keep the fever down, all the more since I'm looking to a series of less than pleasant days in the near future.

Colonel Bentivegni was as good as his word, and by noon he was heading back for Berlin, having as sole consolation prize a carbon copy of Platonov's questionnaire and my notes on the irrelevant conversations I had with Khan–Uncle Terry. Poor Uncle Terry: what an inglorious end – and I do not yet know what exactly killed him, how, who is responsible and where his body might lie. Bentivegni doesn't exclude a move by RSHA to deprive us of a first-rate coup that would have improved the *Abwehr*'s standing in the Führer's eyes. The assassination would have been carried out against *Leibstandarte*'s interest in pumping a star tank commander all they could. But we do snarl at one another; we do crazily feed on one another.

When Avrora Glebovna and I left Hospital 169 last night, someone was shouting at the top of his voice on one of the wards. *War's a fucking ballerina* was the most intelligible sentence, repeated over and over. She covered her ears to avoid listening. From her, not one word on the moments she spent before seeing her father's body – not to me. Tomorrow I have a choice: either I tell them they're off to a detention camp, or I send them off without telling them. I haven't yet decided what it'll be.

All afternoon, I drove from one medical point to another, from hospitals to army morgues. Khan's body is nowhere to be found – or else they're not telling me. Came back low on fuel (although the only positive thing of my additional task is that I am to be allowed all the fuel I want), nearly ready to draw my horns in and eat humble pie with the *Oberstarzt* at Hospital 169. He could be useful in locating the corpse, so I must prepare myself to come down a peg or two and give him what he'll undoubtedly ask for in exchange. If I choose to believe what Weller told me about him, Mayr is recovering from jaundice and suffers from debilitating neuralgia attacks. In Stalingrad army surgeons would do anything to lay their hands on morphine for their patients – or themselves, what do I know? I saw some aberrant behaviour there towards the end. Had I wanted to answer Terry when he asked me if any of ours had gone mad, I could have described a chamber of horrors.

Enough. The regiment's accoutrements are coming in, good home-built material, plus some excellent tackle from heterogeneous sources: Polish saddles and harnesses from four years ago (where did we keep them all this time?), Russian equipment (including M-40 and M-41 mortars and 4-A radios that average 150 km in reception), which makes up for its simplicity with its ruggedness. Speaking of which, I asked my officers to break with cavalry tradition enough to switch from P08s to P38s. As handguns go, they're less fiddly, and preferable to Lugers in these extreme climates. I switched as far back as Poland, although in those days it was seen as heretical eccentricity.

In the mail, a letter from the celebrated writer Dr Ernst Jünger, whom I met in Probstheida at my grandparents' home eight years ago and with whom I have been corresponding intermittently. This was sent in September, when our hopes were still up. I'm sure it can wait a little more before I answer it. I have toed the line all day, and now I deserve to open Dikta's letter.

He'd read in novels and seen in movies how unanticipated news can cause people to drop the letter they are reading. It seemed like a cheap dramatic device, but Bora did exactly that with the contents of his wife's envelope, and then stood staring at it without picking it up.

There was no letter, no text at all, save "To Martin" and Dikta's signature on the photograph. Taken at Magdalena Ziemke's famous studio in Dresden, where actresses and top party officials had their pictures taken, it portrayed her completely nude.

In a suffused light (the artist's trademark *glow*), Dikta crouched in a three-quarter pose with her chin on her hand, the ash-blonde knot of her hair nearly undone, wisps from it seemingly ablaze in stunning black and white contrast. Neck, breasts, nipples were crispness itself, and there was a powdery mist where lines swelled into curves. In the smooth, twisted pose a tendril of blondeness flickered in the shade of her thighs, but so that the viewer had to search for it and become an accomplice. She was looking elsewhere, to an invisible point at the lower left corner of the image's scalloped edge, yet something in her lids and eyelashes seemed on the verge of a trembling upward motion, so that she'd look straight at him; and it'd be unbearable. In the shade of her thighs that blonde mark – more than glimpsed, less than seen – guarded the tender petal of her sex, subtly lit from somewhere so that it, too, glowed like a white flame.

Bora didn't know how to react other than physically: a desperate automatism that mortified him at being aroused by his wife, as if it were base and indecent. Of all the arguments Dikta had used to keep him from going back to Russia, this was the cruellest. As if he didn't know what he was giving up. *What does she think, what does she expect: that I should masturbate in front of it? You can't do anything else with a photo like this. It's what it's for. She wants my desire to regress, for me not to have another object of affection if not herself. Why? I have no other object of affection besides her.*

This was the last straw after a hopeless day. Angrily Bora swept the portrait off the floor and shoved it inside his diary so that he'd be screened from it, protected somehow. It was what Platonov had tried to do by flipping his women's photograph upside down. And he, Bora, had heartlessly returned it face up.

The diary's tough canvas-bound cover, worn at the corners and stained, was now all that separated him from those neat and muted forms, marvellous where light and flesh and golden-fleece became one. In yesterday's dream Dikta had knelt on the bed with nothing but a garter belt on, lovingly taking his clothes off in a similar glorious glow.

I will not open it again to look at the picture inside. I will not.
But of course he did.

5

In the morning, Bora felt drunk. There was no apparent reason for it; it wasn't imputable to alcohol, and he hadn't taken anything stronger than aspirin the night before. Instead, for the first time in quite a while, he'd had a wet dream: little surprise there. It hadn't soiled the camp bed only because he'd gone to sleep with his uniform on. *And I haven't even masturbated for it,* he thought irritably. The need to wash his underwear and riding breeches brought to mind the babushkas, dead and alive, Stark's promise to get him "five more" if necessary, and the entire bungle of Khan's death, Platonov's women, Mantau and his SS colleagues. *Well, Kostya is a married man: if I soak my clothes and let him take it from there, he'll handle it just fine. I'd be more embarrassed to have an old woman touch my mess.* Last night he'd slipped Dikta's photograph back inside the envelope it had come in and resealed it by pasting a strip of glued paper along the cut edge. The envelope now lay at the bottom of his trunk, although he didn't plan on leaving it behind whenever he travelled away from the command post.

If last night his wretchedness had failed to abate his desire, this morning something close to self-righteous resentment in him tried to fight back. Why in God's name did she make things so difficult for him? Without any fuss or complication, his brother's girl had let him marry her, make her pregnant, and now sent photos upon which she described herself to her husband as "fat Duckie" (Duckie being her nickname, and the birth expected in late June). Peter showed them to everyone, ecstatic as he'd been ecstatic about the full moon seen through the telescope when they were boys at Trakhenen.

Not Dikta's way at all, Bora knew. Her seductive image had nothing to do with child-bearing. Deep down, Dikta with a child was unimaginable, even for him. He was unable to say whether he would even like it, given the times they were living in. He said he would, but it was a statement expected of a young National Socialist husband. And although before Stalingrad his anxious mother had resorted to writing "Dikta doesn't feel well" – an obvious hint at a possible pregnancy, as if the prospect would make him more prudent, or eager for a transfer away from Russia – Dikta had never confirmed it. And if he hadn't impregnated her before Stalingrad (when he'd been sure he had), or in Prague a few weeks ago – No.

No, no. Making love to his wife was an end in itself, and as such *not* sterile, not needing to create life. His impractical, confident longing was that they would both remain forever young, forever at the height of vigour, fit to pour themselves into each other incomparably, out of a ferocious existential joy of doing it. He didn't need to be reminded of this by the photo Dikta had sent him via her mother's lover.

The seminal fluid that had seeped through the army cloth had had time to dry; still it left a telltale halo. Bora looked out of the door to see if Kostya was around. He wasn't, and the sentry sat half-turned, rolling himself a cigarette. He decided he'd walk past the schoolyard, beyond the graves and the fence, where a small canal brimmed with water after the rain. There he could bathe with his breeches on, and effect a first laundering.

The canal banks had been cleared of mines when they'd first arrived in the area; but still, one never knew. Bora stepped with brisk carelessness, taking off his army shirt. The downpour had made the mud black and very soft; slippery once he had removed his boots on the incline to enter the cloudy water.

The early hour, glass-like, crisp, made objects near and far visible in detail. Wherever Kostya had gone, he'd be back soon; noise would come from engines and whatever else functioned in the Ukrainian countryside these days; but at the moment silence was priceless.

Cold and lazy, the current reached to his waist. In both directions, the narrow ribbon of water ran on, reflecting the brilliant turquoise of the May sky. In his groggy state of mind, the impression was of standing in a flow of liquid air. Cupping his hands, Bora leaned forward to scrub his face and neck. Suspended particles of diluted soil tasted slightly bitter on his tongue; fine grit met his teeth. The leather sheath of his ID tag, dangling from a braided cord around his neck, grew dark with dampness; his grey braces formed two floating loops at his sides. Cold water awakened his skin through the soaking cloth. How far away now were the summarily executed babushkas, never to know the texture of his man-dirty uniform in the wash. How far Platonov's body at Hospital 169, Khan's unobtainable body, the tank safely in the Field Marshal's headquarters, Mantau, the Karabakh horse, the slaughtered hens, Dikta's thighs, the dead at Krasny Yar...

When, still bent at the waist, Bora tilted his head to rub his neck, his eye met the square edge of a wood-cased Russian mine sticking out of the mud along the bank. Rain had partially exposed it, like a strange geometric tongue or insane deadly mushroom. He found himself entirely indifferent to its presence. *Oh well, we'll take it out sometime,* he thought without the least alarm. *It belongs there, after all.* He was no longer used to landscapes free from the marks of war, and risk made life worth biting into.

In March, leaving the hospital in Prague, the intact state of the city had taken him aback. Houses, palaces, towers, belfries still standing appeared artificial to his eyes; there was something of a theatre backdrop or movie set in the flawlessness of the ancient skyline. Free of rubble, the streets gaped, empty. Out of

142

place were the windows with intact panes, each of their frames in its rightful place. Bora recalled how he had looked around, trying not to act surprised, although he had furtively grazed the corner of a sound wall, the solid surface of a portal, to verify its reality. His wonder had only lasted minutes. But in the handful of minutes Bora had imagined the fall of the city – not of *that* city: of any city – according to the rules of war. And so the Gunpowder Tower began to crumble from the top down and fell apart one cornerstone at a time, a blackened gold angel at a time; the cathedral on Hradschin Hill dissolved like a termite hill under a violent rain. Streets filled with debris, recreating the familiar obstacle course, the known, claustrophobic sense of impediment.

Only then had he been able to accept Prague still untouched, with the proviso that it would not stay so forever: knowing this comforted him. Dikta, walking at his side, had noticed nothing. She hugged his arm with her whole perfumed, haughty self: ultimately unreachable, for all that she was about to be mightily possessed. The woman present and unattainable, bliss prolonged through time. Even his wife's absolute beauty, her physical perfection, their peerless carnal rapport had for a moment been acceptable to him only in view of their end. *Only that which ends is precious*, he'd thought, and had stopped to kiss her in the street.

In Prague he'd realized how much he was loved. By his wife, his mother, his stepfather, his brother. Peter, en route to a furlough home, stopped by to ask if he wanted him to stay. Bora had said, "Are you out of your mind? Go and see Duckie, knucklehead. I'm not dying."

It surprised him now that he remembered the episode. Only through his diary entries had he been able to reconstruct the last days in Stalingrad, when a high fever had made him forget many details. He hazily recalled the end of the long trail out of the siege, in the winter snow, when he'd reached German lines with however many he'd managed to drag along, and a colonel in a sheepskin coat had shaken his hand, crying out,

"Thank God, thank God!" But it was possible he'd forgotten it, and someone had told him afterwards. Of his stay in the infectious disease ward in Prague he remembered two or three days clearly, although it had been close to a month.

The rumble of aeroplanes taking off from Rogany brought him back to reality. Bora wondered what he was doing half-dressed in a canal with his skin bristling when he had so many chores to attend to.

After rubbing himself dry and changing into a clean uniform he felt worse. *I hope it isn't another bout of pneumonia,* he told himself. It felt like it: fever and a sick headache. In spite of it he laid out the day's routine, beginning with a fact-checking request to Bruno Lattmann. Lattmann had ready access to colleagues at Offices III D and III Q, and the inordinate ability to collect data at a moment's notice. Then came three solid hours with a prospective Russian-born officer, formerly of the 5th Don Cossack Regiment. From Odilo Mantau and the *Leibstandarte* folks complete silence. It was possible, as Bentivegni had said, that Mantau had had to answer to RSHA Amt IV "Gestapo" Müller for losing Khan Tibyetsky, and the SS tank men might still be searching the Tractor Factory for the long-since-removed T-34.

At midday, he was at Hospital 169. They told him Dr Mayr couldn't leave the medication room immediately, but Bora was allowed to wait in his office.

It was a small dark space, with a clothes stand by the door and a camp bed that looked no more comfortable than Bora's at Merefa. A badly ironed uniform and rolls of underwear were stacked inside a cardboard box, medical equipment sat on a shelf no doubt inherited from the Soviet tenants; some of the medicines too, labelled in Cyrillic or in English, if they were lend-lease material from America. The window had been blasted and repaired, its panes replaced by sheets of waxed paper that trembled in the breeze and concealed the view. Only extreme cleanliness mitigated the impression of squalor given by this interior. Unframed family photos (a wife, a boy in uniform, a garden scene) had been tacked on to a pressed wood bulletin board, and this hung on the wall facing the desk. By habit and training Bora reviewed his surroundings, but made sure to be found standing idly in the middle of the floor when the surgeon joined him.

"You were prescribed this medication, Major, were you not? Why are you returning it?"

"Because I do not need painkillers any more, Herr Oberstarzt. Someone else may put them to better use."

Mayr brought the containers close to his face to read the contents. "I doubt you've come here to deliver a handful of drugs or to return my gown. Is it the body you're after?"

Bora was startled. He was about to say *I can't imagine how you could know*, and then he realized it was Platonov's corpse, not Khan's, to which Mayr was referring. "Yes, it is." He corrected himself. "I plan to see that he's buried tomorrow."

"You're late. It's already been done. Outside, here in the park. A number was assigned to the grave; you may attach a name to it or leave it as it is. I am accustomed to running a tight ship, Major, which I assure you is anything but easy under the circumstances. Something else I can help you with? Otherwise I'll bid you good day."

Already buried. One more promise to the Platonov women I won't be able to keep. Bora made no comment. There was no time to waste, so he said what he'd really come for: access to or information about Tibyetsky's body. When he finished the sentence, the surgeon's faded eyebrows met at a frowning angle; surprise lent his jaundiced yellow eyes a dull, reptilian look. "Why would I do such a thing?"

"Because you can; and because *I* can't."

"Let me rephrase, Major Bora: why *should* I? I don't even like you."

Bora had prepared for the likelihood of such a response. This was where his hurried checking through Lattmann's *Abwehr* contacts would come in useful, and allow him to stay the course.

"Herr Oberstarzt, you may be unaware that your wife's son, Officer Cadet Karl-Philipp Neuhaus, is under surveillance. Some imprudent statements of his in the presence of the wrong army school colleagues could place him in hot water, but if he toes the line from now on, he may get away with no more than an admonition. I suggest you instruct him to toe the line."

An intake of air, less than a gasp, whistled in Mayr's throat.

"Is this blackmail?"

"Not even close. It'd be blackmail if I had something to do with Officer Cadet Neuhaus' troubles. I do not. And I am asking a favour, not something in exchange for the advice I just gave you."

The surgeon clenched his jaw. Again that dejected slope of the shoulders, surrendering to the evidence. He slowly opened the glass cabinet to store away the medicines Bora had brought. When the door yawned open, an image of the room was reflected in it, like a transitory glance at an alternative world from underwater. "You are used to people doting on you, I can tell. Your looks; your smile. It annoys me that you count on it."

Bora was fascinated by the reflection in the glass, where a headless copy of himself lived ephemerally. "If that's so, it hasn't done me a lot of good lately. The complete results of a postmortem on the deceased in question would be greatly appreciated if available, although in a pinch I'm ready to settle for the cause of death, or even the location of the Russian officer's body. In case it helps with identification, I can describe recognizable scars from wounds the man suffered in the Great War."

The cabinet door closed, shutting out the alternative world. Turning to face him, Mayr lit himself a cigarette. Repeated washing and bathing in alcohol had dried and worn out the skin on his hands until they were red-raw. The match's small flame seemed capable of setting them on fire. "I was informed that someone had telephoned this hospital about a victim of poisoning yesterday. Was it you?"

"It was."

"Since you say your advice was free and it is a favour you're asking me, Major Bora, I feel entitled to reciprocity. I will take steps in the direction you ask; in exchange, find a way to annul Sanitätsoberfeldwebel Weller's unjustified reassignment."

Thank God it's all he's asking, Bora thought. "I'll do my best, Herr Oberstarzt."

A convoy bound for Donbas Station forced Bora to take a detour when he left the hospital. He negotiated through minor streets where bomb craters had been insufficiently filled and the removal of anti-aircraft posts had left ruts and gashes on the pavement. His headache was becoming oppressive; he should have asked the surgeon for a remedy, but after telling him he no longer needed painkillers it would not do. If only he had at least kept the Dolofin handy! Clenching his teeth relieved the ache only so much; listing what he had to do next distracted him, but not enough to lessen the discomfort. *So now I have to start looking for Sanitätsoberfeldwebel Weller too,* he thought. *Another nuisance, even though I have Bruno Lattmann to assist me. I had to watch my tongue when the* Oberstarzt *gave me a song and dance about the medic being severely depressed (he simply seemed sombre to me), and how "this sudden transfer, seen as a punishment, may push him over the edge." Bunk. Impatient as I was to enlist his help, I had to agree. I could have brought up the story of Bauml's brother, or how in Stalingrad I saw a tank corps surgeon shoot himself in the head, or how I had looked into a packed shelter after Siberian troops simply threw in hand grenades to finish off those inside. We must keep our cool, all of us. As for the awful acts so many of us witnessed, I could have told Officer Cadet Neuhaus' stepfather that we committed crimes comparable to the Reds' across Russia, not least in Kharkov. If the military judge ever comes, I have an earful for him, and that's a fact.*

The afternoon took him eventually to Oseryanka, and to Platonov's women. Bora's headache worsened in the process; it was blinding by the time he rummaged through the teacher's desk at Merefa for aspirin. The small orange tube was half-filled with tablets, and he took them all.

Kostya, still mourning for his hens, had laundered Bora's breeches and underwear and hung them to dry. Through the open window, in his shapeless fatigues, he cut a Petrushka-like figure while he felt for dryness and then folded the officer's linen shorts. Kostya had asked to report to him, so Bora waited for the pain to subside enough to listen. On an empty stomach, the medicine should have some effect, especially reinforced by the swig of nameless aquavit from Lattmann's once well-stocked supply. In Poland his friend had been able to share French cognac and American bourbon, but now he was down to what he could surreptitiously sweep up, one step away from cheap vodka or kvass.

When he felt he might be able to stand the sound of a human voice, Bora called Kostya in.

The orderly wiped his muddy boots before entering the classroom that served as Bora's office. "*Povazhany* Major, there's chicken for dinner."

"Yes, yes." Nauseous with pain, Bora couldn't bear the thought of food. "What else, Kostya?"

"You wanted me to ask around about Krasny Yar, so I did." Kostya spoke at attention, cap in hand, the way of a factory worker reporting to his superintendent. "Father Victor's sexton, over at Ozeryanka – he has a family. Seeing that we have so much chicken meat to get rid of, early this morning I brought him two of my poor hens. My poor hens, esteemed Major! My consolation on this earth. When you open them up they've got a tree of eggs inside, some tiny and soft, and some almost ready to be laid."

"I'll get you some more. Tell me what happened at the sexton's."

"Kapitolina Nefedovna – that's Father Victor's mother – told the sexton's wife, who told him. And *he* says the trouble in the

Yar began when Makhno's counter-revolutionary troops arrived in the Kharkov Oblast twenty-three years ago. He caused a lot of grief, Makhno did. Old Nefedovna was a matchmaker then: she told the sexton's wife that the Whites took girls in the woods and then killed them; there's no telling how many."

Plausible. Sitting on a corner of the desk, determined to conceal how under the weather he felt, Bora assented. Makhno was a bogeyman in Ukraine, but an anarchist, not a counter-revolutionary per se. Led by Frunze, Trotsky's forces had turned against his bloody Black Army, and he'd ferociously fought back until he was beaten and driven into exile. "Were their bodies found?"

"Most of them, later. The Bolshevik forces arrived eventually; they fought tooth and nail over the Yar, and they took it over."

"And did the killings stop?"

"Yes and no."

"What does that mean? Did the killings stop or not?"

"They no longer killed women, but a man was bludgeoned there in '22."

"Ah. And what about the years between the civil war and now?"

"That's what I asked the sexton. What about those years?"

Bora had a great desire to close his eyes to relieve the migraine. "Come, Kostya, say it all in one go."

The orderly relaxed his stance a little. His beardless, rosy-cheeked face had to Bora's mind the anonymity of a hundred such faces he'd shot at, or whose owners he'd taken prisoner, interrogated, seen go to the gallows. "They were hard times, *povazhany* Major, no food. It must be said the Party kept its stores full of Ukrainian grain but gave none to the people. I don't know if it was good or bad, if it had to be done or not. People starved; they ate the grass on the roofs of their houses and even clumps of dirt. And so, as they always do, they took to the woods…"

"And Krasny Yar?"

"It was the last piece of forest folks went foraging into, owing to what happened in Makhno's day. Kapitolina Nefedovna told the sexton's wife that in the '30s, folks from nearby farms and villages slaughtered children for food in the Yar." Kostya must have taken Bora's physical restlessness for impatience or disbelief. "I don't know if that's true," he hastened to add. "Fact is, people have kept well away from the Yar ever since the civil war. If you go there, it's because you're desperate. Mushrooms and berries are what you're liable to find, but are they worth your life?"

"Somebody must live in the woods or occasionally roam them now to have killed those who've died lately at Krasny Yar."

"The sexton sees it one way, *povazhany* Major, and old Nefedovna another way. The sexton says Makhno's men never really went away, and they took to living like animals in the Yar. Kapitolina Nefedovna, who lost a niece to the Whites, says it's a spirit, an unclean force. That's proven, she says, by the way folks are killed, with their eyes put out and heads cut off."

"You don't need to be an unclean force to behave that way."

"She thinks so, *povazhany* Major. As a matter of fact, no assassin was ever found when the farmers organized searches to look for the bodies. And since it's not as if everyone who goes into the Yar is killed, those who come back say they haven't met or seen anybody or anything. So that's no help. This time around, the sexton says, the killings began again in the winter of '41."

It had been a hard winter, that of the German invasion, a starvation winter. Although the presence of malignant spirits was unlikely, compasses did malfunction in the woods, as Bora had heard from those of the 241st and seen for himself. It could point to a magnetic anomaly: around Kursk the phenomenon was related to huge magnetite deposits. But magnetic fields don't drive people to murder. Starvation on the other hand might, although none of the recent victims had been harvested for meat.

Kostya uneasily shifted his weight from one leg to the other, because the officer was giving him no sign of appreciating or rejecting the report. "Old Nefedovna's niece," he added, "before the Whites killed her – this is all from the sexton, through his wife – well, Father Victor, who was then learning his trade in the Kharkov Seminary, was sweet on her. The sexton says he was crazily jealous in those days, that he'd beat her and then go and pray with his face on the floor in front of Our Lady of Oseryan. He never married after she died, and although in Merefa they say it's because he wants to reach a high rank within the Church, the sexton says it's because he lost his intended back then. And he dreams of the Yar, the dead in the Yar."

The dead girlfriend is one detail the priest never gave me. He volunteered to talk about the trouble in the woods, but kept out this titbit, along with several others. He wants Krasny Yar burned to the ground; I wonder if it's because of the unclean spirits he and his mother believe in, or for some other reason. "Did you ask if that girl's body was ever found, Kostya?"

"I did, *povazhany* Major. Never was. If there's anything left of it, it has to be still in the woods."

Yes, old matchmaking Nefedovna would never tell me any of this, and probably neither would the sexton. Kostya's hens came in handy. Still, I can't tell him we should be thankful they shot his pets; he's surely nonplussed that I'm interested in Krasny Yar. Bora left the corner of the desk. "You've done a good job, Kostya. Keep your ears open, and if you track down somebody who survived going into the Yar, see that you bring him – or her – here for questioning."

There was still time before evening to receive a politically uncomfortable visit. Bora dealt with it as well as he could. His headache lasted into the night, and he was able to fall asleep only after finishing the aquavit Lattmann had given him.

Sunday 9 May

Jubilate Sunday at the Merefa outpost; Mothering Sunday in the Reich. If I recall well, today's introit to the Mass reads, "Let all the

Earth rejoice unto God". Leibnizian optimism about us living "in the best of all possible worlds". Too sick last night to put down the day's events, which I summarize below.

1. Regarding Platonov's wife and daughter, I saw no advantage in dilly-dallying or sweetening the pill, much less in blaming it on orders I'd received. The worst of it was that both of them took the news of their relative's hasty burial and their future detention as if they expected nothing else of us. Selina Nikolayevna coldly reminded me that I had lied to them all along, first by letting them believe her husband was still alive, then by promising they would remain free. As for Avrora Glebovna, I can't blame her for the contempt she showed towards me. Within the hour, they were both on a southbound train, under armed escort. Why is it that I get nauseous when I'm under stress? Good thing I'd skipped the midday meal, otherwise I'd have vomited it and half my stomach up as soon as I'd left Nitichenko's *shatka* with the two of them.

2. My problem then was what to do with the old biddy, the priest's mother. I specifically asked Avrora Glebovna how much she and her mother had shared with Nefedovna concerning their relative (imprisonment, death, etc). She answered, "Nothing. Possible." As former "enemies of the people" they must have learnt to hold their tongues with friends and foes alike. The hag, busybody and matchmaker to the end, seems to think I had a fling with Avrora, or at least tried to. Well, she looks so much like my wife that I had difficulty keeping my eyes off her, but I'm faithful to Dikta, and that's all I have to say about it. I think I'll let old Nefedovna be, on account of what else I might discover about the Krasny Yar mystery through her, and because I'd complicate my life even more if I had her arrested. I dislike her a great deal, though. If her house stood on chicken legs and rotated at will, I'd say she was the witch from the Russian tale.

3. In this warm climate you soon won't be able to stand under the balcony where Mantau's unfortunate babushkas are hanging. If, as he says, one or more of them were Soviet agents, before even gaining access to the prisoner's cell they would have had

to know he would only eat candy bars and also have managed to plant a poisoned piece among the others – coincidentally, the very one he happened to bite into the following day. If there's any official Russian responsibility for the incident (here I disagree with Colonel Bentivegni) they will claim it soon, as they always admit to the punishment of traitors and diversionists. In that case, the task given me by the colonel will find an automatic solution, and Mantau will face the blame of losing a prize defector during his watch (and thank God the babushkas ended up going to him and not to me). This would imply: a. Soviet decision-makers knew Khan was in German hands *and* had been forcibly transferred into an RSHA facility, and b. a team of their workers/agents was quickly infiltrated and diverted to the place where the execution could be carried out. We'll see.

4. Thanks to the set of keys I kept for my own use, I returned to our former detention centre and went through it in detail, to ensure that neither of our prize inmates had left anything others could discover and use. It's been my experience that detainees (and even special guests on occasion) often idle away the time scribbling numbers or names. They're seldom of use, but I wanted to make sure. All I could find – and it avails me nothing – were the Platonov women's initials on the edge of the general's table, traced by him with the pencil I left him the evening before his death. Khan, who at least three times during our brief conversation looked on the verge of telling me something (maybe only that he acknowledged our distant tie), left nothing behind. But then, why should he? He had every reason to expect he'd be soon transferred with all honours to Berlin.

Regarding my lie to Mantau about the T-34's location, still no news from Badger Face, although before nightfall I did receive a visit from a *Leibstandarte* captain who didn't bother to introduce himself by name. He threatened me (nothing specific: he must know Schallenberg is my quasi-father-in-law), just the usual "You watch yourself", "Mind your step", "We know you" and the like, the array of innuendos I've collected in the past two years. "For what?" I replied. "It's true that I had the tank taken to the Tractor Factory." He limps and has a birthmark on his cheek, so I'll be able to track him down, and as God is my witness, I will gather some dirt on him for future reference.

Note: last Friday Metropolitan Aleksei of the Ukrainian Autonomous Orthodox Church was murdered, apparently at the orders of the Ukrainian Insurgent Army (UPA), for having withdrawn his support from a treaty with the Ukrainian Autocephalous Orthodox Church, its rival in the region. Can we ever hope to make sense of all this?

Major Boeselager sent me a Cossack captain, who came complete with red stripes on his breeches and *shashka* sabre, and potentially brings a squadron (*sotnia*) with him. He's (according to Boeselager) the touchstone against which the prowess of Russian-born elements is to be measured. His spoken German is so flawless that at first one is enchanted, and then grows suspicious. *Why* does he know our language so well? I wasn't at my best, so my feelers were only working part-time. I'll have to do some thorough background checking on him. Not because I don't trust Boeselager's judgement (he's an outstanding officer), but because under Old White Head I learnt to be wary.

When the day was done, I fell asleep doing paperwork (thanks also to Bruno's aquavit). A chair being worse than a camp bed, I had nightmares all night. This morning, the headache's gone; no more fever as far as I can tell. I feel shaky like a sick cat, but it'll pass.

The sound of a car engine interrupted him. Bora rose to his feet, released the safety catch on his pistol and finished writing in haste.

Must close it here: I can see a staff car approaching the schoolyard.

He slipped a sheet of blotting paper into the diary before closing it, and threw it into his trunk.

Wine-red piping identified the newcomer as a member of the judiciary even before he said, "Heeresrichter Kaspar Bernoulli, of the Armed Forces War Crimes Bureau. I think I know your stepfather."

Bora saluted, and shook the hand the judge stretched out to him. Surprised as he was, he thought, *Ah, yes. The world is divided between those who know my stepfather and those who knew my natural father.* He bowed his head in acknowledgement, as he always did in these cases, because a son necessarily stands for the absent.

"He'd have made Field Marshal, had he not retired."

The observation made Bora uncomfortable. General Sickingen's political unorthodoxy was a sore point, although less now than in the past. Ever since the war had started, the old man had learnt to watch his outspokenness in order not to harm his son and stepson's careers. Still, it was highly unlikely that he would have agreed to become a Field Marshal in the National Socialist army. "My stepfather belongs to his day," he limited himself to saying. And then he added, so as not to appear discourteous, "Welcome to Merefa, Dr Bernoulli. May I ask on what occasion you happened to meet him?"

The military judge glanced towards the graves at the end of the schoolyard, a quick, acute glance. "Oh, centuries ago. Well, not centuries – twenty years ago, at least. Your stepfather was just back from his anti-Bolshevik post-war duties in Finland and Poland... I'd served in East Prussia, myself."

Bora made another curt bow of the head. It all kept revolving around those early years somehow: Uncle Terry's beginnings, the dead at Krasny Yar; Platonov too, who'd reaped his first military successes at that time. A pinch of seconds sufficed for him to conjure up the balalaikas, Cossack ammunition belts and other tasteless souvenirs from Sickingen's *Freikorps* adventure, stuff his mother graciously agreed to keep – but in the smoking room, where actually no one went, given the general's aversion to tobacco. For a moment he was standing simultaneously here and in the tall-ceilinged hall, where hunting trophies from Grandfather Wilhelm Heinrich (who'd made it to Field Marshal, and how!) also decked the walls. It was possible to imagine a military judge in the *Freikorps*, but barely. That venture had managed to prolong the Great War bloodshed by four years at least.

"What brings me here," Bernoulli went on, "I believe you know, as it was your report that called our attention to the Merefa schoolyard matter."

Almost too good to be true. "Consider me at your complete disposal," Bora said. "I can show you the site at once if you wish – it's right here. Or, if you prefer, I can first share the additional photographs and notes I've taken since the bodies were discovered early in April."

The schoolyard matter, of course, meant the shallow mass grave where executed German prisoners had been buried, some of them apparently still alive; Bora's men had found them in the process of cleaning up rubble to set up the outpost. From under those bodies, two packed layers of civilian victims had been unearthed, still unidentified save the highly decorated remains of the Alexandrovka schoolmaster, whom a local peasant had recognized thanks to – *Georgji, Vladimir and Anna* – his Great War medals.

Bernoulli, who had come alone with nothing but a briefcase, driving a small car, displayed a rare lack of officialdom. He courteously said, "Show me the evidence first, please," adding, "The Bureau takes all reports very seriously," perhaps to explain his errand in Russia at this stage of the war, when millions had already perished. "This instance in particular – two distinct cases of mass execution – could not be ignored. I was sent directly from Berlin: Dr Goldsche's office. You seem surprised, Major Bora: why?"

Leading the way to the burials, Bora explained. "I hardly dared hope the Bureau Chief himself would send an enquirer."

"Yes? Did you not repeatedly notify us of violations committed by the Soviet Army and the NKVD? Your name figures on reports you have written ever since your headquarters days in Cracow. The Soviets' massacre of Polish officers at Tomaszow, the Skalny Pagorek incident at the hands of our own Security Service – you see I have a good memory. It struck me when in one case you mentioned the principle of *actio libera in causa*. It's not often that a young company commander recognizes a soldier's responsibility for his acts even when the man's under the influence of alcohol."

"If he chose to become intoxicated, he's doubly responsible as far as I'm concerned."

An enigmatic expression appeared on the judge's face. "The voice of one who cries in the wilderness, eh?"

If those deliberate words weren't underlined by discouragement, then it was pity, or else impotence: Bora didn't dare wish for doggedness. Having reached the row of graves, he stated the obvious. "I could not wait to have our men's bodies re-buried. We had an early thaw, and it had to be done."

"I understand. Dr Goldsche sent me as soon as he heard, but I was delayed on the way. I should have been here two weeks ago."

Bernoulli had a severe, narrow-chinned face, somewhat sad. Shaven-headed, dark-eyed, he seemed to Bora for some reason the kind of controlled man who is not ashamed of shedding tears in private over what moves him. If he thought about how he'd learnt in the past two years to show less and less, even though he felt more and more… *We all have our ways of coping*, he told himself. He watched the judge put down the briefcase and take out his spectacles as he stood by him near the graves, in the shade of the trees at this hour of the morning.

"Well, Major Bora, I think it was Goethe who said, 'The highest thing man can achieve is wonderment.' Wonderment as an astonished state, beyond which one is not to reach. The Romantics' Sublime, maybe, to be found in extreme beauty as well as in horror. My legally trained mind rejects extremes, plays literally by the rules, but it's whatever informs the rules – the *Principle* – that brings me here."

"I imagined as much, especially as the Soviets did not sign the 1929 Geneva Convention."

"You knew that as far back as Poland."

"I knew that as far back as Spain, Dr Bernoulli, which is when I first faced the Reds as enemies. In Poland – well, the truce with them was mutually agreed upon."

Fourteen markers delineated spaces like beds in a dormitory; the narrow interval between one and the next was just enough to rest one's boots in. Dirt had been packed onto the mounds with the backs of shovels; pebbles lined their perimeter. On each neatly cut pinewood cross a shingle was nailed, reading "German Soldier" on it, but not the dead man's helmet; helmets were more useful these days to preserve those who were still living. Bernoulli leant over to pick up a storm-tossed leaf from the ground.

"I was working in a dismal wooded place near Smolensk from early April until last week. Let us say that Poland's case is best left alone for now."

Smolensk? Bora had heard rumours of a massacre when he'd gone through that area in 1941, from Russian switchmen interrogated after taking over the railroads during the invasion. He'd passed the report along without comment, as had his colleagues, noting merely that the prisoners had mentioned the Polish uniforms worn by those supposedly led to their deaths. So it had taken two years to find the spot, or maybe even to look for it. It made sense, given all that had happened in the interim. On a scale of one to ten, what the judge was telling him registered about a six, which these days was rather high for a response from Bora, but still far from wonder, or astonishment. Bernoulli avoided looking at him, playing with the leaf; he studiously tore it to ribbons, following the fibres lengthwise. "The question is whether it's more egregious to abstain from the Convention or to violate it systematically."

"A sin of omission versus a sin of commission?"

"For us Catholics, at least, Major."

With something between annoyance and fascination Bora watched Bernoulli accurately tearing the leaf into equal strips, truly a lawman's overcritical attempt to coerce nature, an imperfect and ultimately futile endeavour. Beyond the single mounds of earth beneath which he'd buried the soldiers, to the left of the mass grave, the unpaved road breathed dust, impalpable and the colour of face powder, at every waft of wind. His wife, his mother used such pale colour on their skin; he had an urge to feel it under his fingertips, close as he was (with different kinds of affection) to both of them. "The trench just beyond is where we found our men," he said. "We left the civilian corpses there because they were in a state that precluded handling, other than a minimal search and approximate count. We unloaded a truckful of quicklime on them, and shovelled clean earth from the rise by the road, over there. If it isn't enough, by the summer we might have to dig everything up again, or else pour cement over it."

By the summer the entire region could be securely back in German hands all the way to the Don, or else be lost as far back as the Dnieper. Bora mentioned summer as if they could predict that they would all be here four weeks or forty months from now. "Badges and identification discs were removed from our soldiers before death," he went on, "so it is laborious work trying to reconstruct what units they might have belonged to, or how long they'd been in Soviet hands. I believe I wrote that in my report."

"Indeed. Some of our soldiers captured early in February were kept in a Kharkov temporary camp, you said."

"In the Yasna Polyana district, as far as we know. Our forces rushed there even as the city was being recaptured. It's useless to add that they got there too late." Bora turned and gestured without pointing directly to the school building. "Our soldiers were shot with 7.62 calibre Soviet rifles there against the wall, which I purposely have neither painted nor stuccoed over." When the judge turned slowly to look, he added, "When I arrived on 10 April, my impression was that the wall had been used before for the same purpose, and for a larger group of people – possibly the three dozen civilians whose bodies already half-filled the trench. Our soldiers were covered with snow and debris, mixed with a veil of dirt from the recently dug mass grave. Excess soil from the trench had been scattered in the expanse between the fence and the canal over there, but was unreachable at the time because of the snow cover. Our divisional medical chief was unable to establish the amount of time elapsed between executions as it had been unseasonably cold prior to the most recent use of the grave."

"I read he had suggested five to six weeks. How could anyone dig a trench during the hard freeze?"

"The trench had been dug much earlier for defensive purposes. The field beyond was mined." Bora watched the judge drop what remained of the leaf, and take off and wipe his spectacles with small circular motions. "According to official sources, the Russian units holding this sector belonged to the 179th Armoured Brigade. Shafarenko's 25th Rifle Guards certainly held out against our forces south of here on the Mosh River. I don't know why coups de grâce were not administered after the execution. In any case, torture seems to have been applied at the Yasna Polyana prison camp."

"I saw the photographs you took there."

Bora knew his next sentence would sound dismissive, but did not modify his tone. "I only arrived when *Das Reich* vacated it after using it for a week." Disregarding the judge's curious stare, he stepped past the individual burial mounds to the edge of the mass grave. "Regarding the civilians, there's a detail I didn't include in my written report, because it's based on hearsay and I couldn't find eyewitnesses. The schoolmaster, Janzen by name, was of Mennonite descent, and there's a strong likelihood the others were ethnic Germans as well. From what I can gather, their community in nearby Alexandrovka – already decimated by Makhno's Black Army during the civil war – disappeared at the end of January."

An imperceptible sign of uneasiness, a narrowing of eyes, was all that came from the judge. "Out of the ordinary, a peace-loving Mennonite wearing war medals."

"The Tsar rescinded their exemption from military service over seventy years ago. Those German Protestants who didn't leave the country had to adapt. Like other German minorities, Janzen and his men might have been scheduled by *Reich* authorities for transfer to the Warthegau/Warthe District and executed by the Soviets during that first week in February when they retook Kharkov."

A stubby cross reading *Cornelius Janzen and others known only to God* was the sole identifier on the long mound of beaten earth. Bernoulli did not encourage further comments. "Have you retrieved evidence from the civilian bodies?"

"What I could: shreds of paper items, cartridge parts. Here: I carry a couple of spent shells in my map case."

Hefting the metal casings in his hand, for a moment the judge resembled a buyer dissatisfied with the change he was given. "These aren't...Soviet rifle shells have bottleneck cases, Major."

"Yes, sir. 7.62 calibre, 76.6 mm long."

"And aren't these Mauser 7.63 mm, only 25 mm in length?"

Bora remained expressionless. "As you know, the 7.63 can fit most Soviet Tokarev handguns."

"Surely you don't mean to tell me the holes on that wall were produced by single pistol shots?... Major Bora? I asked you a question."

"Yes, Dr Bernoulli. Then it could have been our own M712 *Schnellfeuer*. It shoots in rapid-fire bursts of ten to twenty."

Bernoulli pocketed the metal bits, retrieved the briefcase and turned around to leave the graveside. "Let's go inside."

In the classroom, with the sun having been up for two hours, it was already warm. Through the open window, a ghostly sliver of moon showed as it arced down to set. On the bank of the canal, well out of earshot, Kostya was tending the droshky's draught horses.

"Tell me, Major Bora, which German units were operative in this particular location during the retaking of Kharkov?"

Bora chose from a selection and partly unfolded a large map marked M-37-X-West, smoothing it out on the teacher's desk. "Well, SS General Hausser raised a battle group from a *Das Reich* regiment, a *Leibstandarte Adolf Hitler* regiment, plus one motorcycle battalion from either division. Kharkov was in our hands until 2 February, when the Soviets took it and held it until 16 March. We began our counterattack the third week of February, and by 10 March Hausser, who'd been energetically pushing north this way, was already back in Merefa. Our soldiers had apparently been shot one to two days previously, but in the thick of battle their burial went undetected. By mid-March, all of Kharkov was reconquered."

"So, if our soldiers were executed around 8 March, the lower estimate given by your divisional medical chief for the civilians' deaths gives us a date around 1 February. The higher estimate would go back one week, to 24 January or thereabouts."

Bora refolded the map. "It must be said that in the first three months of the year units of all kinds were roaming this countryside, both ours and theirs."

Lost in thought at his side, Bernoulli stood with his face low, pinching the bridge of his nose with thumb and forefinger. "Are you aware of any special units attached to Hausser's battle group?"

"Not directly." As he said the words, raising his eyes to the window, Bora watched his orderly vigorously brushing the horses by the water. Suddenly he realized he'd forgotten all about the anti-personnel mine on the canal bank. The thought went through him like whiplash. From here he was unable to tell whether Kostya was drawing close to the explosive charge or not. The doubt split his attention between here and there, indoors and outside. As if someone else were speaking in his place, he heard himself say, "SS *Einsatzkommandos* are constantly being created and disbanded ad hoc, Dr Bernoulli. Informants told me a patrol took time in mid-March to search this area for the last *Dorfjuden*, but I have no confirmation whatever."

"'Village Jews'? I thought they were long since disposed of."

"Right." It was curious how he could make sense when he was no longer paying attention to the conversation. Bora couldn't turn his eyes away from the window. Alertness bordering on panic, and an odd, sluggish inability to turn it into action nailed him where he was, fascinated by the sight of man and animals in harm's way. *Where did I see the mine? Where was it?* He felt as at times he did in dreams, rooted to the spot despite his anguished need to move. "All I can say is that hereabouts they don't care for Jews much, and, if anything, they'd help search for them. It could be true, or not."

"Is this informant available for further questioning?"

"Yes."

The mine was more to the right of where he's standing. Or maybe not. If Kostya leads the roan down that way, where the young tree bends to touch the water... That's where I saw the mine, less than a foot down the bank.

"Major, is there something of interest outside?"

It took a direct question for Bora to snap out of his entrancement, sprint to the windowsill and call back the oblivious orderly along with the horses. "There are unexploded charges still lying around," he said to justify himself, summarizing things to a puzzled Bernoulli. (*Why didn't I move right away? How could I even think the mine "belonged there"?*) "I can't afford losses."

"Yes, of course," the judge agreed. "If I am not mistaken, you were speaking of paper items from the civilian layers..."

Bora was eager to dispel any notion of negligence on his part. "I was." From the desk drawer he promptly took out a battered tin box. Inside he'd collected blackened, rotted bits of printed paper, which he carefully laid out on the wooden surface. "The shreds definitely belong to a Protestant Bible, and this scrap – I believe it's relevant. Someone had time to pencil on it a few words in *Plaudietsch*. It's a Low Saxon dialect, and all I could make out is *lot dien Rikjdom kome,* 'Thy Kingdom come'. Perhaps Janzen and the Mennonites were rounded up and killed to keep them from being transferred to Germany."

"By whom?"

"That, sir, depends on whether it happened while the Red Army had Merefa or not. I do not possess that information."

Frowning, Bernoulli studied the remnants of soiled paper. "But we're not talking about *Dorfjuden* here: it's ethnic Germans, our own people. You say the Mennonite community disappeared at the end of January: Kharkov was ours then. For all your *Abwehr* methods of relating data without interpreting it, Major Bora, you're suggesting the possibility that the Soviets shot and buried our soldiers in a grave dug for ethnic Germans executed by German troops! Why would German troops —"

"As the teacher's medals suggest, the Mennonites' Russification comes to mind as a reason, but it's guesswork. I gave you the evidence I have, sir." A pause between them, where flies slowly circling in the room could be heard, threatened to become an uncomfortable silence. Bora would not allow it. Out of the same tin box, he retrieved two cases of film roll. "Taken near the gully known as Drobytsky Yar, and in the Pyatikhatky woods, north of Kharkov. It's best if I don't keep them here."

Bernoulli seemed to slump a little. "I see." He sat down in the only chair, looking at the metal cylinders on the palm of Bora's hand. "And *why* did you photograph those two places?"

For the next ten minutes or so, he listened without interrupting to what Bora had to say, running his eyes across the thickly written notebook pages laid one by one in front of him. His long-fingered, nervous hands, joined in concentration, reminded Bora of priests who'd heard his confession through the years. He leant across from the judge with his elbows on the desk, so as not to have to raise his voice to be heard. And although there was no penance given, a formula was followed when their conversation was through.

"Major," Bernoulli told him, "there's no time now to take a detailed, extensive deposition from you. Technically, I should not administer the oath until our written protocol is signed, but the instances you relate are potentially very serious, and – although I in no way doubt your sincerity – I wish to warn you about the consequences of perjury." He rose to his feet. "You will please raise the three oath fingers of your right hand and repeat after me: *I swear by God the Almighty and All-knowing, that I have spoken the pure truth and withheld nothing. So help me God.*"

"I swear by God the Almighty and All-knowing that I have spoken the pure truth and withheld nothing. So help me God."

"Very well." The visit seemed about to end, judging by the snap of locks as Bernoulli opened his briefcase and placed a selection of Bora's evidence inside the folders he'd brought along. "Anything else, Major?"

Until now, Bora had wondered whether he should add Krasny Yar to the load already placed on the judge's shoulders. He made up his mind because he had the impression he might not have a chance to see Bernoulli in person again, and he might as well say it all. From his trunk, he retrieved his handwritten notes about the dead in the woods, duly carbon-copied. "It probably has nothing to do with war crimes, sir, but I am bringing this incident to your attention as well."

Bernoulli glanced at the papers. "Fine," he said with a patient expression, on this side of weariness. "Fine. We'll take a look at this as well. And now, Major, if you don't mind, treat me to a cup of coffee."

Kostya always had a pot ready on the stove. Bernoulli could have had his cup of coffee straight away, but the judge gently refused Bora's offer to drink it there.

"Do you own a Thermos?" he asked, and when Bora said yes, he added, "Let's take your vehicle and have coffee on the road. First, however, you had better instruct your Russian orderly more thoroughly where he shouldn't tread."

So Bernoulli was aware of how imminent the danger had been. Did he speak Russian? It was more than probable, given his profession and with the majority of violations having been committed on this front.

Bora went to speak to Kostya at the edge of the dirt road skirting the schoolhouse, where he'd gone to stand with the horses, a safe area gone over for mines with a fine-tooth comb. When he returned, the judge had already taken his place in the personnel carrier. Bora started the engine and began to ask, "Where would you like —?" when Bernoulli interrupted him.

"I cannot hide from you, Major, that the obstacles to this enquiry – or enquiries, I should say – will be many. For the sake of simplicity, I am asking you to refrain from disclosing my presence here to your colleagues and superiors. There's enough for me to follow up in this area without further interference. I'll come and go as required by my investigation, which means you will not necessarily be informed of my arrival ahead of time."

"As the Judge wishes."

"I'm ready for my coffee now; and if it's not too far, let us drive to the lost Mennonite colony of Alexandrovka."

In the afternoon, Bora was still overwhelmed by the outcome of his meeting with Bernoulli. He'd all but given up hope that his reports would be followed up on, and now this positive sign of attention had come. He hadn't felt so encouraged in at least six months. Stalingrad might finally become a ferocious parenthesis between times of war; a parenthesis where *some* rules still applied.

Bora's good mood reached such an extent that he walked to the canal and dug out the Russian mine himself. He light-heartedly handled the flat-topped wooden case to expose it, and followed the tripwire to its anchor deep inside the dirt bank. Keeping it slack, he fingered it without feeling the slightest rancour against those who had laid it across his path. It never crossed his mind that it might go off and blast his arms, or kill him outright. Once he had inserted a makeshift pin in the fuse and cut the wire, his satisfaction ran close to a sense of invincibility, although it was no more than a single mine out of millions laid by the enemy.

Seeing Father Victor in the distance heading a procession of old parishioners singing and bearing icons – it was Sunday, after all – failed to annoy him, even though they were probably heading to some harebrained exorcism, the priest's speciality.

In the middle of a sterile field lying between the canal and the dirt road, where a pile of rubble marked the last remnants of a small shed ruined by war, Bora found a surface upon which to rest the explosive device to defuse it. One of Kostya's hens must have used the debris as a nest, because there was an orphaned egg still lying on the ground. Whether edible or not, it had kept its intact fragility, surviving the creature that had produced it. Bora crouched to pick it up, with the same controlled reach of fingers he'd used to raise the landmine. A pointer to what, this solitary egg? The children in the fairy tale had had crumbs to mark their way home through the deadly woods. *If somebody ever asks me what I learnt in Stalingrad – were he even Ernst Jünger, who's likely to do so and expect a sophisticated, abstract answer – I'll answer: the value of crumbs. The crumbs we gathered up with our fingers after eating, so that we'd leave nothing unconsumed, and those I scattered for the sparrows in the snow, simply to avoid feeling so miserable and beyond salvation that I couldn't afford to spare any crumbs. We were crumbs ourselves, left over from the bloody table of war: never mind that we started it all. Should Jünger insist on a more elaborate synthesis, I'll say: Chronos devoured his children there.*

From the road across the field Father Victor's deep basso drew closer as he led his followers' untrained, tense voices in a prayer where the words "unclean force" and *koldun* – sorcerer – were repeated like a litany. His invention, no doubt (twenty-five years of materialism notwithstanding); and if a German patrol didn't stop him first, he might be intending to walk the kilometres to Krasny Yar from here. Some of the elders in tow carried accordions strapped across their chests, ready to accompany the march or to celebrate the success of whatever propitiatory rite would be performed later on. Bora, whose love of music excluded bellows-based instruments, changed his mind about finishing work on the landmine. He headed back towards the schoolyard, and went indoors to avoid the risk of hearing them play.

An hour later, having secured a dinner appointment with Lieutenant Colonel von Salomon at divisional headquarters in Kharkov, Bora was preparing to spend the night in town and perhaps take in a concert as well. He needed the diversion after an intense week. Where Judge Bernoulli might be quartering, he hadn't said, although it was possible he'd chosen Kharkov as well, given its centrality to the cases he'd flown in to investigate. A man strictly there on business, Bernoulli, whose only reference to anything personal had been a mention of his days in a *Freikorps*. Whether he was of Swiss origin – as his last name suggested, or even related to the family of eighteenth-century mathematicians – he hadn't specified, and Bora had not enquired. The latter could be the case, since at one point, while visiting the demolished farms of the Alexandrovka Mennonites, the judge had turned to Bora and – apparently out of context – asked him, "Are you familiar with the St Petersburg Paradox?"

As he drove to Kharkov, Bora remembered quoting from memory something about the value of an object: how it should be determined not by its price, but by its utility. Bernoulli had said yes, and dropped the subject. In fact, Bora was thinking now, the mathematical principle also dealt with risk-taking. Risk-averse, risk-neutral, risk-loving: those were the categories deriving from the discourse about value. Was Bernoulli giving him hints, warning him, or did he simply refer to a judge's moral task in times of war?

It was odd how, despite its sombre reason, Bernoulli's visit had had a calming effect. Most of what they'd discussed was more dangerous than any explosive device; but for Bora, speaking about what he'd witnessed or gathered information about had truly acted as a confession of sorts, whatever might come of it.

The hour before sunset was especially sweet in this season: still bright but already combing the land with longer shadows. Ditches and ravines, long straight *balkas* wide enough to contain villages like separate worlds below, broke the greenness with the rhythm of waves and undertow.

At the pleasant turn-off that led to Babai and other villages south of Kharkov, Bora's personnel carrier was overtaken by a staff car, an unusual event in itself given the lack of traffic. Not so unusual that it should be Mantau's Opel, whose driver pulled over a few metres ahead, next to a low retaining wall at the side of the road. From the lowered window of the back seat, a gloved hand emerged, signalling for Bora to halt. He slowed down and came to a stop, careful to remain in idle behind the other vehicle, so he had some control over what might happen next.

For a change, Odilo Mantau was in uniform; a walking-out uniform too, a rare sight in Russia. When he exited the car on the shoulder of the road, Bora turned off the engine and also got out. Given that Mantau did not draw closer, and waited there, pulling off his gloves, Bora decided to approach him. *Is this risk-averse or risk-neutral?* Neither of them greeted the other. A glance inside the car revealed an SD private at the wheel, and in the back, on the passenger's side, a box tied with a garish red ribbon, as out of place as the spruce outfit Mantau had on. Unlikely that it was a present for the Russian beautician he was bedding. Bora judged it to be either for the girls of the popular Dutch brothel in town or for one of the Ukrainian dancers due to perform that night in Kharkov.

"Hello, Hauptsturmführer," he said. He fully expected the story of the misplaced T-34 to come out, but Mantau had something else in mind.

As was his habit, Odilo Mantau started in the middle. "Didn't I warn you?" He wagged his finger in metronome fashion. "A little squeezing of her girlfriends, and I find out that one of *your* babushkas – Agrafena whatever her last name is, the first bitch I hanged – was a nurse, fully qualified to handle poison. Now tell me you're not behind it, and that mine was a knee-jerk response."

Bora was only mildly surprised. After all, forced labour came from all walks of life, as Platonov's wife went to prove. Mostly, he didn't want to give Mantau the satisfaction of scoring a point. "I'm not behind it, but won't argue that now. Did they identify the alkaloid?"

"Nicotine: enough to kill a horse."

Standing by the car a step away from Mantau, Bora carelessly ran his forefinger along the edge of the Opel's door, where a scrape of the paint betrayed the slam against his vehicle in the *Kombinat* parking lot. "There's certainly enough tobacco grown around here. All you need now is for the NKVD to claim they ordered Khan Tibyetsky's execution. Unless it was the Ukrainian Insurgent Army: they detest Soviet officers more than they do us."

Edgily, Mantau looked away. He was of medium height, and facing Bora accentuated the difference in size between them. A sidestep reduced the contrast. "You know, there's nothing whatsoever to smile about, Major."

"I'm not smiling."

In the setting sun contours and shapes were particularly crisp. When he turned, Mantau's pupils shrank to pinholes in the light, so that his grey eyes had a flat sheen, singularly animalistic. "On the contrary: you look like you're having fun with this."

"I assure you I am not."

A few irritated steps around the car took the captain to the middle of the lonely road and back. His well-manicured hands on his hips, he seemed to be measuring the space at his disposal, all the while glancing over his shoulder. Three times he walked to and fro before stopping halfway through an about-face and darting a spiteful glare in Bora's direction.

"Try this one for size: my sources report that in '41 at Gomel you bartered a Jew for a grand piano."

Now what? I knew Mantau didn't stop me to talk about Soviet nurses. He's looking for a confrontation, or he's just frustrated and doesn't know what to do with his impotence. Bora savoured the small gathering of saliva in his mouth that meant physical readiness for anything, from a fistfight to the disarming of a landmine. *Risk-loving, definitely.* "Actually, it's the other way around; I bartered a grand piano for a Jew. My counterpart profited on the deal: the piano was a prize concert Petrov."

"They say the Jew was your old piano teacher."

"Do they? I think it'd be foolish to pick up a piano teacher and get rid of a piano."

"And then you bartered him again, with the International Red Cross."

In the stillness of the hour, a bell tolling somewhere sent waves of clear sound outwards, like circles in a pond. Bora recognized it. It was the schoolhouse bell that Father Victor had nagged him for and obtained two weeks earlier; if the priest was out on a procession, it must be his old mother, the busybody Nefedovna, who was ringing it. Still, the small hammering echo was pleasing to the ear. Bora drove his hands into the pockets of his breeches in an impudent show of easiness. He was growing accustomed to these exchanges, somewhere between gossip and threat, not being above them himself when necessary.

"Well, I needed medical supplies for my unit, and they needed a Yiddish speaker." Each sarcastic word rolled off his tongue like tart fruit, not altogether unpleasant. "It was expedient. We all barter on the Eastern Front, as you know. It's the rage. Don't they call it *Tauschmanie?*"

The approach of two soldiers on bicycle patrol – eyes right, salute, regular motion of knees and booted feet – gave Mantau a reason to return to the side of the road, where (as Bora had expected) he nonchalantly stepped on to the low retaining wall as if it were a podium, gaining instant eye-level parity with his colleague.

"It seems to me you'll barter your Saxon arse for a lot of trouble one of these days."

Bora did smile this time. *When they come out in the open they're less dangerous: you can squash them because you can see them.* "Did I commit an irregularity? I'm told that district commissioners and even SS commanders keep Jews for special positions they can't fill in this desolate neck of the woods: accountants, office machinery technicians, or hairdressers for their wives. We can't all be so improper. May I enquire whether you asked for and received clearance from Gebietskommissar Stark before you ordered the hanging? It would be an irregularity otherwise."

The mention of the hanging was sure to irritate. Mantau fell for it, immediately saying what he might have meant to add piecemeal for effect. "Do you deny the Jew's name was Weiss, like your piano teacher? His old woman had already been packed off to Palestine through the Polack consulate in Leipzig back in '38."

"Not by me. I was then a twenty-five-year-old at the War Academy in Berlin."

"*Well!* See that it doesn't go to your head being a twenty-nine-year-old with your own personal regiment."

"I'm obliged to you for the helpful advice, and I'll see to it. Did you get clearance from Commissioner Stark?"

"Go get screwed."

"Literally? *I* wish." Smiling came from somewhere deep, amused and secure. Bora let Mantau stew for a while, because Mantau's real problem was not the babushkas' hanging; it was losing Khan Tibyetsky. Without further exacerbating matters, he simply said, "We're in the same boat, but I might be able to help."

"How so? By admitting that you're behind the murder?"

"You'll have to abandon that notion. No. Discovering how it happened; short of Tibyetsky having committed suicide."

"He did no such thing. And I don't need your help."

You do, you do. That's why you stopped me. Unhurriedly Bora turned to head for his vehicle. "Look, Hauptsturmführer, my agency and yours will be exchanging potshots over losing the man, but it's at your place that he died. In case you should modify your views, you know where to find me."

Predictably, Mantau's voice reached him after a brief pause. "It won't do any good, but speak."

Still with hands in pockets, Bora pretended to hesitate. He stopped, turned, walked back. Critically he kicked the front tyre of Mantau's car. "Don't keep them so full; on these roads they're better off slightly deflated."

"I'm not asking you for mechanical advice!"

"Right. But you shouldn't keep the tyres so full."

"Major Bora —"

"I'm coming to it. The babushka you executed first, Agrafena – are you positive she could have introduced the poison during the time she was cleaning Khan's cell?"

"As if you didn't know the chocolate bars are lend-lease provisions. The NKVD or whomever could have supplied her with a sealed, poisoned ration to use."

That means they didn't search local labourers working at the jail. I can see why Mantau gets in hot water: he's a dolt. "But she would have had to add a poisoned bar to Khan's lot, and she would have had to be very clever not to be noticed. He was suspicious of everyone. You said you let him keep all the D rations in his cell. Do you still have what remains?"

"What a question! Yes. You can believe that none of us would taste it."

"Good, because I itemized the food and drink Khan Tibyetsky brought along. We can determine whether a poisoned piece was introduced from the outside without him knowing."

Mantau looked unconvinced. "We've been through that. It only works if you know how many of those damned treats he ate daily."

"As far as I know, they pack 600 calories each, and three of them make up a day's minimum energy requirement."

"But he was also regularly eating his provisions at your place, was he not? He told me he'd only have one bar in the morning, and stay on hunger strike the rest of the day. That damned candy being all he had on hand, he might have consumed more than one ration overnight."

"It's still worth a shot trying to do some maths, Hauptsturm-führer. I can tell you right off that when Khan first arrived I counted fourteen D-rations. When I brought his trunk to your place, there were twelve: fourteen minus the two bars he'd eaten in the two intervening days. He ate the poisoned one on the morning of 7 May, so there ought to be eleven bars left in all. If there are twelve, it means someone brought a poisoned ration in and mixed it with the original stock, even though it'd be chancy placing *one* poisoned piece of food among many others. It could have been days before Tibyetsky ate the lethal one. If the plan was to keep him from talking —"

"We don't know that, Bora. The Reds might simply have wanted to punish him for defecting."

"True. Is there a lamp that can be turned on from inside the cell?"

"You forget it was originally a Soviet jail."

"I take that as a No. So in the dawn light Tibyetsky might not have noticed there were thirteen chocolate bars instead of twelve."

Mantau did not comment. Whether he felt anxious to verify the theory, or was simply running late for his appointment, he told Bora "I'll see you later," entered the car and ordered the driver to get going.

Once the Opel was out of sight along the road, Bora once again took his place behind the wheel and followed it towards Kharkov.

*

All went well with von Salomon, who had good news regarding equipment and mounts for Bora's regiment. The two of them dined on the upper floor of a building meant for Soviet *apparatchiks*, on Red Army plates and with Red Army tableware. The small price for Bora to pay was listening to the colonel's nostalgic tales of his younger days. Georgian wine led to polite familiarity, and at other tables officers had already gone beyond the adjective *polite*.

Von Salomon came from landowning stock (Bora's own), but unlike Bora's people, the dreadful decade stretching from 1919 to 1929, not to speak of the years that had followed, had played havoc with his family's finances. He saw the loss of the family's East Prussian estate as a personal slight; he regarded it (and, worse, the fact that Poles had eventually bought the property) as a wrong to be righted. Discovering after the invasion of Poland that the mansion had been turned into a hospital had devastated him. The fact that German soldiers were treated or convalesced there these days didn't make up for his dejection. Wherever he went, even in Russia, he carried a watercolour of the estate, painted before the Great War.

"I'll show it to you," he said, "after the Ukrainian dance."

Courteously Bora objected that he had an engagement for the evening already, namely to listen to an all-Brahms *Lieder* concert.

"And what, hear that 'In Heaven, too, Power is permitted'? No, Major Bora. I require your company this evening, and you will do me the favour of obeying. No arguing, please."

It meant sitting for over three hours downstairs, where a stage had been set up for the dozen energetic folk dancers District Commissioner Stark had in his providence brought to town. Buxom, big-legged, booted girls who twirled in unison, looking for all the world like decorated dinner bells in their short flared skirts. Nothing but accordions in the orchestra; nothing but uniforms in the audience. Stark sat in the first row, and Mantau was there too, at the extreme right of the second row, where Bora and von Salomon also had their seats.

During the interval Bora had nearly succeeded in sneaking away when Stark saw him and loudly insisted on having a drink with him. He, too, was merrily in his cups. The district commissioner pointed to some of the overheated girls cosying up to some of the men present. "They're desperate to come along if the fortunes of war change again," he said philosophically, as if Bora didn't know. "Whoever stays here after we're gone will get a bullet in his head for collaborating. Imagine the gals. My dear Major, I'm a good man and married to boot, and don't sleep around, but there are some first-rate movables here tonight."

Cosiness with any kind of woman was just what Bora meant to avoid. Still, he had to sit through the second half of the show, and when Mantau at lights on signalled to him that he wanted to speak, he jumped at the opportunity to absent himself from von Salomon.

"Remember you're to stay at my lodgings tonight," the colonel said, dashing his hopes. "I mean to show you the watercolour of the family estate; and besides, I don't feel like sleeping."

Mantau led the way outside, where the night was mild and field gendarmes everywhere made it safe for the public to disperse. In the dim glare of screened headlights, some officers idled, lighting themselves cigarettes and cigars; others chatted and laughed. Many of them would be dead in two months' time, but tonight Kursk was still merely the name of a Ukrainian city north of here.

"Fucking accordions; I hate them," Mantau grumbled.

"Not as much as I do, Hauptsturmführer. Ten more minutes and I'd have opened fire on the orchestra."

"Well, let's waste no more time tonight. What I wanted to tell you is that there are *ten* rations left: not twelve, and not even eleven."

Bora was at a loss to understand. "It suggests that the poisoned item was in the original stock, and that Khan ate two of them between the sunset of 6 May and the following dawn."

"Whatever. The one he ate the morning of 7 May was what killed him."

"So it seems. It continues to sound like suicide. Did you check how many discarded wrappers were lying around in the cell?"

"Of course. You must think I'm stupid. There was one wrapper."

"*One?*"

"That's what I'm telling you. It consists of aluminium foil and a parchment paper shell."

"But that makes no sense." To Bora, Mantau's ill-humour was as annoying as the added complication of numbers. He'd argue, if it would do any good. "Whether he did it in one sitting or not, if Khan ate two rations between the time you delivered them to his cell and the time he died, there ought to be *two* discarded wrappers: two foil pieces and two parchment paper jackets."

"Well, there was one double wrapper, and that's all."

"I wonder what happened to the other one. Did the babushka clean the cell before or after you gave Khan the D rations?"

Mantau yawned. All around, staff cars and personnel carriers were slowly beginning to move, drawing narrow trails of glare across the tarmac, like slime from oversized snails. "I told you he made a scene the evening of 6 May, on account of 'being held against his will': as if we cared. He threw his bedding around, kicked the furniture, and worked himself up so much that we had to check his blood pressure and then send in the cleaning woman to tidy up. So you see, if he'd already eaten a ration, she had time not only to sweep up any discarded wrappers lying around, but also the opportunity to plant a poisoned piece. Besides, when they came from the Sumskaya first-aid station in the morning to pick up the body from the floor, there was a lot of confusion, and they could have inadvertently removed any piece of trash lying around as well. It'll be lost by now."

Bora stepped aside when a pennant-bearing staff car drove dangerously close to him, carrying its high-ranking cargo. "Didn't you have medical personnel on hand at the prison to intervene as soon as he became ill?"

"I told you already. No, they're short-handed at Sumskaya, and their personnel return to the first-aid station overnight. Not that it'd have made a difference; Khan was gone in minutes."

"Well, ask the folks at Sumskaya anyway. Anything might help at this point."

"Why don't you go ask them yourself?"

As God is my witness, I'll punch him in the public square. Bora held his breath to avoid physically reacting to Mantau's rudeness. "Naturally you have access to the toxicological test, and to the remaining double wrapper."

"Yes, but the foil and paper shell were torn in the process of opening, so there's no telling for sure whether the poison was injected through the wrapper or in some other way."

"Hm. And do you happen to know whether the contents of Khan's stomach equalled the amount of one or two bars?"

Mantau waved for his driver, standing at attention by the Opel, to bring the car closer to where he stood with Bora. "Come on, Major! We're talking a small amount of food, and Khan vomited part of what he'd ingested. The surgeon wouldn't be able to tell. For Christ's sake, he's just a military bonesetter."

"That's true, and it might make little difference now. As you say, Khan could have broken his rules and consumed a ration the night before his death – it'd have been digested by the morning. We're back where we started. Short of what you might learn from the other babushkas, we can only guess how the poison got into the chocolate, or when."

"Well, thanks for nothing, Bora. I knew you'd just waste my time."

Never as you did mine, you bastard. The Opel had silently drawn close, and waited nearby. Bora recognized von Salomon's slope-shouldered outline pacing impatiently at the exit of the building, and took his leave from Mantau less than amiably. "Keep waiting for the NKVD or the Ukrainian Insurgent Army to claim the murder, then."

6

WEDNESDAY 12 MAY

Bora didn't know how prophetic he was. Moscow claimed responsibility for the assassination just after he'd spent two days in the woods south of Bespalovka with three-quarters of his cavalry unit assembled and the filling of his officer and non-com positions nearly completed. It was Bruno Lattmann who first intercepted the Russian communication via radio, although leaflets of the Moscow-run Partisan Movement had also appeared overnight in Kharkov, celebrating the "People's stern and righteous reckoning". Khan was indicted as a Trotskyite, Zinovievist traitor and enemy spy, whose death while in the hands of the "Nazi hangman hordes" had proved how far Soviet justice could reach.

Early Wednesday morning, during a stop at Borovoye on his way back to Merefa (officially to see Lattmann before he left with the Platonov papers for the Kiev Branch Office, unofficially to hear if he had news about the medic's reassignment), all Bora could do was note Lattmann's words. "Hell, Mantau was right on the mark. I still don't understand how exactly they managed it, and I'd have wagered the UPA would get to Khan first, given his long Bolshevik career. But Ukraine is becoming more acronym-ridden than Spain six years ago. I wonder how long the NKVD knew Tibyetsky was in Kharkov."

Lattmann kept his outlook philosophical. "They must have found out where he'd crossed over early enough. Count your blessings the babushkas got to him when he was no longer at your place."

"That's puzzling, too. Whoever diverted them to Mantau's supervision did it *before* the defector was taken from us. Either Sydir Kovpak's Moscow-run partisans have a crystal ball, or they have a mole inside Mantau's SD, which would be egregious. I would *love* that. By the way, does *Narodnaya Slava* mean anything to you?"

"'National Glory', or 'Glory of the People' – what is it, a slogan?"

"I don't know. Khan pencilled it behind a photo of himself standing in his tank, wearing an impressive array of medals."

"It might refer to the T-34."

"Or to himself, knowing the type. See what else you can find out about those claims, Bruno."

"Won't be easy; I'll do what I can. The communiqué doesn't specify the names of the 'patriots' who carried out the punitive action. It means nothing per se, but you'd expect it."

"Yes, especially since we had a list including the women's patronymics to begin with. If they were operatives, theirs could have been aliases. Still, why not identify the two who were publicly hanged, at least? Language-wise, I can't argue with the authenticity of the claim – *Down with the brown plague to mankind and culture! The hangman hordes shall perish!* The rhetoric is all there." It was warm out here; both men were perspiring heavily. Bora removed the camouflage smock he used on patrol, and unbuttoned the neck of his summer shirt. "Have there been any official German reactions thus far?"

"I'll say. The Ukrainian railway personnel were brought to task for the arrival of the babushkas at Pokatilovka instead of Merefa. Yesterday the Security Service shot them all: at both stops, from the assistants to the German stationmasters to the last signalman and switchman. At Pokatilovka some resistance was attempted, understandably, and an SD man was wounded. Now they're dragging people out of bread lines at random and machine-gunning those who try to escape. And since some Ukrainian gendarmes are lending a hand here and there, there's got to be some heavy-duty settling of old accounts going on." Lattmann followed Bora as he hurried to the personnel carrier, and watched him toss his smock on the front seat. "They'll stop you north of Khoroshevo if you continue from here. I wouldn't go to Kharkov if I were you, Martin."

Bora shook his friend's hand, where every other fingertip was bandaged. "You would, Bruno, and so will I."

Lattmann had been conservative in his estimate. Entering the city was impossible from all sides; not even the usual dirt lanes between dismantled factories could be traversed. Trying his fortune from Merefa, Bora found that roadblocks began at the *Kombinat*; vehicles were being turned back regardless of their business in Kharkov. He decided to walk inside and ask the Commissioner's permission to phone the 161st Division headquarters for last-minute information. The suite of offices was deserted, however, with the exception of Stark's assistant and piles of medical supplies no one had been able to pick up. Bora was permitted one call. When von Salomon's phone rang, the colonel's answer came husky and anguished. "I have no time to talk to you, Major. This is appalling – right below my windows! Appalling, appalling."

Bora couldn't get anything else out of him; other extensions at headquarters rang out. Without knowing whether von Salomon's hesitation was due to actions by German troops or directed against them, he tried unsuccessfully for an hour to be let through at the checkpoint. At mid-morning, in the wake of a staff car whose provoked passengers prevailed, he was finally allowed past the heavily armed patrol, but the journey lasted only until the next security stop, five kilometres from the city limits. While those in the staff car – one of them a general's aide – took up a heated confrontation with the Security Service men, Bora stealthily backed up a good way, put the camouflage smock back on, left the personnel carrier at the side of the road and went around the roadblock on foot, at his own risk.

Cutting unseen across the field, he traversed a wet, deeply furrowed area just the distance needed to get back on the tarmac to the north and out of sight of the patrol. Here he soon managed to get a lift from the driver of an army truck, which had originally been travelling southbound and had been forced to turn back at the same checkpoint. The driver's depot was at Jassna Polyana. Bora got off there, crossed the tracks to the park beyond, and twenty minutes later reached downtown Kharkov. Behind him were desolate, empty streets. Here and there a small shop in the traditional Russian style – below street level and reachable by climbing down a few steps – had broken windows and no one inside.

Under the sun, in the canvas camouflage garment that heightened the heat of day, Bora dripped with sweat. Rifle shots – a dry *pock, pock* sound that echoed between buildings – guided him to the curving avenue and square that until the Stalingrad disaster had been named after General von Paulus, near the marble-striped Cathedral of the Annunciation. A round-up was in progress there. Bora couldn't say he wasn't used to the scene. He wished he could say it troubled him; in fact, nothing seemed to trouble him any more. It was all already seen, done, experienced. Crowds lost individuality; it came down to shoves and rifle butts pushing or dividing or striking, quick turns on the heel as someone sprinted to get away and the weapon was righted, aimed and fired without missing. Everyone played their role perfectly, victims included. Bodies lay around, blood pooled under them. Only his anger (which was something other than a feeling of pity) was stirred, like a thick liquid that needed mixing and scooping but in the end agitated on its own. Principle, not people; not feeling what he didn't feel. Virtue had nothing to do with it. Bora stepped up to the SD non-com directing the operation, who looked over impatiently even before he was questioned.

"Who authorized this?"

"Gruppenführer Müller's orders, authorized by the Gebiets-kommissar."

"Aren't these Ukrainian nationals? The assassination was claimed by Russian Soviets."

"It was Ukrainian rail workers who attacked a German soldier. And anyhow, Major, check your sources. UPA counterclaimed the terrorist action this morning."

That was news, but not to be looked into now. Von Salomon's office not being far away, Bora walked there. He couldn't see anything in the street overlooked by his windows that was "appalling" or that justified the colonel's anguish, so he changed his mind and decided not to waste time on someone else's squeamishness. It was when he turned into the lane near the cathedral, between the textile works and the old Palace of Labour, that he understood. There Army units were deployed alongside the Security Service and were corralling terrified men and women into waiting trucks for deportation, or worse.

If hierarchy meant precious little to the SS and SD, it did carry weight with Army ranks. Bora remembered he still had a copy of the babushkas' name list with him. He eyed a fairly young artillery lieutenant busy lining up civilians on the sidewalk, approached the line and without a word jerked a woman at random out of the long row.

Unhesitatingly, the lieutenant pushed the woman back in line. "What are you doing, Herr Major?"

Bora flashed the sheet in front of him with the women's names on it, rubber-stamped by Stark's office. "No: what are *you* doing, Lieutenant? You have my five female labourers. I'll hold you accountable if I can't collect them."

The subordinate read the Commissioner's signature – not the date, because Bora's thumb was concealing it – and took a resentful step back. "Well, sir, pick them up quickly, then. We have work to do."

Striding along the line of civilians Bora reclaimed the first woman he'd chosen and pulled out four more instinctively, not knowing why he selected this anguished face, that unresisting wrist instead of another. No kindness whatever was in his gestures; he was simply angry and uncomfortable. *Is this how we die, at random? Is this how we are chosen to be born in the first place? What role am I playing before God as I mindlessly reach to save one and condemn the others?*

Afterwards, on foot as he was, he didn't know what to do with the women. He forbade himself to become emotionally involved, to the extent that he couldn't have said what their ages were or described their faces. It was not relevant. He pushed them ahead of himself around a corner, down a narrow street lined with tram tracks, until he came to a crossroads, where he stopped. Because his pistol holster was unlatched, the women stood before him in a knot, weeping, and only when he shouted at them, "*Davai!*" did they understand they should run for it.

In the confusion, Bora was twice more able to pull the stunt of the name list with Army patrols in the reticule of streets and ruinous public buildings between the cathedral and the Trade Guilds Park. A fourth time would have been far too risky. By the time he climbed the stairs to von Salomon's office, he had little desire and no patience for an earful of gloomy recriminations.

The colonel's restless pacing was audible at the end of the hallway. It did not cease when Bora appeared on the threshold and saluted. On the contrary, it widened to include the window in its path.

"This is all very bad, Major. Very bad." Von Salomon didn't enquire how Bora had managed to enter Kharkov, and Bora said nothing whatever. "At this time, very bad."

Sporadic shooting continued outside; the window panes rattled feebly in their frames. Bora was still angry. Concealing it was not the difficult part; getting rid of his anger was. He watched von Salomon press his hands to his cheeks as he paced. "Psychostasis," he heard him mutter. "Psychostasis. The dreadful weighing of souls after death. Can anyone escape it?"

The guilt-sharing words sounded elegant and empty. To Bora, the colonel's resemblance to a large unhappy dog was more evident and credible than his inner turmoil. Lowering his eyes, he noticed now that in pulling one of the women out of one of the round-ups a small length of yarn from her frayed blouse had become stuck to his right sleeve. Quickly he removed it, pushing it with his forefinger out of sight, under the buttoned tab of his cuff. Whether von Salomon's question was rhetorical, Bora answered it. "If one believes in psychostasis, Herr Oberst, no one may escape it."

"Yes." The colonel halted by the window, and leant against the sill. "My opinion as well. You know, I have it from reputable sources that SS and Police General von dem Bach-Zelewski, who led special operations in Riga, has been having hallucinations about Jews ever since. Some say instead that it's because his sisters married Jews. Both circumstances would – eh? What do you think?"

The dilemma sounded sincere, insofar as von Salomon might wonder whether mass executions or marrying into Jewish blood could have caused the SS general's mental strain. Bora kept his eyes on the occasionally trembling window glass, beyond the colonel. Years before he'd got wariness down to a fine art. And even though of late there were moments when without reason he abandoned it altogether, this was not such a time. He said, impassively, "I think I needn't remind the colonel of the Führer's 13 May 1941 decree regarding the summary nature of collective reprisal measures on this front. And may I also point out that General Erich von dem Bach renounced his Polish surname Zelewski two years ago."

Most security checks had been raised when Bora left Kharkov in the company of a supply officer headed for the commissioner's office. The checkpoint north of the *Kombinat*, still manned, was now being dismantled, and they were allowed through. Beyond, Bora asked to be let off where his personnel carrier was still parked as he had left it, but for the folded piece of paper stuck between windshield and wiper. It read, above an illegible signature in green pencil, *A note has been made of this vehicle's licence. Abandoning* Wehrmacht *property unguarded in occupied territory is not only unadvisable, it violates rules. The driver may expect disciplinary measures.*

Of all the things that had happened during the day – perhaps because he was objectively responsible for it – the admonition was the one that came close to making Bora blow his top. Because the Security Service men were looking on he did no more than accurately refold the paper along its creases and pocket it, but he was fuming as he drove without other incident towards Merefa.

Merefa, 7.15 p.m.

The words that come to mind are "vicarious" and "metonymy". In moments of stress, substituting one sentiment for another, or taking something for something else, allows us to appease and tranquillize anxiety. The object that crosses our path then is invested with a larger meaning, and triggers a response proportionate to its role.

The Nitichenko priest, Father Victor, couldn't have chosen a better way of precipitating events half an hour ago, although from the outside it merely looked like the return procession from whatever superstitious mumbo-jumbo he started out for two days ago. News travels much faster in this countryside than the supposed elimination of all radio apparatuses would lead us to believe; when the peasants filed past, they were singing and shouting their joy for the reprisal enacted in Kharkov during the past twenty-four hours. Communists, Russians, Jews, it's all the same to that primitive, bigoted Nitichenko: God wants them dead, and good riddance.

Had I not been submitted to three hours of accordions last night, and had the Ukrainians not used the same as an accompaniment blared at full volume, I believe I would have taken things in my stride. As it was, I stormed out of the schoolhouse, halted the procession and commanded that the instruments be turned in. They've learnt by now that if my holster is unlatched, there's no discussion. I got the elders to pile up the accordions in the middle of the uncultivated field flanking the road, and told them to go. They didn't; or rather, they walked until they were far enough away to dare to stop and look what would happen. The priest, holding a good-sized icon, was stationed midway between them and the place where I was.

Having prepared things quickly and efficiently, I set the Russian mine from the canal bank in the nice hollow formed by the bellows and the right-hand keyboard of the nethermost instrument. I then packed it with pebbles and dirt, removed the pin from the fuse and paced to a convenient distance from it. By this time, unlike his flock, Father Victor understood what was afoot, dropped the icon and went scampering after the others. It took me a single gunshot to blast the pile sky-high and make even the least dismembered of the accordions incapable of ever working again.

What will the Merefa peasants think of it? It isn't as if I care. Don't they know that according to the May '41 Führer's decree, paragraph 4, "suspicious elements are to be brought before an officer as soon as possible"? It is up to me as a German officer to decide not only who is suspicious, but also what is suspicious and how to dispose of it. The sentry has no doubt seen worse retribution visited on Russians, because he didn't blink an eye. As for Kostya, he's not one to question officers or Germans. Besides, he wasn't present. I'd sent him to the village to scout out someone who had actually visited Krasny Yar and lived to tell the tale.

Speaking of suspicions, when he gets back from the Kiev Branch Office Lattmann may be able to provide me with an update regarding the newest claim by UPA, the Ukrainian Insurgent Army. As things are, I secured one of their freshly printed leaflets at the Kombinat, where I met with Commissioner Stark for a few moments after returning from Kharkov with the evidence. He had himself arrived from the city shortly before, begrudging – as he said – having had to authorize the police operation "before having the opportunity to look into the wisdom of such measures." Uneasy lies the head, etc… I did two things. Kept my mouth shut about his comment, and remarked that there's no lack of official and clandestine presses in town, so that the Security Service have their work cut out for them in tracking the leaflets to the right printing place. He didn't bring up Khan Tibyetsky's death, and neither did I.

It intrigues me that the UPA claim keeps the specifics of the assassination (we're all assuming it is such, but it remains to be seen) under as much silence as its Russian counterpart did. And it follows rather than precedes the Soviet claim. Genuine in the sense that it must originate in UPA circles, it mentions the Prussian-backed coup d'état against the 1917 Ukrainian National Republic, and promises to visit upon General Skoropadsky – who in his younger days headed the coup – the same fate suffered by Khan. This is an obvious reference to the fact that Skoropadsky is at present in Germany, although it should be said that he chose his residence after falling from power.

At the end of the day, when it comes to responsibilities for Khan's death, Mantau enjoys an embarrassment of riches. From his point of view it is only right to target Ukrainian and Russian Kharkovians alike, so that no culprit goes unpunished. The fate of the babushkas still in SD custody is not to be envied: the risk is that they'll say whatever they think Mantau wants them to say.

A last note: at divisional headquarters there was mail for me. A letter from Dikta, come through the usual army post channels, and an envelope hand-delivered to me by Senior Army Chaplain Father Galette. I'm still sitting on both messages, because I'm not in the right mood to hear from my wife or from my former teacher, Cardinal Hohmann.

A postscript. The Security Service must think me less equipped for certain eventualities than my training has made me: I carry around spare licence plates, and I'm changing them first thing in the morning.

First thing in the morning, the Merefa peasants came to pick up the pieces of their accordions. Bora's animosity had considerably abated, so he told Kostya to distribute handfuls of *karbovanets*. Money being scarce, Kostya returned with the message that if there were other instruments the Major wanted to blow up, they had concertinas and fiddles available as well.

After changing the licence plates, Bora was rinsing his hands in a dainty washbasin left behind by the Russian schoolteacher. He said, without smiling, "Never mind that. Anyone in the village who might be able to tell me about the Yar?"

"*Da-s i nyet-s, povazhany* Major. Yes and no. There's a man from Schubino to see you."

Bora raised his eyes at the mention of a village near Krasny Yar. "Schubino? It's thirty kilometres from here."

"He said he's from Schubino but lives in Merefa now."

Setting aside the enamelled bowl, graced by sprigs of red flowers around the rim, Bora slowly dried his hands with the cloth Kostya held out to him. "And he's here to talk about Krasny Yar?"

"He didn't say that, sir." Kostya picked up the washbasin, avoiding the officer's stare. "I think he might make you mad, though."

Taras Lukjanovitch Tarasov didn't even have to open his mouth to annoy the German officer. He'd dressed in his holiday best and worn the Soviet Badge of Honour reading *Proletarians of the world, unite!* Civilians were shot for much less.

Bora sized up the bony little man who introduced himself as a *rakhivnik*, finding the idea irresistible of a consumptive-looking accountant who dared to confront an army of occupation. "Well, Tarasov," he began, "you lived in Schubino. That's close to Krasny Yar. Are you here to tell me about the woods?"

The question seemed to annoy the visitor. "The woods? No. I'm here to turn myself in for killing the traitor Tibyetsky."

Concealing all that went through him at once (surprise, doubt, disbelief, amusement) forced Bora to exercise self-control so it wouldn't seem artificial. *Old fool, take your place in line: there are others ahead of you* was what he wanted to advise, but in all seriousness he said he appreciated the gesture. And nothing more.

The grey-faced Tarasov stood there awkwardly, with a look of expectation and fear. He watched the German take out a blank sheet of paper from the drawer, and also the UPA leaflet he'd got from Stark, rotated on the wooden surface so that it was readable to the man facing the teacher's desk.

Bora waited. He'd learnt not to indulge in small gestures that could give away puzzlement or impatience. No drumming of fingers on the desk, no playing with his wedding band, no open stare. He sat straight in the chair, looking unconcerned at the place between Tarasov's chin and his chest where the badge pinned on the old suit, nearly three inches across, showed a young couple against a flutter of banners bearing Marx's call to arms. He scented fear in the sickly man, and some other emotion less overt and understandable. A fly lightly settled on the leaflet where a line in bold read *Slava Ukraini*: Glory to Ukraine.

Sensing that a justification for his claim was called for, Tarasov wet his lips. "As political commissar at Kharkov Factory No. 183 and then at the FED photographic camera firm until my retirement, I have a direct ideological share in the moulding of the patriots who carried out the people's vengeance."

Again, silence. The fly took off from the leaflet and landed on Tarasov's right shoulder. Fear, yes. Bora expected that. The other emotion was – what? Not hostility, not arrogance. Not self-delusion, either. Resentment? Hopelessness? *Wouldn't Odilo Mantau give an eye tooth to be in my place.* Bora savoured the strangeness of the moment, whether or not it would lead anywhere. He placidly took the fountain pen from his breast pocket and uncapped it. Holding the nib close to the blank sheet, he asked, "And who are *the patriots?* Names, please."

Tarasov swallowed the need to cough. Between fifty and sixty years of age, hard to tell on an emaciated frame, he seemed confused by this odd reception. "I do not intend to betray my fellow Russians."

"Ah. Not *Slava Ukraini*, then. *Slava Rossii*. The excellent Soviet partisan leaders Sydor Kovpak and Semyon Rudniev, who I understand made general a month ago."

"Major, I thought —"

"Why come to me?" Ready to write, Bora's pen stayed firm, a hair's breadth away from the sheet. "There are other German authorities to whom you should have turned yourself in."

Tarasov gave him a frustrated look. "I'm a Merefa resident. You're the German military authority in Merefa. To whom should I go? This is really – not acceptable."

"*Not acceptable?* I don't care a fig for what is acceptable to you. I asked for information about Krasny Yar, and you strut in with claims you can't support, presuming that a tin badge will cause a German officer to react! Didn't you hear it's the woods I'm seeking information about?"

A fit of hollow coughing shook Tarasov. Disturbed, the fly left his shoulder and sought the ceiling in an undulating semicircle. "I heard." He spoke hoarsely when he regained his breath. "That's what prompted me to come in the first place, but – it gave me an idea to – the opportunity to —"

"Play the braggart over Commander Tibyetsky's death? Do not offend me, accountant."

Unexpectedly the little man struck the desk with his fist. "Well, do not offend *me*, Major! After all, I was a comrade of the traitor Tibyetsky!"

Bora did not move a muscle. *And I was just trying to save this idiot's life.* A suspended wordless pause, very different from the previous silence, went by before he capped his pen and put it away. *Whatever he's up to, whatever he's done or not done, now we're getting somewhere.*

The conversation with Taras Tarasov lasted over an hour and a half. Bora listened with absolute attention, jotting down a few sober, indicative notes that would become an extended memorandum as soon as the accountant left the room. He wrote furiously so as not to leave out a hint, a comment, filling out several sheets on both sides. Had he not promised to report what news he had about Sanitätsoberfeldwebel Weller to Mayr at Hospital 169, he'd have continued to ponder Tarasov's "confession". But first there were service errands in Kharkov and the matter of Khan Tibyetsky's post-mortem, his exchange goods for the day.

At the hospital, hammering, sawing and refitting continued behind closed doors. While he waited for the surgeon to finish his rounds, Bora took his diary out of the briefcase and retrieved Dikta's letter, placed between the pages as a bookmark. Leaning with his shoulders against the wall, he opened it with trepidation. It was short, because Dikta did not indulge in effusions; she'd sooner send three short letters than a long one. And although she'd received the best in Swiss education, she seldom elaborated in her correspondence on what she certainly felt about him (or others; or the world). For a twenty-six year old, there was always something immature in her words, an adolescent impatience to be done with the writing chore.

Past the affectionate greetings at the start, she wrote:

We've become fast friends, your brother's wife and I. The doctor told Duckie she must walk, so I take her to concerts, lectures, art exhibits, charity fairs...and shopping, because nothing fits her any more. In the evening we sit on the bed in her room to talk and we giggle like little girls, she in her nightgown and myself in a bra and frilly undies, a new set I had Mamma send me from Paris that is really quite indecent but you will love. If Papa Sickingen saw me wearing it! With three women in the house he's exasperated;

doesn't know what to do with himself. Imagine: he who doesn't like dogs takes Wallace every day for a constitutional in Rosenthal Park or goes to pout alone in the smoking room, under those nasty glass-eyed trophies and the balalaikas.

It's amazing how many things Duckie is ignorant of about her own body. She blushes, but she's very curious about the things experienced married people can do. I think she's a little envious of us. She asked me if any of it is a sin, the dear Duckie. I answered her that I wasn't raised Roman Catholic but you certainly were, and that none of it seems to be a problem for you. I believe that as soon as the baby is born and she gets back in shape Peter will be quite grateful for our girlie talks.

By the way, Mamma, your mother and I have volunteered to break horses for the Army; who better than girls like us, with our riding skills and charm that even the dear animals understand?

I miss you – miss you – miss you! Come back soon, my darling Martin, and all in one glorious piece.

Dikta

P.S. Did you receive the Ziemke Studio photo? I was actually looking at a pair of your riding boots Ziemke told me to place on the carpet near me. Of course I adore the man inside those magnificent boots.

Mayr's voice from the end of the hallway startled him. "Major Bora, weren't you here to see me? I haven't got all day."

Bora squirrelled away the letter. Flustered as he always was after reading his wife's messages, in the few steps separating him from the physician's door he regained a polite aloofness, sealed over and to all appearances storm-proof.

He shared what he'd learnt through Bruno Lattmann, which wasn't much.

"This is as far as I have got for now, Herr Oberstarzt. I have confirmation that Master Sergeant Weller did not ask for reassignment. It was by direct order at Army Corps level that he was transferred from this hospital on 6 May. At Army

Detachment Kempf HQ in Poltava, where he was supposed to report three days later for a new assignment, they have no record of his arrival. Which doesn't mean he wasn't there: we know how sometimes bureaucrats bungle things the moment paperwork doesn't fit exactly the norm they're used to. Alternatively, he could still be in transit."

"It's been a week!"

"This is Russia. Rail transport: unreliable. Roads: worse. A flat tyre, and you're stuck; two flat tyres, and you walk."

The surgeon's white gown was missing a button. Seeing Bora's eyes wander to the curl of thread that remained in its place, he took off the garment and tossed it onto the clothes stand by the door. "Well, I did some local checking, and Weller isn't serving in any of the other medical units in Kharkov. My concern is *why* they did this to him."

Bora glanced around the room with non-judgemental, attentive coolness. Cover and pillow were stacked at the head of the camp bed; the glass cabinet still contained some of the painkillers he'd brought last time. From the bulletin board on the wall the surgeon's family photo had been taken down. The four tacks that had held it in place seemed to Bora singularly forlorn, a mark of prudence or pain. He often took his time in answering, and not only because it was typical of his training. It also allowed him to take in – as now – signs of his counterpart's level of comfort. Or lack thereof. "We don't know that *they* did anything to your medic," he observed at last, "other than reassign him. And as far as the incident you seem to entertain as a motive, if there's one who could in any way be brought to task for a prisoner's death it'd be myself, *not* Weller."

"You will agree it's easier to punish a non-com than a regimental commander."

Or a surgeon. A measure of sarcasm was expected, but Bora had no desire to foster an argument. Besides, at the *Abwehr* Branch Office in Kiev they'd taken Platonov's death in bad humour; it was not beyond possibility that they'd sacked Weller for it. *They wouldn't necessarily tell me, either.*

"As promised, I'll keep looking for him, Herr Oberstarzt. There are some other channels I can tap. What about you? Did you have any luck?"

Mayr put an unlit cigarette between his lips, possibly to keep from blurting out what he had in mind. He handed over a summary of Tibyetsky's post-mortem, copied by hand since the colleague who'd filled it out was no doubt forbidden to share it.

Bora thanked him. "I asked for a regional casualty update," he felt the need to volunteer. "In case Weller suffered an accident en route to Poltava. With all the mines being laid overnight, we can't always keep up with the clearing. Not that I think...but one never knows." The gown tossed onto the clothes stand was slowly beginning to slip off the top knob. Without looking at it directly, Bora kept it in his peripheral vision, secretly impatient for it to reach the floor. "About the autopsy: may I ask whether you detected anything out of the ordinary?"

Facing away from the door, the surgeon could not see the lingering downward motion of the white garment behind him. The cigarette he'd put in his mouth stayed there as he spoke, an unlit paper cylinder stuck to his lower lip. "I had no access to the body, but the findings seem consistent with poisoning. Although a small part of the food ingested was regurgitated, the stomach contents revealed enough nicotine to cause death within minutes. Concentrated, it's deadlier than strychnine, and not difficult to find. Farm women everywhere use tobacco leaf solution to kill garden parasites."

On the clothes stand, having silently rounded the top knob, the surgeon's gown slid off it and came to rest on the transverse bar of a lower knob, where its downward progress began again. Bora eyed it with something beyond lack of patience, on the threshold of physical discomfort. "Does nicotine have no odour or taste?"

"It tastes very bitter, which is why most accidental deaths are due to poisoning through the skin. It's amazing the victim ate the whole bar. Was he a smoker?"

"Yes." By the door, the inanimate drama continued. The choice was between waiting for the cloth to creep down until it glided off of the support altogether or stepping in to interrupt the process. Bora kept from intervening because it would give away his impatience, but he refused to keep watching. He lowered his eyes to the handwritten notes. "Forgive one last question. What are the symptoms of this kind of poisoning?"

"Toxicology isn't my field, Major. Alkaloids in general – ergot, hemlock, atropine, strychnine, they're a huge family – can cause anything from extreme agitation, even hallucinations, to a lucid and progressive paralysis, vomit, diarrhoea, convulsions. Not a good death, Socrates notwithstanding."

Bora nodded. When he raised his eyes, the gown had finally reached the floor, and lay in a heap at the foot of the clothes stand.

Unaware of the distraction he'd indirectly provoked, Mayr fished out a lighter from his pocket and lit his cigarette at last. "My part of the bargain was fulfilled, Major. In these difficult times, Oberfeldwebel Weller was a caring and attentive helper, whose well-being I had at heart and for whom I hoped there'd be an opportunity to earn his medical degree. I am truly sorry he's gone. And I hold you responsible for whatever befell him."

Why do I put up with him? I no longer need his help. The ungenerous thought went through Bora's mind while he saluted. "No need to speak of him as if he'd died, Herr Oberstarzt. Weller may have arrived in Poltava as we speak."

His second errand in Kharkov was at divisional headquarters, where he was to pick up the authorization to collect a special shipment of fresh mounts for his unit, due to arrive by rail in Smijeff by the middle of the following week. Von Salomon, however, wasn't at the office. Bora assumed at first the absence might be connected to the debacle in Tunisia: news of over one hundred thousand German prisoners fallen into Allied hands had caused noticeable turmoil in the building. The lieutenant who took care of the colonel's paperwork did not confirm his suspicions either way, and provided some assistance. However, not being empowered to sign for his commander, he could only invite Bora to return in the afternoon.

"Is there a possibility I could find the colonel at his lodgings?"

"You could try, Herr Major."

Von Salomon was staying in the same large flat on Pletnevsky Lane, overlooking the river, where Bora had been a guest the night of the folk dance. Too spacious by his own admission, the colonel often had visitors, mostly colleagues in Kharkov for service-related business, and was known to do some of his work from there. Bora headed there. Here the Kharkov River flowed west, to merge not far away with the Lopany. On the other bank, beyond half-demolished buildings, the Donbas station marked the terminus of the rail line that would bring the regimental mounts from southern Ukraine. Due to the presence of German bureaus and officers' quarters, Army police patrolled this district made up of charming houses from the turn of the century painted in warm colours with stucco festoons above their windows and classical façades. It was very warm, and felt like it would rain again.

In von Salomon's second-floor flat, there was music playing: a radio or a gramophone; Bora could not judge from outside the door. He had to ring twice before someone heard and came to open up. A colonel in an *Organization Todt* uniform, complete with armband and cuff title, stood there and frowned. Clearly not expecting a visit, he said brusquely, "Yes? Who are you?" When Bora introduced himself and gave the reason for his presence, the colonel added, "Lieutenant Colonel von Salomon was up until very late last night, Major. He's resting at present."

Someone else was in the room, invisible to Bora because the OT officer held the door ajar. Behind him, on the wall, the glassed-in watercolour of von Salomon's estate reflected the figure of a middle-aged lady in a morning suit. With more than an impression that he'd interrupted something, Bora apologized. "Forgive me for sounding insistent," he said. "It regards an important shipment, and is somewhat urgent. I do need the colonel's signature at his earliest convenience. Should I call again after lunch?"

The officer glanced at his watch. "Not before 14.30."

Politically well-connected wives and fiancées did visit the higher ranks occasionally, and friends literally made room for those special times if they could. Von Salomon had probably left his flat to this colleague, who – Tunisian news notwithstanding – was making the most of the opportunity. After all, it was Russia; it was wartime. And honestly, even before the war, Bora had laid Dikta wherever he could. He saluted and left. *But the few times I had this luck,* he enviously told himself, *at least I took a hotel room and did not inconvenience colleagues.*

The lunch hour dragged on. Before returning to Pletnevsky Lane at the appointed time, Bora sought the divisional office again, to no avail. "You could try again around 16.30, Herr Major." When he rang the bell at von Salomon's flat (he could have bet money on it, yet still it vexed him), no one answered the door. So he decided to at least get something done and drove to the *Kombinat,* a bit closer to Kharkov than if he had travelled back to Merefa.

Behind closed doors, Commissioner Stark was berating somebody in Russian. Over the telephone, if one was to judge from the lack of other voices and the brief silences during which he most likely was listening to excuses being made at the other end of the wire. The words "black market", "typewriters" and "former Starshin Infantry School" stood out from the others. A longer pause was followed by a less irate conversation in German. Bora waited, and eventually Stark's assistant made the major's presence known to his superior. "Well, let him in," was Stark's reply.

"I can't get any madder than I already am, Major Bora," he added half-seriously when Bora walked in. "What with getting our arses kicked in north Africa, what with nuisances here… So if you want to pester me, this is as good a time as any. These Russkis are the same as ever – they work for you but they'll rob you blind the moment they can. And then this unseasonable warmth, this damned humidity. It's about the cavalry mounts, right? Have you got the signed authorization?"

Without giving details, Bora explained there had been a delay in the paperwork, which he hoped to obtain before office closing time.

"I understand what you're saying, Major, but we can't make exceptions. You'll have to come back when you have the signed authorization. While I have you here, though, let me tell you that we haven't forgotten about your babushkas, and are looking into the confusion. Both you and Hauptsturmführer Mantau requested female personnel at the same time. Are you sure you didn't swap lists with him?"

"Positive. Why should I do such a thing, Commissioner? I wasn't even aware that he'd asked for labourers until you mentioned it the day he and I had words."

Stark set aside a number of folders, slapping their covers closed and securing them with their elastic bands. "In that case, the mix-up must have occurred after the two requests left this office. Imagine, the women originally assigned to him arrived this morning. In light of all that happened, I believe they should by rights be turned over to your unit." Around him, little by little as his role took shape, the accoutrements and signs of political standing coalesced. Flag, portrait of the Führer, a brand-new map on the wall. "Speaking of the devil, Major Bora, you don't happen to know where Mantau is, do you? He isn't returning telephone calls, and I just heard he's been out of the office since he was summoned to Kiev on Wednesday night."

More likely than not, Kiev meant Gestapo Headquarters. Bora had to make an effort to resist a malicious smile at the news. "I don't know where he is, Herr Gebietskommissar. May I take a look at the list of labourers?"

Stark showed him a typewritten sheet of names and patronymics, and rose to open the window. "I wish it'd rain; the mugginess is unbearable." A view of the old factory beyond the gravelled area of machinery and stacked materiel became visible; the brick building where Bora had seen the Karabakh stallion stood etched against a thundery sky. "As you'll judge from the first names, Major, they're a younger lot than last time: Barrikada and Revolutsya aren't anything they'd call females in the old days. You haven't got anything against young washerwomen, have you?"

"Not at all. When may I send for them?"

"As soon as I inform Mantau – which is why I'd like to get hold of him."

Bora returned the sheet. He'd actually looked for Avrora Glebovna's name on the list, unsure whether it was because he wished it would be there, or else because he'd ask to remove it if it was.

Shaking his head, the commissioner placed a paperweight (it was actually a large pebble) on the sheet. "This being in effect still Army-administered Ukraine," he continued, rocking in his swivel chair and staring at his desk, "I may have arrogated to myself a role that doesn't belong to me, but I demanded that the two women executed last Friday be taken down from the improvised gallows. I never authorized that hanging, you know."

It was the very thing Bora had thrown in Mantau's face. He said, "A little kindness goes a long way, even in Russia."

"Hm. Like it or not, nominally at least, the welfare of the population is within my purview."

It remained to be seen – Bora was curious but did not ask – whether Stark had also protested against Mantau's decision to carry out a reprisal without following protocol. Equally, Hans Kietz, who was Gestapo head in Kharkov, could have reported him. At any rate, if Mantau was sitting in the hot seat at the

Vladimirskaya Street headquarters in Kiev at this time, he wasn't about to shed tears over it. "There's something else I'd like to discuss, Herr Gebietskommissar."

Behind the desk, below Hitler's photograph, a framed map of the *Reichskommissariat Ukraine* showed the general and regional districts, and a dotted line the prospective additions to the administration, including Kharkov and its region. Bora kept it in mind as he said, "I'm trying to locate a recently transferred Medical Service NCO. The name is Weller, Arnim Anton. These are his data. He's hopefully en route from Kharkov to his next assignment, but it would help me to know where that is, since at Army Detachment Kempf headquarters they do not possess that information. I went as far as I could through military channels. Given that Poltava falls under *Reichskommissariat Ukraine*, I thought I might try the administrative procedure."

Stark lifted his spectacles above his eyebrows, and peered closely at the card Bora had given him. "Is the man a friend? A relative?"

"No."

"Is he meant for your unit, then?"

"Yes."

Bora was lying, but Stark asked nothing else. Curbing inquisitiveness was second nature for all of them, even at the highest levels. He put down the card next to his telephone. "No promises, Major. As you know, there are thousands of men being redeployed at this time. I'll see what can be done, and have you contacted should his name turn up."

"I appreciate it, Herr Gebietskommissar. May I make a phone call from your assistant's office?"

Stark said he could. "And try to get that authorization signed by today."

The divisional headquarters update was that von Salomon had not yet come in to the office. When he arrived on Pletnevsky Lane, with thunder rumbling across the river and not a drop of rain under a sky still largely cloudless, the sound of conversation inside the second-floor flat told Bora he wasn't about to barge into a tête-à-tête. In fact, the door opened on several officers having drinks, and not one but two ladies. The OT colonel, more annoyed than the first time, disclosed at last that von Salomon had taken a sleeping pill, and wouldn't wake up before 6 or 7 p.m.

It effectively meant having to stay in Kharkov overnight. A disgruntled Bora walked the tranquil street back to Donski Avenue, where he'd left his vehicle by the bridge. Between banks of sloping earth, the Kharkov River carried bits of leaves on its unhurried current, a sign that somewhere to the north-east heavy rains had been falling. Mosquitoes gathered in dancing clouds above the water. *One more month, and we'll butcher one another between these stuccoed residences, across towns and villages, up and down this front. This quiet, this silence is like pausing for a moment before shooting oneself.*

With time to burn, Bora drove to the west end of town, and went to have a bite at the eatery on Kubitsky Alley, not far from the RSHA prison. At a long table, SS and *Leibstandarte* officers – some about to finish their coffee, some standing and ready to leave – turned to look when he entered. Among them was the captain with a birthmark who'd threatened Bora the previous Saturday. Leaving the others behind, he walked haltingly towards the major's place and tossed the dinner bill on his table. "Here. You Army folks owe us for giving you back Kharkov after you lost it."

Blood rose to Bora's head to the extent that he saw the room through a swimming veil. But he'd done his homework, and the urge to strike back was resisted in the time needed to collect himself. When the captain returned to his colleagues, he picked up the bill from his still-empty plate, folded it carefully, and with it in hand calmly stood up from his chair. Ignoring the tense waiters, he crossed the floor to the long table where the group was waiting to see what happened. A glance around to see who was highest in rank, a well-mannered nod in that direction, and the bill found its way on to the tablecloth, near the captain's crumpled napkin.

"Forgive me; I believe this is yours. The Army takes no lessons from officers who got their injuries driving drunk from a Paris whorehouse. If the Sturmbannführer at the head of the table allows, however, even on this day of temporary setbacks I will toast *Leibstandarte Adolf Hitler* for their success in Kharkov during the month of March. Russian wine or German champagne?"

An incident had only been avoided because the Sturmbannführer had a sense of humour, and the restaurant did serve German champagne. Bora sat at his table until he was the only one left in the restaurant. It took that long for his agitation to settle. The waiter's discreet cough, a mild reminder that they'd have to close soon, brought Taras Tarasov to Bora's preoccupied mind, who less than ten hours earlier had stood before him with the bold claim of having murdered Khan Tibyetsky. *Some days are endless,* he told himself. *You don't get much done, but they go on forever.*

At divisional headquarters, the paper-pushing lieutenant was apologetic. "It'll have to be in the morning, Herr Major. Lieutenant Colonel von Salomon sent word he won't be receiving tonight. And tomorrow it'll have to be before 08.30, because the lieutenant colonel will be out of the office after that time."

Bora gave up. He left a phone message for Stark to that effect, and although in a pinch lodgings could be had at headquarters, he decided to use his extra keys and go to the special detention centre on Mykolaivska, where as far as he knew things had been left how they were when they'd closed it up on Bentivegni's orders. If the bed in Khan's room (his own temporary room during overnight interrogations) was still in place, it beat an army camp bed or a colleague's sofa any time.

Not only were the furnishings of Khan's room untouched, electric power and water were still hooked up – a luxury that permitted Bora a welcome shower in the sultriness of the evening. With the change in the weather, the hallway and stairs smelt of dog hair, as if Mina were still guarding the place instead of sitting fat in a Kharkov barracks. The door to Khan's room, smashed by rifle butts and nearly jerked off its hinges, leaned useless, but the bed – minus the sheets and pillowcase – could be comfortably laid on.

When Bora, freshly washed and shaved, switched on the bedside lamp, the wallpaper depicting factories and smokestacks came alive with its zigzag lines as it had for western engineers and businessmen of the past generation, and for his remarkable relative until the week before. With the acute sensibility of his evening fever, he fancied he smelt one of Tibyetsky's Soyuzie cigars, containing a fraction of the nicotine that was to kill him. And although he had no emotional reason to mourn him, Bora did feel sorry for the way he'd died, so far from his glorious exploits. He took the diary out of his briefcase and, sitting cross-legged on the mattress in his underwear, he prepared to put down on paper the tale old Tarasov had told him this morning, on the promise of being shot like a hero.

Thursday 13 May, evening, at the former special detention centre on Mykolaivska Street, the right place to summarize my strange meeting with Taras Lukjanovitch Tarasov, a rakhivnik and political commissar pensioned for health reasons after working at the FED camera factory and Zavod No.183, previously known as the Kharkov Comintern Locomotive Factory.

Despite his outlandish claim to assassination, the man no more killed Uncle Terry than I did. He is a staunch Soviet, and as such contiguous with those who possibly carried out the deed. Mostly, he has a foot in the grave (see below), and an immense amount of grudges. Our latest reprisals, the dubious reputation for mass shootings my Merefa schoolhouse enjoys, and especially the blasting of the accordions yesterday, have convinced him I am the man to give him a quick, glorious death. Which, in his mind, is preferable to dragging through the last stage of blood-spitting consumption.

Tarasov's unsustainable self-accusation faded the moment I

assured him that his political allegiance and Soviet Badge would suffice to have him shot. Despite two years of war in his homeland, he has a fairly romantic vision of execution, of which I decided to disabuse him. I should know: on armed patrol we take no prisoners; when attacked by partisans, we hang them. I then proceeded (am I not a black soul?) to cultivate his venom regarding Khan Tibyetsky, against the promise to duly have him shot in three days' time. "Unless," I said, "you come before then with hat in hand to tell me you have changed your mind."

After a long conversation interspersed with his sick cough, I began to perceive how wrong I may have been in seeing coincidences where there were none. Things and people seldom happen to be in the same place at the same time. Perhaps Khan had a reason for defecting where he did, for insisting on detention in Kharkov, for smiling when he heard of Platonov's death, and for not wanting to die at all (Mantau is right in this). Platonov might have had something other than a military reason for flying over this region with detailed maps, and perhaps for offering to bribe me. And not even Tarasov coming to me was a coincidence, since it was my request for information on Krasny Yar that first prompted him.

The role of the Yar, this patch of woodland I regarded as an accessory to the great events, emerges as potentially pivotal. Still obscure, but central somehow. Eye of the storm, middle of the labyrinth. If only I could kick myself for not letting Platonov articulate his offer to bribe me, instead of coming within a whisker of shooting him dead.

Summing up, Tarasov described Khan's exploits during the Bolshevik Revolution, and although it is difficult to picture this pencil-necked accountant as a firebrand, he sounds as though he really was there. Either that, or he's memorized the small volume of memoirs, *From the Baltic to Mongolia*, that Khan authored circa 1938, a copy of which I myself picked up in Moscow shortly before the war. But Tarasov added details I wasn't aware of, details that smack of truth and go to prove that sometimes, in our blessed arrogance as information-gatherers, we don't see the forest for the trees. Literally.

Example: Khan and Platonov knew each other as far back as 1919. Khan's memoirs having been published during the Purge, he'd go out of his way to avoid mentioning a colleague presently in disgrace, if ever his ego allowed him to make room for others. Tarasov brought up Platonov (whom he believes alive and free) merely because he was part of the same close group of revolutionary fighters.

Less surprising (but I didn't know this either), Khan and Platonov operated in the Kharkov Oblast in 1920–1, against the same Nestor Makhno whose men reportedly raped and killed young girls at Krasny Yar. Indeed, the two comrades were engaged against Ukrainian anarchists, under the command of the mythical Red Army founder Mikhail Frunze, then commander of the Southern Front. They fought a fierce guerrilla war in the Voronezh–Kharkov area until Makhno, defeated and badly wounded, had to retreat and flee abroad. Tarasov at this time worked as an accountant for the printers of K Svetu ("Towards the Light", a Cheka-backed publication) in Kharkov, and moonlighted at the Free Brotherhood Bookshop, which the Bolsheviks used as a trap to lure and capture Makhnovists.

Out in the field, it was a matter of ambushes and violent reprisals, with mutual pleasantries such as cutting off and stuffing one's genital organs into one's mouth, burning one another's farms and fields, kidnapping, et cetera. If only half of it is true, the lot of them deserve to be strung up by the neck. As expected, many Ukrainians took advantage of ideology to get even with neighbours they had a quarrel with: the usual civil war scenario. I saw it in Spain with my own eyes.

The really interesting part comes now, because Krasny Yar has a role in it. Tarasov repeated the bad press about Makhno, and told me that once the Bolsheviks had stormed the woods (where some of the anarchists had their lair), Khan and Platonov set up a makeshift command there. The occupation lasted a month, during which they lived off the land. Then Platonov suddenly left the Yar, following a furious disagreement with Khan that created a rift in the group. More about this later. What puzzles me is that the two were once again good comrades by the time the Purge came about. As is known, Platonov quickly rose in rank and became a protégé of fabled revolutionary hero Tukhachevsky (the wrong horse, in view of the later Purge), while Khan apparently played second fiddle.

Tarasov is firmly on Platonov's side. From all I heard, however, I wonder if Platonov was callously stepping on his friend's toes to get ahead, or if Khan had to support him because Platonov knew something about him that could cost him dearly. In light of this, it'd make sense if he eventually trumped up the charges against Platonov: it didn't take much in those days. But why wouldn't Platonov spill the beans when he was tried by Stalin? He could have helped his case, had he been able to accuse Khan of anything. At the very least, they'd both have ended up in the Lubyanka. But he didn't talk.

Now I take all this with a grain of salt, but according to Tarasov, throughout the '20s Khan was often in Kharkov, owing to his interest in the Komintern Locomotive (later Tractor) Factory, where tanks were first built in 1928. Tarasov was then an accountant at the factory. Khan enjoyed a good stipend and all kinds of bourgeois privileges, including a dacha back in Moscow with servants and a private car. In town, he frequented the best of post-revolutionary society, including artists and the new intelligentsia. Platonov visited too, occasionally, but he stuck to army-related business and his lifestyle was much more sober. Enterprising fellow that he always was, after Lenin's New Economic Policy (NEP) opened up Russia to foreign concessions, Khan used the Komintern Factory as a base to strike semi-private deals with European and American technicians and businessmen who came to advise or to grub (Tarasov's expression) for Russia's natural resources, including ore from Krivoy Rog and coal from Lugansk.

So far, it's all information I can use: if Tarasov is an example, the long-standing grudge against Khan's lifestyle could well have exploded into ideological hatred after he defected to the enemy. What's more, both the local Bolsheviks and the Ukrainian nationalists had excellent reasons to assassinate him.

One last detail: during the NEP years, at least once every summer Khan visited Krasny Yar. How does Tarasov know? His family lived in Schubino at the time, within walking distance of the woods. The excursions could have been made to reminisce about the Red October glory days, but I doubt it. Tarasov himself doesn't know. Then, one fine day in the mid-1920s, it was Gleb Platonov who arrived without Khan at Krasny Yar, in the company of a stranger. Given the bad name the Yar already had, the locals were curious about this and the other tours, but it ended there. The stranger remains unidentified; the motive for his trip to Krasny Yar also. Tarasov is convinced that Khan (and perhaps also Platonov, I might add) profited during or right after the guerrilla war against Makhno. This is what incenses him to this day. When asked why he didn't act on his suspicions, he gave no answer. It seems obvious he was afraid: brilliant career officers pulled much more weight than a former comrade who'd gone back to book-keeping.

Back to my initial observation: is it purely for military reasons that Platonov was flying a plane in this area when he crash-landed, and is it by accident that Khan crossed the Donets no more than twenty kilometres from Krasny Yar? What is – or was – in those woods that lured the two officers back here through the years? Are the deaths there in any way related? Too bad the date of the last visit by one or the other, or both, is unknown! I will not build hypotheses on shaky premises, but I am intrigued. How intrigued? Enough to secure an updated map of the mined sections of the woods, and plan a trip to Krasny Yar myself.

Meanwhile, time permitting, I will follow up on Khan's NEP years' frequentation of famous theatre performers, stars of the Kharkov opera and the handful of well-heeled foreigners in town, including some Americans. The seemingly auxiliary titbit gives me in fact a precious clue, thanks to which, if I know how to go about it, I might find out much more than I expected. As Bruno Lattmann says, I should no longer delay my visit to Larisa Malinovskaya.

7

FRIDAY 14 MAY, FORMER *ABWEHR* SPECIAL
DETENTION CENTRE IN KHARKOV

At half past midnight, Bora had just fallen asleep. What awoke
him was the clicking open of the street door, four floors down.
Heard despite the distance, not imagined, it roused him completely so that he went from deep dreamless slumber to a state
of lucid alert. Darkness was unbroken in the building. Outside,
sheet lightning briefly drew the rectangle of the window grille
high on the wall, against a night sky where clouds scudded
in front of the stars. On the opposite side of the room, Bora
perceived – dark on dark – the crooked rim of the damaged
door open on the hallway.

He stretched his left arm, reaching out and groping for the
pistol holder on the floor by the bed; he lifted it noiselessly and
unlatched it. The heft of steel hardened his wrist as he passed
the weapon into his right hand; in a single motion his fingers
moulded around the grip and released the safety catch. Tensely
he elaborated on thoughts of what was needed to prepare for
every eventuality, without giving himself to dangerous flights
of fancy. The entire building was untenanted; this much he
knew. The block it belonged to, damaged during the battle of
the spring, had been evacuated and the German authorities
had kept it empty for future use.

From downstairs another distant sound came, consistent
with the previous one – the click of a bolt as the door shut

automatically. Bora sat up. There's a difference between the sound of someone exiting and pulling the door behind him and the small noise of the mechanism when, from the inside, someone gently pushes it closed. This sound was of the second kind. Had the flash-lit window been a mouth panting in suspense, it couldn't have better matched his state of mind. The thunder was like thunder in dreams. Bora rehearsed the familiar layout of the entryway to determine and anticipate the movements anyone would have to make in order to reach this floor.

His sense of a soldier's dignity could be impractical at times. *I'm not about to be shot in my underpants,* he thought absurdly, and felt around for his breeches. *The time it takes him to climb to this level trying not to be overheard is the time I need to button them and pull up my braces.*

He'd gone through the process of clothing his lower half and retrieving his gun when the light in the third-floor hallway was turned on. Bora got to his bare feet at once, too highly strung to feel the glass shard he'd stepped on, a remnant of Khan's ornate goblet. Downstairs, steps moved around, the progress of someone who walked from room to room, looking inside, searching. One man, wearing boots. Bora reached the threshold and listened. *I made the same sound when I walked to Platonov's door – that's Platonov's door he's going to. It's as if my own ghost were moving downstairs.*

Having seemingly completed his search below, the booted man resumed his climb. Steadily he trod the steps to this level, a careful but secure soft thud of footfalls. Bora counted. There were eight steps to each flight of stairs, two flights per floor.

Someone who slept more heavily than me would have noticed neither the glare from below nor the sound of his climb. Best not reveal I'm here. He's searching, but doesn't necessarily know there's anybody in the building. Bora leant out of Khan's room aiming the P38 at the top of the stairs, ready to open fire.

"Major Bora, are you up there?"

Bora raised the muzzle of his pistol as he released the trigger. "Doctor Bernoulli! For God's sake, I was about to shoot you!"

Bernoulli found the light switch in the fourth-floor hallway. "I can't believe you left the street door unlocked, Major. It was hugely imprudent."

"I thought – I'd have sworn – I'd locked it. But how did you possibly —"

"How? I billet here. This building is now being used as temporary quarters: weren't you told? You wouldn't have found electricity and running water otherwise. On the second floor, the rooms are all furnished – you'd be more comfortable in one of them, I'd say." The judge seemed urbanely amused by Bora's confusion. "You're not as mysterious as you think, either, Major. I was driving by as you walked in from the street earlier this evening. You didn't see me, and I didn't care to make myself known. Until a few minutes ago I was dining with colleagues. When I returned and found the place unlocked – well, I imagined that you or another officer rooming here had forgotten to bolt the door. An army vehicle with a different licence plate from yours was parked in the courtyard below, so I deduced it might or might not be you. Then I noticed that on the second floor none but my room was occupied, which made me curious to know where the other tenant might be. I didn't think you'd choose to sleep up here in an unmade bed. Sorry if I alarmed you."

"Not at all. I – didn't realize the rooms below had been refurbished." His foot hurt. Bora looked down, and saw blood on the floor tiles.

Bernoulli shook his head. "I did startle you, didn't I? You'll need a plaster on that heel. Come; I have a small first-aid kit below."

The incident turned into a chance to talk. Bernoulli had a Thermos full of strong coffee, and after they had downed a couple of mugs each, sleep didn't seem important to either of them. They sat in what had been the guard room on the ground floor, a square whitewashed space that doubled as a kitchen, with a table and chairs. The judge sounded well informed about the building's previous designation and its inmates. Without asking, Bora volunteered that he'd conferred with Colonel Bentivegni, and very recently too. *Why not? They both serve in Greater Berlin; their duties are to an extent contiguous. It means he knows far more about me than I imagined: that's why he brought up the St Petersburg Paradox.* The fact could be dangerous or consoling, depending.

Unlike Bora, who drank out of an aluminium mess kit cup, Bernoulli sipped from a ceramic mug with a Greek fret on it. He said, "I'm looking into the episodes we discussed when we first met, Major Bora. I've requested the support of Judge Knobloch, who is, however, busy dealing with the reported February killings of German prisoners at Grischino, and the murder and rape of Red Cross nurses. It will take time, and you may never actually hear what our findings are."

"I'm not in the position of being in a hurry, Dr Bernoulli."

"The Bureau is. It is fair to let you know, nonetheless, that your immediate superior in the *Abwehr* doesn't seem particularly in favour of your photographic hobby."

Bora would not have expected the close-mouthed Bentivegni to have let out that much to a military judge, but stranger things happened at central office level. "I'm sorry to hear it," he noted. "Because I intend to keep it up."

The guard room had no windows. A sense of privacy and isolation – again the image of a confessional came to mind – was derived from the lack of openings. The sound of thunder came muffled from outside; from time to time the overhead lamp flickered as lightning struck the line somewhere. With the coffee mug between his hands Bernoulli sat across from Bora, who had insisted on dressing fully in his superior's presence. Whether reacting to the young man's words or to the tone in which they were pronounced, he assumed the frown of a disappointed teacher. "Allow me the privilege of age and experience, Major: it's this elitist cavalry mode, this Junker mode, that gets many of you into hot water in times when circumspection is called for. You're not as pristine as you pretend, either. I listened carefully to your report when we first met. My observation is that you're aggravated when things don't go the way you think they should."

"I follow my sense of ethics."

"Ethics? Need I remind you of the root of the word? *Ethos* is man's attitude before hardship. Don't take the word in vain, Major Bora."

"I know what ethics means in philosophy, sir. I grasp what it means in the religious sense. Please do not patronize me to this extent."

Impertinent as it was, Bora's reply must have betrayed his concern at not being taken seriously. The judge could have reprimanded him for it. He chose instead to indulge in the paternalism that had caused the reaction to begin with. "I was told you travel alone across distances in an occupied country —"

"I notice the *Heeresrichter* does the same."

"— and you do not shrink from open conflict with political colleagues. There is a difference between loving risk and ignoring it: didn't your stepfather instruct you in that regard?"

"The general and I do not see eye to eye on many things. We don't speak much."

Bernoulli poured the last of the coffee first into Bora's mug, then his own. "So long as you know that the object's value, its *utility*, might demand a very high price. Turning in other Germans for what appears to have happened at the Pyatikhatky forest and Drobytsky Yar exceeds risk; but it may be your way of following ethics. As for Colonel Bentivegni, I believe he's getting bored with his charge and may ask for front-line duty before year's end."

"Well, he'll get there as a major general."

"Yes. All things considered – it is technically none of my business, but judges do dabble in ethics themselves – it would help your credibility with your superiors if you were able to offer them a clear theory on Commander Tibyetsky's death, which was such a serious loss to your agency. It's irrelevant how I know, Major: suffice to say I'm fully informed. And I heard you were encouraged to look into it."

I was told to solve the problem *and* tidy up *afterwards*. Bora gave up trying to fathom the judge's sources. The quivering light bulb, a reminder of the precariousness of his holed-up Stalingrad days, when a man could count on nothing and darkness was frightful, put him in a strange state of compliance. He said, "There isn't much to build a theory on, I'm afraid. Two groups credibly claim his assassination; the supposed culprit is dead, and her companions are out of my reach. I came here tonight because... I don't know what I was hoping to discover, to understand. If only Khan Tibyetsky had given me a clue."

"To what? Why should he? A defector takes into account that he's forfeiting his life."

"Precisely. A man who played as complicated a game as I believe he played, and probably for quite some time, is a man who on the one hand asks for collateral, and on the other keeps something that will serve him as security, if not as life insurance."

"My understanding is that the tank model he came in *was* Tibyetsky's security."

"His *iron horse*: right."

There's something in a judge – if he's an able judge – that invites disclosure. I shouldn't trust him before (or until) I learn his motives. The oilcloth on the table, held in place by tacks, had a faint criss-cross of cuts on it, caused by those who'd sliced bread or other food on its surface. Heedful of signs and meanings (and portents, at times), Bora ran his eyes over the faint lines. The world was readable: or else it was his mental habit to think that he could read it. Everything was significant; coincidences ceased to be such when the latent design was exposed. Sitting here, lowering his defences... He felt the small sting of the wound on his heel as a marker of sorts. *I, too, am written upon.* He said, "You might know Tibyetsky was distantly related to me."

Bernoulli nodded. A shadow of stubble on his razor-bald head betrayed a receding hairline, an antithesis to Bora's thick skullcap of dark hair. "I was told, yes. We're not liable for our relatives. Why, sometimes we can't be held liable for the friends we have. Are you sure Tibyetsky gave you no hints during his residence here?"

"None that I caught. Neither of us was ready to acknowledge our connection."

"Would he have mentioned his *collateral* to the RSHA?"

"I doubt it. Over there he refused to talk altogether. The fact that while in their custody he asked for Colonel Bentivegni – and for me, too – made me hope. Now it's too late."

The storm was directly above Kharkov. Thunderclaps boomed close enough to indicate that lightning must be striking the neighbourhood. The metal-roofed sheds where Kostya had stolen gasoline came to mind, lined up along the river southeast of here. In the muggy guardroom, Bernoulli unhooked the clasp of his collar, revealing a dazzlingly white shirt. "I needn't tell an interrogator that lack of oral communication can be replaced by the written word."

"Tibyetsky had no time. His forcible removal from this centre —"

"Yet even under great duress those who want to leave a clue will try to scrawl it quickly on virtually any surface, using any means available. I speak from courtroom experience, and you yourself showed me the prayer pencilled on a scrap of paper by the Alexandrovka Mennonites."

"I went through Khan's room carefully, tonight for the third time. Wallpaper, furniture, even the door: there's no message scribbled anywhere."

Bernoulli sighed; or else let out a deep breath. "Right. And the room was not his security. His tank was."

Rain had begun to fall outside, hopefully breaking the lightning storm. Slowly the two men finished their coffee; when the light went off, they sat in silence with their thoughts

(Bora wondering whether he should mention Taras Tarasov, and deciding against it).

"I'm back where I started from, Dr Bernoulli."

In the morning, the military judge left before Bora got up. When they'd parted ways five hours earlier, he'd said he had several matters to look into, and would start in good time. By 8 a.m., through flooded streets, Bora drove to divisional headquarters, where a still-drowsy von Salomon received him, signed not one but two authorization sheets and dismissed him, having exchanged no more than a "Good day" with him.

Outside the colonel's office, the paper-pushing lieutenant supplied Bora with the most recent map of the minefields between Kharkov and the river. "We can vouch for those we laid, Herr Major. The wooded areas by the Donets remain iffy even after clearing. Partisan gangs are known to switch around our actual and dummy minefield signs often enough, so you can't really trust them. Same for the right bank of the Udy, too."

"Not the Udy at Kharkov, I take it."

"No, sir. Much further down, past Borovoye and Schubino."

The meandering, boggy course of the Donets tributary, full of islets and false rivers, bordered Krasny Yar from a west-north-west direction. Bora scanned the map and told himself he'd worry about it when he got there. Meanwhile, before heading for the *Kombinat*, there was enough time for him to drive to the northern suburb of Pomorki.

Just before the turn-off from the Belgorod road, across a field smothered by wild hyacinth, he saw the wooded rise where a half-hidden cluster of small *novyi burzhuy* villas stood, built in the '20s for the members of a reborn commercial and artistic middle class. Most had fallen into disrepair, but Larisa's less than others. Bora entered (in low gear) her overgrown garden, marked by a narrow corduroy path that allowed him not to get stuck in the muddy grass. A lean-to hut of unpainted logs had been added to the one-floored *dacha*, and deeply contrasted with it. The side of the original house was graced with a wooden terrace; only part of its trellis remained standing, but even the segment that had collapsed was covered with blooming vines.

In front of the log cabin, a florid young woman in a white kerchief was tending chickens. She froze with her hands full of feed at the arrival of the German vehicle. Not wanting to alarm her even more, Bora stopped several metres back and addressed her in Russian. It took a few minutes for the girl to feel safe enough to answer his questions and let him in.

At the *Kombinat*, Russian prisoners poured buckets of crushed bricks out at the edge of the green in front of Stark's office, where puddles gaped in the dirt of the parking spaces.

"Wipe your boots on the rag out there, will you?" was the first thing the commissioner said, the moment he heard the front door opening. He read the paperwork Bora had delivered, told his assistant to process it, and resumed what he'd been doing: applying his signature in indelible pencil onto blank documents. "I don't have much time, Major, as we're beginning to gear up: I'm expecting my agriculture and forestry specialists to report in at last. But do sit down a moment. You're doubly in luck today. There are two hundred horses in this shipment, a good part of them Budenny and Chernomor breed or half-breed, the tough rangy mounts you want to have on this terrain. Even though you have to thank that old bastard Russki marshal for it, he always did know his cavalry animals."

Bora declined a seat. "It didn't do him any good when the Poles bowled him over at Komarov, *Konarmiya* or not. But I'm very grateful to Budenny for breeding mounts we'll use against him."

"And that's not the best news. Or rather, given that someone's death is somebody else's gain – how do you say it in Latin? You young intellectual officers were given the opportunity of studying these fancy sentences, while in my time we had to make do with business school."

"*Mors tua vita mea*, Herr Gebietskommissar?"

"Exactly. The *mors* in question is Brigadeführer Reger-Saint Pierre's. His staff car struck an anti-tank mine near Mirgorod two days ago. He's done with this vale of tears, horses included: the biggest piece of him left is a booted right foot."

"That's highly unfortunate."

"Why, did you know him? Before expressing your sympathy, consider that I'm having the Karabakh stallion, barely arrived in Mirgorod, shipped back here. I can, I can – of course I can! What am I district commissioner for, if I can't pull strings the way I see fit? The two general officers next in line to receive him don't need to hear about it. Turian-Chai is getting an Olympic equestrian to ride him, or he becomes horse stew."

"Don't even say it in jest. How soon can he be here?"

"It might be ten days to two weeks." Stark drove his pencil into a tabletop sharpener, and quickly turned the wheel. "I've got some pull, but I'm not a miracle-worker. And so that you're not tempted to take it as a favour, I expect you and your army colleagues to think and speak well of this administration. Now that Army Group Kempf is moving to Kharkov, we politicians need all the military support we can get."

Bora hadn't heard the news; a clear sign that the attack on the Kursk salient was drawing near. The possibility secretly electrified him.

Glancing at his out-mail basket, Geko Stark checked the end of his pencil with the tip of his tongue. "Are you bound back to town, by any chance? If so, I'll entrust you with hand-delivering these letters at your earliest convenience to the Southern Railway Station *Feldpost*. They're important, and you'll notice one of them is going to the General Army Office Medical Inspectorate, Personnel Branch, to track down that medic of yours."

Bora had not anticipated another whirl through Kharkov, but one would have never known by the promptness of his assent. "Will do, Commissioner. Thanks for the trust."

Trust was a term used elastically by *Abwehr* officers. From the *Kombinat*, Bora drove straight to divisional headquarters; there he opened the letters, read them and ably re-sealed them before taking them to the Field Post Office. Not one to waste time, he then called at the SS first-aid station on Sumskaya, and asked to meet the surgeon there.

Merefa, 2.10 p.m.

I'm really back where I began. At the SS first-aid station on Sumskaya they lied to me again, feigning ignorance, which means I couldn't speak to the man they had over at the RSHA jail the evening of 6 May. Worse: when I told them I know for a fact (from Odilo Mantau) that their medic was one of the last to see the prisoner alive, they flat-out denied it. It's a pattern. Khan's body was on the premises on 7 May, when they told me to my face they knew nothing about it; his post-mortem was carried out by their head surgeon, and only by a stratagem was I able to secure a copy of it. This reticence, along with my doubts about the role of UPA and NKVD (with or without the babushkas), leads me to wonder whether and to what extent the Security Service might be involved in this operation. All they'll admit is that there was a candy wrapper in the victim's pocket, which they threw away! On the other hand, do I really know what Dr Mayr at Hospital 169 is all about? Was he really too busy to do a post-mortem on Platonov when I asked him to? Is he unaware of Weller's destination, as he says, or – as I suspect – is he behind it, for reasons of his own? He surely buried the old man in a hurry; and in the hospital garden, to boot. I may be reading too much into this, but I haven't much to go on.

To all appearances, Khan ingested poison hours after the man sent from Sumskaya measured his blood pressure (the tantrum occasioned the check-up). A deadly dose of nicotine laced a lend-lease American D ration, identical to those Khan brought with him when he defected. Are we sure? Could things have gone otherwise? And what's "otherwise"?

Here are some of the possibilities:

a. The poison was administered in a different manner, for example by injection or other means, the night before Khan's death. Objections: does such a delayed-action poison exist, and did anyone other than an SS medic have access to the cell? Most of all, traces of the poison were found in Khan's stomach: hence he'd eaten it.

b. For whatever unrelated reason, Khan became ill after waking up on 7 May, and was opportunistically administered the lethal dose during first aid. Objections: if Mantau can be believed, Khan was already beyond help by the time the medical personnel arrived from Sumskaya. And in any case, how did the killers know Khan would conveniently take sick, and what would have occasioned his illness in the first place?

c. Khan did away with himself, and I'm butting my head against a wall. Objection: would a man of his temperament choose suicide, and ask for help in addition?

At any rate, lips are sealed over at Sumskaya, and I cannot fathom why someone inside the Security Service or the RSHA would kill a precious element like Khan Tibyetsky.

By mail last week a former colleague communicated bad news from the days with the 1st Cavalry Division. Our old regimental sergeant went on emergency leave three months ago because his wife, severely wounded in an air raid, had had both arms amputated. They'd been married twenty-two loving years, no children. He carried her photograph everywhere (we teased him for it). Well, on the anniversary of their wedding day last February he shot her and himself in the clinic where she was recovering.

Accustomed to bad news as I'm becoming, I was shocked nevertheless, as I knew the man and never expected him to fall apart so completely. Perhaps, as Cardinal Hohmann says, we're all turning brittle in our "delusion of man-made glory". I don't feel brittle, but it may be that I keep my nose to the grindstone and don't indulge much in melancholy. Our old comrade's tragedy, however, induced me to sit down with Bauml during my latest stint at Bespalovka, and talk to him man-to-man about his brother's death in Stalingrad. It is better if he tells, rather than keeps everything inside like our old regimental sergeant.

It was hard: we both fought back our emotions to keep the conversation going. In the end, I hope the meeting was of some help to him. Bauml thanked me, at any rate. As for me, I can only hope nothing like it comes my way; and that's all I can say about it. Incidentally, what he reports of the terrible day his brother was left behind with the desperately injured got me to rethink a little the scenario of Platonov's death.

MEREFA, 3.38 P.M.

"Jesus, Martin, it's the fourth shot you've put away in ten minutes. What's going on?"

"I'm thinking."

Back from delivering the Platonov dossier to the Kiev Branch Office, Lattmann had stopped by with mail and updates for his friend. He now hefted the bottle he'd brought for him from the city. "It's a hell of a strong vodka to use as a thinking aid."

"Well, here's one for the road." Seated in front of the mine-field map, Bora drained another glass. "Scots blood, you know: holds drink well."

"Ah, yes. When it doesn't make you hare-brained."

"Says who?"

"Your brother Peter, for one." Taking advantage of the lowered defences alcohol was likely to cause even in Bora, Lattmann shot from the hip. "I hope it's not true what he says: that you made him swear he'll ask for a transfer away from Russia if you're killed."

"It's not true."

"So Peter made it up? He's worried, for somebody who made it up."

"Pilots exaggerate everything."

Bora's hostility, like all else about him, had a polite, reclusive quality. His friend was aware that it could border on cruelty, not least against himself. It was impenetrable, too. Alcohol or not, a Bora who didn't want to talk was a lost cause for a meaningful conversation. Lattmann knew he'd gone as far as he could with him. He drank a swig directly from the bottle. "So you plan to trek through mined woods?"

"I plan to trek through woods where minefields are marked. I'm not studying this map to entertain myself. Bruno, I've got two weeks before every waking moment I have will be spent with the regiment. By the end of May I must be able to report fully manned and equipped, so anything else I mean to do, I must do now. When did you see Peter?"

"Yesterday, when we stopped for refuelling at the Poltava airfield. He's there, conferring with his KG55 colleagues – working overtime and hoping against hope, depending on the start of the campaign, to snatch a two-day pass in Leipzig when his child is born."

Bora was copying data into a small pocketbook, letters and numbers that meant something for him alone, to overlap on the topographic map as keys to dangerous spots. "I bet he makes it. Kempf is moving to Kharkov, but I see no sign of us moving ahead before the second half of June. What do you have for me regarding the Insurgent Army and Tibyetsky?"

"One interesting titbit: leaflets circulated in Poltava, Zaporozhye and Kiev were worded exactly like the Soviets' claim to having executed Khan in German custody. They are clearly derived from it. We still don't know when his presence in Kharkov became known. It's possible the Gestapo raid on the detention centre, in full daytime, alerted the UPA or NKVD. Both groups are using the defector's death as a piece of internal propaganda, but they can't *both* be behind it. Either the Soviets did it, or – not having done it – beat the Ukrainians to their official claim. And I have another piece of news: Odilo Mantau got his ass fired over Tibyetsky's death. Courtesy of Kharkov

Gestapo chief Hans Kietz, who shipped him to Kiev with his marching orders. They were celebrating at our Branch Office, because it'll be a while before he's substituted."

"That's good news. I wonder how long before they sack me over Platonov's heart attack?"

"I don't think they will, once they see what you got out of him. They'd given up on learning anything from the old man."

"Anyhow, it isn't as if I haven't got another job apart from interrogating higher-ups." Bora held the bottle out to Lattmann. When his colleague said no, he corked it and put it away. "We go by what Russians and Ukrainians claim regarding Tibyetsky, but there's a third possibility: we could be wrong in supposing the existence of an organized enemy plot. The killer could have acted alone, or, at most, on someone's commission. Listen to what a little fellow called Tarasov told me yesterday, standing right where you are now."

It took a little over ten minutes of summary, after which Lattmann didn't appreciably change his views. "Why, he sounds delusional! And you plan to execute him?"

"It'd be merciful. He's at the last stage: coughing blood and so haggard you can see through him. I don't know; I haven't made up my mind on how to keep my part of the bargain according to military rules, so I gave him three days to come back and ask to be spared."

"What if he doesn't?"

"I might turn a blind eye and leave him to his natural destiny. But if he's tattled in Merefa about his extravagant claim and he's believed, I'll have to make an example of him."

"An example. Right; of course." Lattmann looked away from Bora's stern face. "How many times have I heard that? And now from you, too. I'm no philosopher, Martin, but if there's normality somewhere, none of this is it."

"We didn't sign up to lead a normal life. You volunteered for the East as I did. We *chose* to fight 'those who wear their shirts out of their pants'. Now it's consistency and not normality that we must strive for."

"Oh yes?" In his summer uniform, faded khaki shorts and ankle boots, four out of five fingertips bandaged, Lattmann gave the incongruous impression of an overgrown Boy Scout, despite being married and a father of two (and a cousin to Peter's wife). "I wish I had your coolness, Martin. Sometimes I wonder. Well, I might as well say it. I wonder how we'll go back to our families after all this."

"Those of us who go back will have to deal with it." Bora smiled, to lighten the conversation. "And to prove to you that I am more prudent than you make me out to be: before long I am going to thoroughly reconnoitre Krasny Yar. I snatched an authorization from divisional command to proceed; I doubt Lieutenant Colonel von Salomon even read what he was signing this morning. It's a limited area, three kilometres per side, so I'll use the spider-web approach, because even though German troops have met no trouble in that area thus far, six dead civilians point to some kind of hostile activity, and counter-guerrilla methods are justified. If we find nothing, it'll have been good practice."

"Why; do you expect to find somebody or something there that will explain Khan Tibyetsky's death? However the assassination was planned, it didn't originate in that patch of woods!"

Bora resumed writing in his small notebook. "I won't know until I understand more about the place. That blockhead Mantau swore by his babushka's guilt. I don't. And speaking of women, I'm going to spend some time with Larisa after all."

"It's about time."

"Yes, and something else I can't write home about." Bora gave him a piece of paper with the SS surgeon's name on it. "See if you can run a quick check on this officer; whether he's all he says he is. And please keep looking into the matter of that Weller fellow, the army medic. Anything might help. Mayr, the surgeon at Hospital 169, won't drop the subject. Wait – check a little deeper on him, while you're at it. His previous assignments, citations, recent and upcoming furloughs and suchlike. See if he's really got his neuralgia and jaundice. He claims a high exposure to suffering, et cetera, which in his profession and while at war is inescapable. I may be way out of line, but – look into *rumours.*"

"What sort of rumours?"

"I don't know. Stress, combat fatigue… Mercy killing."

Lattmann took notes and pocketed the scrap. "I hope you're barking up the wrong tree, Martin."

Soon Lattmann and Bora were driving together to Borovoye. From there, Bora continued on to Bespalovka, where he'd interview more prospective components of the regiment and plan the Krasny Yar operation.

Monday 17 May, near Bespalovka, 4.30 a.m.

Two intense days with the regiment. Nagel is here! I could have embraced him, I was so happy to see him. As it was, we warmly shook hands for half a minute. Thank God for Nagel. I'd put my life into that man's hands ten times over. He's sure to build a cadre of non-coms I can lead through a ring of fire. If it weren't for Sergeant Major Nagel, I'd have had my head blown off a couple of times in Stalingrad alone. Turns out he'd heard the regiment was in the making, and was taking steps to ask for admittance at the same time I was looking for him.

He and I agree we should impress upon all applicants that our task is not going to be a picnic. Most of us who have anti-guerrilla experience are aware that the dangers for us are higher than on a regular front line. If there's anyone among us (officer, non-com, trooper) who for any reason has had enough, or – worse – anyone whose nerves have given way before, better get rid of them now. This is not going to be for them.

Newcomers who labour under the illusion that partisan = bandit = improvised fighter had better be disabused quickly of the idea. I circulated diagrams of the typical partisan regiment, as tightly organized and hierarchically arranged as any unit but wholly disinclined to observe the rules of fair fighting. I explained how squads similar to *Einsatzkommandos* come in tow, with leeway to exterminate as necessary. This isn't to say I haven't had occasion to negotiate with partisan leaders: some of those who come from the regular army are not bereft of decency. Yet this summer, as we move out, the regiment needs to be prepared for unpleasant duty. I mean to keep civilians out of the mess as much as possible (it's good policy, and morally preferable), but if we're to keep the flanks of our advancing army safe, we'll have to be equal to anything. The evangelist Matthew writes *Estote parati;* and ready we must be.

As I write, my officers are informed that the entire unit will carry out an exercise next week. I calculate it will take 2 mounted platoons patrolling the river side of the woods, with 3 stationary machine gun positions; the other two sides of Krasny Yar will require 1 squadron each, plus machine gunners every 60 m. The entry side, where I'll go in, will involve 2 squadrons, plus 2 platoons. Technically, this means that each of us will "cover" about 11 m^2 of the woodland: unless the killer is a troll or a creature who lives in the bowels of the earth, we ought to be able to flush him out. If not, we're sure to find evidence of his having been there.

For now, I'm due to go back to Merefa, where Kostya is to give me an update about Taras Tarasov: has he shown up to ask for mercy in the last two days? Time's up. Taras Tarasov has a rendezvous with destiny (or with Martin Bora, who plays that role as far as the little accountant is concerned).

Five kilometres out, at the crossroads by the Diptany farm, Bora met a Security Service patrol and had to stop. Armoured cars and half-tracks, with *Leibstandarte* and Army trucks in tow, clogged the dusty fork in the road. Dark mud clung to their tyres. Had there not been smoke rising from the north-eastern horizon, that alone would have said they were back from some mopping-up operation or other on the banks of the Mosh River.

"Where are you headed? We're not done," the Hauptsturmführer in command told him, adding, "Why are you alone, Major?"

Bora answered the first question; as for the second, he pointed to the sub-machine gun he kept to hand. It annoyed him – as it did every time, no matter how many times it happened – when his papers were taken a few steps away and pored over. Unfailingly, they were given back with a nod, as happened now.

"Very well. Keep left, at your own risk."

Open fields, undulating terrain and grassy ravines led to the river. "To my *left?*"

"That's what I said. Wait here if you're afraid, Major."

Bora stepped on the gas, and headed in the direction indicated. As soon as he was out of sight beyond a rise and a dip, he turned right at the very next crossroads. The morning breeze carried the smell of smoke from the burning sheds, whiffs and ravels of odours – lumber, charred grain, ticking. Shooting still sounded from less than a kilometre away, in short bursts of machine-gun fire. Marksmen's rifles, sniper rifles cracked at intervals from beyond the river, as it seemed. Slowing down to a halt came as easy as it was foolish. Bora took out his field glasses to look. It was all a green haze while he focused the lenses, and then the clarity of motion as soldiers became visible, stealthily approaching a cluster of farm buildings. Whatever was going on, no one on either side was paying any attention to him.

Which was interesting, because a shot was aimed straight in his direction. Bora felt it, heard it glance the metal frame of his windshield at the top left corner, missing him where he stood behind the wheel by a span at most. He froze for the stunned instant needed to run a mental check and make sure he hadn't been hit. Somehow he managed not to react outwardly by lowering his field glasses. *Not a Tokarev, not a Mosin. Nothing Soviet. And they're not firing from the farm, or from across the river.* The thought was still taking shape in his head as he turned slowly and refocused his field glasses on the rise he'd climbed and driven down to reach this spot. The steadiness of his hands seemed strange even to him, because he was enraged. And although he couldn't make out the sharpshooter, he did see the trembling heads of fescue where he lay in the grass. *He's keeping me in his sights as I look his way. Won't fire at me now that he knows I'm on to him, and he wouldn't have fired in the first place had I not stopped to look. At my own risk: is this what they meant? I could go back to the Diptany fork and call his commander to account, but it's enough to have shown them I'm not in the least "afraid". I have stacks of more important work to do.*

He was understandably put out when he reached the Merefa schoolhouse. There, Kostya made things worse by reporting that Taras Tarasov, far from coming with cap in hand in the last two days, had been bragging all over Merefa. Bora didn't need to hear what about. *I'll shoot the bastard myself; I'll drag him out of the house and shoot him myself.* And whether or not in town they knew that today was the day of reckoning, once there Bora couldn't find a soul in the streets to tell him where Taras Tarasov lived. His anger increased in the process of banging on doors and demanding a response. Seeing Father Victor Nitichenko stroll over from the road to Ozeryanka effected the incredible result of making Bora's wrath peak and at the same time returning him to a measure of calm.

"It's over there, *povazhany* Major: the house down the street with the faded shutters." And given that Bora was already stalking toward the place, the priest added (out of spite, or relief, or as an apology?), "But you're late, *bratyetz*. Taras Tarasov had a gush of blood overnight and died a sinner, as he lived. My mother, sainted woman, is there washing him for burial now. We thought you'd have been here earlier to have him shot for what he claims he did."

There wasn't much that could be done. Doing nothing was not an alternative in view of Tarasov's brag about having killed Tibyetsky. Bora had the priest's mother reclothe the miserable Tarasov, and while Father Victor was instructed to circulate news of the upcoming reprisal, at gunpoint he commandeered the accountant's neighbours to lay the body out in the street and to set his house on fire. He wouldn't leave the scene until the building was too far gone for the bystanders to salvage anything. And it was only 9 a.m. by the time he took the road to Kharkov.

Elsewhere, he told himself as he moodily stopped at the inevitable checkpoint, *they shoot everyone and raze villages to the ground for less than this. So why is it that what I just did doesn't please me at all?*

In Kharkov, at the military exchange, he had to wait for the arrival of a supply mule dray in order to secure what he needed for his visit to Larisa Malinovskaya. Maximizing every moment, he used the unwelcome delay to open Cardinal Hohmann's letter.

He received a message from his old ethics professor once a month, as other former philosophy students no doubt did. Written in Latin (the Latin of an erudite man, not of a priest), the briefs ideally brought together the university students who now served the Fatherland in different places of the earth: at least, those who hadn't already fallen in battle. Not that it was the same letter for all: Hohmann was not a man to repeat himself, or, worse, have a secretary compose a single text for everyone. He wrote personally, using a fountain pen, addressing in every officer the boy who had been sitting in front of him in the Leipzig classroom, whose change from those days he could not ignore.

The use of a dead language barely toned down the severity of his moral comments, which were only not directly political because they made use of Gospel quotations: still, he had them hand-delivered by army chaplains, avoiding censorship. Bora sometimes kept the letter sealed for more than a week, irritated at the idea of having to look inside himself from the moment he opened it to read. Then, without exception, he cut the edge of the envelope and took out the two sheets written in a slanted elegant hand, which never asked for a reply: this because they were lectures, and because answering in writing could endanger young men belonging to an ideological army.

Bora, however, always replied, using if needed the pocket dictionary his family firm had published at the end of the 1800s, the *Lexicon for Latin Correspondence, with Examples from the Classics*. He replied as he'd done in his student days, with logical arguments of an off-putting stubbornness, all the more unshakeable since he felt deep down that Hohmann was right and he was wrong. To the letter he'd received after Stalingrad, exasperated by the cardinal's anguished appeals to faith, he'd answered by translating into Latin a single lapidary sentence by Oswald Spengler, confident it would irritate: *Factum mutat facientem.* "Every action changes he who commits the action." And then the signature with his military rank.

This morning, waiting for the mule dray to come clopping down the street from the rail station, he read the cardinal's words and found them so beautifully irrelevant to his present plight (or perhaps so relevant to it) that he tore the letter to shreds.

Pomorki, 1.45 p.m., north of the Kharkov Aerodrome

Old people's houses all smell alike. Tolstoy would say something like it. He wrote that it's happy families that resemble one another: true, but... it's this odour of dusty carpets, clogged drains and milk that has overflowed while boiling.

The opening of the front door caused a yawn of bright green squares in the twilight of the interior, as glassed-in photographs or paintings reflected the glare from the wild garden behind Bora's back. He stepped into a small anteroom, wood-panelled like a closet or a bathing hut. The space beyond was the parlour. Bora felt the absurdity of standing here with a pat of butter in his hand eight hours after being shot at at a crossroads by other Germans, and less than five hours after ordering a dead man's house to be set on fire.

How do we go back to our families after this, Lattmann had wondered. It was an exercise in rhetoric for Lattmann, and for everyone else. As far as Bora was concerned, Dikta didn't want to hear about the war, his stepfather knew everything there was to know about it, and from his mother he would intentionally keep all details. *And none of us will really "go back". It's someone different and new who returns, if and when he does. Factum mutat facientem.*

From inside the parlour, he heard a sonorous, trained female voice saying, "So, you're Friderik Vilgemovitch Bora's son, Martyn Friderikovich. You don't look at all like him. I was hoping you would."

"Good afternoon, *gospozha.*"

"Ah, you speak Russian. Enter."

As his eyes grew accustomed to the dimness of the house, Bora realized that no one was in the cluttered parlour; or rather that the woman addressing him sat behind a folding screen. The cloth-covered paper of the screen showed Japanese cranes in flight on a gilded background.

"You must be five *pud* in weight," she observed, unseen. "And tall: how much?"

She was right about his weight, three kilos below the norm after Stalingrad and pneumonia. "One ninety-two last time I checked," Bora said to the screen.

"Your father didn't come quite to that, but the weight is the same. Eyes?"

"Green."

"Green. From The Little One, your mother. Ih. Not dark like your father's. Dark eyes – more passion in them. I'm not one of those Russians who mistrust dark eyes. But I should have mistrusted them. Without a moustache, without a beard, you all look like boys. Come forward, Martyn Friderikovich: stand where I can see you."

There was a hole in the eye of one of the painted cranes, about the size of a coin. She must be sitting to peep through it. Having come not knowing what to expect, Bora took every moment as it came. "I brought you butter, *gospozha.*"

Some agitation behind the screen; a small stubby hand in a lace glove extended from behind it. "Give here. Give here."

Bora took a step forward, and the hand grasped the waxed paper wrap.

"Nyusha! Nyusha!"

The summons was to the florid girl in a white kerchief, whom Bora had met three days earlier to ask what he might bring to please Larisa Malinovskaya. The same girl who today, while Bora was parting trailing branches and creepers to walk up to the house, had opened the door to him and touched her temple with a smile of understanding.

Nyusha came rushing in.

"Plate, Nyusha. Quick."

The girl followed a maze through the furniture-crowded room to a glass cabinet, from which she took a dessert plate. She handed it to the woman behind the screen and walked back outside.

An interval followed, during which the small, impatient sounds of unwrapping were all that came from the paper and silk barrier. Bora waited. He'd meant ever since 1941 to meet his father's old lover, and now that he finally was there, impulsiveness would not do.

He looked around the parlour, taking in details. As if ranked in order of importance, furniture and many odds and ends clustered around a concert piano, like huts around a cathedral. Draped with shawls, congested with framed images of all sizes, it had caught Bora's attention from the moment he walked in. A glory of redundancy everywhere he looked. Disguised as it was, the piano stood for his father, for his link with the invisible old woman; it beckoned from within the reef of small tables and stands, chalk genre figures, houseplants that obliterated corners and reduced the floor space. Not a square inch of the papered walls was unoccupied, either. Old studio portraits pictured Larisa as the buxom beauty once so prized by male admirers, especially turn-of-the-century opera enthusiasts. The Edwardian-fashion blouses made her look all breast, like a handsome pigeon, small-headed and with an egret plume in her dark hair. In fact, all about her in those fading likenesses resembled a glorious bird. She'd been thirty-six in 1911, when Friedrich von Bora had left Russia after a seven-year affair. A much-reproduced (and scarcely credible) Karl Bulla studio portrait of herself in the garb of an Orthodox nun with a skull in her hands, taken shortly after the conductor's death in 1914, exceeded all the rest in size.

Bora looked without judging; he expected theatricality in her on- and off-stage poses and expressions, whether she wore braids as Wagner's Isolde, or a lace cap as *Faust*'s Margaret. There she was, Amelia in *Simon Boccanegra*, Chimène in Massenet's *Le Cid*, possibly Natasha in *Rusalka* and more, in other chief roles from lesser-known operas (Rubinstein's? Tchaikovsky's?) unfamiliar to him. And then the later Malinovskaya, violinist and revolutionary, with Frunze and without Frunze, with Trotsky and without Trotsky, and eventually without male companions at all, portrayed with her instrument against a watercolour backdrop of moonlight on the sea.

The voice from behind the screen came out sticky, as if the woman were chewing a large mouthful. "Yes, you're taller – and you look *modern*. Only your hands are like his. Your father was an intellectual, for an aristocrat. And he was exceedingly talented. Are you talented?"

"Not really."

"And do you have brothers or sisters?"

"Not by him, *gospozha*. I have a younger brother by my stepfather."

"How could La Petite, your mother, remarry after *him*?"

"Well, she was widowed at twenty, and my stepfather had sought her hand before Father did."

"Is he an artist, at least?"

Generaloberst Sickingen? The thought of it! Bora smiled inwardly. "He's a soldier. A very good husband to my mother, and a good father to me."

"Of course it's much easier to claim a *soldier* as a father than a genius. Your mother should have remained faithful to his memory, as I did."

Bora didn't show what he was thinking: every opera aficionado knew Larisa Malinovskaya had counted sexual partners before and after his father: Debussy, Mucha… Mikhail Frunze, for example. As for the exclusivity of that love affair, the Maestro might have lived for years with his premier soprano, but in the end had gone back to Germany and married his young cousin. Pretensions to loyalty on the part of a forsaken lover were touching, but altogether unnecessary.

She didn't even ask for a spoon. Is she gobbling butter back there? It seemed so plain that she was, Bora didn't know what to make of it. War drove people to desperate cravings, he was aware, but the oddity of this reception, the vanity of a screen set between them, and now the greedy smacking sounds from behind it, threw him off-balance. He'd entered, not for the first time, a space suspended from daily experience, a dimension dangerously close to normality, where daily rules, however, did not apply.

"You remind me of Frunze," the sticky voice said.

"The founder of the Red Army, *gospozha*? I hope not."

"Not your features. The glance, the way you hold your head. *Frunzik* was outrageously handsome."

Ah yes, there it was. One of the portraits on the concert piano was of the young Russo-Romanian firebrand, a bright-eyed and moustached disciplinarian. Bora had studied Mikhail Frunze's campaigns and innovations ("The Red Army was created by the workers and peasants and is led by the will of the working class. That will is being carried out by the Communist Party…") It made sense, if she could capture his fancy, that a soprano compromised with the old regime should seek a relationship with Frunze to prove her change of heart. But for all his valour and organizing virtues, Frunze had run afoul of Stalin and officially succumbed to an ulcer, although *Abwehr* operatives knew for a fact he'd been purposely administered an excess of anaesthetic before surgery. If Frunze had been Larisa Malinovskaya's protector in the early 1920s, one had to wonder how she'd managed to survive his disgrace. Had she distanced herself from him towards the end, or had she found other supporters within the Party? Most of all, had she known Khan Tibyetsky in Kharkov? It was this consideration that had most influenced Bora's choice to visit her now.

"And so you're called Martyn, yourself. Martynka the Widow's Son, like the character in the Russian fairy tale. Your father wrote a *Lied* for me by that title. A triumph. He was thinking of *me* when he named you."

Bora spoke to the hole in the screen. "I was coincidentally born on Martinmas."

"In the old days only illegitimate children and foundlings were named after the saint of the day. Your father was thinking of *me* when he baptized you Martyn, which was the name we planned to give our son, should we have one. Naturally, for us, it would have been bourgeois to marry. We both thought so. *I* thought so. And then he returned to Germany in 1911 after his father's death. And there he met his little cousin, his young cousin, La Petite, who could have been his daughter in age. She was a child when he left for Russia. She was seventeen when he returned. What do you want from me, Martyn Friderikovich? You Bora males don't come to a woman without wanting something."

"Forgive me for protecting my father's good name, Larisa Vasilievna. I don't believe he sought anything of you, apart from your affection. Which I understand he reciprocated."

The muffled clack behind the flight of cranes betrayed the unsteady setting of the plate down on the floor. "You're not seeking affection here. You would have done back then, be certain of that. He was old enough then to have had a son your age.

Father and son, both of you would have 'sought my affection' then. It happened other times. Father and son." The plump gloved hand emerged left of the screen, forefinger and thumb lifted, a sort of lay blessing. "Father *and* son. A rich merchant from Nizhny Novgorod and his first-born ruined themselves over me. The son set fire to the Odessa warehouses to spite his father; the father turned his son in to the Okhrana as a subversive."

I must flatter her judiciously. She's clever and suspicious, and rightly so given the circumstances. Father did fall head over heels for Nina, as if he'd never lived with his prima donna as man and wife. This could turn into a very long interlude, if I am to obtain information from her. Knowing that she was prying, Bora nodded his head towards the piano. "Did you own it back then, *gospozha*?"

"When I lived in Moscow? Yes. What you want to know is whether your father played on it. It was his. He played on it. Do *you* play?"

"Actually, I do."

"Who was your teacher?"

"Weiss, from Leipzig."

"Ih! Weiss, the best. He is the best in Germany."

Yes, and I traded him like a piece of furniture for a Petrov grand piano, which was the only way to get him to the Red Cross. "My parents thought so, *gospozha*."

"Your parents? They're not 'your parents'! The Little One, La Petite, she's your mother. Your father is dead." The screen trembled; she was perhaps getting to her feet, or maybe only crossing her legs or changing position behind it. "You're itching to play; you wonder if it's in tune. It's in tune. Let me hear you. And don't think I don't have an excellent ear left."

"What should I play?"

"Something he wrote."

There was a brief composition, less than two minutes in all, called *The Bells of Novgorod*, dedicated by Friedrich von Bora to his disagreeable but genial colleague Balakirev. Difficult as it was minimal in duration, Bora knew it by heart, including the finger-straining *ossias* that would make or break his chances of gaining her confidence.

He freed the piano of shawls and fringes, aware of his own eagerness. His motions felt even to him (and to her, no doubt) like a suitor's haste to undress his beloved. In the dusty room, no dust flew about from the silk he parted, lifted and pulled back to expose the gleaming key lid.

Afterwards, no sign of life came from behind the screen for a time that exceeded the showpiece's duration. Bora lowered the key lid slowly. He was already replacing the bright shawls over the instrument when she observed at last, "So, you do have talent after all, Martyn Friderikovich. You play better than your own father. He was a *god* before the orchestra, but played the piano no more than very well. You play more than very well: Weiss taught you right. *The Bells of Novgorod*, no less: difficult as *Islamey*, a worthy tribute to old Mily Balakirev. You are wasted in a uniform."

"Hardly, Larisa Vasilievna. I like being a soldier."

"Nonsense your mother's second bed-mate has put into you. You are wasted in a uniform."

"With all due respect, I have no intention whatever of making music my career."

A swish of clothes and she emerged from behind the screen, a stocky, domineering grey-eyed woman with curls and a Queen Victoria jowl, in a lace-collared black gown reaching down to her feet. Her feet were small, swollen and bare. Bora was careful to exhibit no response other than a nod; he estimated her to be in her late sixties, and she was no longer beautiful. The butter she'd just finished eating rimmed her lips in greasy slickness, and the fatty folds of her cheeks were also shiny. The detail embarrassed him, but he remained unmoved.

"Killing for a career is better, I suppose." Larisa waded among odds and ends, docking at last into a wicker armchair, whose overstuffed cushions she dropped on the floor before heavily sitting down. "Come, what do you want? Other than wanting to meet me, yes, yes. Nimble-fingered as you are, you're a Bora; you're up to something else."

He turned on his heel to face her where she sat. It was a challenge looking her in the eye and keeping his mind off the oily smears on her face. "Very well, Larisa Vasilievna, but I'm up to something very small. I read in articles about your relocation to Kharkov during the Great War, about your work with Lysenko and the Ukrainian People's Opera. You led the music scene. So I was wondering whether you recall ever meeting a celebrated revolutionary officer who went by the name of Khan Tibyetsky. During the 1920s he frequented Kharkov's brightest and most artistic. He might alternatively have used the name —"

Larisa interrupted him. "I met everybody who was anybody, back then."

Yes, and Redundant Lives *is the title of the memoir she wrote in 1915, so scandalous that only the French would publish it. After the Revolution she must have eaten humble pie to be forgiven for it, and all that remains is this parlour crawling with souvenirs. I don't see my father's portraits, but if I know her type, she has a shrine to him somewhere in this house.*

"*Khan*, you said?" Seated like a barbarian queen among her trophies, she visibly searched her memory. "Khan Tibyetsky... Khan Tibyetsky. Khan! My red-headed sybarite!" Pulling another cushion from behind her back, she tossed it without looking, knocked a metal ewer from a fragile stand and sent both clattering on to the floor. In the time it took Bora to retrieve the ewer and return the stand to its feet, an alarmed Nyusha showed up from the garden, asking if *gospozha* Larisa needed anything.

"No, dear, thank you. I don't need anything." Larisa waved the girl away. To Bora, she added, "Nyusha lost her husband in the war. She is devoted to me, takes care of things. I will leave her all I have, even though she's a peasant, a peasant through and through. Poor dove, droplet of my heart's blood, she won't know what to do with what I leave her. But to *you* I'll give nothing; not even things that belonged to your father, if that's what you came for."

"I'm not here for that reason, Larisa Vasilievna."

"We'll see. Well, you asked about Khan Tibyetsky. Why; what about him? He lived large. It felt delicious after the difficult years of the civil war and the months following Frunzik's death to have champagne and butter. There were buckets of butter in the pantry, back then."

In the sultriness of the cluttered parlour, Bora stood stock-still, conveying an image of comfort that did not remotely correspond to the way he felt. The concept he had of his father – formal, free of affection – was bruised by the sight of slovenliness mixed with remnants of vanity. *Where I stand, in the uniform in which I stand, I am empowered to do as I will. I could order this house to be torched with her inside it. I could. I live in a world where a son can with impunity destroy his father's lover.* But when she charged him, "Why do you want to know? Why are you asking me these questions? You Boras always have an ulterior motive," instead of anger he felt a near excess of pity.

"Esteemed Larisa Vasilievna, *gospozha*, I will bring you all the butter I can find if you talk to me about Khan Tibyetsky."

"And sugar."

"And sugar."

Aware as she must be that he wouldn't sit down until invited, Larisa let him stand. "It was in Makhno's days, when his Black Army stole from rich estates, convents, barracks, farms. I know: I used to spend time in Kharkov even before the Revolution bought me a town house on Kusnetschnaya Street. Kulaks and other landowners entrusted valuables to their former servants, but Makhno hunted for and found the stuff in their huts. Makhno was like a sieve winnowing grain. The good things remained in the sieve. Only the chaff was scattered."

"But that's Makhno, not Tibyetsky."

"Well, what do you know about Tibyetsky's business? He took

over where Makhno left off. We made merry when he came. We had buckets of butter and buckets of champagne."

"I don't understand, Larisa Vasilievna: he *took over* how?"

"The valuables, funds for the Revolution. It all flowed through Kharkov, the year Frunzik died."

1925. Yes. Tarasov had told him how throughout the 1920s Khan had often visited the Komintern tractor factory in Kharkov, but perhaps that was not his sole interest in the region.

"When you made merry, *gospozha*, was there a man called Platonov, too?"

The lacy hand indicated for him to sit, and Bora pulled out the piano stool to do so.

"Ih! Gleb Platonov: how long since I have heard that name. 'Honest Platonov', 'Platonov the Righteous'. Gleb the Contrary, I called him. Scarcely smiled, scarcely drank: a tedious comrade if ever there was one. You see, I have an excellent ear and an excellent memory, Martyn Friderikovich. Now, Platonov acted soberly, but I saw through him. He was like you Boras: ambitious, single-minded. It wasn't wealth with him, it was success. He knew exactly how to secure it. My good-natured Khan was afraid of him."

Hard to imagine Tibyetsky in fear. "Physically afraid?"

"I don't know that! He was afraid, that's all. Platonov knew things. He kept secrets."

And how, Bora thought. "What sort of secrets, *gospozha*?"

"They wouldn't be secrets if I knew. If I knew, it'd mean he didn't know how to keep secrets. Secrets about Tibyetsky. Secrets about Frunze, even."

"Khan was not Russian-born: could his past be one of the secrets?"

Where her armchair was, the corner of a frayed carpet drew a triangle on the wooden floor. She tapped her feet where rug and parquet met, a drumming of swollen toes. "Are you familiar with the Russian saying, 'What's good for a Russian kills the foreigner'? Do you know what *shirokaya natura* means? We have *superabundance of spirit,* Martyn Friderikovich. The way Khan lived in Kharkov tells me he was more Russian than I am, born in Moscow and raised by a father of the ninth administrative rank, an art collector who could honour a million roubles' debt and outdrink a Cossack."

"Please tell me more about Platonov."

"Boring subject. Platonov made his career, surpassed Khan, stepped on Khan. And Khan had to keep on his good side. Khan's legwork helped Platonov become a member of the Revolutionary Military Council. Of the two, saint and sinner, I'd take the sinner any day."

It was what he'd heard from Tarasov, more or less in the same words. Bora smoothed a crease of the piano shawl near Frunze's photograph. "But the 'secrets': could there have been goods involved? Property requisitioned during the Revolution, perhaps by Makhno, snatched from him and stashed away? Have you ever heard of a place called Krasny Yar?"

"No. I've never heard of the place. It must be a very small place if I've never heard of it. During those years Khan and Platonov argued like street dogs, but they never mentioned Krasny Yar."

"You saw them arguing, *gospozha?* And why would a man with an ego like Khan Tibyetsky's allow a seemingly less brilliant colleague to get ahead? Was it really, as you say, that Platonov knew secrets about him?"

"What else? Once when they had a fracas in my town house, he called Khan a 'thief's thief', and only by throwing myself between them was I able to keep them from killing each other. They made up, as they always did. Khan was like embers under ash, though. After that time they never visited together any more."

"And did one or the other, as far as you remember…"

Larisa sank in her armchair, nodding. "I remember everything, provided I want to. But not now. Now I'm tired. It tires me to look at you, you're a Bora: five *pud* of manly arrogance.

I know your blood. Go. Come back when you have plenty of butter. Sugar, too."

She might be pretending; or not. It was unlikely that he'd get anything else out of her in either case. Bora watched her sit looking elsewhere (or nowhere) in the room, disregarding him, an old person's technique for dismissing the young. He left the parlour and the house, and the overgrown garden, not feeling wholly himself until he reached his army vehicle and sat behind the wheel. It relieved him to see the nick on the windshield frame: a testimony that it was still the same day, and the same life, in which he'd been shot at near the Diptany crossroads.

Tuesday 18 May, Merefa.

Good thing I remembered "The Bells of Novgorod", "Tristan chord" and all. As a composer, my natural father had a predilection for the pentatonic scale and chromaticism. Weiss told me he had nothing more to teach me when I mastered that piece. I doubt it was true. But we were in 1934, and there was a new obligation for Leipzig residents to exhibit their racial papers. I'd just graduated with high honours from cavalry school at Hanover, and was about to enter the Dresden Army Infantry School. I was hardly home any more, whether or not I'd received enough piano lessons from a Jew.

As for *La Malinovskaya*, what did I expect? What was my impression? I believe it was Seneca who said, *Nullum magnum ingenium sine mixtura dementiae*, pointing to a link between genius and madness. Although we didn't mention her much at home for obvious reasons, I was always curious about her life and career. Her art connoisseur father might have honoured his huge debt, as she says; but, gambler that he was, he shot himself in a Marienbad casino a few years later. This detail she passed over in silence, while blaming "those two upstart merchants Ostruchov and Tetryakov" for his downfall (as if I should know them; I didn't ask, to avoid going off on another wild goose chase). Larisa's offstage rows with Odessite Maria Kuznetsova, also very beautiful, made the headlines. Not to speak of her (reciprocated) jealousy of Salomea Kruszelnicka (if I am spelling her name right), at least until Salomea had to flee abroad for political reasons some 40 years ago. 1925 must have been a difficult time for Larisa, because, as well as Frunze, she also lost her young friend Jurjevskaya to a spectacular drowning suicide in a Swiss mountain stream. But much as she pined after faithless Friedrich von Bora and Mikhail Frunze, Larisa never even considered doing away with herself. Of course it would have been a loss to world music, as her remarkable coloratura was and is rare in large voices. In her generation, only Felia Litvinne comes to mind.

She has added a possibly significant square to the Tibyetsky puzzle thus far: namely that the open quarrelling between Khan and Platonov was about theft, or that stick-in-the-mud Platonov's idea of theft. It begs the question as to whether Khan's luxurious living in Kharkov (Larisa called him a sybarite!) was wholly derived from the Party's gratitude to a hero, or had other sources as well (his audacious business deals with foreigners, for example). The expression she used, "a thief's thief", points to an appropriation of goods from someone who owned them illegally or unjustly in the first place. Makhno? The landed gentry themselves? I mean to go back to Pomorki as soon as possible and wheedle out of her all she remembers about those days. She's right as far as I am concerned: I did visit her with an ulterior motive.

Note: not far from her house, on the grounds of the Biological Institute, totally abandoned, there are shafts leading to underground gas pipes. As I saw when I briefly stopped there on my way back – curiosity being my second name – I noticed that except for one, their iron lids are bolted shut. Rightly so, because otherwise they'd make a perfect hideout for undesirables. If the lidless one is a typical example, they're 7 or 8 metres deep!

Another note: upon my return to the schoolhouse, Kostya was as moody as one like Kostya can be moody, surely on account of my burning Tarasov's place. Well, what do these Russians want? Can't they appreciate that one is sparing them worse trouble? Peasants through and through; Larisa was right.

8

WEDNESDAY 19 MAY, KALEKINA FARM,
NEAR KRASNY YAR

At the edge of the woods, the red-stemmed dogwood they called *deren* in Ukraine was in full bloom. Pollen from other plants, shaken by the wind, fell across the sunbeams where the trees grew sparsely, although in other spots the shade was deep and blue-green. Along the dirt lane white poplars shed their down. It was like a snowstorm in places, bits of white fluff becoming caught in the unripe ears of wheat until the fields were covered with a layer that made their bristling, tender green look cottony. Bora and Nagel arrived on horseback. They stopped by the desolate farm marked on their maps as Kalekina; long collectivized under the name "Friendship of Peoples", it was nothing now but a set of ramshackle buildings where hollyhock grew rank to the height of a man, and the fences had been burnt as firewood. The wheat meagrely sown before the last battle for Kharkov might not ripen before the next battle took place.

Nagel looked at the shabbiness of the farm. "They have the woods less than half a kilometre away," he observed, "and they've pulled up pickets and gates. They *are* afraid of going into the Yar."

"Can't blame them, Nagel. They are afraid of that, and of us, and of everything else at this time. You've seen the women by the old man's grave; they bowed deeply to us as they would have done when the tsar or landowner went by."

The women at the grave were the ones who'd sent the Germans to the Kalekina farm. According to them, the beheaded corpse belonged to old man Kalekin, who had two adolescent grandsons and had ventured into Krasny Yar "only because of the boys, because the boys were the first to go missing during the spring thaw". Missing where? In the Yar, of course. After his death, two sisters whose husbands had died at the front moved into the Kalekina farmhouse. The siblings were thought to know other details that Bora and Nagel were seeking before entering the woods.

Bora was never formal or predictable on these occasions, and that's why he wanted Nagel with him, who knew him best and went along with him whatever the errand. He approached the main house from the side, where a small four-paned window, blue with the reflection of the sky from afar, turned darker and more transparent as he drew near. Bora discreetly rapped on the glass with his knuckles, in part because he didn't want to alarm those inside (although Nagel kept a sub-machine gun at the ready), and in part because the fragile bubble-specked pane, beyond which shadows were perceivable in the glare from another small window opposite, divided the everyday world from a realm inside. Reflections and transitory images: if Bora moved his head slightly he could see the sergeant standing watch behind him; if he only tilted it, the interior of the house came into view with the liquid semi-darkness of a water tank. Enchantresses, witches, fairy women were as likely to live inside the Kalekina farm as peasant girls whose men had gone to die. It wasn't Larisa Malinovskaya Bora was reminded of – she was mundane even in her solitude – but Remedios in Spain, whom he'd physically loved like no other (*Martin-Heinz Bora… died and went to heaven,* he'd written in his diary after meeting her for the first time), and whose essence he wondered about to this day. She was to him what she wasn't to other men; other men saw her and tasted her in wholly different ways. What she'd given him she'd given no one else. Circe, Calypso, Melusina: she'd been the sorceress who is far from everyone and to whom men must go begging, or come stumbling to from foreign lands.

He rapped three times on the pane, a magic number, and the shadows within gave something like a shiver, less than a motion. A woman's face floated within two steps of the window, looking out. Plain as it was to both of them that he could have smashed the window instead or barged in unbidden, she made a small gesture of her left hand that invited him to come around the corner and reach the doorstep.

They looked to be in their late thirties, homely and clean, so fair that the blonde hairline showing from under the white kerchiefs on their heads seemed white. One was tall and stocky, smelling of cheap drink, the other minute; both had eyes of that peculiar blue-grey, dark to the extent of simulating blackness. When Bora told them what he was here to do – find out details about those who hadn't died, necessarily, but had gone missing in the Yar – they both looked suddenly grief-stricken, as if wilting under his question. He realized the boys lost were their own before they told him, and was briefly angry at the others, those by the grave, who hadn't informed him of this. But the sisters did not weep. *They're like springs that have given all the water there was to give*, he thought, *and I stand here digging for wetness.* He chose not to step indoors, speaking to them in full view by the threshold. Once he made it clear that he and his man hadn't come looking for labourers or recruits (in case the boys had been found and were presently in hiding), they told him the story.

For perhaps half an hour the three of them spoke, in a storm of fluff raining from the poplars. The seed-bearing tufts, blinding in the warm sun, wafted and became caught on every surface, vertical or flat. They reminded Bora of the cinders hovering, impalpable, around the steel of Khan's T-34: lightness over difficulty and peril, as now. Mankind complicates everything, and nature literally makes light of it, with twirling ashes and hairy seeds. Nagel kept watch and Bora tactfully questioned the women, nodding at their words, until the stocky one withdrew and he conversed with the small sister alone.

Kalekin had been their father-in-law. Their sons, aged thirteen and fourteen respectively, had never come back from a trip to the Udy River, on the other side of Krasny Yar. The old man had taken it even harder than the mothers; once his own sons had fallen at the front, the grandsons had become a reason for living: he doted on them, spoilt them all he could under the circumstances. They'd gone fishing in the Udy, and never come back. The Russian army was quartered at Papskaya Ternovka then, so Kalekin had trekked to enquire of their commander if by chance the boys had been recruited or hurt by a mine. The officer, who was a good fellow and also a local, told the old man the boys hadn't been seen. Yes, they might have strayed into the woods; however, the comrades didn't have time now to go looking for them – he could readily understand this, couldn't he? Kalekin said he could, but it wasn't true. He became ill with the loss, obsessed with searching for his grandsons despite the battles that were being fought everywhere around him, until he'd left the farm early on 1 May for the woods, and had died there.

"But there's no proof your boys went into the Yar," Bora objected, "much less that they were killed." He showed the wooden button he still carried in his pocket. "Was this your father-in-law's?"

How could he have known? The small sister was staggered; she covered her mouth, glancing back as if to make sure her sibling was out of earshot. "It comes from my nephew's coat, the coat that used to belong to his father. Where did you find it, *poshany* Major?"

Bora felt an inner chill, and wouldn't say. He modified the statement he'd been about to make to "There's no proof he was killed" because it seemed obvious that at least one of the boys had ended up in the woods, and also possible that his grandfather had been killed just after he'd found the clue.

"Don't frighten your sister for now. Stay away from the Yar, both of you, and tell me what else you know about it."

The rest was whispered to him away from the house, where the farm woman stood to avoid being overheard by her sister, and where, of his own accord, Bora righted a spindly gate, fallen in from the last gaping, rickety fence.

He learnt that in Makhno's days the older sister, twelve at the time, had been taken from her parents' farm at Sharkov, brought to Krasny Yar and raped, which was why she also had another child, a daughter twenty-two years of age, now an army nurse. "Father went looking for her, and Makhno's men shot him. My sister won't talk of those days, *poshany* Major, not even to us. She's so scared of the dark even now, you have to keep the candle burning at night." (*Or else she gets drunk to be able to fall asleep,* Bora told himself.) "She won't go near the woods, be sure of that, not even for her son. When the priest from Losukovka came a few days ago and walked with his procession around the Yar, she wouldn't look out of the window."

"In the years after that war, did you live here?"

She shook her head. "We moved. Our husbands worked at the warehouse in Smijeff. We came back to our father-in-law's when we were widowed, but were in Sharkov when he died."

Afterwards, summarizing things to the sergeant, Bora wondered out loud, "About the kidnapping: what can the dark have to do with it? The Yar is anything but a dark forest, even at its thickest. Was the girl raped overnight? Night is dark everywhere."

"They might have thrown a cloth over her head, or kept her hooded the time she was with Makhno's men. How did she escape, Herr Major?"

"The younger sister was quite small at the time, and doesn't remember. She is aware the Bolsheviks replaced the Black Army, but can't tell for sure whether it was they who freed the girl or if she had picked her way out of the woods. On the other hand, both women were familiar with a boy who went missing at that time. He was found hanging from a tree at the edge of the woods, stripped naked."

Nagel glanced at the house, at the woods, and back at the house. "It's all very strange, Herr Major. Looks as if discouraging folks from going into the Yar is the main idea. But there are towns and collective farms that could have organized expeditions through the years, not to speak of the government or the Red Army. They could have resolved the matter had they wanted to. Or were the woods declared off limits for whatever reason?"

"That's what I think. But if they were, it wasn't done officially. Which is why I wanted you here today: I have no clearance to do so, but I'm going to take another look before we go in with the regiment."

With the privilege of a senior non-com, Nagel shook his head. "Well, sir, I'm not about to wait out here. We've been through worse things than a patch of Russian woods, the Major and I. And if the women can keep an eye on our mounts, I'm ready when the Major is."

Considering the irregularity of the errand, it was a mark of Nagel's regard for him. And Bora, usually so spare with effusions, went as far as allowing himself a friendly tap on the sergeant's shoulder. "Let's go, then."

Entering Krasny Yar from the once well-kept "Friendship of the Peoples" confines, he understood at once how the accumulation of leaves over the seasons concealed the irregularity of the terrain throughout the woods. Days after the rain the low-lying areas were still wet if not soggy, while others, rock-strewn, stayed scrubby and dry. Overgrown fruit trees, long returned to the wild, had survived their extinct farmsteads (the place had been settled in the late 1700s, and kept as pasture then), while elsewhere one stumbled upon rotten planks and stumps that had once sustained sheds or lean-tos, beyond living memory. No trace of man-made paths remained. Still, the dismantled structures pointed to a possible reason for the locals to come foraging here during the Great War, and later in the years of the Famine: scrap wood to burn or reuse, small apples, berries, mushrooms. The Russian peasant's ability to live off the barest essentials made even the Yar a promising – if scary – place to come beggaring through. After all, not all those who'd strayed into Krasny Yar had died, despite Father Victor's dreams and tales of wild creatures and ghosts.

Ahead, the thin, trilling chatter of small birds drew festoons of sound from tree to tree, as green as their striped livery; deeper in, woodpeckers' calls sounded like people whistling insistently for their dogs. The Germans proceeded in view of each other, cutting through the Yar at a ninety-degree angle from Bora's first visit, when he'd met Father Victor. Although their compasses functioned for the time being, both snapped branches or blazed young trees with pocket knives to mark their trail. Seeking to pick up signs of human presence, they followed a north-north-west direction, towards the blasted tree where those of the 241st had recovered Kalekin's remains. Muddy spots were checked for footprints; heaped leaves for signs of discomposure.

Absence of recognizable tracks meant nothing per se in Russian forests: those who did frequent them knew how to mask their passage. Russian partisans hid well, not to mention the small *razvedchiki* units, no doubt making forays on this side of the Donets as much as their counterparts, German scouts, did on the other side. Depending on their cleverness and training, partisans were either less or more accurate at erasing their traces than Red Army soldiers.

The blasted tree, the dark line of firs were still distant. Birches and nut-bearing trees, nameless shrubs alternated all around. A boundary legible on Bora's map and notes, and marked on the ground only by a shallow, narrow gully that fallen leaves concealed, marked the German minefield some three hundred paces to the men's right. Depending on Manstein's plans, it would either be cleared next month or added to.

Approaching as he did today, but not so much from the

direction he'd come from the first time, Bora could see how the ridge where lightning had struck the tree and Kalekin had been found was in fact circumscribed. Skirting it gave the impression of a rise or mound with a ditch on three sides rather than what in Russia was usually called – depending on its dimensions – a *yar*, *balka*, or *ovrag*. Today, the shape reminded Bora of ancient or medieval earthworks. Even the Great War trenches he and his brother had explored as vacationing boys in the woods of East Prussia had more in common with this kind of trough than a natural rift in the land did.

He gestured for Nagel to pause, and snapped photographs of the rise and of the hollow over which the blasted tree reclined bridge-wise. This, too, was interesting upon closer examination. Bora crouched to see if it was merely a cleft gaping at the foot of the large stump or if there was more to it. He got down on his hands and knees, moving aside creepers and brush. It seemed to be no more than a dip in the land, crowded with dead leaves, overarched by long-branched thorn bushes. But if he parted the tangle (a horseman's gloves came in handy) a burrow was revealed, yawning in the flank of the rise. Larger than a fox hole but not by much, choked by brambles, it measured maybe forty centimetres top to bottom, and little more from side to side.

Again Bora signalled, this time for Nagel to stand watch while he continued to explore. Nagel, who had a penchant for worrying about him, didn't seem enthusiastic, but obeyed.

Shining an electric torch inside the hole revealed nothing but clumped soil and a jumble of hairy roots. From the pasted-down texture of the dirt ledge, it appeared as if the animal it must be a home to had recently squeezed through. Entering was out of the question for a man of Bora's size. He was about to resign himself to lying on his belly and peering as far as he could crane his neck, when on a whim he decided to strip the thorn branches where they hung thickest, to the left of the small opening. A not so cramped gap came into view then, sufficient – with some effort – to allow the passage of someone who did not suffer from claustrophobia. Bora put his head in, then his arm holding the electric torch, and squeezed himself forward enough to illuminate the dark space. By that very motion, the woods above, Nagel, the world at large became instantly far away and foreign. It was irresistible. Bora pulled himself back and changed direction so as to put his booted legs in first, and sank out of sight.

Open German army food cans were the first objects he recognized on the ground, then a razor case, unstitched, of the type Soviet soldiers carried, a half-rotted wooden box or lidless crate against the dirt wall, with nothing inside. Bora couldn't stand up in the small space, maybe a metre and a half in height and twice that much across, partly timbered. A cave-in of soil and planks as the vault had given way, towards the centre of the rise, further reduced the available room. At his feet, in the dark wet dirt, Bora glimpsed the bowl of a hand-carved spoon, typical of the resourceful Russian infantryman. The break on the shaft was new, sharp. A soggy tatter turned out to be a triangular canvas bag resembling a holster, its upper loop and lower buckle gone, which he identified as a Red Army axe cover. The round tin with something inside that had been scooped out like food contained in fact German boot grease. He recalled the soldiers of the 241st telling him about pieces of equipment and material disappearing around Krasny Yar.

He regretted not having a flash on his Kodak camera. With his foot he turned over the tins to shine a light on the impressed dates, double-checked the dilapidated wooden box for markings, and pried as far as he could into the timber-and-dirt collapse. Once he had finished, he had to admit that, as for many enterprises, it was easier getting in than out. There was nothing to grab on to to clamber out into the open; dirt crumbled and fell in chunks. When Bora did squeeze through at last, the greenness outside and Nagel's sturdy figure a few steps away welcomed him back into a dangerous but less oppressive world.

"They used it recently, Nagel, although the hole has been there a long time. The wooden box – an ammunition crate, I think – goes back to the Great War at least. It makes you wonder whether the older sister was kept in a similar hideout twenty years ago. It's dark enough, even in daytime." He described the shelter, listing the objects inside. "All our army tins bear the 1942 date, so they might be the pilfered items the 241st Company men told me about. What do you make of it?"

Nagel wore a habitual frown. One had to know his careworn face as well as Bora had learnt to in order to recognize a lack of real concern on it. "There's not many of them at any rate, Herr Major – five at most, from what you said. Either that, or they have other such holes in the woods. They tried to eat boot grease? Could be untrained irregulars, or civilians hiding for whatever reason. It could be runaway Jews."

Neither of them spoke the word *deserters*. Neither of them mentioned to what excesses sieges and starvation had brought German and Russian soldiers in the past two years. Nagel skirted the subject. "If it happens to be anyone left over from the civil war, he'd be in his forties, minimum, and pretty out of his mind by now."

"Just the right combination to get you to hack up or dismember your victims."

"Or eat them, Herr Major. On this front we've seen that, too."

There, Nagel had said it. "Christ, let's hope not." Irregulars, civilians, deserters. Jews. Hadn't the Security Service been on the lookout for *Dorfjuden*? Bora formulated the thought and found it highly unpleasant. *Would desperate rural Jews in hiding eat tinned pork meat? Probably. Would they steal it in the first place? If they don't read German, yes. And why wouldn't they kill?* "Jews would go out of their way to avoid being discovered," he reasoned.

"Yes, sir. Although as long as German soldiers aren't harmed, it's not automatic that we'd intervene. We haven't thus far."

Together they climbed the rise and looked around as far as the curtain of trees allowed. The wind, still blowing over the woods, mimicked the fresh sound of running water. Bora pointed out where he'd found the wooden button, and the spot where the soldiers had retrieved Kalekin's corpse. "I wonder what they did with the old fellow's head," he grumbled. "The truth is, we could be facing the same individual – or individuals – who have holed up here and committed murder for the past twenty-odd years, or else entirely different people who have found shelter in the Yar ever since. It could be someone who only occasionally frequents the woods. As you say, Nagel, if there's any pattern, the aim seems to be to keep folks away. What for? What are they guarding?"

"Maybe just their own hides, Herr Major."

"Right."

In a zigzag they kept heading north, careful to note any evidence on the forest floor that might reveal sinkholes, caves, trenches. From the quadrant where the woods became thicker as they followed an imperceptible slope, gradually extending to the Udy River and its mined banks, Bora had the impression for a moment of smelling an open fire somewhere. Abstinence from cigarettes ever since the start of Barbarossa had granted him a keen sense of smell, useful in the field although a definite disadvantage in unclean quarters (not to mention the horrific stench of death at Stalingrad, the memory of which sickened him to this day). Depending on the direction of the wind over the Yar, ragging the heads of the higher trees and making the sombre edge of firs boom like a sea cliff, the odour of smoke could come from one of the farms toward Krasnaya Polyana or Schubino, or even from across the Donets, as on the day Khan had arrived and cinders of the grass fire he'd himself set had fallen all around like snow.

Bora recalled the woods on the enemy bank, where the half-blind old woman had mistaken him for a Russian recruit, and how he'd thought then she resembled the deadly hag of the fairy tale, Baba Yaga. Khan compared himself to the witch, flying in her magical iron mortar and rowing with a broom that sweeps the air behind it. But no Baba Yaga, no *koldun*, ghosts or goblins made fires. Nagel signalled that he smelt it too. The odour of burning wood on a warm day might not necessarily indicate a man-made fire, either, much less a hearth. On the rocky outcrops dry brush could go up in smoke by itself.

Now and then one or the other looked quickly in the direction of where sounds like small animals scuttling about crinkled the air. Nothing was ever seen. Were there partisans lying in wait, watching them, their invisibility would be the same: the unforgiving, seldom-failing crack of SVT rifles would have long ago made all the difference. Or it might soon. Bora regretted allowing Nagel to come along. *The risk is mine; why involve a family man in all this?* As for himself, he felt remarkably at peace. *If they shoot me now, my spirit will fly at once out of here, back to Merefa and into my trunk and inside the envelope where Dikta's naked photo is. If there's a heaven, that's heaven. In a sealed envelope with my wife, because what I desire most is to put my hand between her legs as I did in Prague – just my hand, so my fingers may nudge the breath-thin silk away from the tender well of her flesh.* It surprised him how sober and lucid he could remain while thinking about it, aware of the smallest detail around him and yet just as authentically in the Prague room where they'd wantonly touched and savoured each other half the night before making love for the long other half. At one point the scent of woodbine wafted overwhelmingly to him from a cluster of dead trees, and Bora breathed it in to the bottom of his lungs (you never know which scent is the last you're going to inhale); the questioning call of a *cuckooshka* from its perch, so much like a mechanical bird's in a German clock, sounded to his ears familiar and unnerving at the same time.

Nagel's figure came and went behind the trees as he kept to Bora's right. It felt lonely in spite of him. *He and I could get lost and not know it for a while,* Bora thought. *I could already be dead and not know it. If God loved me, I'd have died in Prague, when Dikta sat astride my knees, facing me, letting me search her with my hand, kissing me. But here I am.* Inside the compass, which had functioned well until now, the needle had begun to tremble and become aimless. Bora pointed to the small round case on his palm, and the sergeant, who was looking his way, nodded to show he'd noticed the same.

On they went, orienting themselves exclusively by landmarks. A negligible ditch indicated on maps as Orekhovy became important, with its namesake, a growth of walnut trees, alongside it. For the compass, north was everywhere and nowhere, but the nut-tree ditch stayed still. The land dipped and rose; uncharted lesser mounds were perceivable. Bora marked them on his map without stopping to explore them now. At one point they had to cross the ditch to continue, and it was a threshold. The mid-morning hour and its warmth took on a new garb, a new face: the wind fell; a stillness was created where birds turned silent first around the men, and then, like a widening circle in a pond, the singing ceased further and further away from them, until the entire woodland became soundless.

"Herr Major," Nagel said, and nothing else.

A storm of flies raged noiselessly ahead, where a small clearing outlined a patch of green light. Steady-hearted as he judged himself to be, Bora felt a rise of anxiety, a kind of superstitious repugnance at going further. *But I'll go, I'll go. Whatever it is, I'll register it on camera, too. It could be anything from a creature that died a natural death to an animal sacrifice that dingbat priest has carried out, if he dared come this deep into the Yar.* As if he didn't know what it most likely was.

On his part, Nagel fully anticipated matters, because he halted after calling Bora's attention to the flies. Bora kept walking.

That it was a putrefying human head impaled on a stake he realized when he was still six or seven steps away from it, more than close enough to judge it had belonged to old Kalekin. Something fearfully primitive, belonging to a medieval Dance of Death: drawing nearer would be an exercise in morbidity. Bora did it only to look for evidence around the grim trophy.

What Bruno Lattmann had said, *How will we go back to our families after this,* held true. Bora covered his nose and mouth. Embracing his mother, lying with his wife after this, after everything, give or take, that had happened in the last four years! *It's not just what we've done or was done to us, but what we've seen others do, what we haven't been able to keep our eyes away from.* He held back his nausea, but barely. Bitter saliva came up and had to be spat out while he photographed the shreds of flesh, the chunks of hair on the pitiful remains. *That's what the axe was for, whose soggy cover I saw in the underground shelter.* He turned away so as not to smell or see more than he had, and marked with an X the approximate spot on his map. To Nagel, who'd drawn closer and was frowning hard, he said, "It's been there nearly three weeks. No point in removing it, or making the daughters-in-law see *that*."

Nagel, who never spoke unless it was necessary, hinted a nod that fell short of an assent. They were now two-thirds of the way to the bends of the Udy, where the boys had got lost. False rivers and oxbows that had turned into sickle-shaped ponds hugged the rim of the wood on that side. No more than a hundred paces further, water seeped and surfaced in places, and beyond – but not much – according to Bora's notes the Russian minefield formed a wide belt. The Red Army had laid it during their withdrawal in March, so it was as likely as not that the children had blown themselves up with anti-personnel charges, if they hadn't been killed before.

Still looking for tracks, Bora and Nagel halted at the edge of the minefield, turned away from the sloping ground. As long as their compasses remained unreliable, they retraced their steps following the blazed trunks and the walnut growth along the ditch. As soon as the instruments agreed on where north was, they allowed themselves to deviate a hundred or so metres from the way they'd come in, covering new ground. Tension kept them spasmodically alert, although neither one of them showed more than a soldier's watchfulness. Birches past blooming and new grass, overgrown stumps, moss: none showed the presence – much less the frequentation – of man. Yet someone had killed and beheaded old Kalekin; someone had made a warning or an altar of his severed skull.

Bora kept a close-mouthed sullenness. Attentive as he seemed to be, his thoughts were straying like restless dogs. *I hope the Mahdi embalmed my great-grandfather's head, and that it was a tidy, bony bundle his wife claimed and took away in her little Victorian trunk. Why is it that a severed limb, a gory shred is more frightful than a whole corpse? Losing a limb must be doubly awful, because a piece of the man is buried in advance of the man, or left rotting on the ground.* To his right, where the uneven forest floor made him suspect the existence of earthworks similar to the one he'd investigated but smaller in size, he paused to look for holes and passageways. A grove of blooming *deren* not far away matched the place on his map where he'd pencilled a check and added in the margin, *Here according to the priest the girl was found with her throat cut a year ago. She was deaf mute, a refugee living near Schubino at the time.*

Finally, at the foot of a sprawling bush, the sergeant pointed out human waste, a fly-ridden handful studded with undigested berries and small feathers, as if the diet included raw bird meat and small fruit gobbled whole. Poking it with a stick he'd broken off the shrub, he seemed overly thoughtful. "It does make you think it could be a crackpot from the old days, Herr Major."

Bora kept from nodding, and from saying no. *Flies every-where,* he was thinking. *The men, the mounts resent them, biblical plague that they are. Skin food excrement wounds rubbish are to them all the same, all appetizing. Chasing them makes no difference: they're like a noxious thought you can wave off but not eliminate. Not even cleanliness keeps them away, just like virtue isn't enough to keep away evil thoughts. I can see why Satan is called Lord of the Flies. This is, and always was, war. We are, in the year of Our Lord 1943, like our counterparts in the year 1943 before Christ was born, in Sumer or Egypt, chasing flies and killing lice.*

"What do you think, Herr Major?"

"Nothing worthwhile. Let's get out."

They had returned within sight of the sombre fir line (the wind bellowed in that direction, still raging over the woods) and were negotiating a rough escarpment when the sergeant tripped on a root and lost his balance.

"Everything all right, Nagel?" Bora called out.

"Everything all right, sir." In a half-crouch among the leaves he'd discomposed by stumbling and steadying himself, Nagel searched around with his hand. "Wait. I thought I saw something: a shoe or a belt or something."

Bora joined him. He stood keeping an eye on the surroundings while Nagel combed the bed of leaves with a pronged stick, back and forth until he picked up by its frayed strap a small broken sandal, hand-stitched. "I'm afraid the boys were done in too, Herr Major."

They emerged from Krasny Yar not far from where they'd entered it, at the edge of the "Friendship of Peoples" communal farm. The sun was high, and gusts of rabid breeze alternated with absolute calm. To Bora the tumbledown view of sheds and empty barns seemed novel, as though centuries had gone by since he'd turned his back to them to enter the woods. It had been two hours by his watch, but he wondered if at times watches lie.

Nagel, experienced soldier that he was, walked casually with the sub-machine gun always at the ready. "Did you smell a fire in the woods, Herr Major? There was definitely an odour of smoke drifting through the woods."

"I smelt it. God willing, we'll go back in with the regiment as soon we are fully mounted."

They went to untie their mounts, Frohsinn and Totila, grazing on dandelions behind the old Kalekina homestead. As they did, the farm women anxiously peered out through a crack in the door. Nagel glanced at Bora, wondering whether he'd say anything about the small sandal or the old man's head, but Bora was tight-lipped, looking elsewhere as he became smoothly, impeccably saddled.

* * *

Thursday 20 May, 5 a.m., Bespalovka.

The topographic map I have, 1:25,000 in scale, does not show Krasny Yar as featuring a ravine, despite its name. This I already observed. The legend does indicate the moderate height within it as *mogila*, which our cartographers translate as "hillock". It is the rise with the lightning-blasted tree on it and the hideout below ground. However, I'm wondering whether the correct term on the Russian map should be *kurgan*, and on ours "burial mound". It is true that, as far as I know, these ancient earthworks are more typical of southern Ukraine, but not exclusive to that area. In Stalingrad, the day after our division reached the city centre, other comrades fought tooth and nail to take Height 102.0, which according to the Russians was and is a large burial mound, Mamayev Kurgan.

Does it make a difference? It might. The "hollow" by the blasted tree the men of the 241st spoke of is in fact man-made. It could be the partly collapsed entrance to an inner chamber (the cave-in has been there a very long time), perhaps enlarged by those who God knows when entered it to steal. You'd need equipment to remove the fallen beams and earth, and a stronger torchlight than the one I took along to look into the jumble.

Burial mounds of the ancient steppe peoples are rumoured to contain precious objects, mostly gold. It could have been the reason behind Makhno's choice to set up his command at Krasny Yar. Chased out of there in 1920, he could have been forced to abandon the goods to the Bolsheviks. I don't want to go off at a tangent. Still, the presence of valuables – of any sort, important documents included – would justify Platonov and Khan's trips to the woods, together and separately (and at least on one occasion with an unidentified outsider). Were they hauling out things? Neither Tarasov nor Larisa mentioned that, and someone has definitely been guarding the Yar, discouraging access to it before and since. It could have been over the destination and use of those valuables that Khan and Platonov had argued. The Bolshevik revolution is full of such tales: witness the fable that Admiral Kolchak sank or lost Tsar Nicholas' tons of gold bullion in a Siberian lake!

Question (I'm back to it, with variations): whatever it is that attracted the generals to Krasny Yar, was it removed entirely or just in part? Did it play any role in Khan's death? I hypothesized a lone assassin, when in fact the tank commander's presence here as a defector could have alarmed those who knew about Krasny Yar. If only I'd let Platonov tell me what it was he wanted to offer!

As for the broken sandal Nagel found, it's either a woman's or a boy's, and looks as though it's been there longer than a couple of months. Be that as it may, Nagel deduces from it that the Kalekin boys were killed in the Yar. I'm starting to form a rather different idea.

Things are coming together slowly, although I could be completely off course. Being nothing but a self-made investigator, I tend to draw conclusions from very disparate clues by intuition rather than logic. Uncle Terry would have saved me lots of trouble if he'd only trusted me, left me a message and let me understand whom he feared on this side of the Donets.

I'm readying to leave Bespalovka. Before I return to Merefa I will stop at Borovoye to retrieve my vehicle, seek Bruno Lattmann's advice on something and see if he's got any more news for me; depending on what I learn from him, it's off to Kharkov then, and/or to Gebietskommissar Stark's to procure butter for my next errand.

20 MAY, 7.15 A.M., BOROVOYE

Bruno Lattmann's success in securing – among other things – a phone number at Odilo Mantau's new assignment (an unglamorous, inconvenient task with *Sonderkommando* 4a in the boonies due south of Kharkov) was a welcome surprise. Bora made the most of it at once, taking advantage of his colleague's spartan but well-equipped facilities.

Soon enough, Mantau's tone came grudgingly through the receiver. "I know it's you: I recognized your voice. What do you want, Major?"

"Only to be useful."

"I don't need your usefulness."

"Look, I have nothing to do with your transfer. I couldn't have had even if I'd wanted to."

"I don't feel like talking to you. And how did you find me here, anyway?"

It was sweltering in the hut, and Bora was grateful when Lattmann handed him a canteen.

"We're in the same line of business, Hauptsturmführer. And we could both use a solution to Khan's death. Give me a hand, I'll give you the whole arm."

A mumbled "Go to hell" did not discourage Bora, who held the line while counting to himself the seconds that would pass before Mantau asked for details.

"Give me the arm first, Bora."

"I can't do it without getting a hand from you – it's physiological. Are you there?"

"I'm here."

"I need to know whether you were present when Khan's blood pressure was taken after his tantrum, the evening before he died. You were: good. Did they come from the Sumskaya first-aid station? Yes? That's odd; at Sumskaya they deny it. Well, Hauptsturmführer, I don't know if they'll oblige you and go and get fucked, but they deny it. You suspected the Soviets sent a babushka; but what if they sent someone else? It seems someone is playing with our medics: I lost one over a prisoner's death; you might have been given one you didn't ask for. I'm looking for mine. Maybe you ought to be looking for yours. Do you have his name?"

"Not here. It's not like I took along the jail passes and other papers when I left Kharkov."

"In your place I'd make an effort to at least retrieve the man's name."

More grumbling, followed by "Contact me on Saturday. I might have the information."

Bora put down the receiver. "That jackass," he told Lattmann.

"There are more grey cells in his buffed fingernails than in his head. How did somebody so dense get a commission?"

His friend, who'd listened while chewing for a change on something edible, unsuccessfully offered Bora a handful of sunflower seeds. Before answering, he crossed the small floor space to turn the radio on. Tuning it in to a music station to increase their privacy, he said contemptuously, "For what the shithead has to do in his present job, all he needs is a lack of conscience."

"Well, monitored as these calls are likely to be, Mantau won't look too sharp even to his boss Theodor Christensen." Bora uncorked the canteen and avidly drank from it. The old song that came from the radio warbled *It happens only once / It will not come again...* "Speaking of conscience and lack thereof," he added, "if you're wondering about the little accountant who had a rendezvous with the firing squad, he beat me to it by dying first. I got there just as the local priest's mother was preparing him for burial."

"Good: it spared you a hard choice."

"But you understand I had to teach the village *some* lesson, so I ordered that his house be burnt down. And then I heard the hag had stolen a suitcase from the dead man as recompense for her Christian duty, so I requisitioned it. Nothing of interest inside, only old ledgers from Tarasov's days at the FED camera factory and Kharkov Factory No. 183: political commissar and accountant to the last. Say, Bruno, where can I find hens around here? I need a dozen chicks for my Russian orderly."

Lattmann choked on his sunflower seeds, laughing. "What are you setting up, a farmstead over at Merefa?"

"I could answer that we have to pretend we'll be here forever, but in fact I just want to be nice to the poor fellow. *Leibstandarte* shot his last batch."

The statement sobered Bora's colleague considerably. The radio went *It happens only once / It will not come again...* Taking back the canteen Bora handed him, he washed down the seeds with lukewarm water. "Dead chickens, a marksman's bullet on your windshield: Martin, we're down to gangster methods. Do you think it's wise to report to Dr Mayr what information you now have? After all, what I could pick up about him and the Sumskaya SS surgeon is fragmentary, the best I could do."

"I'll report at the hospital as soon as it's practical, and to the devil with the rest. They can't do worse than take potshots at me."

"No?"

"Not at this time."

It will not come again / It's too grand to be true sang Lilian Harvey. Lattmann turned the radio off. "Hope I don't have to tell Benedikta they were your famous last words. How did it go with Larisa?"

"She's a formidable old woman; I wouldn't be surprised if she had hexed my inconstant father so he'd die."

20 MAY, 11.49 A.M., MEREFA KOMBINAT

"It's a joke, right?" Geko Stark spoke sitting back in his chair, hands on its armrests, spectacles across his smooth forehead. "Throwing a party, or is it for a lady friend?"

"I simply need it, Herr Gebietskommissar."

"A kilo of butter?"

"Yes. I'm willing to give all these ration cards for it, pay in occupation money or Reichsmarks."

"You're serious, aren't you?" Behind Stark, the wall map of the *Reichskommissariat Ukraine*, conveniently without glass in its frame, showed an update. The addition of the Kharkov region with a dotted line had been coloured in pale orange, and the location of the *Kombinat* marked with a small paper flag. "Why, it *is* a woman!" he added with a mock frown. "I took you to be one of those married fellows who keep abstinence *in venere* while away from home. See, I do know some Latin! What will Standartenführer Schallenberg say?"

"Neither he nor my wife would have anything to say about it."

"It won't be easy – it's an inordinate amount. We have rules." Stark tapped his fingers on the armrests, pursing his lips. "She must be very special. Not a Russki, either. It's not allowed to give prized foodstuff to Russkis."

Bora took the ration cards back. "Never mind, Herr Gebietskommissar. I'll see to it some other way."

"There is no other way in this district. So, she's Russian to boot. Fascinating. Fascinating." From the upper floor, where one by one offices were being filled, there came frantic clicking and the ding of carriage bells, a duel between typewriters. "I suppose an exception *could* be made, since you're taking the Karabakh off my hands and out of the stew pot." He took out a sheet of letterhead and uncapped his fountain pen.

Bora's hopes were up. "She's older than my mother, if you must know."

Stark began to write, smirking. "And has ten children to feed?"

"She eats butter by the mouthful."

A pause in the writing gave way to a loud burst of laughter. Stark wheeled around in his swivel chair, guffawing with his back to the desk and to the annoyed visitor. He had to wipe the nib and start again on a fresh sheet to continue. "You horse fellows are priceless! Next time you hear from Standartenführer Schallenberg, magnify my generosity to him: he has Bormann's ear. Your ration cards stay here, along with one thousand *karbovanets*. And no fuel allowance for a month. Turn those ration cards in, as well."

It was exorbitant, but Bora did as he was told. *Thank God I have Bentivegni's special signed permit for extra fuel.*

"Keep in mind you cannot collect a kilo all in one place, Major. My power doesn't extend from army stores to divisional commands, which is where there's a small chance you might find that amount. It's up to you to figure out how."

After two disappointing stops at the same number of Kharkov army exchanges, Bora tried his luck with the 161st Division quartermaster, where a long negotiation obtained him the butter. Also, having refused to part with his Ray-Ban sunglasses, he had to swap his smart British-made cigarette lighter to obtain half a kilo of refined white sugar.

3 P.M., POMORKI

Since his last visit, pomegranate trees had blossomed in Larisa's overgrown garden. The scarlet buds were unmistakable against the enamelled greenness of their shiny leaves. Trees and fruit of the dead according to myth, notwithstanding their merry colour. Bora acknowledged Nyusha's greeting (*Another young widow – do I meet anyone but widows in this country?*) and gave her the box of food he'd brought, instructing her to take it at once to Larisa Vasilievna. He'd already put out of his mind that he'd paid the German currency equivalent of a labourer's monthly pay for it in *karbovanets.*

The room beyond the parlour, where he was received this time, was nothing short of a reliquary, a gleaming box where three walls were covered with icons: brightly coloured, gilded, encased in copper and silvery metal, studded with paste jewels, an icon corner – *beautiful corner*, the Russians called it – gone mad; Bora had seen Orthodox chapels with less than one tenth of the icons Larisa kept in her bedroom.

Reclining in a wicker chaise longue, she liberally rained sugar over the cardboard vat of butter. "You kept your word," she said. The sleeveless vest she wore was unmerciful on the loose flesh of her upper arms and neck. Bora did not stare, letting his eyes wander instead over the biblical carousel around her cumbersome person. Our Lady of Kazan, Our Lady of Oseryan, Our Lady of Vladimir – those Bora recognized. The three angels visiting Abraham, the Dormition of the Virgin, all the soldier–saints of the Eastern Church, George, Dmitri, Hadrian... down to the Archangel Michael. With an electric lamp on, or by candlelight, the gilding and silver-wash of their revetments must shoot reflections back and forth, a mute lightning storm.

On the fourth wall, over the bed, oil portraits and photographs of his own father formed an altar of their own. He'd imagined something of the sort; still, he was taken aback. Not even at Trakhenen, where his parents had made the house into a memorial to the defunct Friedrich von Bora, did one see such a proliferation of likenesses. The trimmed beard, the thoughtful dark eyes some Boras had got from the Salm-Nogendorf line (and presumably what had fascinated his seventeen-year-old mother, along with the conductor's world fame), stared back at him with the same elegant unconcern he might have exhibited looking at Moscow devotees in the luxury theatre boxes costing fifteen old roubles, or at the zealous waiters of the famed Strelnia restaurant.

Larisa drove a tablespoon into the fat, detaching ivory-coloured lumps which she brought to her mouth and took in whole. The gluttonous half-sucking, half-chewing motion was impossible to ignore. Standing at the edge of a threadbare *kilim*, Bora glanced her way and then had to look elsewhere. *Well, Friedrich*, he told himself, *thank God you're long dead, and see none of this. That ancient cow a former seductress? My father kissed her, lay with her for seven years. Like Homer's heroes, he was in her thrall. He'd have given a son by her the name he gave me.* Standing here mortified him, but he hadn't been asked to leave while she ate, and had come with work to do. *Please let her have enough for now; it sickens me to think of what she was, and what she is now.* Bora forgot about his fit, decent grandfather, his soberly elegant grandmother, his energetic stepfather. *If this is what it's like, I don't want to grow old.*

When he looked again, the spoon had carved a well in the butter. With her mouth full, the old woman stared at the glass top of her tea table with the fixed, unthinking gaze of a ruminant that savours her feed. Grease lined her lips, turning pink with the rouge she'd hastily layered on them upon his arrival. Only when she was satisfied with her snack did she dab her chin with a crumpled handkerchief. Other than that her teeth were still slick with fat when she smiled and invited him to sit across from her, she had regained a bearable – and even coquettish – appearance.

Bora saw there was only an ottoman available, or her bed, so he chose to remain standing.

"*Gospozha*, I do need the rest of the information I came for. As you see, I'm upfront about it."

Without answering him, Larisa ogled the butter. Fortunately she did not reach for it again. Bora risked losing his patience when she wagged a finger at him, reminiscing. "The voice of Felia Litvinne in the body of Ganna Walska. Talent *and* beauty. Do you know who said it of me?"

"No, Larisa Vasilievna, I do not."

"Khan Tibyetsky. It was the year after I lost Frunzik, whom I'd last seen in the spring of '24. After I lost Frunzik I wanted to die. Which is less than what happened when your father abandoned me: then, I wanted to do worse than dying – I wanted to die to the world and keep living as a nun. I would have, had the war and the revolution not distracted me. Khan came to visit on Frunzik's suggestion, and continued even after his mentor's death. We made merry, and though we were only friends, I loved every minute of his visits. I even put up with Gleb 'The Contrary' Platonov."

Bora was impressed. Bad eating habits aside, she recalled precisely when they'd left off. She spoke about 1926, five years after the events of the civil war in Ukraine. He had to listen to more supplementary details about vigorous guerrilla commanders entering bit by bit into the Soviet political system, building careers. Khan was constantly on the move while in the Kharkov area, Platonov kept his nose to the office grindstone…

Taras Tarasov had implied the same. Bora, too, continued with the question he'd left unanswered the first time. "And did one or the other bring along or travel with someone else, Larisa Vasilievna?"

She wet her forefinger with her tongue. Gathering grains of sugar fallen on the surface of the tea table, she crossed her swollen ankles and spread her toes. "If I gave a soiree where I sang or played the violin, Khan would bring engineers, businessmen, capitalists from Europe and America. I never saw someone so capable of making friends. Generous: he brought gifts. We'd drink until the men fell under the table. Khan became too good for words then. Ih, the stories he told, the yarns, the jokes… He talked too much. His guests listened. I wouldn't be surprised if some of them went right to Platonov and added fuel to the fire of their cockfight. In fact, it was Platonov who came one year with some of them – without Khan."

"Who were these men, do you know?"

She spoke with her finger in her mouth, staring at him. She'd been a dark beauty, with glittering, light blue eyes that now contrasted with the fleshiness and decay of her face. Madame Blavatsky came to mind, with her frog-like magnetic glance. "Foreign carpetbaggers, all of them. They didn't come for the music but for the caviar and drink. And the salmon *koulibiak*, which Khan had an army courier bring on horseback all the way from Tschuguyev. Men who represented – you name it: buyers interested in the FED camera factory, managers of the Economic Office you called *Wirtschaftskontor*, of the German–Russian Transport Partnership, of American mining concerns… I don't recall their names, none of which were good Russian names. And with Platonov the Sombre, Platonov the Honest, the Contrary, there wasn't even drink, much less *koulibiak* or caviar. I see you're married, Martyn Friderikovich. Are you a faithful husband?"

"Why, yes."

"You shouldn't tell her if you're not."

"But I am, *gospozha.*"

Whether she disbelieved it or dismissed his loyalty, Larisa shrugged. "Some things you only tell lovers, you know. Anyhow. Then, after Ukraine was no longer independent, the Hunger

Time came. Kiev replaced Kharkov as the capital city. No more salmon pie. No butter, no sugar, no bread. People dropped dead in the street, Martyn Friderikovich. None of the visitors stopped by any more. That was the last of it."

"This is just incidental, Larisa Vasilievna, but does the expression *Narodnaya Slava* have a meaning that you know of, regarding Khan or Platonov?"

"No. There were too many slogans and bywords those days to remember them all."

"Did Khan or Platonov ever mention what the 'funds for the revolution' consisted of that were taken from Makhno, and what it was that brought about the accusation of 'thief's thief'?"

She shook her head. "Women who don't ask questions meet more favour with men than those who do. The same goes for men, you know."

As if I cared to meet her favour. "Sorry if I have to ask so many questions, *gospozha.*"

Nyusha had poured the sugar into a shell-shaped porcelain bowl. "Before I answer anything else," Larisa said, sticking her forefinger in the bowl, "I'll give you a sample of the things you only tell lovers. In the late 1870s, when your father was a cadet in Dresden and a pupil of Friedrich Wieck's, things happened that changed his life."

Bora was aware of the facts. Clara Schumann's father, enthused by the young man's talent, praised him to the great von Bülow, who shortly thereafter, while *Hofkapellmeister* at Meiningen, spoke to Johannes Brahms. "Yes, *gospozha*, but my mother knows this."

"Wait. Brahms met your father, was impressed. He remembered that a year earlier, while he had conducted the German Requiem for the tenth victory anniversary of the war against the French, your general-rank grandfather was present. He was so moved, he asked Brahms how he could return such a precious homage to the veterans."

"It was a famous performance, Larisa Vasilievna."

She silenced him. "Brahms could be witty, at times. He replied, 'Could I ask for anything?' and your grandfather said, 'Anything at all.' So in 1882 Brahms reminded him of his promise, asking that he release his young son from an army career and let him follow his musical gift. 'Germany may have in your son another brave officer, but the entire world would lose a unique musician.' You never heard this story, did you?"

Bora had (it had been a scandal in Leipzig society, until it resulted in unprecedented fame and wealth), but politely said he hadn't. His eyes lingered on a small icon of Mary the Melter of the Hard Hearts, encased in a gilded *riza* that let only her face and hands show through windows in the chased metal. *Larisa's father could have parted with these religious knick-knacks before committing suicide in Marienbad,* he reasoned. Even his grandparents had made sacrifices at the expense of their vast collection during the great economic crisis, to keep the family publishing firm going despite the bad times: mostly to retain all the employees in the days when the jobless amounted to six million in Germany. But old man Malinovsky would have got little for the icons; besides, he might have been as excessive (*shirokaya natura*: superabundance of spirit) as his daughter, even, in his attachment to material objects.

Larisa gloated. "See? There are things I know about your father that your mother ignores. It was to me, not to her, that your father wrote from America, to tell me that he was dying. He kept it from The Little One, and his last letter was to *me*."

Half true. Bora looked down from the icon. Under the pretence of an overseas tour, the Maestro had kept his terminal illness from Nina, but his deathbed note was addressed to Oberst Edwin Sickingen, recommending his young wife and son to him. Not that the colonel needed encouragement to pursue his first love, but he was married to Donna Maria Ascanio at the time. Even after his annulment, the widowed Nina had made him wait two more years before agreeing to wed him.

With unexpected energy, Larisa lifted her legs down from the chaise longue and fumbled around the floor with her stubby feet until she drove them into a pair of embroidered slippers. "Give me a hand to get up; we'll go to the parlour. Before we return to boring subjects, we must make music. You on the piano, I on the violin. Your father's music you know how to play. But do you play Mozart? Do you play Schumann?"

"I'd say so, *gospozha*."

She led the way to the other room. Opening the violin case, she half-turned. "*Narodnaya Slava* – you asked about it. It's an expression, as you say, a generic expression. To us who lived in Kharkov, though, in the old days it was a cinema off Voennaya, by the Horse Market. If it means anything else, I am not familiar with its significance. Where did you hear it?"

"It doesn't matter, Larisa Vasilievna. I was hoping it would have a deeper meaning."

20 May, 7.20 p.m., Merefa.

It was a blessing. I couldn't have taken it if she had played badly. Instead, she is a consummate violinist. We did a Schumann "Kinderszene" and a fantasia from César Franck's "Accursed Huntsman", transcribed for piano and violin by my father (his manuscript was what I read from). The third work was the charming Mozart set of variations on Antonio Albanese's "Hélas, j'ai perdu mon amant". Larisa wept as she played: it is a moving, nostalgic piece; you needn't have lost someone or be far from the one you love to feel it. Decayed physically as she is, there was a moment when she nearly looked as she must have appeared then. Somehow, the weight and sagging skin fell off her and she made my heart race with emotion. I briefly understood why Friedrich von Bora had loved her.

"We were gods" is the controversial chapter in her autobiography where she describes her relationship with him. If she sang as she plays, and if he conducted as we all know he did, the hubris of her words is less unforgivable. And so is her risqué account of their mutual passion, which so troubled me at seventeen when I first read about it, on the sly. A notorious acquaintance of the family, R. v. Ch., unmarried and beautiful, lent it to me from her private library, because we certainly did not keep a copy at home. What is it that Dante writes about the lovers seduced by the story of Tristan and Isolde? Precocious six-footer that I was, I gloried in my brazenness, proposing to the lady by the bookshelf when the intention had been there all along on R. v. Ch.'s part. Brief but intense, and no doubt more fun for me than for her. Luckily six years later she was still available, because it was Peter's turn, and my parents (the general first, Nina second) made me understand that as the older brother I had to "think of it". So I brought him along with a bouquet of roses and left him there with an excuse. Thank God she had a sense of humour!

Anyhow, as soon as Larisa and I finished playing, the short-lived enchantment dissolved entirely. I was glad to leave her house. I doubt I'll ever go back. She followed up on her decision to give me none of the objects that were Friedrich's and that she has managed to keep through these thirty-two terrible years. Not his conductor's baton (the ebony one Brahms had made for Gaspare Spontini and then ensured his pupil would receive), not his musical scores, not the photograph where they are portrayed together at Tsarskoe Selo… But it is also true what I said: that I wanted none of those things. Friedrich von Bora is a musical legend to me as to everyone else. My father, really, is the rock-solid Generaloberst Edwin Sickingen. He made me what I am, and I am grateful to him.

When all was said and done, I came away from *La Malinovskaya* with the following considerations (which I have integrated with Tarasov's testimony):

1. In 1920, Khan and Platonov conquered Krasny Yar and for a month set up a makeshift command there (remember the Great War wooden crate I saw in the hideout). They also took over what Makhno left behind, meant as "funds for the revolution", and started arguing about the matter. At this point it

could have been anything from bank drafts to jewels to gold ingots – not cash, because it would have lost its value. It could have been documents, if they had market value.

2. Beginning in 1926, when their respective revolutionary duties slackened and Lenin's NEP opened up Russia to foreign investments, the two comrades – having apparently made up – returned to Kharkov; through their friendship with dashing Mikhail Frunze they started to frequent Larisa's privileged townhouse. Officially they had errands in or around Kharkov. According to Tarasov, Khan visited the Yar, possibly because the goods were still hidden there. Fact is, Khan spent lavishly and Platonov reprehended him for it; their renewed disagreement went beyond his lifestyle (see the accusation of being a "thief's thief"), so Khan might have helped himself to the entirety of those funds.

3. In the see-saw of their relationship, the two officers seemed tied by a mutually unbreakable bond: Khan because he was blackmailed, maybe, and Platonov due to his career ambition, which Khan helped fulfil.

4. Shortly before the Famine, when waters were becoming dangerous in no-longer-independent Ukraine, Khan was the first to cease visiting Larisa. Platonov came at least once on his own, according to Larisa, with generic "foreigners" and opportunists. At least one could be the man accompanied to Krasny Yar. Who was he? One of the Western (including American) engineers, managers and technicians, who in Tarasov's words came to "grub for Russia's natural resources, including ore from Krivoy Rog and coal from Lugansk"? If it makes a difference, Tarasov said *neznakomets* (stranger), which is not identical to *inostranets* (foreigner), the word Larisa used. A stranger may not necessarily be from outside Russia. Whatever: does this man have anything to do with any of this? Did our honest Platonov relent and try to further his ambitions by buying off a foreign investor? Unlikely: I don't see how. Did he plan to punish Khan, the "thief's thief", by making it impossible for him to keep using the funds? How so? I even thought the existence of a visitor

might simply be dangled before his colleague's eyes, so that Khan would be afraid of putting his fingers into the till again.

5. The Purge trials began in 1936. Suddenly, all games were up. The two comrades, bound hand and foot to each other, were sucked into the vortex that would kill over a million Russians. The show trials followed one another. Finally Khan saw his chance to break free, and either directly or indirectly brought about Platonov's fall. The rest is history: by the time Platonov was rehabilitated, broken in body if not in soul, Khan had surpassed him in glory and fame, becoming the star he was when I saw him towering on the T-34 that so enthralled my colleague Scherer.

Questions: are the murders at Krasny Yar connected with the events listed above? What valuables (if any), what secrets, remain hidden there? If there's one or more guardian (I use the term for lack of a better word) in the woods, his reach and ability must be limited, as some who venture into the Yar do so undisturbed: the priest, the men from the 241st, Nagel and myself...

I was never convinced that Khan's death was a vendetta by the NKVD, or by the Ukrainians: they're only exploiting a done deal. But who's behind it, then? Only the RSHA and *Abwehr* were informed of Khan's presence in Kharkov. Colonel Bentivegni, Gestapo Müller – do they know what this is all about and are keeping silent? Mantau and I could be nothing but pawns in a far larger game.

Were old Platonov still alive right now, I'd dangle his pretty daughter by her ankles out of the window to make him tell.

Unrelated note: Hurrah, the regimental mounts are due tomorrow morning. Lippe and Nagel are already at the Smijeff–Gottendorf rail station to oversee the operation, and I'm joining them on Saturday at the latest to see the quality of the shipment for myself.

Other note: Kostya is close to worshipping the ground I walk on, on account of the dozen chicks I brought back from Borovoye (it was interesting driving back with them peeping inside a basket on the front seat). I told him to spare the altars and get me a working shower instead.

9

FRIDAY 21 MAY, KHARKOV

In his second-storey office at Hospital 169, Dr Mayr stood up from the chair behind his desk on hearing Bora's words. He gave the impression of being cut in two by the blade of light coming through the sheets of wax paper glued across the broken window. Hammering on the same floor, the whine of electric saws lent an air of added confusion to the moment.

"Are you sure?"

"Quite sure. Barring accidents, Sanitätsoberfeldwebel Weller will be safely Fatherland-bound come next Sunday."

"May I ask how you found out?"

"You may not." *As if you didn't know.* Bora expected some official statement of surprised relief in the order of *thank God*, or *that's a weight off my chest.* The enigmatic reaction annoyed him. He noticed that the medicines he'd brought in were gone from the glass cabinet; the bulletin board was empty as well, and on the clothes stand an army shirt on a hanger badly needed ironing. The man before him, too, seemed in dire need of smoothing out, hot-pressing or whatever could take the psychological and physical wrinkles off him. And yet he'd asked Geko Stark in writing to urge Weller's repatriation. Not so much on the spur of the moment, Bora chose to provoke.

"Since I kept my part of the bargain, we're even, Herr Oberstarzt. While I'm here, though, and since I heard that you too, coincidentally, are due for a furlough soon – just out of curiosity: is there really no doubt in your professional mind that my prisoner died a natural death?"

The weariness in the surgeon's glance quickened a little. "What, that again, Major? Will you not let it go? Didn't I perform a post-mortem for you, although there was no reason for it?"

Receiving three questions as answers to one further ill-disposed Bora. "So you said. But I was talking to someone recently, and Mikhail Frunze came into the conversation. The Bolshevik, yes, the founder of the Red Army. He died of an overdose of chloroform in a Soviet hospital eighteen years ago."

"So? What does it have to do with us?"

"Please do not misunderstand me, and do not read into my words more than I am specifically asking: is there *any* possibility my prisoner was accidentally administered the wrong medicine, or an excess of medication?"

The blade of outdoor light drew a jagged line across the surgeon's figure as he waved his hands to dismiss the idea. "Oberfeldwebel Weller is trained and experienced —"

"Yes, and so are you. Please answer my question."

"I really don't understand you, Major. In a severe cardiac crisis, with a patient whose general health is so gravely compromised —"

"What was he given?"

"What I had on hand: camphor in a 20 per cent solution."

Bora retrieved a small notebook from his breast pocket, flipped it open and pencilled a note. "Camphor, 20 per cent. Not something else? What about aconitine, for example?"

"Aconitine!" Mayr burst out. "Are you mad? On a cardiac patient? Besides, an excess of medication would be detectable right away in an autopsy."

"*Right away.* And you did the post-mortem when? Twenty-four hours after the decease, did you not? Isn't it true that a lapse of hours would make a difference to the detection and measurement of some substances?"

In the segmented light from the window, Mayr's field-grey uniform, murky between the flaps of his white coat, had the colour of water at winter's end. It was the tinge of ice-melt, when brooks run along snowy banks. His agitated face looked pale yellow. "This is totally out of order!" He raised his voice. "This is *unconscionable* behaviour!"

Why is he so alarmed? He knows more than he says. Bora slipped the notebook's thin pencil back into its leather loop. He kept his tone under control. "You're reading too much into my words. Take – say – a substance like aconitine nitrate, a remedy against neuralgia as far as I know, hypodermically injected: could a lapse of hours make it undetectable?"

"I contest your assumption! It's unheard of, Major Bora! Are you by any chance accusing me of negligence or conspiracy, or worse?"

"Could a lapse of twenty-four hours be enough?"

"I have no idea. Maybe. But —"

The notebook slid back into Bora's breast pocket. "That's all I needed to know for now, Herr Oberstarzt. Thank you."

Mayr was trembling in a cold rage when Bora left the office. Down the hallway he went, and to the ground floor. There through an open doorway he glimpsed a white-stockinged nurse leaning over someone's bedside, her stout calves wholly unattractive, and, passing by another ward, an army chaplain administering the last sacrament. His hands, in the process of draping the stole over his shoulders, were waxy and long-fingered. Everything reeked of phenol, as if cleanliness were the sole bastion against death.

Provocation seldom failed. The surgeon's reaction – officially on Weller's account, but in fact self-defensive – was at the same time both admissible and curious. He had skeletons in his closet, and how. Lattmann's latest titbits about him amounted to more than hearsay, and after the phone conversation with Mantau it was important for Bora to understand whether Platonov too might coincidentally have died before his time. Murder is different to an error or an unintentional overdose, and he had to know.

When he opened the main door, a whiff of phenol tried to follow him outside. The lindens in the hospital garden, however, some of them precociously in bloom, would allow for no other aroma, so that Bora felt he was diving into the heady, honeyed scent. At the family place in Borna the ancient linden tree bloomed in June, its scent filtering day and night into the rooms. In his childhood the scent had heralded the summer holidays for him; ever since childhood it had meant slipping away to those same rooms with Dikta before their marriage. *She is made of love.* He surprised himself by humming a tune as he walked towards his parked vehicle. *From head to toe, just as the song says. There's no denying it... Bless the linden trees that remind me of her.*

He'd already started the engine before he changed his mind and made an about-face. He stepped down a shady path of upheaved gravel instead, towards the nameless grave where Platonov, husband and father to women who looked like the one Bora loved, had been buried. He spent ten or so minutes there, pondering things under the perfumed clusters of the old trees.

From Kharkov, the terrain between the villages of Beryozovoye and Babai rose and fell, deeply seamed by gullies and ravines. Mostly green, often treed, sometimes they opened up into stone quarries like pale wounds, invariably marked as *karyer* on the map. Bora, who always left on time when he had an appointment but was also always in haste, before long found himself blocked by a long convoy of Panzer IV and armoured half-tracks occupying most of the road. Overtaking them was out of the question. After steaming behind the slow-moving vehicles for the best part of ten minutes, he decided to turn around and try his luck down a lesser lane; from Lednoye, however, no more than a hundred metres behind him, another convoy was joining the main road.

This too was positioning and repositioning in view of the coming battle. Standing to be sandwiched between mastodons, Bora wished he'd known about the contretemps. Had the slope on both sides of the road not been so steep, he would have long since taken to the fields. As things were, the tail of the convoy behind him accelerated (if anything resembling high speed could be said of it) to join the head vehicles. So he had to bide his time at thirty kilometres per hour, smelling fumes and eating dust until the next turn-off or a spot where the left or right shoulder flattened out enough to be negotiated on four wheels.

Like the rails not far away, the road followed a rather long crest between *balkas*, no wider than the pavement. Small ponds shone far below. Huts, wooded areas, fences lay sparsely alongside them, at the foot of the grassy ravine or sat strewn along the opposite slope, unreachable by car. Overhead, two escort fighter planes from Rogany shuttled from one end of the convoy to the other.

In Bora's memory, at one point the ridge did broaden out for maybe a hundred metres to the left of one driving south: enough to dare a pass and maybe hit the detour towards Rshavetz. Impatiently he counted the minutes and paid close attention to the slightest sign of a manoeuvring space opening for him to steer into. The margin of compact gravel remained narrow for what seemed to be an endless stretch of time, marked by the racket of steel tracks all around and by the skimming passage of the watchful aeroplanes. Eventually Bora saw the thirsty strip of land at the edge of the road inch wider, and grew hopeful.

Just then, the tank in front of him came to a dead stop. The driver of the SPW half-track behind him kept rolling, unaware. Bora had been in the process of attempting his hazardous getaway when the half-track's armoured cowling ever so gently touched him, applying the pressure of seven tons against the rear of a vehicle one-tenth its weight. The small, sturdy frame of the personnel carrier catapulted forward, its front tyres not carefully seeking the edge of the descent but heading straight into the void. Bora saw sky–horizon–earth tilt downwards before his eyes; negotiating the fall was impossible for the decisive seconds during which the vehicle spun out of control and then brusquely nosed downwards. A merry row of birches flashed into view; was gone. The impact against the escarpment risked flipping the vehicle sideways, although it bounced back and righted itself at once, and Bora kept his seat, more or less, by holding on to the steering wheel.

Down he went, quicker now than he could think (he wasn't thinking at all; merely registering events with surprise), straight down, brakes useless, if not dangerous, on long grass and at that angle. The row of birches, white and tender green, seemed far away and yet within arm's reach. Within seconds, stolid abandonment and the frantic need to intervene competed for Bora's attention, too brief a time to make a difference to action or to the lack thereof. Papers he'd laid on the front seat went fluttering; anything loose flew its own way. By leaps, the personnel carrier careened downwards until it struck the bottom of the escarpment, where a deeper ditch marked the foot of the ravine. There it wedged itself front-first into the trench, rearing up and coming to a halt almost vertically. Bora bumped every part of his body that was in contact with any surface and leapt out, only to roll back inside the ditch. The right-hand door, stuck open, pinned him down, but not enough that he couldn't wiggle and scramble out from under it.

His left elbow and both his knees bled profusely where the skin was bruised and torn. Bora realized he'd have spared himself injury had he not worn the summer uniform with shorts and rolled-up sleeves, but there's no dressing for an accident. The little time it took him to get to his feet after creeping to safety made him furious. *As in Cracow*, he thought, *only worse. Dumb tanks. Of all the stupid ways...* On the ridge above, slowly proceeding, the two ends of the convoy had meanwhile reunited.

Faces were looking outside turrets and cabins in the rumble of engines; hands gestured, so it was likely they'd send for help before long. One of the fighter planes swept low over the crash site, like a big fly on spilt milk.

Bora glanced around. At least he knew exactly where he found himself on the map. It was a matter of no more than three to four kilometres to any one of several communities: the checkpoint at the turn-off to Artyomovka was probably where the drivers who'd seen him go down would leave word to have him picked up. He might as well wait here.

He limped back to the ditch and crawled in to retrieve his briefcase, stuck under the pedals; his sub-machine gun, maps, loose documents, cap and what few other things he carried lay scattered up and down the slope. His wristwatch, the glass on its face scratched but unbroken, read 9.51 a.m.

Looking at it, the personnel carrier did not appear particularly damaged; once straightened and hauled out, it would continue to do its job. The same was true of him, although his elbow and knees were beginning to hurt as the excitement of the moment subsided. Bora clambered the steep incline to recover what had fallen out and got lost. For close to ten minutes he searched the grass collecting odds and ends, while the tail of the convoy above rattled southwards and freed the road at last. The fighter planes followed. In the silence, a *cuckooshka* called mockingly from a tall pine; the birches caught a breath of wind and trembled from first to last. At the edge of the road, where Bora climbed and went to sit, the shoulder appeared bitten off where the rear wheels had briefly dragged as the vehicle left the ramp.

He was plastering a strip of bloody skin back onto the meagre flesh of his elbow when the explosion came. Directly below him, he saw his upended vehicle blow apart as if a rocket had centred it, a spectacular burst and report that crumpled him where he was in a reaction of self-defence. Metal and rubber, glass jetted in all directions; tyres and the front seat;

less recognizable elements of engine and chassis, a fiery dismemberment that shot some fragments sky-high while others struck the escarpment and the road like projectiles. Pipes and chunks of metal flew past, bounced next to him; bolts and twisted lumps whirled through the air. The steering wheel rained from above, and the heavy-treaded spare wheel that sat on the hood followed, soon to roll and tumble down the slope towards the birch line. Smoke and flames fanned up. Bora sat up, breathing in the acrid smell, and could think of nothing better than checking the time. It was 10 a.m. sharp, and a crater gaped where his vehicle had until that point stood planted in the ditch.

Five minutes later, from the direction of Artyomovka and Merefa, an ambulance and a staff car approached at a good clip. The first belonged to one of the army hospitals in Kharkov; the second had been sent from Gebietskommissar Stark's *Kombinat*, where news of the accident must have been relayed by those at the checkpoint. Bora, who'd meanwhile circled what remained of his means of transportation and was just getting back to the road, paid scant attention to them. He said as little as he could, angry and overwrought to the extent that he felt no pain whatever when they disinfected and stitched his limbs. They kept posing dumb questions to judge if he was alert, until finally he blurted out in bad humour, "I'm fine. Get off me. All I need is a goddamn ride to Merefa."

In fact, on the way he asked that they stop at the *Kombinat*, to thank the district commissioner for the attention and to place a telephone call to Lieutenant Colonel von Salomon. Von Salomon was in low spirits and made much of the accident; even more of the loss of a vehicle "at a time like this, Major Bora", as if it were Bora's fault. Bora bit his tongue. Everything was beginning to ache in earnest: under the summer shirt his neck and shoulders felt bruised and sore. "I don't believe this command will be in the position to supply you with another personnel carrier, Major. It will be unavoidable for you to rely on one of the vehicles already assigned to Cavalry Regiment Gothland, or your own mount. Really, I am surprised at you, who I expect, above the others, to be clear-minded!"

It was difficult not to think that von Salomon would have felt exactly the same had Bora not survived the crash. From across the hallway Geko Stark, busy at his desk with an orderly pile of papers, raised his head enough to say, "Judging by your face, you met with no sympathy at headquarters."

Bora deemed it prudent to keep to himself what he thought of the lieutenant colonel at this time. He gloomily put down the receiver. The ambulance driver, who happened to have been at the *Kombinat* picking up hospital supplies when the news of the crash was brought in, walked out of the office across from Stark's with a large box in his arms. He gave Bora what Bora took to be the secretly amused stare of a low-ranker at a crestfallen officer. Bora could have kicked him. Stark didn't help matters when he called out, dialling a number on his telephone, "Did you at least scrape together the kilo of butter you were looking for the other day?"

"No."

"No?"

"No." It was a meagre satisfaction lying because he was in a contrary mood. Bora decided he'd asked for enough favours today, and chose to walk the handful of kilometres to the schoolhouse. As luck had it, Kostya was driving back from Yakovlevka on his droshky after having stolen an oil drum and fittings from God knows where. He overtook Bora less than two hundred metres from the *Kombinat*.

"*Yisouse*! *Povazhany* Major, what happened to you?"

Well, it beat limping along the road with a briefcase, a submachine gun and bandages everywhere. Bora threw everything in the carriage and climbed up next to his concerned orderly.

"What happened, *povazhany* Major? Where's the car?"

"Oh, shut up, Kostya."

MEREFA, 6.27 P.M.

That evening, it took four aspirins and a glass of Lattmann's
vodka for the fever to stop bothering him, if not to decrease.
Kostya and the sentry were out at the edge of the field in the
low sun, tinkering with the oil drum; the big-headed, big-footed
draught horses grazed nearby. Inside the schoolhouse, Bora
began his diary entry for the day.

> On a day when I might have died, I'm writing under a reel of flies.
> My great-grandfather, the Field Marshal, told us about the flies in the
> letters he wrote during the Seven Weeks' War against the Austrians,
> not to speak of the insects he met in the Cameroon when the Came-
> roon was German. Flies no doubt crowded around my Scottish great-
> grandfather's severed head at Khartoum. It is so bad that cleanliness
> becomes an obsession with some of us, although others give up the
> struggle and simply live with the vermin. Horses shake their tails,
> whip their sides, hoof the ground and turn back their heads to bite
> at horseflies (*tabanum* or *tabanus*: I can't recall the exact name in Lat-
> in). Men swat them with anything that will swat (folded newspaper,
> map, notebook, open hand…), catch them in their fist, trap them
> under a drinking glass or a cup, and finally ignore them.
>
> From a great altitude we probably look like flies ourselves, on the
> great body of Russia. And God knows she is trying to shake us off,
> or squash us. I should know: I was one of the German flies caught
> on the flypaper, inside the choking trap that was Stalingrad. One of
> the handful of flies that got away. They say flies have ten thousand
> eyes, or composite eyes that amount to that much fragmentary (but
> immense) complementary vision. Don't they see the hand coming
> down to smash them? And when hundreds, thousands of them are
> smashed all around, why do they keep circling?
>
> *Besprizornye* (or *besprizorniki*) is a Russian term…

The sound of an engine coming to a halt in the gravelly yard
outside the schoolhouse, the dull click of a door opening as

285

someone alighted from it, caused him to pause and cap the gold-tipped pen. Weeks ago, it had been the *Heeresrichter*'s unannounced arrival, but other visitors were just as likely. Warily Bora unlatched the holster and moulded his fingers around the P38.

"Major, it's Bernoulli."

Bora breathed out. One look at him through the door, and the judge was merciful enough not to remark on the scant security of the premises. "I found eyewitnesses in support of your statements about Alexandrovka and the other places," he added as the younger officer stood to greet him. "The paperwork is here for you to review before you sign."

Bora didn't look forward to entertaining, although of all possible intrusions, the military judge's was the least likely to indispose him. "Take a chair, Dr Bernoulli. Make yourself comfortable." He then mentioned the car accident (remaining testily vague about it) only because he had to justify the presence of noticeable cuts and bruises.

Seated across from him, Bernoulli refrained from asking questions. Only an unconvinced pressing together of the lips, on this side of a sympathetic smile, remained on his face.

Was his making light of the crash believable? Bora closed his diary on the drying ink. He was aware of the obstinate impression he was giving. Without modifying it, he turned thoughts over in his mind, careful not to express them. If he closed his eyes, he saw the slender row of birches at the foot of the ravine, pencilled white against the green shadow and delicate in the face of his rudely plunging vehicle. *What lovely, feminine trees,* he thought, under Bernoulli's serene scrutiny. *As charming a set of witnesses to an accident as I could hope for.* But also *I will not share the rest with him: why give details?*

Judges are by necessity used to facing reticence. Bernoulli rested his briefcase on the floor, leaning it against the leg of his chair. He let his attention wander from the weathered, canvas-bound diary to the small framed photo Bora kept on the teacher's desk. The portrait seemed to intrigue him: short-sighted as he was, he removed his eyeglasses and held it close to his face to observe it.

"A fine-looking young woman," he commented. "Your wife?"

"Benedikta, yes."

Any worldly-wise man would readily perceive how the close call of the morning had played a part in him taking out his girl's photo. Bora felt exposed. He realized with trepidation that he risked slipping into one of those moods when you couldn't lie if you wanted to; his obstinacy was geared to make him keep his silence, because he needed instead to talk.

All Bernoulli was doing amounted to a rather paternal contemplation of Dikta's portrait. "Congratulations. She appears to be a fitting German counterpart to you, such as we're taught to recognize these days."

Bora set his face hard. His stubbornness was more than a veneer over different feelings. It was a family trait, cultivated to an art without ever becoming ill-mannered. He was therefore very surprised by the impulse to capitulate and talk simply because a seven-tonner had nudged him off the road and prevented him from being surely as dead at this time as anybody who was destined to die. He slowly but jealously took the framed photo from the judge's hand. Dikta was and remained his aesthetic, athletic ideal. Whether it *was* love, well… he was convinced it was passionate love, although it could be physical enchantment for all he knew, because he himself had had no great time to devote to the building of a solid relationship. And Dikta adored him to the extent that she could adore anything.

It was raining elsewhere, not nearby. At Pomorki, maybe, on Larisa's pomegranates and wild hyacinths. The coolness of early evening was doing his fever good, even though the flies revelled in it. Bernoulli seemed to have forgotten about paperwork, and the risk of revealing himself a little seemed small to Bora in the face of greater things.

"She and I," he said, "I don't know how to put it, we're somewhat… *perfect* at this time."

"I can tell."

"The thought of it worries me. Or, rather, the thought that we won't remain such for long. That I might not, due to the war…" As he moved the diary on the table aside, the sealed envelope with Dikta's naked photo inside, which Bora had been tempted to open and worship tonight, fell out and lay on the surface between them. He felt foolish. "Forgive me, Dr Bernoulli: I don't know what I'm saying, or why I'm even saying this."

The judge's glance migrated from the framed picture to the envelope with Bora's name penned on it. "Because it's on your mind; it's understandable. But perfection as a state or condition is in itself a question of *lack*: lack of error, of faults, of flaws. You and your wife might be too closely identifying your relationship with the illusion of such absence of flaws. Young couples – handsome couples – often live on the tethering edge of their fear of losing what they have, what they are."

"I know; I'm aware." Bora stared at the envelope. It was too complicated to explain that insecurity heightened the preciousness of his relationship with Dikta, simultaneously eroding it. Love remained in the middle of it like a seed in the husk, wholly dependent upon the quality of the soil to determine whether it will wither or bear fruit. "But it doesn't help."

Two handsome young people, thus far without the tedium of daily routine. Dikta always impeccable – smile, skin, hair, nails. He couldn't imagine her less than perfect. And she probably couldn't imagine him less than the spruce, whole, good-looking cavalry officer. A polite world, sensible but aesthetic; orderly routines, where even divorces were polite; voices seldom raised. Homes where breakfast was served on silver trays, a change was required for dinner, rooms kept their dustless immaculate appearance; even the roughness of the boys' sports and the unfailing practice of horsemanship did not soil that world. Discipline, respect, holiday schedules, rank and propriety kept in mind always; generosity, charity part of that world as forms of duty. Flowers fresh on the table, manners kept throughout.

Bora inconspicuously (he thought) replaced the powder-blue envelope inside his diary.

"Is that an unopened letter from her?"

Bora had seldom felt so vulnerable; it seemed to him that everything around could bruise his already battered self. "No, it's – a photograph she sent."

"And you resealed it?" Under the dance of flies, Bernoulli patiently sat on the other side of the table, wiping his eyeglasses. He was no more expecting an answer than Bora was about to give one.

It thundered, so far away that the low rumbling seemed to come from another world, much further than Pomorki. Bora wearily latched his holster.

"There are still too many ties, Dr Bernoulli, too many attachments. After Stalingrad, I thought I'd cut loose of everything and everyone; for my own egotistical good, because it hurt so much to keep caring in the face of disaster. But it was enough to see her again in Prague, see my mother... I'm sure you confront such feelings, or have done in the past."

"I let go of my eagerness for perfection long ago, Major. Which doesn't mean I don't suffer: it's my human lot. I no longer suffer the dread of the Fall. Losing a bit of perfection – which means of course losing it all – opens the way to wisdom." The small cloth the judge used to wipe the lenses was folded neatly, put away. "If I may make an observation, you are going about it yourself, although in a headlong way: you court disaster by risking a lot, by risking more than your war career demands, even. Accept the fact that trouble will come looking even if you do not actively court it. Unless you'd rather be a part in your own undoing." Bernoulli paused, straight in his chair and yet without rigidity. "That's it, isn't? Perfection lost through self-immolation attains a heroic quality that accidents do not afford. You are – forgive me – an arrogant young man."

"Yes. And it's no excuse to say that I was brought up to be arrogant. Arrogant and polite, which is less of an oxymoron in my family than it seems." It shamed him to be seen through so precisely, yet there was a sense of release as well, bordering on comfort. Bora wanted to look away, but didn't.

The judge did it for him, changing the subject to help him, or because he'd come to discuss very different matters after all. "I brought sworn statements from Ukrainian witnesses, one of them a physician, confirming what you observed at Drobytsky Yar."

"Good."

"If you say so." Bernoulli unclasped his briefcase. "Within months," he added slowly, "everything leads us to believe that army counterintelligence will be taken over. Your *amicus curiae* reports to the War Crimes Bureau; the new ones and those you sent in from Poland and Russia in the past three years may fall into the wrong hands." From a folder, he took out typewritten sheets with the photographs taken by Bora clipped to them, bearing the headings *Alexandrovka–Merefa, Drobytsky Yar, Pyatikhatky Forest.* "Think it over, Major."

"I have. I want these to go in. I want someone to pay attention to them."

The papers were turned so that Bora could read what they said, although he merely scanned them.

"Unless you revise your position, then, the die will be cast for good."

"It was cast long ago."

Bernoulli tightened his lips before saying, "Sign here, then."

Bora did, with an ear on the mutter of distant thunder. He watched the judge place the sheets in a folder, and this inside his briefcase. From the open door, a delicate, penetrating scent of flowers flowed in. Bernoulli inhaled. "Are there linden trees in the neighbourhood?"

"Not too close. It's the evening and the damp in the air that makes them perceptible at a distance."

"Makes it good to be alive, don't you think?"

Bora nodded. Saying *I can't see myself growing old, Dr Bernoulli* was unthinkable. They were all in God's hands, each one of them: the judge, his brother, their loved ones. For him, having signed his name belonged to this moment of scented air as much as anything else. *It's raining on Pomorki and my father's old lover, who used to race in a sleigh through the snow to reach him at night wherever he was in Russia because their physical love was excessive like mine and Dikta's. It is good to be alive, but only because I've signed off on those papers.*

Before long, thickening clouds would hasten the close of day. The presence of a visitor insured against interruptions, but a downpour would force Kostya and the careless sentry under the lean-to roof behind the building, within earshot. "Doctor Bernoulli," Bora began, "I'd appreciate your opinion on something in relation to Khan Tibyetsky's death. Are you in haste?"

Bernoulli answered that he wasn't. In silence he listened to Bora's summary of his exchange with the SS medical personnel and phone conversation with Odilo Mantau, commenting eventually, "I see. It all points to a variety of scenarios. Have you entertained the possibility that they were speaking the truth at the Sumskaya first-aid station?"

"How so? Khan's body was taken there, and they outright denied it."

"Not about Khan's body, Major. About sending a medic to the RSHA jail the night before he died."

Aching all over, Bora uncomfortably shifted position in his chair. "Well, what else could have happened? Are you suggesting that an intruder infiltrated the system, unbeknown to the RSHA?" He'd hinted that much to Mantau, so he acted scandalized for the sake of appearances. "It'd be egregious!"

"We live in egregious times, Major. It all depends on what Khan knew about what, or whom, and how important it was to silence him. Didn't Hauptsturmführer Mantau tell you the prisoner clamoured to be returned to *Abwehr* custody?"

"From the moment he was brought in. Apparently he threw a tantrum about it the evening of 6 May."

"In that case…" Bernoulli seemed for a moment absorbed by the echo of thunder outside, or by the growing scent of trees in full bloom. A fly landed on the spotless cuff of his shirt, and he calmly waved it away. "In that case, once he made it into the jail, it would be conceivable that an operative, in the enemy's pay or not, could have gained a suspicious prisoner's trust by claiming to come from you, or from Colonel Bentivegni. The RSHA is not wholly impermeable; the request for medical intervention could be intercepted and acted upon. Wasn't there a mix-up with the Russian cleaning women as well? The right man might have succeeded in leading Khan to believe a plan was afoot to return him to *Abwehr* custody."

Yes. Unbelievable as it sounded, Mantau didn't even have a name to hand. There was no telling what had really happened in Khan Tibyetsky's cell the evening of 6 May. Bora was torn between a desire to disregard the suggestion and a desire to strongly latch on to it. "But this is 1943 Kharkov, Dr Bernoulli, not the island of Montecristo!"

"Or Shakespeare's Verona. Yes. But we needn't suppose the plan was for Khan to feign death like Edmond Dantès or fair Juliet in order to escape. Become ill enough to be transported out of the jail, maybe."

"That would imply administering some kind of medication in advance. I had thought of it. But the fact is, the D ration contained enough nicotine to kill him outright."

"Or so reads the post-mortem." Bernoulli leaned over to snap the clasps of his briefcase shut. "There are precedents in criminal history. If you have someone's trust, Major, you can lure him into chewing a poisoned D ration. But you can just as well trick him into swallowing a deadly pill after ingesting a perfectly harmless candy bar. That way, chocolate *and* poison would be present in the oral cavity and in the stomach."

It would soon be too dark to drive safely, especially alone. Bora decided he would invite his guest to stay, and relinquish him his cot overnight. He pondered the judge's words and noted the sting of the sutures on his knees and elbow, in a singular alertness of mind and body. "The scenario would solve the dilemma I ran up against," he admitted. "Namely, how could the intended victim pick a poisoned ration out of several available to him in the cell? As you suggest, perhaps he didn't. Provided that Khan was directed to ingest a capsule or pill *after* eating a candy bar at daybreak, and that he obeyed, it's possible that none of the rations were ever poisoned, by the babushkas or anyone else. The whole set-up could be intended to hide the fact that he was handed the poison the night before by the sole person he'd trust, someone he believed had been sent by the *Abwehr*. But whether or not they're involved at the Sumskaya first-aid station, I can't prove any of it."

Bernoulli set the briefcase on the table and stood up from his chair, imitated at once by Bora. "You can't prove any of it unless you catch the murderer."

"Right." Taller than the judge, Bora found himself at eye-level with the bare, unlit light bulb (there was no power in the building). When he'd first entered the schoolhouse weeks earlier, above the lamp had hung a blackened strip of flypaper, close to saturation. It had disgusted him to hear and see the swarm of flies buzzing as they starved on the gluey spiral, and he hadn't replaced it. Now, despite Kostya's scouring, the flies and mosquitoes came in, as it was too warm not to keep the door and windows open most of the time. "I apologize for the flies, Dr Bernoulli."

"We do our job, insects do theirs – such as it is. I don't like flypaper, either. Anything else before I go?"

"Actually, yes. I'm not sure the army surgeon at Hospital 169, Oberstarzt Mayr, is telling it as it is, either. He asked me to track down his non-com assistant, who was reassigned after General Platonov's death. At the same time he covertly pulled strings with Gebietskommissar Stark to get him shipped homewards as soon as possible."

"Ah." Bernoulli sat down again. "May I ask how you found out?"

It was the same question Mayr had posed to Bora in the morning, receiving no answer. This time he said, "Yes. Last Friday, after the overnight conversation you and I had at the special detention centre, the *opportunity* presented itself for me to read what the district commissioner had recommended in a letter to the General Army Office Medical Inspectorate, Personnel Branch." It was a neutral way of admitting he'd unsealed the correspondence Stark entrusted to him. Bernoulli frowned, but said nothing. "At first I even suspected the Commissioner of playing some sinister role, and surprised a colleague by downing a few drinks over it to clear my mind. All Geko Stark did was honour a request by Dr Mayr, the medic's direct supervisor, to have him reassigned, and to keep the detail from me. Understandable: after all, I was officially trying to enrol Sanitätsoberfeldwebel Weller in my regiment. This morning, the surgeon had an oddly cool reaction when I informed him of Weller's upcoming repatriation. By implication, I was suggesting that I knew there'd been political manoeuvring on his part. The question is: why does Dr Mayr want Weller spirited out of here? You'd think he fears the young man might blow the whistle on him, or something of the sort."

The dim hour, along with the moisture and electricity in the scented air outside, laid a strange siege to the room. The judge, however, stayed Bora's motion to light a kerosene lamp. "Blow the whistle concerning what, Major Bora? Sit down, please. You do not surmise Platonov was done in as well?"

The stitches pulled and hurt when Bora sat. "I ask myself what I *do not* surmise at this point, Dr Bernoulli. I have it from a credible source that Oberstarzt Mayr received a less than stellar performance report while on the Western Front, for openly refusing to continue treatment of a badly burnt and mutilated pilot. During his unit's stint near Pyatigorsk, casualties who could not be transported died coincidentally on the eve of being left behind."

"So? As a philosophy major with an interest in ethics, you of all people should know there's a higher law – higher than a physician's oath, even."

"I also know that Dr Mayr waited twenty-four hours or more to perform Platonov's autopsy. During IC training, we were taught that some substances become undetectable in a corpse after a given lapse of time. Aconitine nitrate, for example, which a surgeon suffering from neuralgia might keep handy, or castor oil plant derivatives. All highly toxic if you only vary amounts and proportions by a hair."

Bernoulli squinted behind his eyeglasses. "But if it was Mayr who carried out the post-mortem, what need did he have to wait? He could have lied to you about the toxicological findings all along."

"Except that I could have asked for a second opinion and caught him in the lie. By waiting a safe amount of time, it would no longer make a difference."

"Granted. Still, the rule of *cui prodest* seems to apply here: who stands to gain from killing one or the other high-ranking Soviet? From what you told me, Major, it doesn't convince me that either one of the surgeons had a motive."

"Unless they acted under orders, or could be blackmailed." Bora stared at the whiteness pencilling the judge's collar, a sign of the perfect shirt beneath his blouse. "Dr Mayr did mention blackmail at one point."

"Spontaneously, or in reply to something you said?"

"To something I said. But he is rumoured to be politically unreliable."

"Politically unreliable… So are the two of us, in a manner of speaking. I mean, when our findings relate to German crimes of war." Bernoulli hinted a tight-lipped smile. "Does it make you uncomfortable that I'm saying this?"

"It makes me very uncomfortable, Judge."

"And less than *perfect*, probably. Anyhow, why would the SS medical personnel at the first-aid station send someone to murder Khan Tibyetsky? Political unreliability scarcely applies to that quarter."

"Well, one can exceed political zeal. My information is that the SS surgeon at Sumskaya, far from being a 'bonesetter' as Hauptsturmführer Mantau seems to think, was lately a euthanasia expert at the Central Office for Race and Resettlement."

"Which doesn't explain why Tibyetsky, who wasn't even a *subhuman Slav*, should be done away with. Is this all you have in terms of evidence, Major?"

If I were a defendant in his courtroom, he couldn't be more successful at making me tell. Will I regret trusting him? Bora had to force himself to look Bernoulli in the eye. "This morning's accident to my vehicle – there was a time bomb involved. No doubt about it; I recognize an explosion when I see one. As far as I can make out, the charge was placed under the chassis, and timed to go off when I'd most likely be driving. I'd have been, too, if I hadn't gone off the road shortly after leaving the hospital. I've got pieces of the clockwork mechanism there."

Bernoulli glanced at the trunk, where Bora was pointing. He gave no sign of wanting to examine the fragments. Slowly, he said, "I take it you don't believe it was Soviet sabotage."

"Don't know. It went off exactly half an hour after I'd had a rather heated exchange with Dr Mayr at Hospital 169."

"Think of what you're saying, Major! Did you only visit Hospital 169 in the morning?"

"No."

"So where else did you stop?"

Bora lowered his eyes to Dikta's small portrait. Her pouting young face had an incredible fairness under the narrow, inclined brim of her summer hat. In the silky shade, she was radiant. He'd taken the photo in Berlin two years earlier and it remained his favourite, although not hers. "After I signed off on a shipment of remounts, I drove by the first-aid station on Sumskaya, then to divisional headquarters, and then to the riverside fuel depot. There, I admit, I left the vehicle unattended for maybe a quarter of an hour, because they created some difficulty around my lack of gas rations. I carry Colonel Bentivegni's special permit for extra fuel, but it didn't fly with them until I'd made a couple of phone calls. Everywhere, excepting of course headquarters and the hospital, where all told I must have absented myself from the vehicle for half an hour, I stayed only a matter of minutes."

"Which is all it takes for a trained hand to plant a bomb. I'm no connoisseur, but to my knowledge such charges can be timed to go off in several hours' time. Theoretically, the device could have been primed yesterday. How many places did you visit since then, and how many times was your vehicle left unguarded? It's still only circumstantial evidence, Major. The pursuit of justice requires more than that, and I can't help you."

"I believe I would have heard it ticking over a period of hours, but it makes sense." The idea of having driven the day before from one Kharkov army store to the next in search of butter and sugar, and then to Larisa's house on and off roads, with a bomb more than just theoretically waiting to explode under his seat, was a sobering one. Bora tried uselessly to imagine himself in Berlin with Dikta, the day of the photo. "Thanks for hearing me out, Dr Bernoulli. That's a big help already."

The stormy, declining hour enhanced the pallor of the judge's shaven skull, the veins marking his temples making him look frailer than he was. He'd rested the briefcase on his lap, and toyed with the brass clasps, opening and closing them. "What will you do now without transportation?"

"I'm having my senior non-com drive up from Bespalovka to Borovoye in a captured GAZ-64 meant for the regiment. If I don't find a mount in Merefa, I'll have to ride one of the draught horses from my *Hiwi*'s droshky to meet him there. Even a draught horse is preferable to no horse at all."

Bernoulli stood. Accompanied by Bora, he reached the doorstep, where he stopped to breathe the air. The wind had changed, however, and in lieu of the scent from the trees, wet gusts of air blew against the schoolhouse in advance of the rain. "There are more details about the Alexandrovka Mennonites I might be seeking for reasons of my own, Major. In case I need to see you again, will I find you here?"

Bora nodded. "If orders to the contrary don't reach me before then, until the end of the month at least. It's getting late, and it's about to pour. May I suggest you spend the night with us, Dr Bernoulli?"

"Thank you, no. Regardless of the weather, I mean to reach Kharkov before dark."

After Bernoulli left, Bora – for all his being a disciplinarian – chose not to make an issue of the sentry's inattention. It meant in turn carelessness on his part, but after Stalingrad he had rare moments of invincibility; this was one such one, especially after surviving the morning's incident. He opened his diary again, because he'd been in the process of verbalizing something relevant when the judge had entered the room.

Besprizornye (or *besprizorniki*) is a Russian term that indicates waifs, homeless and destitute children.

I first read it in Josef Roth's *Reise in Russland*, a collection of the articles he wrote while travelling through the Soviet Union in the 1920s. It struck me then because the author described his subject as living on nothing but "air and misery". Summing up what little I've heard about Krasny Yar's mysterious dwellers – their lack of real weapons and the ghastly awkwardness of the murders, the choice of feeble or elderly victims, the pilfering pranks – I came to the conclusion that they are not Soviet partisans. It's also very unlikely that they should be deserters (ours or Red), or civilians in hiding, who'd go out of their way to keep unnoticed. The small sandal Nagel found had the appearance of having lain in the Yar for more than a few weeks: it could belong to a girl as well as to a male child. Besides, would the Kalekin boys wear *sandals* in the ice-melting season?

By exclusion, that leaves the possibility of one or more madmen (witness Kalekin's head stuck on a pole) holing up in the Yar for the past generation, or else (given the cyclical nature of the murders, whose timing coincides with periods of serious crisis) a periodical frequentation of the woods by different groups, perhaps by stray youngsters, or *besprizornye*. After all, the man of the 241st reported seeing and being followed by a boy while at Krasny Yar.

Officially, I will not give an opinion until there's real proof. Jotting down my notes this evening (it's raining at last), I can easily imagine a band of wild, lawless youths who've survived the past two years of war as best they could, stopping at nothing to protect their turf. Why not? Some of Russia's best and cruellest fighters are 17 years old or thereabouts. If I'm right, those presently at Krasny Yar have nothing to do with the crimes committed before 1941, much less with the rape and mayhem of the civil war days (*that* has to do with Makhno and the hidden valuables).

What if the Kalekin boys (orphaned of their fathers and spoilt by their grandfather, as their mothers told me) ventured into the woods and were killed by contemporaries because they might tell of the hideout? What if the Kalekin boys themselves joined the gang instead, and (directly or indirectly) were involved in their inquisitive grandfather's death? It would explain the presence of the wooden button at the spot where he was attacked.

Making a trophy of the severed head is no more aberrant than some practices already enacted on the Russian front, on both sides. Colonel von Salomon balks at fetishism, but out of superstition will not walk on the shady side of the road. Here we all have to do our utmost to keep sane: sanity is the exception, not a lack thereof!

Besprizornye or not, I plan to enter the Yar at the head of the regiment, without indicating the possible presence of youngsters to the officers and the men, as if it were a regular mopping-up operation. It can at the very least be an excellent exercise.

Note: Unless I'm mistaken, the FED camera factory in Kharkov, where Taras Tarasov worked for a time under educator–entrepreneur Anton Makarenko, employed rehabilitated waifs. I should take another look inside the little accountant's suitcase, to see if there are references to *besprizornye* from Krasny Yar in the 1920s–30s labour force.

Addendum, written later on the same evening: I went through Tarasov's musty old papers again. And because once in a while I must get lucky, I did find the carbon copy of a letter from Makarenko himself, dated 1928, where he indulges in a nifty bit of self-serving propaganda for his Labour Commune. He claims ever since 1920 to have returned "several youngsters" to civilized living, to the Soviet Union, and to dedicated manual labour from many (11) locations in the Kharkov region, including "the desolate patch of woods lately a refuge to them, and before them to the enemies of the Revolution and the State".

He doesn't mention the name of the place, but I'm willing to bet it's Krasny Yar. The same process possibly took place in the 1930s, when the famine occasioned another round-up of waifs on the part of government agencies in Ukraine. Why couldn't there be yet another batch of wild boys who took to the woods when we invaded this region?

It does not solve my problems – that is, it doesn't tell me what was concealed in the Yar, and whether *besprizornye* have had or have anything to do with it. Nor does it help me solve Uncle Terry's murder or disprove or confirm my suspicions about Platonov's own timely death; much less understand who might want to blow me to kingdom come. At any rate, I should send a thank you note to the SPW half-track crew, whose nudge off the road saved my hide.

Shortly before midnight, when he was unsuccessfully trying to get to sleep, Hospital 169 called in. It was Dr Mayr, the last person Bora expected to hear from. *Egregious times*, Judge Bernoulli would say. The army surgeon sounded no friendlier than he'd been when they'd stormily parted ways in the morning.

It's interesting that he's calling, Bora thought. *He's either very clever or very dull: if he's behind it, asking about the car accident would give him away, so he won't. On the other hand, there was an ambulance at the wreck; he might pretend to have heard about it from its driver.*

Mayr premised that he was calling out of a sense of duty, and nothing else.

"I appreciate it, Herr Oberstarzt."

"You don't even know what I'm going to say."

"Whatever it is, I appreciate your calling at such a late hour."

"I'm on duty, Major." In the dark, with rain falling outside, the surgeon's tone came distant, resentful. Lightning caused static; sounds surged and waned. What he said next wholly surprised Bora. "An hour ago, when I went to pick up some glucose from my office cabinet, on a hunch I checked its other contents. As you know, we're working at this building and local labourers have been coming and going for weeks. The glass cabinet in my office – I don't know if you noticed – has no key, and doesn't lock. Yes, it's true of most of the furniture we inherited when we moved in. No keys, and locks that don't work." Mayr paused, but Bora didn't step in with any observations of his own. "Well, a container of Russian-produced aconitine nitrate is missing from my personal supply." Again, Bora kept silent. "This afternoon work began to install new windowpanes in my office. I was at my desk, but must admit I stepped out when the noise became particularly loud. You may be aware that I suffer from neuralgia; in any event, loud noises bother me. In the hallway, I never stood more than three steps from the door while the labourers hammered the old shutters out of their hinges. All the same, tonight I discovered the aconitine nitrate was gone."

Bora breathed in. *A risky move: he's more cool-headed than I thought. True or not, the story allows him to come across as an innocent and helpful bystander, while in practice it doesn't make any difference to my understanding of Platonov's end.* "Is anything else missing?"

"A nearly empty pack of cigarettes, which I'd left in the pocket of my gown on the clothes stand."

"I mean from the cabinet, Dr Mayr."

"Nothing else."

"And when was your last neuralgia attack?"

"My last – somewhere in mid-April. Here, I marked the date on my desk calendar: 17 April."

"Actually, then, there's no telling how long the substance has been gone from the cabinet. Am I correct?"

Mayr's answer, coming through in waves, at times drowned out by low crackling noises, only partially agreed. "The cigarettes were taken this afternoon. It's a fact that we've had native workers in the hospital for nearly two months. A few odds and ends have gone missing. Searching the men when they leave for the day is of little use: in other cases, we surmise they must have dropped what they've stolen out of the window, to a pal waiting below. After all, aconitine nitrate may be dangerous, but remains a valid antineuralgic, especially these days."

Bora felt it useless to comment. It was all too timely and one-sided, this announcement that of all the medications in the cabinet, only aconitine had been taken. For all his brusqueness, an edge in the surgeon's voice revealed his anxiety to make up, when in fact it had been Bora who had asked questions beyond the limits of good grace. *He's sounding me out. Pretending that he had nothing to do with Weller's repatriation isn't enough, and he's adding weight to the scale. Was he counting on the well-placed explosive, and doesn't know what to do now? Mayr fears I'll put a crimp in his protégé's Sunday homecoming – something which I am already actively pursuing. All the more since his own upcoming furlough to Germany follows a week from that date.*

Keeping on the vague side was preferable at this time, and Bora excelled at it. He said, "Well, Herr Oberstarzt, I do thank you for the information. Good night."

"Good night my foot, Major! Is this all you have to say? You dropped a rock in the pond this morning with your conjectures, and can't pretend indifference now."

The thunder was becoming loudest on the side of Osery-anka, as the storm pivoted counterclockwise around Kharkov, its centre. Bora listened to the rain. *If he wants to play, I'll play, but he'll regret it.* "Why didn't you tell me you asked District Commissioner Stark to write to the General Army Office Medical Inspectorate so that Master Sergeant Weller would be repatriated?"

"I wouldn't have asked you to track him down if I knew he would be travelling home!"

"Unless you had an interest in keeping quiet about your request."

"That's nonsense! I was hoping Weller would remain under my wing so that I could help him recover from his Stalingrad trauma. I have no confidence they'll be able or willing to assist him once he's back with thousands of others as traumatized as he is. If he's to enter a medical career, he needs to stay in the field with a good mentor, not flee home and indulge his melancholia – which I know is a temptation for him."

"Herr Oberstarzt, your name is specifically mentioned in a letter sent to the Medical Inspectorate."

The confused stammer at the other end of the line had nothing to do with the bad connection. Mayr was searching for words, or thinking out loud. The only intelligible phrases that came Bora's way were, "You're free to think what you will. I have nothing to do with this, and I'm not even pleased Weller is home-bound."

"Forgive me if I doubt you, Dr Mayr. You're speaking to someone who was in Stalingrad from start to end. I've seen colleagues, including a surgeon, kill themselves. I have friends whose kin were left to die in their filth when their units withdrew. Few sights were spared those of us who survived, whether or not we served in the sanitary corps. And I'm sure it's a hell of a lot better to have medical personnel put you to sleep than to rot in your own pus and excrement. There will be an investigation, Herr Oberstarzt, so you might as well tell me. I'm more capable of silence than most." Static filled the lack of response on the surgeon's side. Bora counted to ten in his mind before saying, "Let me rephrase the question for you, Dr Mayr: did you send Weller back to Germany because he discovered that aconitine nitrate was used on my prisoner?"

Some of Mayr's words were inaudible. "…Why are you doing this? Weller is a fine medic. Being desperate to go home – I admit he is, and has been for a long time – he'd never behave so as to get in trouble, and risk being sanctioned. Would he have helped me, had he known I'd contravened the rules of good practice out of mercy? Yes. Did he do it? No." Static followed the pulsating bursts of lightning outside. "I don't know what kind of case you're building here, Major Bora, but I strongly advise you to leave me *and* Master Sergeant Weller out of it."

Unrequested advice, like threats (or even car bombs) had the peculiarity of obtaining the opposite result with Bora. "Sorry. I can't do it."

Mayr slammed the receiver down.

10

It was still raining in the morning, from clouds stretched thin like haze and about to exhaust themselves. Humidity was high: rock piles and the few paved stretches of the road steamed in the heat as soon as the sun filtered through.

Bruno Lattmann came to the doorstep of his radio shack bare-chested and in army shorts.

"Jesus, Martin, how can you wear breeches and boots in this weather – is the General Staff coming to visit? Oh, you *rode* here. Why?"

Covering his bruises under cloth and leather would keep Lattmann from enquiring, and himself from explanations. "I went off the road," Bora said indifferently. "Car's demolished."

Inside, the reek of pipe smoke was strong. Bora said nothing, but his colleague volunteered, "I picked up the vice for Eva's sake, so that I'll have some fingernails left when I go home."

Bora laughed. "A hard choice for a wife: nailless or with a pipe in his mouth. Bruno, Nagel's coming to pick me up: do you mind if I wait here? There's something I need to figure out." While honouring Bernoulli's request not to mention him personally, he recounted his phone conversation with Mayr, and his suspicions. "Nothing definite, you understand, and I know I'm sticking my neck out. But somebody has to do it."

Officiously Lattmann reached for a packet of Blue Bird, and began filling the Bakelite bowl of his pipe. "Will you do the same thing with the SS surgeon on Sumskaya, or limit yourself to locking horns with the army medical corps? Yes, I *am* being sarcastic, Martin."

"The SS surgeon promises to be a tougher nut to crack, even with the best effort. When I stopped by Sumskaya yesterday, you could tell they'd have gladly kicked me down the stairs if they thought they'd get away with it. As I found out at our headquarters soon thereafter, it appears their head surgeon was transferred to the Army Group Centre, in Mogilev."

"Well, excellent. He'll work for that beastly Franz Kutschera: a marriage made in heaven."

"Whatever, he's conveniently out of my reach. At headquarters I also saw Lieutenant Colonel von Salomon."

"Good news or bad news?"

Bora unhooked the collar of his tunic, the sole concession to the discomfort he felt in the hot room. "A mixed bag. First of all he gave me a spiel about Oswald Bumke, who is his new messiah. He's head of psychiatric and neurological services at *Wehrkreis* VII, and was even called to consult on Lenin's health in the early 1920s. The colonel is thoroughly fascinated with schizophrenia at the moment, and he wouldn't even broach military subjects before lecturing me. The disappointing news is that the regiment will not be going into Krasny Yar at this time, as I hoped. We're to patrol the Donets instead. On the positive side, they're officially conferring the decorations awarded at Stalingrad, so – provided that my schedule allows it – I'm off to Kiev for the ceremony next Thursday. Generaloberst Kempf is purposely flying there from Poltava. The best news of all is that Peter volunteered to be his pilot, so if I make it we'll get to see each other."

Unsuccessfully puffing to light his pipe, Lattmann wasted one match after another. He said, "Dinner's on you the next time we're in a civilized restaurant. Along with losing one's virginity, the Knight's Cross is a big achievement for a man."

"Yes, if I don't stop to think how many had to die in Stalingrad for a handful of us to be decorated. What's worse, it tickles my pride. Here, in anticipation of dinner." Bora took a bottle of pepper-flavoured vodka and a round tin of caviar out of his briefcase. "Smoked sturgeon, I couldn't find."

"Why, that's neighbourly." Lattmann perked up. "Shall we try it? Store-bought Pertsovka, no less!"

Bora amicably shook his head. "*Z pertsem* in Ukrainian. No, thank you. Enjoy." The sticky weather made the cuts pull and sting; the friction of cloth over them added to the unease he more or less successfully concealed. "There's something I need to get done quickly, Bruno, and that's to find a way of keeping Sanitätsoberfeldwebel Arnim Weller in Ukraine until I have a chance to question him about Dr Mayr, in reference to Platonov. On Thursday I contacted the personnel branch of the Medical Inspectorate. Unlike the first time – when they said they knew nothing about it – they confirmed Weller is in fact billeting in Kiev, from where he's due to leave tomorrow. The regular channels are no help in such cases. I approached Lieutenant Colonel von Salomon, but he doesn't want to hear of 'out of the ordinary interventions' regarding scheduled transfers, and turned me down."

"The poor bastard needs to grow a pair of balls if he wants to make full colonel." The pipe was laid aside for good. And so, for the time being, was the liquor. Lattmann dug out a cylindrical can of bread. He opened it, cut two round slices and fished a bit of butter out of a water-filled washbasin, which he spread on the slices. Next came a spoonful of caviar on each slice. "Anyway, do you expect Weller to talk? He's likely to be loyal to Mayr."

Bora said no to the offer of food. "And he could be more involved in this than I thought, despite his security clearance. I'm in a devil of a hurry to try to block him here. How would you go about delaying someone's departure?"

"In less than twenty-four hours' time? Don't know. It's got to come from high up. Hm-m, caviar's good. Sure you don't want some? All right, all right, I'm thinking. What about Geko Stark? It was he who forwarded the recommendation in the first place."

"Yes, but on Mayr's request, and I only found out because I opened the letter Stark entrusted to me. It'd be tantamount to admitting I tampered with his correspondence."

"You could tap the Kiev Branch Office for a credible excuse."

"Such as?"

Lattmann polished off the home-made canapés. "If they agree to do it, they'll think of one. All you actually need to do is bump Weller for someone else who's got travel priority over him. I'll work on it if you want me to."

"As soon as possible, Bruno."

"Where is Weller staying in Kiev, do we know?"

"At a lodging in the Solomenka district for transiting members of the armed forces, across from the Hungarian barracks. We should also have someone keep an eye on him, in case Mayr tries to get in touch and alert him."

Waiting for a radio reply from his "man in Kiev", as Lattmann referred to his *Abwehr* counterpart there, Bora had time to contact Odilo Mantau, whose mood hadn't improved since their last conversation. "Thanks to you, Major, I had an argument with the staff at the SS medical station on Sumskaya. Did you know their surgeon was assigned to Mogilev?"

"Yes. So? Did you get them to admit they sent a medic over to the jail the evening of 6 May?"

"No."

"Well, either they did or they didn't. You said he was a Security Service medic —"

"I didn't say he was a Security Service medic, I said he came from the Sumskaya first-aid station."

"Whatever. Did you at least get his name from the jail ledger?"

"Interesting that you should ask. The name is Lutz, Karl Albert. Lutz, right. And since you know it can't be, don't pretend you'll make a note of it."

"What do you mean? Why not?"

"Come on, Major!"

Bora was tempted to strike the radio with his fist. "Christ, Mantau: *why not?*"

"Because Lutz died during the spring battle for Kharkov."

"Lutz did *what?* There's something wrong with the connection: I thought I heard that he died."

"As if it was news to you. After you started making a fuss about 'someone playing with our medics', I thought I'd double-check the name and ID entered in our ledger. I discovered that Karl Albert Lutz, same rank, date and place of birth, fell on 2 March near Merefa. So I still think you or yours are behind Khan's death. However you laid your hands on a Sumskaya pass with Lutz's name on it, you must have."

"I give up, Mantau. You can't be made to see reason. We were both tricked, don't you understand?"

Lattmann nudged Bora, mouthing the words *I've got Kiev on the other radio*, and that communication took absolute priority over an argument with Odilo Mantau.

Bespalovka, 22 May, mess time.

The remounts are excellent: broken in and trained. They range from RI category for officers (one of these goes to Nagel by my specific order – the *Spiess* is a grand rider) to KR for the troop, plus heavy and extra-heavy horses of the SZK and SSZ class. In addition to the grazing opportunities this land offers, we're also well supplied with fodder. I checked the quality of our 5-kilo fodder cakes, to make sure the proportions of oats, potato parts, hay and yeast are right.

All this is good and opportune news, as our divisional HQ was requested by the commanders of the 198th and 15th IDs, Generals von Horn and Buschenhagen, to supply armed reconnaissance (and engagement against partisans if necessary) on the right bank of the Donets, where the concave bend of the river forms a wide salient on the Russian side that goes from Novo Andreyevka to the north to Novo Borisoglebsk to the south. Just the sort of operation tailor-made for the regiment. Given our orders, and the discretion I was granted, we're off in patrols to reconnoitre the vast area (50 km in length, 5 km in depth) assigned to us.

We'll leave one squadron at a time, at dusk and shortly after dark, with the usual equipment, silenced rifles at the top of the list. Depending on the weather, being five days after the full moon, if it's clear starting out after sunset on Sunday 23 we'll have about three hours of complete dark before the moon rises, at around half-midnight. If it's overcast, as I hope, the hours of dark will stretch to seven all told, because dawn will break by 4 a.m. on Monday. The same pattern will be followed the rest of the week, or however many days it'll take to achieve our objective. We expect to discover partisan nests and possibly catch some of their units on the move. Whatever we find, we're to destroy. I'm calling the operation Warm Gates, after the ancient stronghold at Thermopylae.

In other, no less important matters, Bruno was better than his word. I spoke to his counterpart at the Kiev Branch Office, who took it upon himself to delay Weller's return home on a technicality (we're very good at technicalities in today's Germany). The delay buys me only four days, until the next transport (a troop train actually heading for Konotop, where it'll meet a Fatherland-bound hospital train) picks up the medic in Kiev and takes him out of my reach. There's little chance I'll be done with the military operation by next Thursday (which incidentally means I might miss the award ceremony, too), but that's all I could swing at this time.

And there's another problem. If Mantau spoke the truth, and whoever was said to come from the Sumskaya first-aid station gave a false name, discovering what really happened to Platonov could be child's play compared to solving Khan's murder. I asked Bruno to go the whole hog, as they say, and oblige me by forwarding another question to Mantau I didn't have time to ask him today, since Nagel drove in with the GAZ vehicle the moment I was done conferring with the Branch Office.

WEDNESDAY 26 MAY

Weather and circumstances assisted Bora's plan. Acting on a lead from the 15th Division IC officer, on the night of Sunday the twenty-third his advance patrols detected movement from a partisan force heading north after crossing over from the treed area of Zadonetsky Bor. Partly mounted, the Russians advanced stealthily, and then camped without lighting fires. Bora gave orders to hold back. He sat keeping an eye on them, careful not to betray his men's presence until the following night, to understand what the enemy's intentions were. Daytime on the twenty-fourth was spent in the woods, lying low under siege by mosquitoes and flies in the weary moisture padding the terrain that overlooked the river. All contact with locals, untrustworthy or inimical, had to be avoided.

After sundown the partisans moved. With a favourably contrary breeze that kept its sounds and odours undetectable, under scudding clouds and broken moonlight, the regiment started out in pursuit, unit by unit. Fanning out, webbing, taking position. No engines, no radios, dispatch riders on horseback and on foot.

At first daylight on the twenty-fifth the partisans huddled again. Boys comprised the mounted patrols they sent out to scout the surroundings; the invisible Germans let them go past. After stopping at the old Tichonov farm, the Russians changed direction under cover of darkness. They took the dirt lane that led through the woods in a due south direction, possibly to a rendezvous point on the banks of the Gomolischa, a tributary of the Donets. Keeping out of sight, Bora's men followed and skirted the woods from the outside.

His intuition was once more right. Two separate partisan forces were converging to meld men and materiel. The opportunity was so rich, he had to convince his officers not to engage when the enemy exited the woods and to bide their time until the subsequent night. With a waning moon and the occasional overcast, at 2 a.m. on Wednesday 26 May four *Gothland* squadrons drew near an unsuspected country spot called Kurgan Bischkina, not far from the Donets, at the mouth of an east–west ravine – Semionov Yar. There, the combined partisan body, at least three companies' worth of partly mounted men, gathered for the night. Having quietly sealed off the head of the ravine, the Germans disposed of those on watch along the rim using Soviet-made silenced rifles, and by the time the Russians realized what was happening, mortar and machine-gun fire confronted them from three sides. Dawn broke on a fierce shoot-out that precluded escape. Trying to battle their way out the trap and backtrack towards Kurgan Bischkina, the survivors ran into Bora's own squadron, which lay in wait and mowed them down. One by one, stragglers were chased and picked off. The Germans spared the horses whenever possible, and no one else.

As baptisms of fire go, it was a resounding success for *Gothland*. The only disappointment came with the news that a separate partisan force had successfully escaped encirclement by a company of the 198th ID near the Obasnovka farm, and recrossed the Donets without losses. As for Bora, seventeen wounded troopers (three seriously) and a handful of slightly injured mounts weighed like a feather compared to the nearly two hundred casualties on the opposite side, plus prisoners (mostly youngsters and elders), horses and lend-lease materiel.

The morning was spent destroying equipment and ammunition, harvesting maps, cleaning up as needed and drafting notes for the debriefing at Kharkov later on. Bora was elated, but his mind was already running over the next piece of work: flying to Kiev in the morning to interrogate Arnim Anton Weller about his direct superior at Hospital 169. Thank God Lippe, his second-in-command, was a star-quality officer; Bora safely left him in charge and hurried off.

He arrived at Borovoye late in the afternoon, with the sun still blinding at its low angle. Bruno Lattmann placed a shot of pepper vodka in front of him, which Bora did not touch. Had there been an agreement between them not to discuss the operation, they couldn't have acted more evasively about it. Aside from the fact that Bora had hastily shaved without soap, and presented as wrinkled an appearance as one such as him was likely to tolerate, it transpired that things had gone well.

"Any word from Mantau, Bruno?"

"Well, I forwarded to him your request for a description of the 'Sumskaya medic who visited Tibyetsky the evening of 6 May.'"

"And?"

"Judge for yourself." Lattmann picked up a clipboard. "Here's what I jotted down. I doubt it'll take you one step further. First of all, the shithead flew off the handle: 'What does Bora expect – a patch on the eye or a missing tooth?' Then he said the jail personnel, when asked about it, agreed with him that the man was 'average in every sense: height, weight, et cetera.' About 175 cm, about 75 kilos, with dark blond or light brown hair. Herr Anybody or Herr Nobody, your choice."

"He *is* a shithead."

"QED. So I pressured him for details, mannerisms, et cetera. Nothing; or else no one was paying much attention after Khan's temper tantrum." Lattmann tossed the clipboard across the shack floor, on to his bed. "The only detail the genius came up with is a blackened or stubbed thumbnail on the medic's right hand, which Mantau God knows why noticed."

Bora blinked. He automatically reached for the liquor, and gulped it down. *War marks us all, sooner or later.* Mutilations, large marks, minutiae. The Gestapo captain's preoccupation with his own hands and nails overlapped in his mind with the scene at Platonov's bedside, on the day of his death. Odilo Mantau *would* notice. "Pour me another."

"If it helps you swallow disappointment."

Bora downed a second drink. "It'll have to do more than that, Bruno, if the late Karl Albert Lutz turns out to be

Sanitätsoberfeldwebel Arnim Weller." In the convulsed moments after Platonov's death, he recalled staring at details: the surgeon's jaundiced face, the discolouration on the medic's nail as he hastily put away the needle he'd used. Details like pointers to a greater truth. "Holy Christ, I should have thought of it. But how in hell... Quick, see if you can connect me to Dr Mayr at Hospital No. 169."

The conversation that followed, halved as Lattmann heard it, was at the same time bizarre and absolutely consistent, though not necessarily so in the surgeon's opinion. Bora began by saying, "I'll apologize when I have time. Now answer me, Herr Oberstarzt, or as true as God is I'll make sure the Security Service comes knocking on your door. What do you know of Arnim Weller's past history, how long have you known him, and whom did he frequent outside the hospital? There's a remote chance of Weller getting a regular court martial if you answer me." For a few moments Bora listened, nodding to himself. "Was it cowardice under fire, or was it desertion? That's not just *losing one's nerve*, Dr Mayr: abandoning one's post is tantamount to desertion if he left the field hospital and 'hid with Russian folks' for a week! Is that fact known? I don't care how you covered it up: is the fact known to others? Can it be used against him? In the two years you have known him, did you ever suspect him of unprofessional practices? Don't push me; I don't need to define them. No? I doubt it, and I doubt he didn't give you reason to worry: you worried as soon as he was transferred. You feared his past flaws were catching up with him. It doesn't matter what you think, frankly. Clearly he had access to your office cabinet. Whom did he frequent outside the hospital, do you know? He went out three days a week for supplies: and then? Drove the ambulance occasion-ally: and then? Did you confront him for taking longer than his errands required? Why not? The fuel depot, the *Kombinat* and the special detention centre can't be the sole places he frequented. The mess-hall doesn't count. A drinking place:

where? Did he have acquaintances among SS sanitary service colleagues? I am being *perfectly* coherent, Herr Oberstarzt, and excruciatingly clear-minded."

Lattmann sat on a stack of boxes dangling his legs. When Bora was done with his phone call he gave him a thoughtful look. "It's a lucky thing Mayr is in the political doghouse. If he weren't he'd have your ass for doing what you just did."

"As it is, he'll be grateful I didn't sic the State Police on him. He's involved in this by association, whether he knew it or not. All I actually got out of him is that Weller may be open to blackmail. Under blackmail you're prone to do anything. If you 'lost your nerve' besides, and hanker to go home, you can be manoeuvred."

"By whom? Not the Central Security Office!"

"Why 'Not the Central Security Office'? Weller was given security clearance, wasn't he? Mantau isn't told everything that goes on."

"No more than you or I are told on our side. And if they wanted to deprive us of Khan by wiping him out, why would they kill Platonov too?"

Bora washed down the vodka with a long drink of water from his canteen. "Thanks for helping, Bruno. I have to get going. This is in hope they didn't monitor the conversation, because I'm likely to be preceded by the SS to Kiev. Whatever role they play in this story, I wouldn't give a fig for Weller's life then." He turned back from the door. "Wait. That gives me an idea. It's better if they know we know, just in case: it'll keep them from doing something blatantly stupid. Get me Mantau in any way you can."

It was fortuitous that Lattmann found the Gestapo officer at the same radio frequency, given that *Sonderkommando* 4a was branching out and redeploying those days.

Mantau's comment at Bora's news came quick and sour. "Should I be impressed, Major? Of course you know who the man really is: you sent him."

"For God's sake, I did *not* send him. And if we don't act quickly, he'll be leaving Ukraine tomorrow morning."

More explanation had to follow before Mantau grasped the urgency of the situation. "What time is the train departing Kiev, and from which station exactly?" he asked then. "Our people there can detain the locomotive at the platform if necessary, even if it's a troop transport."

The boast was welcome, for a change. "You do that, Hauptsturmführer. The Vinnitsa–Konotop train is expected to leave at 11 a.m. from Kiev's Central Station. With a bit of luck, by that time I'll be in town myself."

Lattmann's wiry crew cut was beaded with sweat. He let his teeth clack around the pipe shaft while Bora, standing on the doorstep, put on his prize Ray-Bans against the merciless low sun and prepared to drive away. "I hope you know what you're doing, Martin."

"I don't. I'll have to figure it out as I go along. If Weller was present when both generals died, he's likely to be the sole executioner. His timely disappearance en route to a sudden assignment, the circumstance of his false documents... too elaborate: it smacks of a larger plan. You're right; it may be too large for me to handle. But what choice do I have? They expect me to solve this at headquarters, and I can't let too many people in on it."

"*If* Weller is your man, for whatever reason and at whomever's orders he's being shipped to Germany, he didn't believe for a moment that he was accidentally bumped from Sunday's train. He's aware he may be under watch. We monitored no calls from Hospital 169 to him, but I wouldn't count on Weller waiting for the next transport at his regular billet, for example. And Kiev's a big place."

"Who is head of police in Kiev?"

"Major Stunde of the *Schupo*. I think there's a Captain Pfahl heading the Ukrainian auxiliary units."

"Since all those en route to Germany from Kiev are temporarily housed in the Solomenka district, this reduces the playing field. Let's hope police units aren't too obvious, not to speak of the local auxiliaries: we don't want to spook Weller. How much discretion does your friend at the Kiev Branch Office have?"

"Enough to keep an eye on departing trains, but at Solomenka it'll have to be *Schupo* or Gestapo. You're off? Hey – wait a second, you didn't say a word on how the patrolling went!"

Bora smiled a little. "Ivan played Leonidas to my Immortals. But they didn't expect us, and it's just the beginning."

In the afterglow, towering clouds fanned into tumultuous, hammer-shaped heads across the western sky, a promise of thunderstorms down Kiev's way. In the basic but reliable GAZ vehicle Bora covered the thirty-something kilometres from Borovoye to Kharkov only to find von Salomon, who was to debrief him, reclining in his chair with a wet towel over his eyes. "It'll have to wait until the morning, Major, as we're flying to the ceremony."

Bora saluted sarcastically, and left the office. Had he known this he'd have spent the night at Merefa, where it was now too dark to travel. A fortunate intuition had made him take along to Borovoye his change, best uniform, medals, all he needed for the trip to Kiev, on his way to Operation Thermopylae. So he had everything with him, and prepared himself to settle for any horizontal surface at headquarters (even the floor would do) to sleep. He was actually exhausted, "running on fumes", as he'd later note in his diary; a wooden bench in the hallway seemed luxurious enough to lie down on, even though he couldn't stretch his full length, and in the morning he discovered he'd fallen off it without even waking up.

THURSDAY 27 MAY

The Kiev-bound officers were expected at the Kharkov Aerodrome in time to leave at 6 a.m. on a Ju-52 that had seen better days. Bora's travel companions included Lieutenant Colonel von Salomon representing ID 161, two members of the 7th Panzer about to receive the German Cross in Gold at the same ceremony, and a major general being repatriated for health reasons. Fighters due to escort the transport plane waited on the runway, their pilots drinking coffee and playing with small hairy dogs.

As they idled near the aircraft, a tense von Salomon enquired about the weather in Kiev. "Oh, I think there's a thunderstorm between here and there, Herr Oberstleutnant," answered the co-pilot light-heartedly. "We'll dance a bit." Bora recognized the amused contempt towards landlubbers on the part of one who loves to fly, because it was also Peter's.

Bora didn't care about the weather. He did worry about the timing, though. While not as old as the one Bentivegni had flown in weeks earlier, the Junkers (formerly a glider tug in Crete, as its nose art went to prove) could take up to three hours to cover the distance to Kiev. Besides, the major general and his recurring ulcer were running late, and while everyone else in the group felt no hurry because the ceremony was scheduled for "16.00 hours sharp", Bora grew silently anxious about catching Weller before the Vinnitsa train pulled in at Kiev Central. Still they waited. The fighter pilots had time to go back to the grassy edge of the runway and toss sticks for their dogs to catch; the westerly thunderheads mounted and spread into an unhealthy-looking rampart, in a repeat of the day Bentivegni had been delayed on the way to Kharkov. Bora fidgeted, trying not to show his discomfort. Not that anyone was paying attention to him: the award recipients beamed in anticipation; pilot and co-pilot stood around chewing on unlit cigars; von Salomon drank from a metal flask too small to contain water.

As God willed, the major general came in at 6.30 a.m., riding to the runway in a staff car black and slick like a whale calf. With him arrived his aide, an excess of luggage and boxed souvenirs, plus a case of first-rate vodka ("That'll do wonders for his ulcer," Bora overheard the pilot comment under his breath).

The general distributed fine cigars to the officers – two each to those about to be honoured – and climbed the short ladder into the plane. While the escort fighters taxied into position and prepared to take off one after the other, the rest of the passengers reached their seats. Bora, in watchful *Abwehr* fashion, was the last to climb on board, and seized the moment to hand his cigars to the young airman waiting to remove the ladder.

It turned out that von Solomon didn't like air travel. The decision to schedule the debriefing today was an excuse to distract himself during the bumpy flight. The moment they gained altitude, the elderly plane began to oblige the co-pilot by "dancing". More than once it hit air pockets and dropped for a few interminable seconds, which turned the colonel's knuckles white on the armrests. Bora did all he could not to check his wristwatch, to avoid giving the impression that he, too, feared flying.

With contrary winds, the Junkers came in sight of sunny Kiev four hours later, having made a wide deviation to avoid the worst of the thunderstorm, and circled over the city before the pilot felt comfortable to approach the Borispol landing field from the west. Fifteen minutes more and it would be 11 a.m., the time when the Vinnitsa train was due to leave *Kiew Hauptbahnhof.* Bora could only rely on the Gestapo's ability (or willingness) to block it at the platform, as Mantau had promised. Under the plane drifted the north-western suburbs of the city, battered by the 1941 battle; the empty fields and scarred upheaval of the ravine by the deserted Jewish cemetery rolled by, as did other graveyards and parks. As they flew low over the Dnieper, Bora saw people basking on the island's river beach, a sign that even in a city largely depopulated and under severe German administration life went on somehow. Girls in bright bathing suits lay on the shingle, German soldiers in black shorts lazing by their side. Even in his preoccupied mindset, Bora felt a sting of foreknowledge and envious regret: *Dikta and I will never be like that; there's nothing like it in store for us.*

Borispol actually lay at least forty-five minutes from Kiev, on the east bank of the Dnieper, and they would have to drive downtown. The worst news was that the cars expected to pick up the officers were not at the airfield. Not even an angry tiff on the part of the major general (himself in no special hurry, but generals aren't made to wait) changed the truth of the matter. It was now past eleven. The escort fighters did a flyover and nosed back towards the storm. There would be no air protection for those returning to Kharkov the day after now that the highest-ranking passenger had been safely deposited in Kiev.

Upon discovering that official transportation was lacking, Bora tried to find other means by which he could reach the city. Whether they suspected he was acting on the general's behalf or not, the airfield folks were not sympathetic. No one could spare a vehicle or the fuel to make it go. Bora seethed and tried to keep calm at the same time. If the Gestapo did its part in Kiev, they might be holding up the train's departure, although it was unlikely they could delay at will troops bound for deployment. And he couldn't swear by Mantau's brag or promises, which heightened his anxiety.

Finally, at 11.28 a.m., the passengers were able to pile up inside a pre-Purge Soviet GAZ-03 staff bus and start for the city. Masonry and rail bridges being destroyed, they crossed the Dnieper over a pontoon bridge. Beyond, the high wooded cliff where Old Kiev stood with its surviving cupolas and sunlit spires resembled a storybook island, although Bora knew all too well the evidence of war behind it. The award ceremony's lead, General Kempf, would be landing with Peter about now. Flying by choice in an inconspicuous Henschel reconnaissance plane, capable of covering the distance from Poltava to Kiev in an hour, he'd selected the Gostomel airstrip, north of the city and closer to it.

Bora's group was bound for a hotel in what had been the banking and mercantile district before the Revolution, when it had been called the Europa. Near a riverside park formerly known as Proletarsky, and Merchant's Park at the turn of the century, the establishment presented the advantages of being downtown but easily reached from Gostomel, and at the farthest end of Kiev's demolished Kreshchatyk Street. Even so, the major general made his own billeting arrangements. He had stayed away from Russian hotels ever since the day in 1941 when the Reds blew up a square mile of officers' lodgings on Kreshchatyk, now appropriately called Eichhornstrasse after the Prussian commander assassinated in Kiev in World War I.

12.15 p.m. Bora literally dropped his scant luggage in the lobby and commandeered the GAZ-03 to Kiev Central Station, a good three kilometres of zigzags across aged French-looking boulevards and blocks of modern housing reduced to rubble. Vegetables grew in the flowerbeds, drinking places for the troops opened at every street corner, cement pillboxes and consignment stores alternated with bolted doorways and broken windows; a babel of street signs in German pointed to headquarters, hospitals, theatres. Bora urged the driver to go faster than he realistically could.

"We're getting there, Herr Major."

In peacetime Kiev Central, with its exotic tent-like central body, had represented the best and worst of Ukrainian Baroque. It had been added on to throughout the years, and now it also showed the wear and tear of seven hundred days of war. It read, starkly black on its masonry, KIEW HBF.

Hurrying inside, Bora saw no sign of a train on the rails and conceded he'd got there far too late. After all, it was nearly half past noon. Soldiers with dogs on leashes patrolled the platform, a usual sight; he recognized the Hungarian military police and – for all of their plain clothes – Gestapo operatives as well. Obviously they hadn't kept the troop transport from leaving. Had they at least detained Arnim Weller? He struggled not to give in to his frustration as he walked to the stationmaster's office.

The reply from the German official heartened him at once. Due to a "technical glitch" (this usually meant trouble on the line because of partisan activity), the train from Vinnitsa was travelling with a two-hour delay. It was now expected to reach Kiev at 1 p.m. and depart half an hour later. Bora also learnt that passengers due to reach Germany would have to get off the train at the junction before Konotop, where the line intersected the railroad to Gomel–Bobruisk–Minsk–Vilna–Kovno–Königsberg.

It was a welcome breather. Bora stepped out of the office and was at once acutely aware of all that surrounded him – temperature, sounds, odours – because the game was still on. He approached a Gestapo plain-clothes man, who didn't expect to be recognized in his Ukrainian labourer garb and reacted sourly. He changed his tune after Bora had identified himself and his errand. Yes, he said, those due for repatriation were still in the waiting room. "They came in time to catch the 11.00 train. Given the delay, some of them could have decided to leave the station and return later. We had orders, so we kept them here. There are thirty-two of them, from Army Groups South and Centre. We were given two names to look out for: Weller and Lutz, but the man isn't here. There's a chance he heard there'd be a delay and he'll be arriving for the 13.00 departure."

Bora inhaled deeply to keep from losing hope again. In the air there was an odour of boiled sausage, warm metal roofs, peeling paint. Scraggy weeds grew out of the ballast between the tracks. The Solomenka district wasn't far from here. On his stepfather's 1918 map, which he carried among his many charts, it looked like a built-in outgrowth of the railroad in a green area bounded by a graveyard and the barracks of the military schools. A settlement on its way to becoming a city neighbourhood, Sichnyevka was its name now, but they all called it by the old name out of habit.

First, however, he had better talk to those in the waiting room. There at a glance he'd had confirmation that Weller was not sitting among them. Asked about him, those who'd shared the same housing with the medic had little to say: on the silent side, kept to himself. They assumed that for whatever reason he hadn't yet reached the station, he'd arrive as the time of departure drew close. Bora had his doubts. The Gestapo plain-clothes man was right: no home-bound soldier – and especially not Weller – would risk missing a train by not being at the station well in advance, as you never know where and how the next one will arrive in wartime.

Across the tracks, a handful of former settlements (Solomenka, First of May, Olexandrovskaya Sloboda) flanked a long road that went to die in the fields four or five kilometres away. The workers' housing across from the Hungarian barracks, now a dormitory for transiting servicemen, was run by garrison administration non-coms. There Bora heard that Master Sergeant Weller had reported in the night before, as he'd done on previous nights. He'd left at 8 a.m., on foot like the others due to take today's transport for Germany.

"Did they all leave so early? The train wouldn't start out before eleven."

"No, sir. Some waited until 09.00 before heading for the station. At most. Anxious as they all were to get home, Herr Major, none wanted to risk missing the transport. And Master Sergeant Weller had been left behind on Sunday, so you *know* he'd make sure he was there on time."

"Did he have his luggage with him?"

"He did."

A distant train whistle from the south-west came in the wind, trembling with its remoteness. Bora glanced at the wall clock behind the non-com. 12.46 p.m. Was the late transport from Vinnitsa arriving already? There was nothing else he could do here, so he said, "Should Weller come back for any reason, keep him here, call the Hotel Europa immediately, and ask for Major Martin Bora."

The troop transport pulled in slightly ahead of schedule at 12.52 p.m., when Bora was back at his place of observation on the platform. The streets outside and all entrances had someone keeping an eye on them. Still no sign of Weller. With orders not to let any of those on board off, Gestapo and military police cordoned the side of the braking train by doing their usual overbearing act, gesticulating and shouting when the travellers, overheated and anxious to stretch their legs after the long journey, protested from the lowered windows. The occasional officer shouldered his way among them to voice his anger. But there were military police aboard the cars as well, so the grumbling eventually simmered down. Faces of men headed for the coming battle and probable death (Bora knew: it was an officer's lot to know these things and keep stern control) crowded to look out at the unattainable platform. It was a long convoy of cars: one could only hope the air force would look after it between here and Konotop, and then watch over those going from Konotop to the German border.

On the platform, dogs barked, snarled and pulled the leashes; their handlers quickly strode back and forth behind them. When Ukrainian girls fluttered in to sell bliny, doughnuts and cornets of cherries, the soldiers in the train whistled and called out to them: arms, hands, banknotes stretched out of the windows. The moment the train had appeared on the tracks, the thirty or so servicemen being repatriated – most of them permanently injured – pressed out of the waiting room, and now stood where the Gestapo had corralled them, waiting for the only door into their car to open. Then, one by one, they filed by the military policemen checking their papers and climbed on board. Supposing Weller might try to rush in at the last moment, Bora stood a step away, watching with his arms crossed, ready to take out his pistol in seconds flat. However, Weller was nowhere; no one resembling Weller came running in the nick of time. At 1.36 p.m., following Bora's nod, the door closed, and after the customary whistle-blowing the train slowly moved out of the station.

The thing that most angered Bora in his disappointment was that, with no more than a cup of coffee in his system since the morning, he was famished. The physical reaction irritated him, as if its presence fouled the unalloyed nature of his displeasure. Anyhow, there would be no more trains for the day, and no more Germany-bound transports for two weeks. He left word with those providing security to the station to control all passes and keep on the lookout for Arnim Weller. Staying here would be no use. At this point the possibilities multiplied instead of diminishing: Weller could have somehow left Kiev (how? from where?) and might try to get on the troop transport at one of its next stops – a dim possibility given the frequent controls and the distance between stations. Alternatively, he'd smelt a trap after being bumped off the Sunday train; he might seek a hideout in this large, partly ruined city in hopes of weathering the storm, but in view of what? Or, again, he'd attempt against all hope to catch another – any – means of transportation out of Ukraine. *He's not armed, as far as I know. But he's a deserter now, and can be shot on sight.*

The idea that Arnim Weller might be hiding out in Kiev was the most likely. From the stationmaster's office, Bora telephoned Major Stunde and Captain Pfahl to alert the German and Ukrainian police of his dilemma. Not that he hoped they could actually solve it: he received confirmation that, given the amount of destroyed and semi-destroyed buildings in Kiev, the possibility of keeping out of sight was immense. The abandoned Central Department Store on Eichhornstrasse, the shell of the old Ginzburg House near Institute Street, the Gorodetsky House on Bismarckstrasse, imperial era flats and Soviet tenements... all places that had to be routinely checked because they attracted "stragglers, undesirables and even leftover Yids". Still, unlike Bora, Stunde and Pfahl were optimistic: they would pass the word on, interact and keep an eye on public transportation.

Bora left the station. Outside, at least the SS had the common sense of not parading their vehicles and alarming anyone on the lookout for them. Too late, in any case. It was hot, late, and he was hungry. So, the Gestapo had lost their man after all.

Sure, Weller could have resorted to any one of several things, including hiding under a different name. Unless of course he'd chosen the ultimate and most successful form of escape: doing away with himself, spontaneously or with someone else's encouragement. Bora would rather not think of it. From their point of view, Stunde and Pfahl had reason for optimism: after all, this was the town where thirty-five thousand would receive the *special treatment* in two days' time. What was one deserter to the system?

From the station, the sweets-and-cherries girls came out counting money, chattering like swallows. On the sidewalk where Bora stood, a newspaper and magazine kiosk featured papers in Cyrillic, Hungarian, German, pencil portraits and caricatures commissioned by soldiers from local street artists, and a healthy choice of pornographic material. The odour of boiled sausage rode the warm breeze from an eating place on Stepankovskaya, or from the old Ukrainian Police Command beyond. Sealing Weller out of his mind for the time being, and for the rest of the day, was a chore that had to be accomplished. Bora shook the dozing driver of the GAZ-03, and had him drive back to the Europa.

1 p.m. Von Salomon and the other award recipients were lingering around the lunch table in the dining room. General Kempf had come in, and so had Captain Peter Sickingen, who was waiting for Bora in the lobby. The brothers exchanged a smiling military salute and a handshake.

"Sorry about keeping you waiting, Peter."

"You didn't; I just came back myself. Had to run to the edge of town and see the street named after the Heroes of the Stratosphere, those of the 1934 balloon disaster: Russians, but pilots all the same." Peter beamed. "Good thing you're here, though: I'm starving. Look, I brought my brand-new film camera: I'm recording the ceremony for our parents and the girls. I bought it to film Duckie's baby after it's born, but it's worth inaugurating it today."

Bora did not comment on the fact that the street mentioned by Peter bordered Solomenka, and they'd risked running into each other. "Nonsense. You should save the camera for Margaretha and the baby."

"No, no. I'm filming the ceremony, and that's that. I shall label the reel 'My Brother, the Bearer of the Knight's Cross.'"

Save for Peter's hazel eyes and auburn hair, they'd always resembled one another; now for both of them it was almost like looking at oneself in a different uniform. Their size and demeanour were the same, with all that Bora was slightly less amiable and more introverted. They were calm, with the steadiness of the first-line officer and squadron commander; the four and a half years between them made a difference, though, in that Bora was morally highly strung, and Peter as doubt-free as Bora had been in 1939.

Having excused themselves from Kempf and the rest of the group, the brothers lunched together in the park-view room they would share overnight.

Had they known that Peter had less than two weeks to live, they wouldn't have spent time chatting about light-hearted things; or perhaps they would have. Bora was anxious for his younger brother as he'd never been for himself, which meant he had to go out of his way to hide his concern. He gave Peter rope because Peter was the picture of confidence, and little by little he began to feel hopeful, too. *One of the two will make it back, of this much I'm sure. It has to be Peter, so all is well.*

"Neinz," (it was Bora's seldom-used nickname, given him by Peter when as a child he hadn't been able to pronounce Marti*n Heinz*) "remember when we were boys and got drunk at Trakhenen? I never had such fun."

"You didn't? We fell off our bikes and the farmers found us passed out at the side of the road."

"Good thing they did, too, and kept us with them until we were presentable."

"Well, we'd drained half a bottle of their home-made Bärenfang. You were eight, I twelve, and the honey brandy 90-proof."

"Glorious, wasn't it? Man, how we sang *The Watch on the Rhine* at the top of our voices while zigzagging towards Gumbinnen! You took the blame then, and also when I wrote to Air Marshal Balbo."

Bora grinned. "I had to. You didn't speak Italian." From the room's French window, beyond the ornate, narrow railing, the wild treetops in the park quivered in the breeze. There, as in other Kiev gardens where girls strolled in cork-soled sandals, rows of German soldiers lay buried. It surprised him to think of it. But then, seen from the air, the ravine by the deserted Jewish cemetery was as tenderly green as those treetops, with its overgrown but detectable long furrow at the bottom, ploughed over, pale with fat tufts of grass. Old Woman's Gorge was its name, a monument to *special treatment*. Bora kept smiling out of courtesy. Like all euphemisms, *special treatment* jarred; it was empty words. Or words too full. Being more informed than most weighed on him and ached at times like this. The wedding band on his brother's right hand and his incipient fatherhood were another cause of surprise, as though they were out of place here and now in their lives: they had nothing to do with the green park, or the ravine north of Kiev, or the childhood they spoke of. "I had to," Bora repeated. "I'd been the translator who sent the letter to him, after all."

"But it'd been I who came up with the 'Excellency! As a young German enthusiast of transoceanic flight and fervid admirer of yours,' never thinking Balbo would answer and invite me to Rome. Father nearly tanned your hide that time, figuratively speaking."

"I could take it; I was out of his reach in Cavalry School." It wasn't like Peter to reminisce about the old days. That Bora had been listed as missing in action and presumed dead at Stalingrad might have made a difference, or else – as was expected – the start of a new family played a part in it. Bora touched his wine glass to Peter's. "Here's to your family, Squadron Commander Sickingen."

"And to the one you'll have. You're a swell brother, Martin."

"So are you."

And then they ate in silence, having come as close as they would to admitting that they worried about each other.

The award ceremony went without a hitch at Von Schleifer Square. The choice of location was a curious, if symbolic one: the former Spartacus Square, where streets named after Marx and Engels had converged until the war. Cobblestoned, faced by respectable buildings with ornate balconies, it was also easy to watch over. Bora went through the motions with the expected aplomb and mixed feelings of pride and melancholy. This was the tail end of Stalingrad for the survivors of the great and annihilated Sixth Army: handshakes, red leather folders, finely tooled black boxes for coveted metal trinkets. Among the others, behind his camera-wielding brother and a dark-clad handful of Panzer Corps officers in the first row, who should be unostentatiously attending but Heeresrichter Kaspar Bernoulli. Bora felt a renewed tinge of unease at his ubiquitous presence. The judge made no effort to approach Bora afterwards, although they eventually happened to come face to face during the expected socializing time.

Bernoulli nodded a greeting. "Congratulations, Major Bora."

"Thank you, sir."

"Quite an accomplishment. The Air Force captain I was standing behind must be your brother. He's my old *Freikorps* colleague Sickingen's son, isn't he? Looks very much like you."

"Yes, we take after our mother." The day, with its tensions and sense of unfinished business, was taking on a stranger and stranger form. Bora stated the obvious, something he did only when he felt insecure. "It's quite a coincidence meeting you, Dr Bernoulli."

Arms relaxed, the military judge kept his hands clasped before his person – a professorial or priestly stance. "Less than it seems. You were in Kiev before; you should know I have some errands here." (The green ravine by the cemetery, like a scar in the land.) "*Veritas liberabit vos.*"

Einsatzgruppe C, *Sonderkommando* 4a. End of September 1941. Bora looked beyond the judge to the spot where his brother stood full of laughter among colleagues like his own positive, sunny double. "Truth doesn't set us free at all."

"Quite the contrary, in fact. But we can't ignore it." In his unadorned field uniform, Bernoulli cut an ordinary figure compared with his highly decorated equals in rank. "It goes without saying that I'm not broadcasting that the ravine at Babi Yar, so visible from the air, is the reason for my presence in Kiev. Let's say I love award ceremonies."

Did it mean the judge had completed his investigation in Kharkov, and was backtracking towards Germany after the scent of other reports? His evasiveness did not invite questions about future plans, so Bora refrained from enquiries. He did say, however, "Notwithstanding a serious setback, I hope to be able to report to Colonel Bentivegni my preliminary findings about the matter which, in your words, I was 'encouraged to look into'."

Lieutenant Colonel von Salomon was approaching with an army photographer, no doubt to have his picture taken alongside Bora. After all, the 161st ID was Regiment *Gothland*'s parent unit. With an indifferent air Bernoulli made a sidestepping move, but not before a last quick exchange. "Does it mean you've discovered who killed Tibyetsky?"

"And Platonov."

"And can you prove it?"

"No."

That evening there was no avoiding an official dinner, after which Bora closeted himself to phone the chiefs of German and Ukrainian police. Not altogether a waste of time, as Major Stunde had a German witness who'd seen Arnim Weller heading *away* from the train station shortly after 8 a.m. Lattmann's "man in Kiev", on the other hand, called at the Europa and sat with him until late.

Close to midnight, climbing the stairs to retire, Bora felt slightly less pessimistic about the chances of securing the army medic for interrogation.

As for Peter, he'd brought along a book of French poetry, Duckie's gift, and was reading in bed when his brother joined him.

"I'd never read this fellow Villon before," he said. "He's not bad at all."

Bora removed the Knight's Cross from around his neck and draped it by its ribbon across the dresser's mirror. He started taking off his uniform. "Is it 'The Ballad of the Hanged Men', or 'The Ladies of Yesteryear'?"

"Don't know: this one's called 'The Regrets of the Pretty Armour-Maker'." Peter reading poetry was as novel as Peter putting a cigar in his mouth. "Do you mind if I smoke? I know you quit."

"Go ahead." While his brother lit the cigar (the seasoned pilot's trademark), Bora glanced at the poem, which he'd read years before. "Les regrets de la belle Heaulmière" bemoaned the loss of youth and beauty, and the poet's final comment was, "That's how we do regret the good old days, / Among us fools… " Four hundred years hadn't made much difference to regret, apparently, or to the objective foolishness of regretting.

After a shower and a shave, Bora prepared to go to bed. Sitting up with the book in his lap, Peter smoked – Russian brand, Khan's aromatic tobacco! – and watched him slip under the sheet in his underwear. "What happened to your knees and elbow?"

"Nothing: a mishap with the car. Don't tell our mother."

"I won't. Remember when we swore we'd never wear pyjamas?"

"As you see, I still don't. Do you?"

"Well, Duckie asked that I wear them at home. I suppose Benedikta lets you do without altogether, lucky dog. She'll change as soon as she's expecting." Peter put out the cigar, laid the book on the bedside table and waited until Bora turned the light off. After a moment, he added, "Duckie and I mean to start working on the next one come Christmas. We plan on five, like her family."

Bora smiled in the dark. "Well, you're on your way. Dikta and I will have some catching up to do."

"It'll be fun."

"It'll be fun."

"You can probably imagine it all already. Grandmother Ashworth-Douglas says you've got the second sight, that it's the Scots in you."

"I thought the Scots in me only made me hold my drink well."

This wing of the hotel was taken over by the award recipients and others who'd participated in the ceremony. Some of them were retiring now: there followed the footfall of boots on runners, the opening and closing of doors. They were talking loudly after the many toasts and after-dinner drinks. At one point Kempf must have made his appearance, because they went suddenly quiet, and then it was a sequence of moderate *Gute Nacht, Herr General*s up and down the corridor.

Bora had nearly finished constructing an elaborate set of reasons why he could share Stunde and Pfahl's trust that they would catch Weller, when Peter, whom he thought fast asleep, broke the silence from across the room.

"It'll be all right, won't it? For you and me and the girls, I mean."

Bora's heart shrank at the words. It felt suddenly small and hard like a marble in his chest, just as easy to toss and play with, or to lose. "What are you talking about, knucklehead? Of course it will." Behind the cheerful reply, he realized he'd seldom felt so sad. All evening he'd fought against the feeling, telling himself it was the let-down of losing Weller, or the anticlimax after the ceremony, or the coming of fever. It was not. It was not, and he wasn't about to look into it, because he had no second sight and because he was afraid. "It'll be all right for all of us, Peter."

"Good night, then."

"Good night."

FRIDAY 28 MAY

In the morning, with General Kempf, who wanted to fly back immediately to Poltava, the brothers said a hurried goodbye on the hotel steps.

"Take care, Peter."

"You too."

Bora was tempted by a physical, aching desire to exchange a hug – unusual for one so reserved – but refrained from it, lest Peter worried. Obscurely, and denying it to himself, he knew it was the last time they would see each other in life. Now and throughout the following week, in order to function, he repeated *The one who will make it back has to be Peter, so all is well* to himself until he became wholly convinced of it. They would talk by phone once again, and again never mention their mutual affection. Ten days from today it would be up to Bora, alerted to a German plane wreck north of Bespalovka, to discover how war *really* left its mark.

11

28 MAY, AFTERNOON, MEREFA

By midday, having safely landed in Kharkov, Bora drove von Salomon to divisional headquarters. There, he heard the unwelcome news that an SS *Totenkopf* battalion had pre-empted his plans to reconnoitre Krasny Yar, and as of dawn on Thursday had been engaged in the operation. Obviously no proprietary claim could be staked on missions. All the same, the timing and choice of target put him on alert. With only a few days left before his time would be absorbed by readying the regiment for full-scale action, Bora chafed at the bit at having once more arrived too late. Units of the 161st ID encamped in the area reported the passage of troops, shooting and random explosions in the woods. The latter detail set Bora off. *If there's a God, the snooping bastards have stepped into our own or Ivan's minefields; more likely, they cleared their path that way, or blew up something in the Yar: what, and what for?*

The use of firearms confirmed the presence of hostiles (although not necessarily, with *Totenkopf*); the blasts could point to a crude mode of getting at whatever might be concealed within the woods. It remained to be seen whether the SS were operating according to routine and had incidentally discovered occupants and materiel, or had been given the specific charge of seeking both at Krasny Yar.

"Do we know who authorized the operation?" Bora asked von Salomon's paper-pushing lieutenant.

"As far as we know, sir, it was planned by SS Oberstgruppenführer Max Simon himself, and entrusted to the 3rd Panzer Engineer Battalion. Our HQ was informed after the operation was under way."

"Why the armoured engineers?"

"Don't know, sir."

Bora had seen members of *Totenkopf* serving as a fire brigade in Kharkov, but knew their reputation for ruthlessness. Simon headed them now that their founding father, General Eicke, had been shot down and killed in the spring. Officially bound for Bespalovka and his regiment to follow up on Thermopylae, Bora left for Borovoye directly from divisional headquarters.

Lattmann couldn't add much information. The SS had maintained radio silence and travelled quickly to the operation zone.

"Would you say in a hurry?"

"I would say they went in seeming to know exactly what they were doing."

"Not the way you reconnoitre."

"Hardly. Trucks and armoured vehicles went by; I could see them from here. I keep informants at Vodyanoy: we'll see what they've got to say."

"Vodyanoy? That's not far from the Kalekina homestead."

"Right. It isn't healthy for my sources to move while *Totenkopf* is around. They'll bring information as soon as the SS clear out."

Bora spoke with his eyes on the map. "That might be too late for details. I met the Kalekin widows; there's an excuse for me to go there. And it is on the way to Bespalovka. Hell, the farm is six kilometres from here; I could *walk*."

"Don't even think of it. You'd appear way too suspicious on foot if they saw you. What business do you have with the widows?"

"Their sons ended up in the Yar. If I'm lucky, they and others like them are the reason for *Totenkopf*'s raid. If I'm not, I've blown my chance of understanding why Khan and Platonov were done in."

The widows were not at the farm. Bora parked the GAZ

vehicle in the tractor shed – added when the place had been collectivized – under a giant sign that read "Friendship of the Peoples" on the wall. Chaff flew with the lightness of dead insects as his boots swept the dirt floor. A ladder led to a mezzanine where implements and spare parts had been stored, now empty. He climbed there and risked falling through the disconnected planks as he picked his steps to a small window, through which the south-western edge of Krasny Yar should be visible. *Through a glass, darkly…* The glass panes, opaque with dust, were in the way. Bora unceremoniously knocked them out with the grip of his handgun. He had to crouch to look through the low opening, balancing on the rickety flooring without being able to hold on, busy focusing his field glasses.

Beyond the one-floored sheds of the farm compound, five Opel trucks sat at the grassy threshold of the woods. Against a parched, tin-white sky, the operation proper must be drawing to a close; Bora had got here just in time. The Death's Head unit was regrouping to leave. Non-coms led them, and the most interesting part was that wooden crates (Bora counted four, but there might be more already loaded) were being hauled towards one of the trucks. From where he was, they resembled the ammunition box he'd seen during his survey with Nagel. Judging by the effort needed to lift them onto the vehicle, they weighed a great deal. No attempt was made to open them, much less look inside. In fact, one of the non-coms made sure the locks were still fast before allowing the containers on board.

At once, Bora was in a hurry to get going. Most of the unpaved country lanes in this area ran roughly north–south. Whether the *Totenkopf* engineers meant to head south toward Smijeff (and the railroad) or north to Kharkov, they first had to travel the only narrow track, white with powdery dust, which linked Kalekina to Vodyanoy. Covering the small distance to Vodyanoy before the SS started out, and waiting there to see which direction they took, became imperative. Bora slid down the ladder, backed the GAZ out of the shed to the threshing floor and drove west from the farm, crossing the open fields at his peril to keep from raising telltale dust on the lane. At Vodyanoy he barely had time to find an unseen lookout point behind a barn. Once the trucks reached the crossroads, the first four without hesitation continued to Borovoye (and the highway to Kharkov); the last truck turned left and motored south toward Smijeff and its railroad junction. Bora paused a moment longer, thinking. With the Donets dividing German and Russian lines, Smijeff was nothing but a rather exposed terminal for the railway from Kharkov: either the truck and its contents would stop in Smijeff, or else the intention was to load the material and ship it by rail with a higher degree of safety to the district capital. The distance from Vodyanoy to Smijeff being at least four times the distance to Borovoye, Bora let the SS trucks go their separate ways and then hightailed to Lattmann's radio shack. There he contacted his regiment. He dispatched Nagel to the Smijeff rail station – twelve kilometres from the cavalry camp – with orders to relate whether any material was loaded by *Totenkopf* men on to a Kharkov-bound train.

After a tense half hour, he was ready to break the seal of his untouched cigarette pack and go back to his smoking habit. It was a gamble, presuming to know the destination of the single truck. And, time being of the essence, he had to depend on Nagel's resourcefulness when it came to communications. Fifteen more minutes went by before Bora's hunch was confirmed. He'd meanwhile memorized the various directions a train could take once it reached the Osnova junction south-east of Kharkov. Some terminals sounded less likely than others (Kharkov South on the Moscow line; Bolashivsky heading back east); the most promising stops for unloading were New Bavaria (to Poltava), Osnova itself (to the Donbas) and Lipovy Gai (to Rostov, via Merefa).

Lattmann assured him there'd be no stop before Osnova, as the Schtcherbiny station was presently unused. "Your best bets are Osnova and then Kuryash, or Osnova and then New Bavaria, or Osnova and then Pokatilovka–Merefa."

In all cases, it meant a twenty-five kilometre foray to the Osnova junction for Bora, where he'd wait for the "locomotive pulling three cars" Nagel had described to him. On the way there, he silently fidgeted through checkpoints; where emotions and beliefs, extraneous thoughts and considerations went at times like this he couldn't tell – somehow they were shelved away or shoved out of range, leaving him capable of single-mindedly taking the next step necessary and nothing else.

At Osnova, when the locomotive from Smijeff did come into view, Bora watched it leave the braid of many tracks and set off along the rail to New Bavaria. Not good. He grew discouraged at the idea it would travel beyond his reach towards Poltava. But New Bavaria didn't only provide a stop between here and Poltava: a switch east of the railway bridge on the Udy River allowed a deviation down a minor, less used set of southbound tracks to a terminal outside Merefa. The problem was that from Osnova there was no practical way for a road vehicle to cross the Udy and the Lopany in advance of the train: he'd waste precious time getting through Kharkov's southern districts before finding a bridge. Bora took a worried swig of water from his canteen. It seemed centuries since he'd stood in the Kiev square, with Peter filming the ceremony. An exhausted bloody sun sank westward, clouds strangely cupped beneath it as if to receive it. Decapitations came to mind: John the Baptist, the French Terror. Gordon in Khartoum, old Kalekin at Krasny Yar. Bora looked away from the lurid red. With nothing to lose, he had to take another wild guess and gamble on the deviation. It meant taking the highway to the small town of Lednoye, crossing both the Lopany River and the Sebastopol rail line south of the Filippovka district, to reach a point where he could discover through his field glasses whether he had been right or wrong.

Dusk had taken on the tinge of lead when he returned to the schoolhouse. A small miracle had been worked there: Bora found a makeshift shower (featuring an oil drum as a water tank) installed in the courtyard, fine netting in the windows to keep insects out. Weariness and the day's excitement vying for dominance inside him turned to abject physical consolation: he stripped and showered and changed in the twilight, standing on planks arranged so that he wouldn't have to walk on dirt to reach the door. Kostya deserved all the compliments he received.

The new comforts and cold beet soup were welcome; less welcome was hearing that the Russian priest had been looking for him and would be trying again soon. Bora opened his diary with an ear to the sound of crickets across the interminable expanse of grassland outside; he counted on Nitichenko's visit before night sealed over. Shortly – because a mention of the devil brings him around – the creaking of peasant boots announced the priest's arrival. Bora addressed him from the window without waiting for the sentry to announce him. "What's up, Victor Panteleievich?"

Nitichenko's looks were more ruffled than usual. He made the sign of the cross three times, mumbling *Gospodi pomiluy* to ask God's mercy as he entered the schoolhouse. "You question me, *bratyetz*, but it should be the other way around. I spent the day at Krasny Yar."

Bora put away his diary. "You did?" The gesture he made, pointing to the chair, was calm in inverse proportion to the rise in tension he experienced. "Well, what of it?"

"*What of it?*" The priest slumped in the chair. "Don't you know what happened there?"

I'll know when Lattmann hears from his informants. Bora kept a moderately curious air, sitting on a corner of the desk with his right foot on the floor.

Merefa, 10.49 p.m.

Man, the priest gave me an earful. He'd ridden to Losukovka on Wednesday for some concern related to his psalm reader (*psalom-shchik*). Early on Thursday, when *Totenkopf*'s operation began around

339

Krasny Yar, he was "in the vicinity of the Kalekina farm". I may be being malicious, but I'll wager he's started bedding the younger Kalekin widow, with whom he familiarly uses her first name without its patronymic. At any rate, from what he said I understood more or less how the operation went. The sporadic shooting reported by our units lasted all morning; next came a set of explosions "to the east, inside the woods": that is, where Ivan placed his mines. It's engineers who draft the minefield maps, so it's probable the SS set the mines off for reasons of their own, possibly to make a safer, wider swatch in which to advance. Nitichenko holed up in the farm throughout the following night. This morning he found another hideout, from where he could not directly observe the Yar (he apparently knows nothing about the removal of the crates). He heard a single, major blast from that direction as soon as it became light enough to see (read below). Until the time I reached the Kalekina farm in the afternoon, more shots were fired intermittently. Only after he glimpsed the SS leaving did the priest pluck up the courage to go into the woods. To make a long story short, he found the bullet-riddled bodies of the Kalekin lads and those of three more youngsters unknown to him lying about; he believes there may be others. The rise, or hillock or *kurgan* I crawled inside was, according to him, partly demolished and "opened up" with explosives. So I'd say the SS went in specifically looking for the crates, surprised and shot anything that moved, in their usual fashion, found what they wanted inside the *kurgan*, searched through lesser holes and lairs to get rid of any witnesses, and went off to the next thing.

Nitichenko is returning to the Yar in the morning; for now, he's chosen not to tell the Kalekin women the bad news. If I know Russians, there'll be a toing and froing in and out of the woods tomorrow and in the days to come until all bodies are recovered. And this is whether or not they know if the dead are their relatives, *besprizornye*, partisans or God knows what else.

I listened, careful not to comment. There's really nothing to say. Our expression "Alles in Ordnung" applies here no less than in other war-related operations. All's in place. The priest speaks of waste, but everything is waste at war. There's nothing but waste. He and I are as disposable as the wild boys and the *Totenkopf* engineers and the millions of Russians waiting beyond the Donets.

To me, it all comes down to this: specific directions were given to the SS (by Max Simon or others); the material recovered as a result was shipped unopened to Merefa's *Kombinat*. Martin Bora is an idiot, and has been grasping at straws while timber was floating right by him.

It seemed for all the world as if Taras Tarasov had grabbed armfuls of paperwork from his places of employment and stuffed them inside the wicker suitcase. Kapitolina Nefedovna must have hoped it would contain better things than old letters and ledgers from Tractor Factory No. 183 and the FED camera factory. In fact, when Bora had unceremoniously taken the suitcase from her on the day of the accountant's death, she'd acted like a woman cheated of her rights until the major snapped it open and exposed reams of old paper.

When he had less to do, Bora would sit down another time and go through the material with an *Abwehr* officer's thoroughness. Tonight, having found some usefulness in the Makarenko note about the employment of Ukrainian waifs (in Poltava up to 1927, and then in Kharkov), he set aside accounts and documents dated between 1919 and 1939.

In the hope of finding traces of the political and social circle around Platonov and Tibyetsky (or Petrov, Dobronin or whichever alias he'd used at the time), he then singled out paperwork from the NEP years, up to 1928. After all, Khan's penchant for doing business in and around Kharkov could have left a paper trail.

The results were disappointing. Bora dug out a copy of a note sent to the government by a Tractor Factory worker called Schtschetinin, lately of the Zaporozhye Metal Works, protesting about the expropriation of a piece of woodland near the Works, the last remnant of the family estate. The recipient, a party official, had scribbled across it "formerly a landed rich man (*pomeshchik* in the text) and exploiter of the people: deny intervention." Nothing to do with Krasny Yar. Another brief originated from the FED camera factory, where an employee, a retired Navy officer, complained that "co-workers who hardly distinguished themselves during the Revolution" affected sailor uniforms, "trying to live off the fame of brave Soviet mariners". Bora even found a note regarding shipments from an American group – Hoover's Relief Association – during the famine; two mentions of The Giant, a massive student dormitory on Pushkin Street, and a request for labourers to be recruited from the political jail for minors in Kharkov. Khan appeared nowhere. Platonov was absent as well.

Bora decided then that if he couldn't find the protagonists of the tale, he'd settle for the supporting actors – that is, the foreigners and other "strangers" who had frequented Kharkov after the Revolution. Naturally, an English, French or German surname did not imply that the individual had gravitated to Khan and Platonov's entourage. *But I am looking for one specific name, after all*, he told himself. It took much renewed leafing through documents in search of non-Russian acronyms and names of firms, governmental agencies, individual businessmen and sales representatives. All were transliterated to accommodate Russian spelling, an added complication. Eventually, he came across some names he'd anticipated, and others he hadn't expected: American Quakers, executives from the newly created Leica factory, Turkish tobacco growers, listed according to the concession granted to them under Lenin's New Economic Policy: "Type I" (pure concessions); "Type II" (mixed concessions); and "Type III" (technical assistance). Under "Type III" were listed German technicians connected with the Locomotive and Tractor Factory, soon to produce tanks in 1928. A joint note from 1926 (signatories, Schmitt and Kravchenko) dealt with the name change of the Association for The Management of German Factories in Russia, "to be known now and henceforth as *Wirtschaftskontor*". On the back of the sheet, in an obvious attempt to save typing paper, the names of the German–Russian Flight and Transport Companies' executives newly appointed in Kharkov had been added. The first, *Deruluft*, listed Abel, Karl; Dahm, EP; Strasser, Bernd; Wilmowsky, Andreas. The second, *Derutra*, gave the names Herzog, Heinz-Joachim; Merker, Gustav; Stark, AL: Ziehm, Werner.

Bora paused. AL: Alfred Lothar. Stark had mentioned his days with Derutra in passing, on the morning he'd shown him the Karabakh horse. He'd added something about Russians robbing you blind the moment you turn your head, or something similar. Finding confirmation of his presence in post-Leninist Ukraine meant nothing per se; still, Bora became aware of each nerve in his body. Instead of accelerating, his search slowed down; it became a deliberate perusing and careful page-turning, looking through the typewritten or neatly penned Cyrillic script across the dreary documents of the past generation. Taras Tarasov, who might simply have salvaged what he could from his old desks upon the Germans' arrival in 1941, showed no specific intent through his choice. On the one hand, he'd grabbed carbon copies on paper as thin as onion peel; on the other, he'd missed the second and third pages of lengthy letters: it all bore witness to the haste of removal.

Does it follow that if the boxes from Krasny Yar travelled to the Kombinat, *Geko Stark was the "stranger" who visited the woods? No. He was in Kharkov back when the generals met in Larisa's town house. And that's all I actually have in hand – unless I consider his signature on the request to ship Weller to Germany to be a clue. If Khan had given me a hint… If I'd let Platonov end his goddamn sentence…*

The sole objects Bora had left from Commander Tibyetsky – having delivered his lend-lease supplies and tanker jacket to the RSHA jail – were an empty trunk and the snapshot that showed him victoriously emerging from the cupola of his T-34. Bora had already examined this to exhaustion. There were no hints to be gained from the image (why should there be?) or from the two lines pencilled on the back of it: *Narodnaya Slava, New Year's, 1943.*

Taken while we were spitting blood in Stalingrad; I recognize some of the buildings behind him. He was justified in bragging, after all.

During their second (and final) conversation, Khan had carelessly placed the goblet full of juice on the photograph, and he, Bora, had removed it. Khan had at once put it back. Small gestures, revealing nothing but a different sense of orderliness between them. And yet it jarred that a man so proud of his achievements would risk soiling a celebratory image of himself with sticky orange juice. *Unless he wanted me to pay particular attention to the photo.* Bora walked to his trunk and took the snapshot in hand once more. Numbers and letters, he'd already noticed, had been written down with the same pencil on two separate occasions: the pressure of the handwriting varied slightly. *Which came first, the date or the name? One is written above the other, but that alone isn't an indication of priority. For all I know,* Narodnaya Slava *is what he called his tank, although he used the Baba Yaga analogy more. I wonder if he added to the original caption before he crossed the Donets, or even after – at the time I was trying to contact Zossen by radio, for example. And if he did, was it to stress the date (our end in Stalingrad), or the Red Army's "national glory"? When I complained of not finding a message or a note of any kind in Khan's room, Dr Bernoulli commented that the room was not Khan's security. His tank was. What if this photo of his tank were a pointer of sorts? I don't see how. No, I don't see how. I wish* Narodnaya Slava *stood for something other than an armoured vehicle presently being dismantled or a vanished Kharkov movie house Larisa thinks was "off Voennaya".*

To Bora's knowledge, several alleys branched off on both sides of the avenue that derived its name – "Military" – from the barracks long standing in the district, on the left bank of the Kharkov River. It stood to reason that a theatre frequented by soldiers would bear a patriotic name of the *National Glory* type.

Of the city maps he kept on hand, none marked cinemas. A folding city plan, dating back five years, actually served as an appendix to a booklet where Kharkov streets and state-run businesses were alphabetically listed. When he looked under "places of entertainment", he saw no movie house called *Narodnaya Slava* existed, which meant it had either closed before 1938, or changed name. *Not that it'll get me anywhere, but the next time I'm in Kharkov, I might as well take a detour to Voennaya. After all, there's a* Wehrmacht *fuel depot in the former Horse Market nearby, and I could kill two birds with one stone.*

The crickets outside were like steel nibs scratching the dark. Bora listened to them with the diary open before him, in a lonely mood somewhere between hope and agitation. Fever was setting in. From the journal's thickness the edge of Dikta's envelope showed, a narrow powder-blue line with the power of lifting him out of his present doubts and anxiety only to give him more doubts and a different anxiety. He wrote no entry for the night. Before retiring, he unsealed the envelope and lifted his wife's photo from it with his thumb and forefinger tenderly, but not all the way.

Saturday the twenty-ninth he spent at Bespalovka, interrogating the Russians captured during Operation Thermopylae. Nothing of real use could be extracted from them: the survivors were young, eager to collaborate if the alternative was the firing squad, but politically ignorant. The sophisticated lend-lease plastique and timers intended for sabotage seemed wasted on those big-limbed boys thrown together without preparation. Bora saw them as a businessman views exchange goods or heads of cattle. They supplied him with an excuse to present himself and offer Stark newly available forced labour.

Everything was blooming early this year. In the fields around the cavalry camp, sunflowers had begun opening up nearly a month in advance, bright yellow like mass-produced stars on an assembly line. Bora – who'd grown used to seeing endless expanses of them in the East – found them newly jarring, on the threshold of disgust. It was curious how they set his teeth on edge. Closer in, on the thirsty rim of the road, crowded the pale bellflowers Russians called *brother and sister* or *Ivan and Maria*. As a child, Bora had known the plant as wolf's tail. According to the pragmatic Kostya it was cow wheat, a weed that made dairy cattle produce more milk, but when added to food or drink intoxicated you or heightened the effect of alcohol in your body.

The prisoners, his barter chattels, squatted or stood against the unripe yellow of the fields. Bora was staring at them when Nagel walked up to him to say something. "Yes," he answered. "Thank you."

The senior master sergeant had set aside the best among the firearms captured from the Reds. Bora walked with him to view, heft and handle them. Targeting the round heads of the most distant sunflowers, they stood side by side shattering them to bits. Some rifles were definitely better than others. Experienced shooters as both were, they eventually did it with relish. Bora examined weapons and equipment to be destroyed, anti-personnel mines and timed demolition charges of the type used to blast Kiev years earlier. Before leaving for Merefa, he selected and picked up one of the SVT-40 sniper rifles, silenced and equipped with a scope.

KHARKOV, SUNDAY 30 MAY

Von Salomon scanned Bora's updated notes on *Partisanentaktik* as he would postcards from a foreign city he'd never visit. His questions were pertinent, and he'd forward the copy as needed, of course. Had he not called him back as he was already leaving his office, Bora's impression of him would have remained one of melancholy zeal. But he did call Bora back, and in all seriousness, he asked, "Did you know that a turtle dove will kill his rival at mating season?"

"No, Herr Oberstleutnant."

"It's a disturbing thought, in view of the opinion we generally have of Ukrainian bonhomie."

"I didn't know we had such an opinion either, Herr Oberstleutnant."

Bora left the command building shaking his head. With the second half of the morning before him free of duties, he planned to steer clear of military bureaucracy and do some scouting of his own. His city map was duly marked, and from divisional headquarters he could walk to his destination.

When he reached it, he saw that the narrow alley off Voennaya was maybe two hundred metres long. It ran south of the Staro–Moskovskaya barracks blocks, not unlike those in the army district of Leipzig–Gohlis, and nothing much distinguished its course. Most houses appeared abandoned, even those war had spared. The cinema Larisa had indicated stood recessed from the other façades, in a dusty little square where four linden trees cast a scented, broken shade. A dilapidated stucco building that seemed to have been out of use for years, it was unreadable style-wise but probably dated to the 1920s. The sign above the entrance had suffered from time and lack of care. The S of *Slava* had fallen off, and now, fittingly for the district, it read *Lava* – a Cossack cavalry attack formation, or, alternatively, volcanic material. In any case, the change reinforced rather than diminished the impact of the patriotic word.

A semicircular vestibule, oddly reminiscent of a Greek temple, with man-sized chalk owls at the sides of the door, led into the *kinoteatr*. It looked as though the place hadn't been frequented in years: the glass panes of the double door were intact, opaque with filth; the leaf itself, merely stuck to the sill, could be pushed open with little effort. Bora stepped inside.

Wartime cities were full of these buildings suspended between life and death: literally, sometimes, when one side or the other booby-trapped them against the unwary. If he was still alive, Weller might be hiding in such a place down in Kiev. *I've come this far*, Bora told himself. *I'm not going to stop now.* He found

347

himself in a small foyer illuminated by two bow windows, one on top of the other, marking the façade above the entrance. Ahead, rows of spartan armchairs could be detected in the dark projection hall. From the foyer, two curving sets of stairs with ornate iron railings led to the balcony, and presumably to the projectionist's cabin as well. Throughout, a pea-green pressed tin ceiling shed crumbling paint. This formed a pale layer on the floor, thinner and nearly transparent where footprints (left how long ago?) had last disturbed it.

Whenever the place had been forsaken, there was no sign of haste or violence to indicate a traumatic process. What with the greenish hues and the old-fashioned intact nature of the surroundings, Bora had the impression of moving underwater, in a sea relict where noise did not travel. It was not beyond possibility that the movie house had ceased functioning well before the war started; for whatever reason (diversionism, the presence of a Jewish manager), it could have been out of commission for up to ten years.

Upstairs, the projectionist's cabin was dark. Bora used his torchlight to snatch glimpses of objects and examine some in detail. All machinery had been removed. A forlorn stack of old labelled reels was still there, piled on the floor. Most of them he identified as propaganda documentaries from ten or so years earlier – the right material for a military audience – although feature films from the 1920s and 1930s were not missing. *Strike, The Cigarette Girl of Mosselprom, Ivan* (with a Ukrainian setting if he remembered correctly), *Happiness* (the image of the polka dot horse on a hilltop!), *And Quiet Flows the Don,* among others. Some Bora had watched in his Russian-learning days.

One item stood out from the rest. Sitting alone on the projectionist's table, it surprised Bora to the point that he suspected German troops had at least temporarily used the theatre, even though it seemed unlikely. A boxed 8 mm reel of the Tobis–Degeto type – on which *Wehrmacht* war documentaries were filmed – was easily recognizable. The cardboard casing,

unmarked, contained a dark brown metal reel about ten centimetres in diameter, three-quarters full. Bora shone his light all
over it to look for a title, finding none. Inside the casing, however,
a paper tape that had apparently come loose from the reel read
"Baba Yaga". Bora tried unsuccessfully not to let his imagination
run away with him. *It could be a children's film,* he reasoned, *a
cartoon, a short satire against the ancient regime, or whatever else. It
could be whatever else.* Why then was the label in Cyrillic *and* Latin
capitals? Unless of course it contained a German newsreel on
the Eastern Front, shown here to Russian-speaking volunteers
at some point, possibly during the second-last occupation of the
city. It was a recent film to be sure, complete with sound stripe.

Bora's mind churned ideas faster than he could evaluate
them for their usefulness. Foremost was the question of where
he could find an 8 mm projector of the right kind. He pocketed
the Tobis–Degeto reel, went downstairs and for a few minutes
sat in the semi-dark projection hall. He needed to gather his
thoughts, calm himself. When he crossed his legs, the stitched
cuts hurt and the entire row of badly anchored chairs moved
with him. As his eyes became accustomed to the dimness, looking up at the tin ceiling he saw it was stamped with a geometric
floral pattern. Loops, petals, leaves always repeated. He realized
now it was warm here, and the place breathed that indefinite
odour old movie houses have. In the heat, flecks of peeling paint
slowly detached themselves from the ceiling, coming down with
the lightness of moths. Outside, the anonymous alley ran into
Voennaya like a dry river bed, and Voennaya's waterless tributary into the seared lake that was the Horse Market. Kharkov,
all around, waited for the next battle to shatter it.

Bora sat in the empty projection hall with his eyes closed.
The strong impression of being close to the solution made him
ache. Not daring to hope that Khan Tibyetsky had reverted to
being Uncle Terry (or simply to being a German officer) to
the extent of directing him here, still he could not dismiss the
coincidence between the words on the back of the photograph

and this abandoned movie house. Hadn't Khan spoken of himself as someone who erased his tracks, like the witch uses a broom to row through the air? Hadn't he answered, when Bora bragged he'd seen all his propaganda films, "You haven't seen *all* of them"?

Yes, but how could he place the reel here, if he crossed over on 4 May and was under custody from that moment on?

Viewing the reel became a physical necessity, although it was easier said than done in wartime Kharkov. Bora stood to leave. Air Force troops being usually well equipped with film, cameras and such, the closest opportunity would be with Peter's former colleagues at Rogany. He'd need his brother's intercession to convince them to lend him a projector, which meant radioing him at the Poltava airfield before he left for his next assignment.

From divisional headquarters Bora was able to contact his brother, but barely. Peter was in a hurry on account of a training session. Friendly as ever, he couldn't see any problem. "Mention my name and bring a case of beer with you, Martin: my colleagues will oblige you."

Finding a case of beer proved to be more complicated than getting the Luftwaffe squadron's communications officer to say yes. It was midday before Bora could effect the barter at the airbase, and then the problem became where to view the film with a measure of privacy. There was no electricity at the Merefa schoolhouse; the divisional headquarters offices were crowded. "I wonder if you could accommodate me..." Bora asked the pilot. "My wife sent me a reel from home: is there a room where I could watch it alone?"

The pilot snickered without malice. "I'm off to the mess-hall for lunch, Major. The building's all yours for the next hour."

Khan's broadcasts to the Sixth Army encircled at Stalingrad had become legend; in German, the general urged the "doomed fascists" to give up the fight and surrender. Over and over Bora had heard the booming words of retribution flow from loudspeakers at ghostly street corners and from the top of gutted casements. It was one of the sickening memories of those desperate weeks. And it had been a double-dealing man about to defect who thundered about Paulus' capitulation to the Reds!

In this reel, too, Khan Tibyetsky spoke in German, reading from a typed manuscript. The film must have been shot in a room of his residence; definitely not in his office. It went without saying that the men filming and recording his speech had no idea what was being said. More likely than not, they'd been told it was another anti-Nazi propaganda pitch. Bora wouldn't give a penny for the amount of time Khan had allowed them to survive beyond their task.

Standing behind a massive desk, in full uniform and an enviable set of medals, Khan opened pragmatically with, "To whom it may concern: in the event that anything befalls my person during my residence among German troops in the Kharkov Oblast, there will be no negative left of this film. My name is Ghenrikh Pavlovich Tibyetsky, and my preference is that the recipient of the following statement be *Abwehr* Colonel Eccard von Bentivegni, of the Office of Foreign Intelligence III. Should the reel instead be viewed by you, my former Red Army comrades, know that it barely concerns you; even if you succeeded in eliminating me before I crossed the Donets. As a matter of fact, it isn't fear of your retaliation that prompts me to speak – you do not in the least suspect I have for years worked in the enemy's employ – but the all but coincidental presence in the Kharkov Oblast of two men from my past: Gleb Gavrilovich Platonov and Alfred Lothar Stark. Learning of my defection, Platonov might attempt to harm my cause by distorting the truth about matters I alone should discuss. As for Stark, whose support Platonov uselessly tried to engage in 1926, he is without scruples and will succeed in assassinating me if he can lay his hands on me."

Bora, who'd been listening with a wary ear, became stock-still.

"If you have come into possession of this reel, to be safely placed in Kharkov by a trusted and anonymous comrade from the glorious days, it stands to reason that you have reconstructed at least part of the story. In summary, it entails the destiny of Makhno's Black Army war booty, which Gleb Platonov and I found in the heady days of the Revolution in Makhno's local refuge, a *kurgan* in the woods of Krasny Yar near the Udy River." Khan's general officer gruffness, surely meant for those filming him, was belied by a certain ironic quality of his voice and by artful pauses. "The rebels' raids against local gentry and churches yielded a significant collection of Russian and foreign currency, bank drafts, stocks, precious metals and jewels. The gold alone came to ten *pud* of weight, the silver to forty. Platonov and I differed on the destination the booty should have. Our arguments made me painfully aware of his truly bourgeois idea of money and its value: he was Robespierre, I was Danton." (Pause.) "During the NEP we frequently visited the Kharkov Oblast, and at least once a year I travelled alone to the Krasny Yar woods, by my orders marked as an off-limits military area. There, in a place most people already avoided for its scary reputation, Makhno's ill-gotten gains functioned as my carefully disguised private lending institution, in my judgement well suited to afford small frivolities and socializing for deserving comrades.

"In 1926, just before the NEP came to an end, it reached my ears that Platonov had revealed the site to a foreigner by the name of Stark. He was a well-connected former journalist, a horse enthusiast then working for the German–Russian Transportation Agency Derutra. No doubt Platonov meant to expose me as a profiteer through the foreign press, thus ending my career and my life. Was he – the eternal number two – ambitious to surpass me, or was he so livid in his small-minded morality that he'd have the enemies of the Revolution profit from his betrayal? I wonder to this day. Thankfully Stark was more interested in Makhno's booty than in an international scoop, and besides, I had most foreign journalists in my back pocket in those days. Platonov's plan miscarried. Soon we were all too caught up in politics to pay attention to Krasny Yar. All the same, I had Stark shadowed by trusted comrades, and learnt he went back several times to the Yar before foreign businesses lost Stalin's support and shut down."

The densely written page was turned over, allowing Khan to read from its reverse.

"In the following years, the chess game between Platonov and myself continued: he blackmailed me by threatening to talk; I played along, allowing him to feed on his ambition. Soon I had an additional reason to keep him on my good side, having begun to work for Germany under the codename *Baba Yaga*. We were in the Thirties: times were dangerous. It was the end of the October Revolution as we who fought for it knew it. Anybody could fall for a negligible reason, or for no reason at all. I and so many others had not fought to replace the tsar with a tyrant from Georgia: thus died my allegiance to the Soviet Union. I could have easily pushed Platonov into the pit where thousands fell, from Alksnis to Zinoviev. I did not: after all, I wouldn't want him to accuse me to save himself. After his arrest during the Purge, I followed events with trepidation, but Platonov never talked. I will not give him credit; he must have kept the secret because he felt he was too compromised by his association with the matter of Krasny Yar.

"In fact, I had long before taken steps to protect myself. At the time of the XV Party Conference of 26 October 1926, which occupied Platonov as head of security, I flew to the Kharkov Oblast under secrecy. Due to Stark's unauthorized withdrawals, two *pud* of gold were already missing. One by one, with the help of naive *besprizornye* squatting in the woods, I emptied the crates of their contents, carted these out, replaced them with ballast and then used a small explosive charge to cause a cave-in that would more effectively conceal them under the *kurgan*: a long labour that sadly could leave no living witnesses. Shortly thereafter snow came; time and nature would do the rest. Even today, 21 April 1943, Platonov and Stark believe that Krasny Yar still holds Makhno's booty.

"For the past week, ever since Platonov was shot down in the Kharkov area and taken prisoner, I have been worrying that he might decide to talk: any revelation about me at this time, just as I am about to cross over, would mean my death at the hands of the Red Army. It seems that thus far Platonov has maintained his silence, but there's no guarantee. As for Alfred Lothar Stark, the extraordinary efforts he has made from the beginning of the war to be assigned specifically to the Kharkov Oblast, renouncing a *Gauleiter*'s post and other career perks, speak volumes. You may or may not be aware that throughout the 1930s he was – and still is today – in the Soviets' employ, codename *Zhestianik*. Check your documents: you'll find ample confirmation. I am convinced he is waiting for the time of summer operations to draw nearer: he will then attempt a *coup de main* on Krasny Yar, and defect as soon as possible. Platonov's captivity in the Kharkov area, and soon my own presence, will be in Stark's eyes impediments to protecting his identity and securing the booty."

A second page, only partially filled, was begun.

"Hence, Colonel Bentivegni, my insistence to be kept in *Abwehr* custody and well away from Stark. As a chess player, I scented him as my most dangerous adversary once I'd waded across the Donets. I realize that I defy destiny by requesting to be escorted to Kharkov upon arrival, but I am a gambler; and besides, a smattering of Makhno's booty is located in Kharkov. If I live, I mean to lay my eyes on it once more.

"This, on the other hand, may well be a posthumous statement on my part. If Stark or someone representing him has meanwhile killed me to 'get to the goods' – well, he won't 'get to the goods'. He'll only think he did. Seven *pud* of gold and thirty-five *pud* of silver – nearly 700 kilos of precious metals – will no more profit Chancellor Hitler than they will Chairman

Stalin. In 1928, Makhno's booty was worked into the steel of the first Red Army tanks built at the Kharkov Komintern Locomotive Factory." It was the first time in the reading that something vaguely resembling a smile lightened Khan's Soviet frown. Looking straight at the viewer, Komandir Tibyetsky became Terry Terborch for the time needed to add, "Living large, Colonel Bentivegni, has long been my philosophy. I do not intend to reveal where the remainder of the booty is kept. I will only add this: despite its gloomy reputation and deaths, what a beautiful nook Krasny Yar, *the beautiful ravine*, has been all these years!"

Bora remained standing by the projector long after the screen ran black with the occasional flashing white number and then flipped with a snapping sound off the spool. He was somehow less bewildered than he was impressed. *Through a glass, darkly...* His mind reeled at the thought of how many times the alloy of steel and precious metals had been reforged through the years, until gold and silver were no more than particles throughout the Red Army's tank corps.

Had he understood the hint to the cinema's name right away, when Khan had first placed his orange drink on the photograph, he could have – what? Not avoided Khan's death – things were already moving too fast – but understood long ago who, having already disposed of Gleb Platonov, plotted to kill the tank commander. Waiting for Bentivegni, Khan had chosen not to share things with him, only that minor hint. "Do you play chess?" he'd asked. Far from being *too impulsive*, as he'd answered, Bora felt now he'd been much too slow. *Zhestianik – Tinman*: well, *Tinman*'s identity had baffled German counterintelligence for years, although as far as he knew his activity had decreased ever since the start of the Russian campaign – a fact that made perfect sense now.

The rectangle on the wall glared blinding white; the spool kept whipping the loose end of the reel. Bora clicked the projector off.

The morning of Khan's death, when I walked into his office, Stark took a phone call and seemed to forget everything around him. He said something like "Good. Only if you confirm." For all I know, Weller was reporting in after the murder. What do I do now? Solve the problem and tidy up afterwards. *If Geko Stark opened the crates, he's aware he risked all for nothing. If he hasn't, he'll guard them tooth and nail. In either case, he can count on* Totenkopf *engineers keeping mum – what the hell, he's clearly manoeuvred more people than I can count within the SS, at the Kharkov switchboards, at the Medical Inspectorate; in the RSHA, for all I know. He's got access to Oberstgruppenführer Simon. None of them know enough to accuse him of anything, if they ever would.*

Daylight returned when Bora walked to the window and rolled up the blinds. Darkness, light, flickering images: it was all metaphorical of his present state. Until the twenty-seventh, Stark could have counted on Weller's absolute silence: not now, necessarily. Now that he felt trapped in Kiev, the medic could just as well burrow into a hole or become a loose cannon. It was imperative to reach him before the Commissioner did. Yes. Even if Stark felt sure enough of the crates' contents to ship them off directly, he couldn't avoid making that one move: eliminating Weller as soon as possible. Bora replaced the film inside its cardboard case and walked out of the office.

He'll deal with me next. Christ, he dared me with the letter to the Medical Inspectorate, knowing I would open it: urging Weller's repatriation on behalf of Oberstarzt Mayr, who actually had nothing to do with the request. He knew I'd either fall for it, which at first I did, or be frightened by the implications. Even with the film in my possession, a district commissioner of the Reich is much too large a mouthful for a newly appointed regiment commander.

When I went to him looking for a kilo of butter on 20 May, he stopped writing at the mention of an old woman who eats it by the mouthful. As one of the opportunist guests in Larisa's house back in the NEP years, he'd remember the detail. He turned around on the swivel chair to hide his discomfort, not his laughter. And there I was, first talking about Arnim Weller and then about Larisa's favourite treat. Forget the random shot from the Leibstandarte *marksman: that was probably just to teach me respect. Stark must have decided on 20 May to dispose of me: after all, someone rigged my vehicle with a timed device the following day. It's a classic: he's aware I'm aware, and vice versa. He does* not *know about the film reel. How do I get it to Colonel Bentivegni, with or without Arnim Weller in tow? If Stark gets to Larisa and she talks, I'm done for. I can't let her do that.*

At the mess hall, where he stopped to thank the communications officer, the pilots invited him to sit with them. Bora foresaw good-natured razzing about the film from home, and answered that he had no time. But he was hungry, so he accepted a glass of wine, and a sandwich on the go. He left the airbase, munching on the sandwich as he drove.

There's no film negative, he thought. *I can't have copies made of it.* Rolling fields and ravines alternated on both sides of the road. At the checkpoint near the Tractor Works, Bora showed his papers indifferently. Every ounce of his brainpower was engaged in thinking over, planning; it was as if Khan Tibyetsky were sitting next to him with his mouth damnably shut. Or maybe not.

Khan said the gold in Makhno's hideout came to eight pud *– that's about one hundred and thirty kilos. The gold that ended up at the Tractor Works – then the Komintern Locomotive Factory – was seven* pud. *Where did the missing sixteen-plus kilos of gold go? They're "located in Kharkov". And Krasny Yar does mean "beautiful ravine", but it's a dismal little wood: why did he compare it to a beautiful nook? Why a "nook"? Is it a generic expression? In Russian, "beautiful nook" translates as* krasny ugol *– "beautiful nook; beautiful corner". Which is also how Russians refer to the spot in the house where holy images are kept. Holy images. Icons.* Icons? *Maybe Larisa Malinovskaya's father did sell off or lose his sacred art collection at the gaming table to "those two upstart merchants Ostruchov and Tetryakov", whoever they were. Is she clever or naive? Sinister or forgetful? Fuck; I can see why Friedrich von Bora had to get away from her in the end. Maybe the "smattering" of Makhno's booty that didn't go into tank steel is hanging in Larisa's house to this day, one whole* pud *of solid gold and precious stones!*

Past the hospital across from the military graveyard, Bora did a U-turn in the middle of the road. He'd just taken Staro–Moskovskaya to return to Merefa, but he now reversed and sped across the Kharkov River to Pomorki. A puzzled Nyusha, hanging sheets out to dry, told him there'd been no visitors after his visit more than ten days earlier.

To Bora, it meant that Stark probably knew Larisa's town house address from the 1920s, not the present one, and that if he couldn't find her in the compulsory German census of Kharkov dwellers he didn't recall her name. *Still, there's no trusting the fat old witch in her parlour. If she talks she's dead; but I'll be in trouble.* Bora waited for Nyusha to go back inside. Then, instead of leaving the garden, he took the sniper rifle from the GAZ and concealed it in the thickness of creepers and shrubs, next to the leaning wire fence.

As he pulled out in reverse on to the corduroy path, Bora checked the fuel gauge. Even by his own judgement, he was wasting an inordinate amount of gasoline; how long Bentivegni's special permit would hold up before the general shortage he'd find out sooner or later. Back to the city limits, he crossed Kharkov once more. *There's no film negative, that's true. I can't have copies made of it. But I can record the soundtrack as many times as I want.*

BOROVOYE, 4.18 P.M.

First off, Lattmann shared with Bora his informants' report about Krasny Yar. It was much as Nitichenko had told it, except that the body count came to a dozen.

"All males. The oldest must have been seventeen or eighteen. Malnourished: they looked like something the cat had dragged in. Your usual Russki band of young savages, given up for dead by their families and now dead for good. Why they'd rather hole up in the woods rather than staying in the farms they came from is more than I can say. The older ones might fear conscription, but the rest?"

In the afternoon heat, Bora rolled up his sleeves. During breaks from listening and wiretapping, Lattmann always had music on, from a powerful little radio of his. *I – have – no need – for – millions*, went a happy, jazzy tune from another life. "It's a form of juvenile delinquency like any other," he agreed, "complete with initiation rites and redress for interlopers. The priest tells me Krasny Yar saw a recurrence of the phenomenon. The first, in his memory, were followers of Makhno's Black Army, left over from the civil war and eventually either shot by the Bolsheviks or rescued by Makarenko for his state factories. The woods remained a place to run to over the years. Father Victor is convinced most murders were committed to frighten outsiders or to keep gang members from tattling – even though he sees the devil's hand in it, and would like us to torch it."

"Well, according to my informants the six crates hauled onto trucks looked like old ammo boxes rather than the devil's work. Whatever is in them, they – rather than the *besprizornye* – were a reason for the operation. *Totenkopf* spared you having to flush them out of the Yar yourself by going in with the regiment."

"I still plan to do it, as an exercise." Bora took the film reel out of his briefcase. "Speaking of the crates at Krasny Yar, Bruno, give me a hand with this. Never mind how I came by it, it contains a potentially explosive statement by Khan Tibyetsky."

"It does?" Sucking on his pipe, Lattmann contemplated the cardboard Tobis–Degeto case in Bora's hand. The song went, *I've only need of music / and only need your love...* "I'll be damned. If he's the same fellow who shot his tank crew point-blank to roll across the Donets, I don't want to know what happened to those who filmed it. But then again, a man needs to sweep up after himself."

Solve the problem and tidy up afterwards. "It's the way Khan saw it," Bora agreed. The scent of Blue Bird tobacco made him long for a cigarette, a need more psychological than physiological. "I'm not sure you should view the film. I'll leave it up to you, though: there could be consequences."

"I'm all grown up and have received all my shots, Martin. If you need a witness, I'd rather know what it's about."

"I do need a witness. But even more than that, I need to lay my hands on a projector. I don't want to go asking the Air Force again. Also, there ought to be two copies made of the soundtrack. I'll keep one. The other, should anything happen to me, you'll do well to forward to the International Red Cross. Failing that, to Senior Army Chaplain Father Galette, in private."

No comments followed, called for as they were. Lattmann nodded. "Hm. So you need a projector *and* a tape recorder. The second I can help you with, it's part of my bag of tricks – a high-fidelity reel-to-reel Magnetophon that works like a charm. The projector isn't so easy."

"Well, I have to have it today."

It took a friend's positive attitude to accommodate Bora's testiness. "I'll see what I can do. Let me think. The Propaganda Branch feeds films to the locals in the old *kolkhoz* projection hall at Konstantinovka. That's only minutes away, but they don't let the equipment out of their sight. What do you have to swap?"

"On me? Only my Ray-Bans, and I'm not giving those up... Well, I also carry a twenty-five-litre can of gasoline."

"They'd rather take the fuel, I'm thinking. Have you got enough to drive back?"

Bora shrugged. "On a wing and a prayer. But my thieving *Hiwi* keeps me well stocked, so I'll be fine once I'm in Merefa. Better borrow a propaganda film too, Bruno, so they don't wonder what we're watching. Say, do you have a ball of string and an adjustable spanner on hand? And the tarpaulin out there: do you need it?"

Lattmann rummaged around. "Shit, you'll ask for my underwear next. Here's the spanner, but I want it back. This is all the string I've got. The tarpaulin you can keep. Anything else?"

"It'll do for now."

They decided to put five litres in the GAZ, and sacrifice the rest of the fuel to their immediate needs. Lattmann returned with the projector within three-quarters of an hour, after which the bona fide work began.

MEREFA

The setting sun cut across the fields in a merciless line, setting the heads of grass, buds and corollas on fire. Indistinct sour yellow blankets lit up in bursts where sunflowers crowded the hollows: from them, Bora had to remove his eyes to avoid feeling nausea rise in his throat. Film and recorded reel lay under his seat in a canvas bag; spanner and string he carried in his briefcase. On the back seat, he'd laid out the tarpaulin, bags of chicken feed on top of it.

Before they parted ways, Lattmann – much sobered by the dramatic contents of Khan's reel – had said, "Do you really think that's who Tin Man is? It'd be *huge*. He gave away our stuff for years!"

In one of his tight-lipped moods, Bora had only answered, "Right."

"For Christ's sake, Martin! What are you going to do about it?"

"Don't know."

Which was not true. He had to deflect Stark's attention. Once in the schoolhouse, he set aside the odds and ends he'd secured at Borovoye, took a quick shower and then telephoned the *Kombinat* with a compelling offer of forced labour. He feared Stark would be gone for the day, but he was still at his desk and answered the call directly. As always, the commissioner sounded positive; to a trained ear, only his breathing came a little laboured, like one who's been exerting himself or has to keep a lid on strong emotions. Bora took note of this. *Has he found out Khan deprived him of the booty?*

"Good evening, Herr Gebietskommissar, Bora here. I have four squads' worth of Russian labourers available if you have use for them, hale and fit to do some heavy hauling."

"Yes? Fine. Excellent. Ah – their gender and age, Major?"

"Males, ranging from seventeen to early twenties, I'd say. Fresh from surrendering to us." Officiously Bora read from his notes. "The exact head count is 123. Where do you want them? They're at our Bespalovka camp at present."

"Let's see… I could use them at Smijeff."

"Will you pick up, or shall I send them over?"

"Have them ready first thing Tuesday morning at the Bespalovka rail station."

"They'll be there."

"Smashing." In the course of the brief exchange, Stark had regained full control over his intake of air. "One good deed deserves another, Major Bora. Your Karabakh will be here the day after tomorrow."

Bora had foreseen the counter-offer, and yet his own feelings were so conflicted at this moment that his reaction came a little slow. He scrambled to make his pause sound like astonishment. "I'm overwhelmed, Herr Gebietskommissar. In the morning I'll stop by to leave a harness and saddle. I'll also need to trouble you for some delicacies again."

"Really? Come early, then: I'm expecting General District Commissioner Magunia at nine."

After the phone call, there was still much to do before he could go to sleep. Bora pulled the drapes across the screened windows and made himself busy for the best part of an hour. To make room, he emptied the briefcase of all that was in it, including his diary. This – along with the film reel, Dikta's letters, photographs and a few other personal items – he placed inside a simple, handy rucksack of the type artillery troops used, and stuffed it in the rafters of the school's back room. Lattmann had instructions to retrieve it from there if needed. Too familiar with Bora to enquire past a certain point, his colleague no doubt suspected a great deal but kept it to himself. He knew what to do and what role to play, should circumstances call for it.

On severe, high-quality Spicers stationery (a gift from his Ashworth-Douglas grandmother) he began to write a letter to his wife, superstitiously planning to complete it on the following night.

My beloved Benedikta,

Yes, I did receive the fine studio portrait you sent via your stepfather. My darling, how could you imagine I would need it in order to have your beauty before me? Our hotel room in Prague is all I can think of; how we checked the time over and over to see how much we had left to keep doing what we were wonderfully doing; how everything that ever befell me in life was ransomed by those hours spent with you. All in you I love: so much so that your photograph is nearly painful to me in our separation. You are with me always, regardless!

The days here are those of men at war. My new regiment is coalescing and behaving well: I trust it will live up to its promise and honour the traditions of German cavalry. Peter and I were briefly together for the Knight's Cross ceremony (film to follow for Father and Nina); he'll tell you all about it when he gets home to see his new child.

Thank you for being such a good friend to Duckie, darling, and thank you for lending your horsewoman's expertise to the training of our remounts. It might make you laugh that I envy them, lucky beasts.

Do you remember the night we met, when you asked me why I was so tanned, and I couldn't answer that I was on furlough from the Spanish front? You probably considered me another dumbstruck dance-floor admirer of yours: how many officers were there trailing you with their eyes? In fact, from the moment we walked outside in the garden I told myself I had to conquer you or die in the attempt. Well, I didn't have to die: you chose me, and not because – as you say – I am perfect. I'm not perfect, Dikta. I'm not. I am anything but perfect.

12

MONDAY 31 MAY

Bora shaved with unusual care that morning, calmly meeting his own eyes in the army-issue folding mirror. *With her scandalous autobiography, Larisa Malinovskaya meant to embarrass my mother. It was 1915: for all its commercial vim, Leipzig was and is a small place. Recently widowed as she was, Nina had to put up with her society friends' false sympathy and sneers. What do I owe my father's discarded lover? Nothing. On the other hand, in less than half an hour I'll meet with Stark, and have to keep a close eye on him. He's on my tail but has no proof against me yet: Abwehr or not, for all he knows I could merely be stupid or foolhardy. If he is or has been a Soviet agent or double agent he won't visibly betray his emotions. Still, he ought to be foaming at the mouth if he's discovered the crates contain nothing but ballast. Likewise, if he hasn't disposed of him already, he'll be extremely nervous about Arnim Weller scared and loose in Kiev. Most of all, even if he doesn't know about Larisa's icons, he's aware she's his last bet to learn about Khan's movements around Kharkov in the old days. So, considering I can't leave witnesses behind...*

Beautifully white clouds sailed with the ease of galleons across the sky. They'd dissolve when it turned warm later on, but at 8 a.m. their fleet was still complete. Bora, who hadn't been in the habit lately, said a Hail Mary before leaving the schoolhouse.

A battleship-size national flag hung from the third-floor window of the *Kombinat,* nearly to the lintel of the building's entrance. Russian prisoners were placing potted plants at the sides of the door, and a Persian runner in tones of red and blue covered the length of the hallway floor. Stark's office was definitely preparing for SA Oberführer Magunia's three-hour visit. Lattmann had been able to give Bora that detail, along with the time of departure from Rogany – twelve noon – of the high official and his retinue, due for lunch with Field Marshal von Manstein at Zaporozhye.

On the district commissioner's wall, a street chart of Kharkov and its environs, 1941 edition, flanked the map of the *Reichskommissariat Ukraine*. Stark sat speaking on the phone. Even before Bora was announced, he glanced at him as he set saddle and harness on the floor in the office across the hallway. He gestured for him to enter without lowering the receiver from his ear. The time needed for the typewriters to engage in a stormy duet upstairs sufficed for him to conclude his call. "Yes, yes, goodbye." And then, because the Knight's Cross around Bora's neck could not go unnoticed, Stark raised his eyebrows. "Well! Where did *that* come from?"

"Stalingrad and Kiev, in that order, Herr Gebietskommissar."

The match was on. Stark sat back in his swivel chair. "Oh, yes – the award ceremony in Kiev. I read about it in the bulletin." He took a pencil in his hand firmly, avoiding playing with it.

Bora added nothing to the subject. He lifted from his briefcase the name list of the prisoners bound for labour duty. "Here they are, one hundred and twenty-three of them. Fifteen received slight gunshot wounds, nothing that'll keep them from shovelling dirt."

"Are you sure?"

"They're a hardy lot: you'll be pleased."

"Good help is hard to find any more." His eyes on the top sheet of Russian names, Geko Stark snorted. "We'd have machine-gunned the lot in the early days – now we make do with partisan dispatch riders and hangers-on."

"Well, my men killed or injured two-thirds of them. They don't avail us much, dead. Alive, you can do something with them." Bora spoke lightly as he countersigned a receipt, no differently from the day he'd been on the receiving end of the cavalry remounts. He raised his eyes, handing back the sheet. "I left saddle and harness in your assistant's office."

"I saw you. Make an appointment with him for tomorrow before you leave. He'll tell you when the transport with Turian-Chai is due in."

"I don't know how to thank you."

Stark settled even more comfortably in his chair. How old was he? Mid-fifties, Bora judged, which meant he'd been a few years older than Bora was now at the time he'd hung around with Khan and Platonov. In honour of Magunia's visit, he was wearing medals and ribbons too, though none as prestigious as a Knight's Cross. All the same, power and connections surrounded him as pieces of furniture and knick-knacks did Larisa – reefs behind which he felt safe. His friendly stare betrayed security. It said, without voicing the words, *I'm sure you'll think of something.*

"So, Major." He placidly chose to raise the ante. "You're also here to secure the goodies you went through so much trouble to obtain the other day, and didn't. What happened? Is she playing hard to get, that elderly girlfriend of yours?"

Bora smiled. He often relied on his smile; the army surgeon was right in that. He smiled to hide anxiety and irritation, because they were getting close to the target now. "My late father's, actually – not mine. It's an old story, Herr Gebietskommissar."

"I love old stories." The commissioner observed him, seeing nothing but a smiling young officer. On both sides, serenity of expression belied lack of scruples and a measure of anger moulded into pragmatism. Stark summoned and directed his assistant upstairs with the name list for retyping. "And who is she?"

"A world-famous soprano: or she was once." The necessity of remaining one-on-one during this part of the conversation did not escape Bora. He faced the desk aware that the day was taking a new, dangerous turn; events would soon need controlling. *If I don't tell him her name, he'll either have to ask for it directly so that he can track her down, or will try to be oblique in his enquiry.*

"A world-famous soprano in downtown Kharkov, Major?"

"Not exactly downtown: she lives in Pomorki."

Stark swivelled the chair around and glanced at the street map of Kharkov behind him. "And you travel all the way to Pomorki to bring her goodies!"

"My father left her at the height of their relationship – it's the least I can do."

"An interesting devotion on your part. I approve. The only thing is that you'll have to wait until tomorrow to get the special permission for extra butter and sugar rations. I'm very busy, and you'll be returning here for Turian-Chai anyhow."

"That'll be fine. I plan to secure first-rate fodder at the Lissa Gora army park today."

He'll check on me after I leave to see if I'm really going there. Fine: I'm going there. After all, the district of Lissa Gora is nowhere near Pomorki.

The phone rang again, a call from Rogany airfield. Bora availed himself of the interval to take his leave. In the hallway, at the foot of the stairs he met Stark's assistant, who pencilled him in for an appointment at 9.30 a.m. the following day.

From Merefa the route to Pomorki was very easy: first Moskalivka and then Sumskaya, little more than ten kilometres across the city, plus five more outside the city's northern limits, past the Aerodrome and the abandoned leather works, and into a wooded area. Bora knew where the checkpoints were between downtown Kharkov and Pomorki. After stopping at Lissa Gora, the only way to avoid them was to take the second-northernmost bridge on the Lopany River from the Vaschtchenkivska Levada district and follow one of the long north–south streets beyond, cutting across to Staraya Pavlivska towards the Dynamo stadium and the public park around it.

At this time – 9.30 a.m. – along Sumskaya, Bezirkskommissar Magunia's arrival had brought about the usual orgasmic activity of flag-waving, security troops and armoured cars. Bora followed the alternative route automatically, sliding from one minute to the next, careful not to think past the single physical gesture he was performing at any one time.

The park around the stadium had gravel paths, narrower than lanes. Past the Sokolniki settlement, deep in the woods, even the paths ended. Closer to Sumskaya, where past the Aerodrome the boulevard became the road to Pomorki (and also the highway to Moscow) there would be security troops, but not above Sokolniki. It was possible to drive up one of the northbound, grassy bridle tracks. However, the lengthy *balka* parting the forested area between here and the Biological Institute was insurmountable on four wheels. Bora returned to the highway for the time needed to travel on the pavement across the dip, and headed back into the park.

The grounds of the Biological Institute stood forlorn; trees besieged its paved piazza when he reached it. Still, he parked the GAZ out of sight. Three hundred or so paces separated him from Pomorki's *novyi burzhuy* little villas. After a look around, Bora transferred what he needed from his briefcase to a canvas haversack, removed the Knight's Cross from around his neck and pocketed it, and continued on foot towards the residential area. He approached it across the field of wild hyacinth, mostly faded now, swarming with small insects. The empty dachas on the rise were all blooming creepers and fallen-down wire fences. Bora laid down the tightly rolled-up tarpaulin he carried under-arm to put his gloves on, stepped over the closest fence and through overgrown flowerbeds into the garden next but one to Larisa's, and across that to Larisa's broken-down enclosure. Every yard was similarly criss-crossed by corduroy paths in the tall grass and abundance of rank flowers.

Through the gap in Larisa's wire fence, he noiselessly entered her property from the south side. Clothes hung on the clothes line; chickens clucked somewhere, but Nyusha was not around. The front door might be closed, but surely not locked. Quickly feeling around in the thick of leafy shrubs, Bora found the sniper rifle. Making sure that Larisa would not talk was far too easy. That she shouldn't be given a chance to meet Stark, much less speak with him, was a given Bora had coolly considered in all its implications. Had he been a man who liked to choose the easiest option, he could have ended matters here and now. Instead, after duly inspecting his weapon, he walked to the open garden gate and, lifting it from a crusty ledge of dirt and weeds, leant it across the path. The rolled tarpaulin he set in the ferns just inside the gate. Larisa's house seemed asleep as he paced back through the shrubbery; there, protected from view, he rested the haversack at his feet and stood waiting by a sturdy pomegranate tree.

If his reckoning was correct, the time needed for Geko Stark to carry out his duties in relation to Magunia's visit, check the accuracy of Larisa's address as given him and drive here varied between two and three hours from now. Waiting could sometimes weigh heavily, but for once Bora was not in a hurry. The warmth of the day, drifting clouds over the tangle of leaves, marked the passing minutes; insects darted all around like specks of bronze and gold. Squinting in the sun, Nyusha came out for a moment to feel the clothes on the line for dryness; went back indoors. With his boots in the shady grass, Bora waited as one who has peeled the thoughts from his mind until only the bare essentials are left.

The highway to Moscow, a short tract of which was perceivable through the foliage, lay empty of traffic at this hour. Magunia was due to leave at noon from the Rogany airfield; if it hadn't already, all the security apparatus would migrate to the eastern end of town, past the Russian army graveyard and the Tractor Works. Slowly a supply truck went through, heading for Kharkov under the escort of a motorcycle and machine-gunner in the sidecar. Then nothing for a long time, during which whatever Bora was – or had been – lost contours and importance. Becoming his own acts, or quiescence itself in wait of carrying them out, was the prerequisite of success. A temporary dissolution, the discomposing of a mosaic that granted freedom from all trammels, including conscience. *Factum mutat facientem*: every action changes he who commits the action. But only afterwards.

Nyusha briefly stepped out of the door, called the chickens, threw feed around. From within the house, Larisa's powerful voice said something incomprehensible in a peevish tone. A *tachanka*, a peasant cart mounted on tyres, travelled north. Barking from invisible dogs on the other side of the highway, where farms had been torched in February, sounded muffled as though coming from creatures of the netherworld. At this hour, by Bora's watch, most army units would be camped down or sitting in their barracks for the noon meal. The shade of trees moved over him, creating a different pattern of speckled light. 1 p.m. At Rogany, Magunia's plane must have taken off for Zaporozhye. Manstein's table, set with porcelain and silver, would grant the illusion of stable normality, as if Ukraine should be German forever. Bora felt neither the heat nor the weariness of immobility. The words *we're all flyspecks on the map of history, but think of ourselves as essential* drifted through his mind.

When at last the glossy black staff car, like a shellacked porpoise, pulled from the highway into Pomorki Bora went from calm to absolute calm. Impossible to judge until it drew closer whether there was a chauffeur at the wheel or not, or how many people sat in the vehicle. The well-balanced Russian rifle was in no more haste than the hand holding it.

Beyond the green filigree of branches the car approached, slowed to a halt and revealed a single occupant in a pheasant-coloured uniform. It stopped a few metres outside the garden gate; the squeal of gravel under the wheels and the sound of the door opening would not be overheard from the house. Gentle dust, thinner than face powder, twirled and hovered behind it. Bareheaded, visibly flushed by the heat, Geko Stark left the driver's seat and closed the door without slamming it. The motion of his right arm was to unlatch his pistol holster. He listened and looked around. The stillness in Larisa's property, in the abandoned gardens right and left, seemed to reassure him. Walking with gun in hand to remove the small impediment of the gate set ajar, he came into full view for a second. At that distance, under ten metres, Bora wouldn't miss with a weapon of far lesser quality.

The silenced SVT-40 went off once. Stark dropped, felled like hefty game. Unlikely the women would hear more than an indistinct *pop* from the dacha, if they even noticed a noise. The garden gate stood in a particularly secluded spot; you couldn't see it from the door. Bora lowered the rifle. *Keep it together. Keep it together. Don't wonder if his eyes are open because he isn't dead. Don't worry, keep it together.* Shooting to kill was lesson number one. Rifle strap across his shoulder, Bora stepped out to check his work. Geko Stark lay curled in his beautiful gold livery, looking as it seemed at the gravel around him through his lenses. The clean, slowly bleeding hole between his brows added a blind third eye to his smooth marzipan face, where neither surprise nor anger had had time to stamp themselves.

The eyes were blind, no life signs whatever. Bora retrieved the pistol from his hand, wiped it clean of dust with his handkerchief, replaced it in the holster and latched it. *Martin, keep it together.* From the bed of ferns by the gate he lifted the tarpaulin, untied and unrolled it, laid the body on it and after folding it in quickly, tied it head and foot. Counting on muscular strength and impeccable coolness, he lifted the heavy burden enough to carry it inside the garden. Doing this outside Larisa's windows, without her knowing, should have prompted in him a mix of emotions, from relief to satisfaction to sweet revenge to self-righteousness, but emotions were a luxury precluded to Bora right now. Adjusting rifle and haversack so they wouldn't encumber his movements, he heaved Stark's body over the corduroy path to the broken fence, through the gap in it, on to the next garden's narrow planking, and without halting across the next forsaken garden to the grounds of the Biological Institute. The gruelling flesh-and-bone effort made three hundred metres feel like three thousand. At the end of the trail the large building, with its barred windows, slept a complicit sleep. Bora laid down his burden under the trees, where grass became a leaf-strewn cement slab around the sealed shafts to the interred gas pipes.

Once loosened with a spanner, the bolts on the nearest iron lid came up easily. From below, a warm odour of clean earth wafted to the surface the moment the covering was pushed aside. Stripping Geko Stark of identification papers, expensive wristwatch and car keys was a matter of less than a minute. The wallet, Bora would look into later. He dragged the tarpaulin wrap to the mouth of the shaft, finding that he had to force the commissioner's meaty bulk into it head first. Down it went, more than seven metres to the dirt floor and pipes below. His gold–yellow cap followed, and the Russian rifle. From the haversack Bora extracted a timed charge, already secured to the string Lattmann had given him. He held the ball in his left fist while slowly lowering the explosive pack down the centre of the hole, gradually unwinding its length until the bottom was reached. Then he let go of his end of the string. Thoughts and motions still coincided; reasoning shrank to necessity. Shaft. Lid. Bolts. No room for errors or regrets.

Returning and tightening the bolts over the lid, sweeping dead leaves across it and righting the stalks of grass disarranged at the sides of the corduroy paths from one garden to the next, Bora returned to Larisa's property, lifted the gate to push it into its original position and walked to Stark's car parked in the lane. He made sure no bloodstain was visible on the gravel. With the handkerchief he rubbed the soles of his boots to cleanse them of grass and bits of dirt before entering the staff car. He then sat in the driver's seat and backed out of Pomorki.

The first checkpoint on the highway to Moscow, entering Kharkov, was over three kilometres south of here, near the racetrack by the Aerodrome. It would be manned regardless of Magunia's departure. Bora travelled no more than half that distance to Solovivska, an isolated turn-off on the left side of the road, which led through a wooded patch to the leather works along the Kharkov River. Bora had camped there with his men in 1941. The leather works, heavily damaged early in the war, had been closed for years. Bora drove the staff car inside the factory yard to a secluded spot between buildings. There he parked. Inside Stark's wallet, he found the key to several radio frequencies (including, among others, that of the RSHA's jail and the SS first-aid station on Sumskaya), German and Ukrainian large-denomination notes, business cards, family photos (a plump lady – *Deine Sefi* – and four blond sons), theatre tickets and Larisa's address scribbled in pencil on today's desk calendar page.

Bora left everything but Larisa's address in the wallet. On the driver's seat he neatly placed Stark's belongings, rolled down the window enough to toss in the car keys after locking the door from the outside, and left on foot. It was the most exposed moment. Once across the highway, he took a shortcut across the park to the Biological Institute and collected his vehicle, where he replaced the Knight's Cross ribbon around his neck. He drove back the same way he'd come, skirting the north side of Kharkov, crossing the Lopany and patiently getting in line behind the army trucks waiting to pass the Lissa Gora checkpoint. He experienced no fear, no guilt, no weariness; much less anger. Basic bodily functions apparently remained on hold as well: not a trace of hunger or thirst. This being the case, he purposely stopped by the Kubitsky Alley eatery across from the RSHA jail. He ordered lunch and made sure he finished it, eyeing the titles on the local paper an officer was reading at the next table. On the doorstep, he used the calendar page with Larisa's address on it to light his first cigarette in two years.

The rest of the day Bora spent at headquarters. He contacted his regiment by radio to have the Russian prisoners ready for transfer and at the Bespalovka station by 7 a.m. Then he began a painstaking review of the press proof of the *Partisan Warfare Handbook*.

Around 6.30 p.m. he had an early dinner in von Salomon's company, patiently listening to the endless story of the lost East Prussian estate. Nodding along to the colonel's anti-Polish invectives, he told himself that it might be two or three days before they found Stark's car at the leather works, although his prolonged absence would be noticed soon enough at the *Kombinat*. The soldiers at the checkpoint had seen the commissioner take the highway to Moscow around 12.30 p.m., and whatever he'd told them, he surely hadn't said he was going to Pomorki to kill an old woman. As for his body, Bora had timed the explosive device to twenty-one days. Even if the device should go off up to a week in advance due to the heat or to the effects of decomposition, German forces in the entire area would be gearing up for the coming battle by then. A dull explosion inside a sealed shaft in the middle of a park, obliterating what remained of the *Gebietskommissar*, would go completely undetected.

"Have you heard?" von Salomon was saying under his breath, although they were alone in the officers' mess hall, "General District Commissioner Waldemar Magunia has been visiting."

"So I heard at the *Kombinat*, Herr Oberstleutnant."

"He was reportedly very put out at the disturbances in town two weeks ago. There'll be hell to pay if he holds Gebietskommissar Stark responsible for the reprisal that occasioned them."

Bora broke a small piece from the bread roll at the side of his plate. "I doubt the commissar can be held responsible for the reprisal. As I understand, the order was issued by Gestapo Gruppenführer Müller."

"And authorized by the *Gebietskommissar*."

"I see." The coincidence of Magunia's displeasure, news to him, was more than useful. "What do you believe might happen, Herr Oberstleutnant?"

"Magunia never wanted an additional district to be created in the Kharkov Oblast. You watch: he'll seize the opportunity to put a spoke in Stark's wheel. Naturally the Army must stay completely out of the fray."

374

"Naturally."

Von Salomon's sad face, low over his plate of bland soup, hardly befitted a man relating military gossip. "He flew from Kiev under the pretence of a scheduled visit, but his opinion of safety in Kharkov is so low, Magunia decided not to speak publicly to the city administrators this morning. Imagine: he arrived with his words pre-recorded, and had them broadcast to all offices."

"Incredible." Bora grazed the wine in his glass with his lips. His own calm was beginning to worry him, as if it were a flaw. The mention of a tape, any tape, should set him on edge, but it didn't. The second recording he'd made of Khan's film at Borovoye intentionally stopped at the paragraph preceding the last page of the commander's statement: *I am convinced he is waiting for the time of summer operations to draw nearer: he will then attempt a* coup de main *on Krasny Yar, and defect as soon as possible. Platonov's captivity in the Kharkov area, and soon my own presence, will be in Stark's eyes impediments to protecting his identity and securing the booty.* Discovered sooner or later, the doctored tape was meant to suggest a reason for Stark's voluntary disappearance. If Magunia had really come with the intention of sacking Geko Stark, all the better. "The district commissioner seemed in good spirits when I saw him early today," he observed.

"Nonsense." Von Salomon swallowed his wine. "You're too open, my boy. If you wish to succeed as a career officer, you must learn not to trust a man's expression."

"I'll make a note of it, Herr Oberstleutnant."

MEREFA

There were three staff cars parked in front of the *Kombinat.* It was not altogether unusual, but, driving by the building, Bora had to wonder. Stark's absence, for which he might or might not have given a justification as he left the office, was now going on for seven hours. High officials enjoyed latitude in their movements, but this was wartime Russia, the equivalent of a wild frontier. By morning the search machine would be in motion.

All was quiet at the schoolhouse, or so it seemed from the road. Beyond the row of graves, out in the field, Kostya was putting the finishing touches to a paddock for Turian-Chai; a grassy area and heterogeneous planks hammered together would serve the purpose until Bora rode to Bespalovka. Turning into the schoolyard, the unexpected sight of a personnel carrier made his heart leap. Parked by the entrance so as to be invisible from the road, it had a licence plate Bora was unfamiliar with. He drove the GAZ to a halt behind its rear bumper, making it impossible for it to back up and leave. *I made no mistakes*, he reasoned, *left no traces. If ever asked, the girls of the Dutch brothel at Lisa Gora will confirm my stay with them from eleven to three* (the madam was a long-time *Abwehr* informant: Bora had stopped there after ordering fodder to secure an alibi from her). He wracked his brain. *Wait. There's the calendar; Christ. If Stark had pressed the tip of the pencil as he wrote, Larisa's address might have left an impression below, on today's page –*

"Oberstarzt Mayr here to see you, Herr Major."

The sentry had no idea of the relief his words brought Bora.

In ankle boots and old-fashioned puttees, the army surgeon was more yellow than ever; the kerosene lamp gave his badly shaven cheeks the tinge of baked clay. Still, out of professional habit, he told Bora right away, "You don't look well. Are you running a fever?"

"I think so."

"Well, that makes two of us."

Bora crossed the classroom floor. Along with a handful of books, the teacher's small cabinet contained the bottle of vodka Lattmann had brought him, still two-thirds full. If ever there was a night to tap it, this was it. Bora thought so as he unbuckled his pistol belt and rested it on the top shelf. "I thought you'd be travelling to Germany by now."

"The train was delayed. Tomorrow, God willing."

Yes, God willing. And Ivan, and the rails, and destiny that hangs over us like an anvil suspended from a spider's web. When Bora showed the bottle questioningly the surgeon nodded, so he poured two small glasses. "What brings you here, Herr Oberstarzt? I take it this isn't a courtesy call."

"It isn't. Arnim Weller contacted me."

For a moment Bora felt as if a rug had been pulled from under his feet. Slipping was forbidden. It was imperative to convey an image of self-assured balance, which he did. "How so?"

"How?" The surgeon dismissed the question with less than a wave, a mere turn of the wrist. "He's in Kiev, as you know. He's desperate."

I'm not impressed, Bora was on the point of saying, but held back. He downed his drink instead.

"Major, he wants to negotiate and live."

"That might not be feasible or even useful at this point."

"Why? Don't you need a confession?"

Bora caught himself. *How close can one come to betraying oneself? Having disposed of the man behind the murders, just now I nearly admitted his hired killer could be more trouble to me than he's worth.* He made an effort to relax his aching shoulders and invited the surgeon to take a seat. "I meant he might not live. I can't promise life to him."

Mayr's slump in the chair was a sign of accumulated weariness, or anguish unresolved. "Weller is willing to risk it. If *others* catch him, it's all over."

Others might mean the Ukrainian police or political authorities, or Stark. It made a difference. Bora put away his empty glass. "How much do *you* know, Herr Oberstarzt?"

"No more than when you and I last spoke by phone; other than at the hospital we do keep nicotine on hand as a medicine against pinworms."

Bora recalled the medical supplies he'd seen at the *Kombinat* time and again: insecticides, disinfectants and such. One sip at a time, not savouring it but as if he were taking medicine, Mayr drank the liquor. Being here, speaking as he did, was risky for him, Bora gave him credit without feeling particular sympathy.

"I'll need a document signed by Weller."

"I have it."

The practice of watching his expression gave way for an instant, the time it took Bora to blink. "Here?"

"Here." A plain, sealed envelope emerged from inside Mayr's blouse. Laying it flat on the desk, he pushed it slowly in Bora's direction and kept his worn fingertips on it. Bora looked at it, and at the surgeon's paleness.

"How long have you had it with you, Dr Mayr?"

"It was hand-delivered to me today by my substitute, who flew in from Kiev. There, as I understand, he was contacted in private by Sanitätsoberfeldwebel Weller, who begged him to bring it to me. Since the outer envelope bore my name, I opened it and found a second envelope inside – this one – as well as a note full of fear and remorse, instructing me to forward his confession to the man in authority I repute 'most likely to listen'."

"So of all people you chose me."

"In a land of blind men, Major, blessed are those —"

"— who have one eye? But I have two good eyes, not one."

"You're doubly blessed, then. Mind you, I ignored the contents of the letter, although I can surmise it after the phone conversation you and I had. What do you say, Major Bora?"

Bora stretched his hand. "I'll read it first."

"No. Your word, first."

"You have my word that if the contents satisfy I'll see what I can do for him."

"Fair enough."

The instant Mayr's fingers relinquished the envelope, Bora picked it up. He tore it open, something that in his meticulousness he never did. There wasn't enough light in the room and he had to walk closer to the kerosene lamp to read it. Weller had obviously written it in hiding after the delay in his repatriation told him he was a marked man. It exuded fear for his life, in contrast with the clinically unadorned language used to describe Platonov and Tibyetsky's deaths. He'd administered Platonov "0.09 gr. of aconitine nitrate in the usual solution of distilled water, glycerin and alcohol", and talked Khan into believing he'd ingest a narcotic in the morning, not one full gram of nicotine in tablet form "as I knew he'd vomit part of it, was a habitual smoker and weighed one hundred kilos besides". In his terror, any guilt and regret were functions of necessity, and of the resentment Weller felt towards the instigator for "exploiting a man's fragility beyond breaking point". Having first met Stark when delivering medical supplies, he'd been "horrified" to learn how much the commissioner knew about his breakdown at Stalingrad. By surrendering to blackmail ("What else could I do?") he'd brought about death only to preserve his own life. "I ask, isn't that what a soldier does? Killing as ordered without questions, that's all everyone did at Stalingrad! Was there conscience anywhere, at Stalingrad? I did what I did, so that I might live. I admit all, I confess all, because I want to live."

The neurotic hopelessness of entrusting others with such a note while Stark was believed still alive and wielding power, struck Bora as the last resort of a man disconnected from reality. All *he* experienced was cold, angry contempt. He raised his eyes from the writing only to see that in his exhaustion Mayr had meanwhile nodded himself to sleep right where he sat. *If I forward this to the police authorities, Weller will be executed, and Stark's role in the murders played down or denied for political reasons. If I don't, Khan's partial tape – which outright accuses Stark of being a sender and a spy – may never be made public, but will "prove" his guilt in-house and justify his disappearance. Von Salomon is right: Magunia's animosity could be helpful in that regard. It all depends on planting the tape in the most suitable place. As for Colonel Bentivegni, well... I'm only cleaning up after myself.*

When Mayr woke up with a start, Bora was finishing the letter to his wife he'd begun the day before. After the signature he capped his pen, setting the sheet aside so the ink would dry on it. "We have an agreement," he said laconically.

With a mumbled apology for falling asleep, the surgeon said, "Weller's nerves gave in after all. My colleague tells me he's delusional."

Bora frowned. "He'll do well continuing to play insane." The handshake they exchanged was dry and warm with fever. "Know that if I meet that gutless Weller anywhere, I'll fire a bullet into his skull with my own hands. Have a safe trip to the Fatherland, Herr Oberstarzt."

Overnight, Bora's fever rose. The objective enormity of his action, the consequences if discovered prompted him – not for the first time in the last three years – to keep a loaded gun under his bed. In a restless state between waking and sleep, he distinctly saw leaves, shadows, the minutiae in Larisa's garden as if he were still there waiting for Stark; he saw himself at Tra-khenen with Peter, when as boys they had lain face up on his stepfather's Great War horse blanket and watched the falling stars. It was summer; the banks of the Rominte were full of frogs. Then there was something else about Peter. The calendar on Stark's desk had nothing to do with East Prussia or child-hood, but there it was, too. The sick worry that the impression on today's date might give Larisa's address away and allow enquirers to reconstruct Stark's itinerary became a very human desire to be as far away from here as possible. Sweat glued the undershirt to his stomach and armpits. In his agitation, Bora was tempted to go to Bespalovka for good and bury himself in his work there, but he had to stay, and present himself at the *Kombinat* besides. He fell into a brutal sleep towards dawn, and forgot he'd dreamt his brother's death.

TUESDAY 1 JUNE

In the morning he was himself again, and the image of dispassion. He waited until 9 a.m. and drove to the *Kombinat*. The absence of Stark's car from the grassy front lot was a given. It was the lack of typing, the breathless silence upstairs that impressed him. Stark's assistant rose from his chair when Bora looked in from the hallway.

"Is the commissioner in?"

"Not yet, Major."

Difficult to judge from his expression; bureaucrats are hard to read and go haywire for any change in routine, regardless of the motive behind it; a prolonged delay is to them as upsetting as a catastrophe. Bora glanced at his saddle on the floor. "Well, I'm here for the Karabakh. If I may, I'll begin by harnessing him."

The assistant looked down uncomfortably. "I'm sorry, Major Bora. General District Commissioner Magunia reviewed matters yesterday and decided to keep the stallion for reproduction. It is presently travelling to the Marbach stud farm. I'm very sorry." He tried to dress his words in empathy, but his mind was evidently elsewhere. This morning everyone at the *Kombinat* must be labouring under the weight of Stark's inexplicable truancy, and possibly Magunia's hostility as well.

Bora replied (and meant it) that he was extremely disappointed about losing Turian-Chai. "I'll have to live with it, I suppose." He didn't add that as a horse lover he couldn't wish the animal a happier future than to enjoy the good life at the head of a stud farm, away from the battlefield. Shamelessly, he added instead, "I'll wait for the commissioner, in any case. There's the matter of my Russian prisoners' destination, and of a permit I need for special food supplies. Will you please look on the commissioner's desk and see if he left any instructions for me?"

"As you know, I don't have the commissioner's permission to look into his desk," the assistant replied, but walked across the hallway to Stark's office. "I'll see what's in the Out box."

For all his internal turmoil, Bora followed calmly. In appearance, he was watching the official run his eyes across the neat array of paperwork. In fact, his attention was all on Stark's desk calendar, open on today's date. The previous leaf, used to scribble Larisa's address, had been hurriedly detached along the perforated line, so much so that frayed bits of paper still hung from it. No other notes or reminders in view. The desk's right-hand drawer was ajar enough to slip something in or out, possibly as Stark had left it after picking up his pistol on his way to Larisa's.

The assistant sounded at a loss. "I don't know, Major. We – have no directions as to the *Gebietskommissar*'s appointments today. It might be better for you to stop by later, or even phone before you come."

"Very well, then. I'll leave him a note." Without waiting for the assistant to agree, Bora snatched a pencil from Stark's desk and vigorously wrote on the calendar page. *Shipment of 123 Russian labourers began from Bespalovka at 04.00 on 1 June; arrival confirmed at rail station at 06.30. Please advise further. Bora (Major, Army).* Whatever impression Stark's note might have left on the paper below, it was now abundantly overwritten. "That's that, then. Please have the saddle and harness replaced in my vehicle."

When he left the *Kombinat*, Bora became aware of how his neck and shoulders ached after the effort of carrying the dead weight of a hefty man; other than that, he was a master of composure. On the highway to Kharkov he crossed SS and unmarked Gestapo vehicles in tow, travelling in the opposite direction. "What's going on?" he indifferently enquired of the soldiers at the checkpoint. They didn't know, but Bora had a strong impression the vehicles might belong to the search party. He stopped by divisional headquarters to have his orders updated and signed, and took the south-east road to Smijeff and Bespalovka. Halfway there he turned off towards Krasny Yar.

Peasants from Schubino and the surrounding area were still gathered in the clearing between the Kalekina farm and the woods, having come to identify and bury their dead sons and grandsons. Fresh graves dug in the thick soil, all fist-sized sods, formed a row along the leaning fence Bora had righted a few days earlier. Once he made them understand he wasn't among those who'd carried out the operation, Bora got the reticent elders and the grieving women to talk. When he asked about the Kalekin widows, they told him the older one had hanged herself in the tractor shed. "So now her whole family is finished, and she's done suffering."

"The younger one?"

"The younger one moved in with the priest at Oseryanka."

In the desolate house, open and probably already stolen from, a warm breeze made the cheap cotton draped across the window flutter as if it were alive. Bora recalled his first impression of the interior as an underwater world, where magic women noiselessly moved; now the trembling rag was like something lost, floating after a wreck. His present sadness seemed excessive, but somehow appropriate to the day.

Three of the *besprizornye* still lay where they'd been dragged by the SS. Grown youths machine-gunned in their tattered clothes, no one claimed them. Unclaimed and unknown, the peasants accused them of all the wrongdoing committed, from pilfering to the murder of old man Kalekin. For that reason, and because of the stench, everyone stayed away. The dead boys lay under a cloud of flies. One had unruly long hair, the other two were shaven close to the skull; all were barefooted, scrawny. Air and misery, as Roth said, was what they'd lived on for months, maybe years. Bora handed out *karbovanets* so the Russians would agree to dig a grave for them too. *The SS did me a favour after all; otherwise I might have had to shoot them myself.*

What puzzled him most was hearing that, contrary to expectations, none of the civilians had ventured into the woods in the past two days. Some of these women and older men, come on foot from a distance, were ready to go back without their children rather than daring Krasny Yar. "There could be other bodies," Bora told them. "Don't you want to know if other missing youngsters were left where they fell?"

They stood around him with their heads low – white kerchiefs and balding or grey brows, mulish and close-mouthed – while the unclaimed boys were shovelled into a shallow hole. Superstition is something you can't argue against. But so are other things, much more pragmatic. Bora continued towards Bespalovka convinced of the rational explanation: it had prompted his request for orders and the stopover, after all. Once at the regimental camp, he commanded his troops to move into Krasny Yar not according to the original plan but as if against a stronghold, an encircling operation whose set-up required most of the day.

Written at Bespalovka, 3 June.

Thank God we Germans learnt our lesson about forest combat in 1941. Something told me not to trust the Yar this time. Yesterday, while committing a company to pretend a frontal advance towards the centre of the woods, I decided to send another to sweep around the northern edge, where the minefields were cleared by the SS. No sooner had they stepped into tree-covered ground than Ivan opened fire with all he had, snipers and mortar, machine guns tearing everything to shreds. It killed two of my troopers right off, and bogged the others down for a time.

In the three days since *Totenkopf* wiped out the *besprizornye*, on the mistaken principle that – like thunderbolts – the SS never strike the same place twice (or need to), Russian partisans had clearly moved into Krasny Yar. Whether they were those who'd escaped the 198th ID near the Obasnovka farm during Warm Gates, or fresh units arrived from across the Donets, it makes no difference. The confusion, wild shouting and volume of fire could have cowed us years ago, but not now. My platoon leaders kept the men from losing heart, although for a moment I think they were overwhelmed. You couldn't see where the shots came from; broken branches rained down, charges went off right and left: Varus at Teutoburg must have faced a similar sense of dismay. Thankfully, we were better equipped and organized than he was. Calling it a fierce battle would be too much, but for a good two hours it was an inferno. It took us that long to reduce their dogged resistance, strongest around the *kurgan* in the middle of the Yar. I made sure I had troopers waiting at the closest ford on the Donets, as I knew the Reds would try to get away in that direction. I positioned men at Schubino and the Kalekina farm as well. As for myself, I chose to advance with the "decoy" company, where, thanks to the experienced troopers, even greenhorns kept their wits about them under fire.

It took us until the afternoon to tighten the net, over ten hours in all. We were all justifiably provoked, and what frustrated us most was that in the end, rather than surrender, some of the partisans held grenades under their chins and made themselves explode. Others were cold-bloodedly killed by their own. We caught only a handful when it was all over, by the ditch near the walnut grove, the place called Orekhovy. Their commanding officer, an army regular gravely wounded, begged to be given his handgun. There were only Nagel and I present. Nagel frowned hard. He looked over for my assent, and because the man was too weak to hold the pistol steady, he mercifully did it for him.

So it's done at last: the last of Krasny Yar's ghosts have been exorcised. Even though it was worth it, it cost me fifteen casualties. After mopping up, I partly retraced the steps Nagel and I had followed when we first went into the woods together, to see what the *Totenkopf* engineers had been up to. Rags up in the air, where they'd blown up other caves and hideouts. Demolition charges were expertly placed in the *kurgan*, so that the collapsed corridor could explode without causing other cave-ins. The blast had revealed what I call an inner chamber for lack of a better expression, 3 x 3 metres in size, where the crates must have been kept these many years. A false treasure cave, as it were. Were the wild boys, the *besprizornye*, even dimly aware of it? It might have been with them as memories of events are handed down in all primitive societies, until they become one with fable. But taboos remain; strange pacts and unwritten laws stay inviolable. Boys little more than children killing or being killed aren't so difficult to understand in this country: no more than a decade ago, Kostya's sickly four-year-old sister was left to starve by his parents in order to save him and another healthy sibling, even though she wept and begged her mother for food! What do we Germans know? How can we judge? Even as a soldier I feel grief-stricken for all this, for everyone involved. As Nagel put it in his concise manner after the battle was over, "It's a sick place where mercy means helping a man kill himself."

Krasny Yar is definitely clear of occupants now. Engineers from the 161st are dismantling the remaining minefields in anticipation of the summer battle. Until our marching orders arrive, Gothland will camp at Bespalovka, ready to move out at any time.

KHARKOV

Debriefing with von Salomon was a concise matter. The lieutenant colonel heard Bora out without sitting for a moment at his desk. Hands behind his back, he paced a straight line between the window and the closed door of his office. The latest news about Commissioner Stark, rocking Kharkov's administrative cadres, was foremost in his mind.

"Haven't you seen them going by? The Gestapo has been at the Commissariat since 10.00 hours. Acting on information from the Central Security Office, its men also visited *Totenkopf*'s headquarters."

Bora hinted at a nod. He'd hoped Stark's disappearance would fuel the tension between the SA and Gestapo; that the state police would also show up on the Armed SS' doorstep was an added bonus. He said, "I did pass staff cars heading to the *Kombinat,* Herr Oberstleutnant. What's the reason? As far as I could see, the district commissioner's car wasn't yet parked there when I drove by."

"Precisely." Von Salomon made an about-face from the window. "He's been absent without *any* justification since the thirty-first, do you understand? His automobile was recovered early this morning in an abandoned industrial area outside Kharkov, with his wallet and pistol inside. Gone of his own accord, it seems. No signs of violence; nothing. The city is rife with rumours. Magunia's visit is seen as the precipitating factor. There's wild gossip going around that a tape was found on Tuesday in Stark's desk accusing him of illicit deals and other such things." (Bora, who'd slipped the tape in the drawer himself, showed mild surprise: "Really?") "And that's not all. The Gestapo went through the District Commissariat's storage and supply areas and supposedly discovered a number of crates – I don't know what kind, Major, *crates* – filled with dirt and rocks, can you believe? Like in the film *Nosferatu,* eh? But the vampire only carried around soil from Transylvania! Rumour has it that the crates used to contain valuables, because bits of gold jewellery were found in the dirt after sifting... It'd be enormous! I have from a reliable source that the suspicion is that Stark kept gold extracted from the Jewish community in Kiev two years ago and plans to run off with it somewhere – some say Switzerland, others over to the Reds... Officially none of it is surfacing, of course. The story of the tape, then! Why would Stark keep a compromising tape in his desk? What do you say, Major?"

"I say we ought to keep clear-minded about hearsay, Herr Oberstleutnant. I don't see how the commissioner could reach Switzerland from here with a load of stolen gold."

"Right."

"And to the *Reds*? Only a defector would go over to the Reds!"

"Right."

"As for the tape in his desk, admitting that it does exist... If it's not the only copy of whatever it is, it'd be useless for him or anyone to destroy it. Others are certainly circulating."

"Right, right." Von Salomon stopped his pacing. He checked the hour on his wristwatch and then cracked his knuckles. "You *are* clear-minded. It's all hearsay, on the whole. They're looking for Stark all over town. Maybe he was upset about Magunia's visit and shot himself."

"Not with his pistol, if – as you say – it was left inside the car."

"Oh, well, not that it matters to us. The Army has everything to gain from staying away from it all. Back to business: when are you off to Bespalovka for good?"

"On Saturday at the latest, Herr Oberstleutnant."

"Excellent. I'll see you in the field, then. And would you do me a favour, Major Bora? Kindly give a ride to Heeresoberpfarrer Galette as you leave the building."

Bora would have done so in any case, for reasons of his own. Senior Army Chaplain Father Galette stopped by divisional headquarters twice a week, Thursday and Sunday. After lunch Bora drove him to his lodgings, and since the chaplain had with him his portable altar and all he needed to say Mass, he volunteered to help him with it to his second-floor room.

It would be a good time to take advantage of the situation and have his confession heard, but Bora was not in a revelatory frame of mind at the moment. He did, however, entrust Khan's film reel and Weller's note to the priest. "Under the seal of the sacrament of penance," he specified. "To be turned in on my behalf to Chief of *Abwehr* Central Office, Colonel Eccard von Bentivegni, when you reach Berlin."

As Hohmann's one-time secretary, Galette seldom enquired of the cardinals' former students beyond the bare minimum. He did not ask why Bora chose to avoid the *Abwehr* chain of command on the eastern front. He safely put away what he'd been given. "His Eminence hasn't heard from you in some time, Major," he said, a reasonable comeback. "He wishes you to remember that for our Holy Mother Church no action is so dire that it forever changes the man who commits it, provided there's repentance."

Bora did not smile, but remained agreeable. "Repentance is where the rub is, *Heeresoberpfarrer*. I feel none whatever."

From Galette's downtown quarters to Pomorki the distance was less than nine kilometres; Bora doubled it by using unguarded minor roads. When he drove through the open gate Nyusha was outside the dacha, searching for eggs where the chickens laid them in the garden. She looked up in alarm before she recognized him. Bora wondered when his arrival would no longer make women react in fear. He watched her wipe her hands on her apron and start towards the door to announce his visit.

"I don't need to come in," he told her. He hadn't been able to scrape up much sugar: there was less than a hundred grams in the paper bag he handed the girl. "Give this to the most esteemed, the *mnogouvazhaemaya* Larisa Vasilievna, from Martyn Friderikovich and with Commander Tibyetsky's compliments."

"… and with Commander Tibyetsky's compliments," Nyusha repeated, spelling the words out. "Yes, sir." Eggs formed little bumps in the pockets of her apron; beads of perspiration dotted the peach fuzz of her young face. Who knows, her soldier husband might have imagined her this way when he died, standing under the sun in a lush garden – minus a German officer.

Bora felt, not for the first time, that he belonged nowhere. The last image he'd somehow prearranged for his own death was Remedios' in Spain, because Remedios stood for all women before and since, including his wife. But he no more fitted in 1937 Spain than in 1943 Ukraine: the awareness made him free, or alone, or both. He said, "Thank the esteemed Larisa Vasilievna ever so much for showing me her 'beautiful corner', and ask her to pray to Our Lady of Oseryan for my brother and myself."

MEREFA

There were still a few things to do before leaving the school-house to radiomen from the 7th Panzer. At 3.45 p.m. Bora called in his orderly.

"Go to the train station, Kostya. Your wife is coming." He ignored the young man's astonishment by continuing to transfer documents from the desk to his briefcase. "Take your things with you. Here are your papers: she has hers. You're to climb on the train and travel with her to my family's in Germany: there's work for you at Borna, which you'll like. Whatever happens, take my advice: don't come back to Russia afterwards – hide out if you have to."

Kostya began to cry. Bora, however, was in a cranky mood and not up to displays of emotion. "Yes, yes, fine. That's enough. You have ten minutes to get there: take the sentry along with you to bring back the droshky. He'll look after the chicks, don't you worry. Be nice to your girl, and let her wear trousers once in a while."

It felt lonely in the building after everyone left. Bora packed the odds and ends he hadn't already transferred to Bespalovka in the past few days. From the open windows the chatter of birds, far and near, entered the room, and it was the only sound. He'd given the sentry the night off in order to collect his thoughts, or to take one last risk. Since Monday, it was the first occasion he'd had to consider things in a less pressing, immediate manner. He anticipated there would be a rise in anxiety as a result, when in fact it was bodily weariness that had crept in; more an irresist-ible, nearly desperate need to rest. In the frantic activity of the last several days he'd burned the candle at both ends; tension and lack of sleep made every muscle feel strained and sore, as if he'd been in a fist fight. His entire system wanted to shut down. Bora sat on his bed telling himself he wasn't one to drop off during the day, much less when he had work to do – which was his last consideration before falling asleep.

In his dream, he lay with Dikta in their Prague room. It was all sweetness, not a back-breaking contest as their lovemaking often turned out to be. In Prague she'd been angry, and yet (to convince him not to go back to Russia? Who knows?) she'd given him more sweetness than he'd ever experienced. They'd shared such love, the recollection on awakening made him feel full of tenderness instead of merely aroused. In the sultry afternoon Bora tried to fall asleep again so that he might recapture fragments of the scene. All that emerged from his drowsiness was the ceiling of the hotel room, not as it was but cheaply ornate, tiles of pressed tin like those in the Narodnaya Slava movie house. Or no, not a ceiling, either: a borderless metal sheet, an immense aeroplane wing hovering down over the bed, a tin sky. It was unpleasant and oppressive and it woke him up for good in a state of foreboding and alert.

An hour later, Bora was burning in the wood stove the handful of papers he wouldn't take along. Kaspar Bernoulli must have parked on the road because he didn't hear the squeal of gravel under the tyres, only the sound of displaced pebbles as someone approached the door.

"Major Bora?"

"Come in, Judge."

In his shirtsleeves and braces, Bora started to reach for his blouse when Bernoulli shook his head. "As you were, please. Continue what you're doing." He was himself severely attired as usual, and the glare from the window drew green and blue twin crescents on the glass of his spectacles. It made one wonder how he could see behind those colourful mirrors.

The heat and stillness in the room, a stunned silence all around, made this no less a ghostly time than the middle of the night. As soon as Bernoulli reached the middle of the room and stood there, his dark eyes became visible behind the lenses. "I'm returning to Berlin, Major Bora."

"I thought you might be."

"Is there anything you'd like me to hand-carry there?"

"No, thank you."

"Not even for Colonel Bentivegni?"

"No."

The burning bits of paper let out a crisp, acidic odour. Bernoulli observed the young man's frowning paleness, his exacting care over the disposal. He said, "You must be aware of Commissioner Stark's disappearance."

"Yes." Bora looked over, stared the military judge straight in the eye. "More than aware, Heeresrichter." He crumpled a typewritten sheet and lit it with a match. "In Kiev you asked me whether I could prove who killed Platonov and my notorious relative, Khan Tibyetsky. Well, I now can."

"So." Bernoulli inhaled deeply, smelling as it seemed the invisible smoke. Outside, flies banged against the netting of the windows, unable to get in. "And I take it that doesn't make you feel better."

"Not one bit."

"Tell me at least there was a higher motivation behind the crimes."

"There wasn't. Forgive me if I don't say more about it, Dr Bernoulli. It's best if we drop the subject."

A fairly long silence followed, during which Bora also burned sketches and half-done watercolours from his trunk. The judge remained standing. Between them, next to its powder-blue envelope, Dikta's studio portrait lay face down on the desk.

"Objectively, Major, you do look and sound rather troubled for one who's solved a difficult case."

Nothing else was said to elicit disclosure of any kind on Bora's part. However, the photograph on the wooden surface automatically became the focus of both men's interest, merely by lying there. Dikta needn't be mentioned to be recognized as a factor or to subjugate their thoughts and channel desire, curiosity, male resentment. Bora acknowledged the guest's attention on the rectangle of matte paper.

"I keep telling myself it's not the case, but I think that by volunteering again I might have lost her."

"Oh?"

"Yes."

"Such things are possible."

Surprisingly, or merely because his grief was beyond shame and well past social conventions, Bora did not react when the judge reached for the photograph and turned it over.

The result was a dispassionate, careful scrutiny. Bernoulli's pensive face lost none of its sternness; it revealed how under his eyes the extreme intimacy of the image, its significance as a means of private seduction disassembled into its elements, becoming nothing else – and nothing more – than crucial evidence. No comments were called for. But clinicians make diagnoses; judges emit sentences. Bernoulli scrupulously replaced the portrait in its envelope. "Allow me," he said. With steady-fingered hands he tore envelope and photo in half, and then in half again. "It is necessary." One step took him next to Bora by the stove. He tossed the fragments in the fire, where they curled into a bluish flame and were gone. "This, too, is measured according to the St Petersburg Paradox."

The determination of the value of an object must be based not on its price, but rather on the utility it can bring.

Bora tasted blood. His lower lip, bitten through, did not hurt, however. He rigorously kept dropping shreds in the stove until he was done. Save a farewell, he and Bernoulli had no further exchange until the judge left the schoolhouse, bound for the Alexandrovka turn-off. From there he'd travel to the Rogany airfield by way of Khoroshevo and Bestyudovka. Up to Alexandrovka, it was the same itinerary Bora himself, having relinquished his post to the radiomen, followed the day after, continuing, however, eastwards to Borovoye.

Lattmann turned down the volume on the radio. Some melancholy tune about homeland and shining stars was being crooned, and once the dial turned to the left the singer sounded far away, lost at the bottom of a solitary well.

He and Bora had no need for explanations or details. Geko Stark's final exit was an accepted given, so much so that Lattmann didn't ask about it, and his first news for his friend was that Krasny Yar had caught fire. "You can see the smoke drifting from the rise out there; it covered the sun at one point. That nutty priest of yours carried out his threat after all. The Ukrainian police caught him red-handed and arrested him, but it's likely the Autocephalous Orthodox Church will plead for his release. It smells like charcoal if you pay attention. Ashes come down when the wind's right."

Bora sensed an odd relief. "When things come to an end around here, they really do."

"Uh-huh. As long as we don't have to memorize *Nyema piva, nyema vina, do svidania Ukraina.* Already there's scarcity of beer and wine – it'd be too bad to have to say 'goodbye to Ukraine' as well."

"I remain optimistic. Here's Russki tobacco – best I could do for you."

"My pipe thanks you. Say, I have a titbit about Odilo Mantau, too, that paragon of brightness: it seems one of his overinflated tyres blew up the other day while he was driving along a ridge road, and he plunged into the ravine with all he had. Well, he didn't die, but he won't see action for the remainder of the war." With a critical grin, Lattmann looked Bora over. "Spurs, leather seat of the pants: off to *Gothland* for keeps, I see."

"Correct. Nagel will be here in an hour to pick me up. The regiment's moving out soon."

Bespalovka, Regimental Camp *Gothland*, 7.29 p.m.

Few things are as beautiful, as deceptively serene as grass fires just before night comes. What breath of wind there is rakes their smoke gently to one side, all in the same direction, close to the ground. Like braids of milk, if milk could be braided. The immensity of this land, where time is absorbed to the extent of ceasing to be, becomes so harmless and tender, I have filial feelings towards it. Was I ever hostile towards it? Not towards this land, per se. I can walk on it and touch it, crumble its soil under my fingertips and recognize its essential goodness. It was the same in Spain, when my boyish fury against the enemy (it was six years ago!) had nothing to do with the mountains and the rock walls among which we killed one another. Riscal Amargo, the *Bitter Cliff*, was sweet to me all the same, and not only because it was there that I first heard about Remedios. And so Palo de la Virgen, so Huerta de Santa Olalla, so Concud, with its heaps of cadavers the wild dogs fought over later on. Poland itself, our foretaste of Russia, resembled my own country too much to despise it. This evening I looked at the Ukrainian grass fires and was at peace for a moment, or at least reconciled with the fact that I will wage war thoroughly against my enemy, without any hatred for the land he lives on.

Has Krasny Yar burnt to the ground? It's the only question I have. I have no curiosity about the way Stark in his greed must have planned Platonov's death but only resorted to killing Uncle Terry as a knee-jerk response (which, however, caused me to investigate). I have none about Colonel von Salomon's capacity to hold out after all (he will), none about the upcoming campaign. The events of the past six months would last many a lifetime, but I no longer wonder about them.

What we underwent last winter in Stalingrad is beyond telling. I couldn't write it down, I couldn't convey it to others in words, and yet I couldn't keep it inside. We all died to ourselves; in that sense none of us will ever go back. Bruno doesn't need to worry about it. Those who go back will be strangers to who they were when they left.

That's why at last the Heeresrichter Kaspar Bernoulli can return where he came from, which isn't Berlin, or anywhere else in Germany or in the world. I no longer need him, and as I summoned him, I can let him go.

In Stalingrad, week after week, in front of my eyes men lost their minds, killed themselves, fell into idiocy, reverted to a brute and beastly state. I didn't. I held out. For myself and for others, I held out days, weeks, months. I never gave up. At what cost?

The right cost for a man like Martin Bora.

I limited myself, as late as the past month of May, to conjuring up an alter ego to keep me going – paradoxically to help me maintain my much vaunted and complimented lucidity.

I had to. In order not to hallucinate, I consciously created him. I fashioned Bernoulli as I needed him, as a thinker and a disciplinarian, a magistrate who would bring forward my protests against the evil committed here. What he was in fact made of, I don't want to know. I do know that the likes of him console men's loneliness and bolster them in vulnerable times, or else lead them into temptation. Providentially, I am not Faust, and he wasn't Mephistopheles. Bernoulli simply spoke to me in my own words, listened to me as I alone can when I go out and *listen*. Thanks to him who never existed, whatever happens next I tell myself I can take: even the realization that my efforts to denounce all that is wrong might come to nothing, or soon turn against me. I tell myself I've got over Stalingrad, and will not miss the judge.

Standing by the folding table in his tent, Bora reread what he'd written and then tore off the diary page. *One more scrap to burn*, he told himself. He stepped outside, where the sunset paled to grey. Odours were strongest at this hour, including the hale, powerful animal scent of the regiment's thousand and more horses. Men moved about the camp. Before long, his officers would arrive for a briefing. From here, the world appeared orderly, laid out according to a readable pattern.

It wasn't beyond imagining that in such a world, under the conniving silence of the *Abwehr*, Arnim Weller would end up in the *VII Wehrkreis* mental hospital. He'd live, if only because it served others that he should – as it served others yet that Stark should never be found.

Bora pocketed the diary page. This afternoon he'd laid out the marching plan to go across the Donets, and eventually north. Tomorrow he'd gather his senior non-coms, speak to the ethnic Germans, look over the equipment. That was enough anticipation for now: he'd learnt not to look beyond tomorrow.

Yes, he congratulated himself, *I am impeccably clear-minded.* He unscrewed the top of his canteen. *Dr Bernoulli, to your health.* There was only water in the metal flask, but before drinking Bora raised it to the tin-coloured, summery sky.

THE MARTIN BORA SERIES

by Ben Pastor

LUMEN

£8.99/$14.95 • ISBN PB 978-1904738-664 • eB 978-1904738-695

October 1939, Cracow, Nazi-occupied Poland. Wehrmacht Captain Martin Bora discovers the abbess, Mother Kazimierza, shot dead in her convent garden. Her alleged power to see the future has brought her a devoted following. But her work and motto, "Lumen Christi Adiuva Nos", appear also, it transpires, to have brought her some enemies. Stunned by the violence of the occupation and the ideology of his colleagues, Bora's sense of Prussian duty is tested to breaking point. The interference of seductive actress Ewa Kowalska does not help matters.

"Pastor's plot is well crafted, her prose sharp… a disturbing mix of detection and reflection." *Publishers Weekly*

LIAR MOON

£8.99/$14.95 • ISBN PB 978-1904738-824 • eB 978-1904738-831

September 1943. The Italian government has switched sides and declared war on Germany. Italy is divided, the North controlled by the Fascists, the South liberated by Allied forces slowly fighting their way up the peninsula. Wehrmacht major and aristocrat Martin Bora is ordered to investigate the murder of a local Fascist: a bizarre death, threatening to discredit the regime's public image. The prime suspect is the victim's twenty-eight-year-old widow Clara.

"Atmospheric, ambitious and cleverly plotted, *Liar Moon* is an original and memorable crime thriller." *Crime Time*